RESOLVE

ROAD TO THE BREAKING
BOOK 10

CHRIS BENNETT

Resolve

Copyright © Christopher A. Bennett – 2025

ISBN: 978-1-955100-15-1 (Trade Paperback)
ISBN: 978-1-955100-16-8 (eBook)

Map of Virginia and West Virginia:

Copyright © d-maps.com
(https://d-maps.com/carte.php?num_car=7766&lang=en)

Names: Bennett, Chris (Chris Arthur), 1959- author.
Title: Resolve / Chris Bennett.
Description: [Wadmalaw Island, South Carolina] : [CPB Publishing, LLC], [2025] | Series: Bennett, Chris (Chris Arthur), 1959- Road to the breaking ; bk. 10.
Identifiers: ISBN: 9781955100151 (trade paperback) | 9781955100168 (ebook)
Subjects: LCSH: United States. Army--Officers--History--19th century--Fiction. | Confederate States of America. Army--Fiction. | Women spies--Southern States--Fiction. | Rescues--Fiction. | Richmond (Va.)--History--Civil War, 1861-1865--Fiction. | United States--History--Civil War, 1861-1865--Fiction. | LCGFT: Historical fiction. | War fiction. | BISAC: FICTION / Historical / Civil War Era. | FICTION / Sagas. | FICTION / War & Military.
Classification: LCC: PS3602.E66446 R47 2025 | DDC: 813/.6--dc23

To sign up for a
no-spam newsletter
about
Road to the Breaking
and
exclusive free bonus material
visit my website:

http://www.ChrisABennett.com

Resolve [ri-zolv] noun:

1. A firmness of purpose or intent; strong determination.

2. A formal resolution or determination made, as to follow some course of action.

3. Something that is resolved.

DEDICATION

To
Abraham Lincoln,
Sixteenth President
without whom there would
likely no longer be a
United States of America.

The heartbreak of his untimely death
still echoes down through the generations,
affecting Americans even today.

It was, and yet remains
the greatest single tragedy
in our nation's long, storied history.

Contents

*"I'd rather be the lowliest private
on the righteous side of history,
than the supreme commander
on the other."*

– Nathaniel Chambers

Key Civil War cities in Virginia and West Virginia

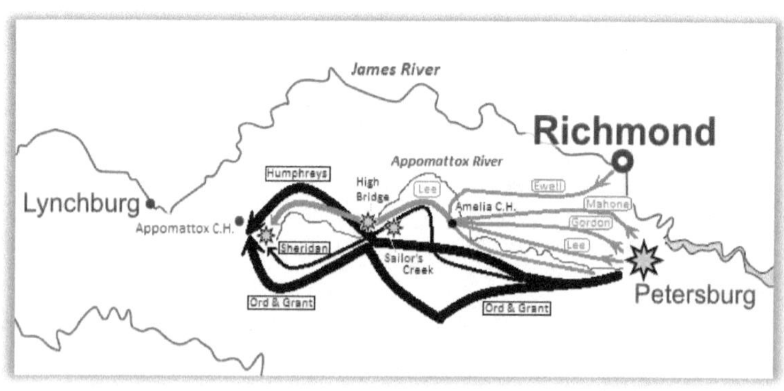

Fall of Petersburg and chase to Appomattox Court House

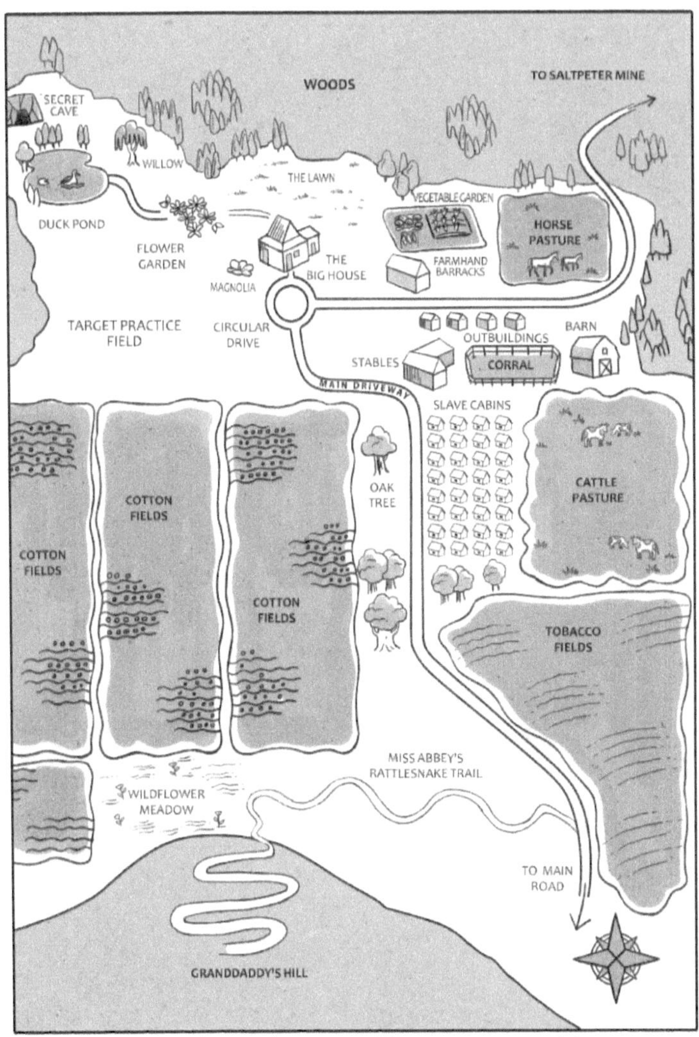

Mountain Meadows Farm (distances not to scale)

Chapter 1. Siege Warfare

"One likes people much better
when they're battered down
by a prodigious siege of misfortune
than when they triumph."
- Virginia Woolf

Saturday January 14, 1865 – Petersburg, Virginia:

Major Jim Wiggins flinched at the sudden blast that splattered his back with mud and pelted it with gravel, knocking his hat off and sending a stream of icy water running down inside the back of his shirt.

"*Damn it!*" he cursed, leaning down and retrieving his hat, then shaking the mud off the brim. "That was a new hat!" he said, turning to Tom and showing him the navy-blue, felt, wide-brimmed officer's hat, which now had a crease across the top, left by the incoming bullet.

Jim scowled as he slapped the hat back onto his head, cranked a round into the chamber of his Henry, then scrambled up the railroad bank, laying prone on his belly. He aimed the rifle up toward where the enemy was dug in along a ridgeline a little more than a hundred yards out, and squeezed off a round, the loud *boom* ringing in Tom's ears where he crouched a few feet away. But to the gun battle currently raging between the Twelfth West Virginia regiment and the enemy, his shot made little difference.

"Damn their mangy, flea-bitten hides, anyway!" Wiggins spun back around and slid down the bank then crouched next to Tom, scowling.

Tom returned a wry smile. "Well, at least they didn't blow your ugly head clean off. I'm sure the quartermaster will give you another hat."

Tom then turned and gazed back out toward the enemy, just visible across the distance through a drizzling rain. When they'd set out just before first light, he'd not expected to end up in this predicament, hunkered down behind the rail line bank with the seven hundred and some odd men of the Twelfth spread out to either side of them.

"Dammit, Jim, this was supposed to be no more than a skirmish. I thought Billy said this rail junction was only lightly defended. No more than a cavalry patrol. That's no cavalry patrol over yonder."

"No, it sure ain't," Jim agreed. "I'd say a full infantry regiment, at the least. Maybe two. And an artillery battery. Must've moved in overnight, 'fore we could get here."

Tom shook his head. "And we didn't even bring any horse-drawn guns."

"Didn't think we'd need them," Jim answered. "But ... with them dug in up on that hill, the guns woulda done us little good anyway. They got the high ground on us, Tom. Artillery'd not do any more than keep their heads down for a moment. They'd never inflict any real damage on 'em."

"True ..." Tom agreed.

They shared a hard look. Then Tom said, "I don't see much choice but to withdraw, though it galls me to go back and tell Nathan we couldn't accomplish this *one* simple thing for him."

Jim snorted a laugh. "*Simple*," he said, and shook his head, causing a new stream of rainwater to run off his hat brim onto his already soaked tunic. "Look, Tom ... even if we was to take the junction—by some miracle—we'd never be able to hold it. Not now that they've decided to give the place some attention. The colonel may be bit disappointed, but it was only a target of opportunity anyway. It won't make no difference in the big picture."

Tom frowned. "Yep. And that's the problem. All this marching around, fighting, and dying ... and none of it seems to make any difference."

Jim reached out and patted him on the back. "C'mon, cheer up, Tom. I'm feeling a bit hungry, not to mention cold and wet. What say we head on back to camp, get ourselves dried off, and get some chow?"

"All right. Guess there's nothing more to do for now," Tom agreed, but he held onto his dark frown.

☙❧☙❧☙❧☙❧☙❧☙❧

Wednesday January 18, 1865 – Dardanelle, Arkansas:

"Well, I hear what you sayin', Captain Matthews … but it still don't seem right," Ned said, a scowl wrinkling his brow as he marched along beside his former commanding officer at the head of a column of more than a hundred freemen. Marching ahead of them, down a muddy road on the south side of the Arkansas River, were several hundred more freemen soldiers, and Ned could just make out another column of black Union soldiers keeping pace over on the north side of the river—the Fifty-Fourth US Colored Regiment. Between the marching soldiers, two Union steamboats slowly plied the Arkansas' placid waters.

"It's *Sergeant* Matthews, now," William Matthews corrected Ned.

"That's the part I'm talkin' 'bout," Ned shot back. "Just 'cause we's now supposedly a federal unit—the *Seventy-Ninth United States Colored Regiment*, rather than our old name, *First Kansas Colored*—and just 'cause you's a black man, now you don't get to be captain no more? That don't make no sense." He shook his head in disgust.

"Yeah, maybe not," Matthews answered. "They don't allow no black officers in the *federal* army. Not yet, anyways. Don't go lettin' that get under your skin now, Ned. Long as I still get to fight them slavers, I'm well satisfied. Besides, Auggie here … uh, I should say, *Lieutenant Gordon*," he met eyes with the handsome, blond-haired young officer who marched alongside them, and the two shared a grin. "He's become a fine officer, and I got no quarrel with letting him take the lead on it."

Ned couldn't argue with that statement, so he just nodded. He also had nothing against Auggie; the situation was clearly not his fault. Aside from that, Ned and Auggie had long ago established a comradeship that had evolved into a strong friendship such as

Ned had never before experienced with another man, black or white.

"Still, I ain't got to like it," Ned concluded.

"Nope, you don't," Matthews agreed. "And neither do I. But we do got to *accept* it … and we got to keep on fightin'."

"Ain't never gonna quit fightin'," Ned grumbled. "Least not 'til this war's over … or I'm dead. Speakin' of," he turned his head and met eyes with Auggie, "What we doin' out here, anyway, Lieutenant? All I knowed was I was sleepin' on my bunk, mindin' my own business, when someone shouted, 'pack up and head out,' and now here we all are."

"Well, from what I understand," Auggie answered, "the rebs have attacked a fort of ours downstream at a place called Dardanelle, a few miles from here. They also fired artillery at a small flotilla of Union steamships, disabling two of them, which are grounded back upstream a ways. We've been called out from Fort Smith to escort these remaining two ships to safety, and to relieve the besieged fort at Dardanelle if we can."

"Oh, is that all? Reckon we can do that with one eye closed," Ned responded with a smirk.

Matthews laughed and nodded as they continued to march.

A half-hour later, they heard the booming of artillery ahead in the distance, followed by the distinctive popping sound of rifle fire. A few minutes later, the order came back down the line that Colonel Williams had ordered the column to march at the double-quick, and to prepare for action against the enemy.

After another quarter hour, they paused in a field overlooking the small town of Dardanelle, Arkansas. From their current vantage point, Ned could see that the so-called "fort" was nothing more than a tall berm of dirt and logs surrounding the town on three sides, with the river making up the fourth. Union troops inside the dirt wall were engaged in a gunfight with rebels, who'd surrounded the town.

He realized this fight didn't amount to much compared to the battles he'd heard about taking place back east — in this case, the Union side had only two cannons, and the rebels only one, and the sum total of soldiers on both sides was likely less than a couple thousand—but still, he knew it could involve some hard fighting, and a man could get himself killed just as dead in this battle as he could in some great monstrous action like the one he'd heard about called *Gettysburg*.

Colonel Williams rode out in front of the men on his horse, and after holding a quick conference with his officers, the men of the Seventy-Ninth US Colored were formed up for action.

"Company will fix bayonets on my command," the colonel called out. "*FIX ... BAYONETS!*" he shouted.

"Forward at the double-quick ... *March!*"

Down the hill they came at the trot, bayonets out front, attacking the right flank of the rebels surrounding the fort. The assault caught the Confederates by surprise, and they turned in a panic to face the new and unexpected foe, whose bayonets hit their front line like a hammer, smashing through and sending them reeling.

Ned found himself immersed in the swirling chaos of battle— stabbing, pounding, pushing—the cacophony of gunfire ringing in his ears, and a thick cloud of smoke stinging his throat as he struggled to maintain his footing in the thick mud made all the slicker by the copious blood splatter.

And then it was over. The men of the Seventy-Ninth Colored leaned on their rifles, catching their breath as the rebels streamed from the field in full retreat. As the ground beyond the town was hilly and thick with trees and underbrush, Colonel Williams called a halt—choosing not to pursue the withdrawing enemy for fear of an ambush or counterattack, Ned assumed.

After setting up a line of pickets, the remainder of the Seventy-Ninth Colored, over four hundred black men, marched in parade formation into the town, to the enthusiastic cheers and heartfelt thanks of the desperate Union cavalrymen who'd endured the rebel siege, all of whom were white men.

❧❦❧❦❧❦❧❦❧❦

Splat! Tony looked over and scowled at the man who'd just dumped a large spoonful of the evening's meal into his tin plate, splattering some of it on his tunic. "Watch what you're doing," he growled at the man, a fellow freeman, who simply turned and did the same for the next man in line.

Tony shook his head and grumbled, "Damned fool," as he turned and walked back toward where the other sergeants of his regiment were gathered, sitting on a set of sawed-off logs to eat their meal. As he approached them, he saw a Union officer step up to the group. Several of them, including Big George and Henry, stood up to greet the newcomer, gathering quickly around him, having set their plates down on the stumps. The men were shaking hands with the officer, and patting him on the back and arms with obvious affection and familiarity.

Tony immediately recognized the officer, then felt the usual warm feelings that seemed so natural now any time he met unexpectedly with Colonel Nathaniel Chambers. He smiled and shook his head at the wonder of it, remembering how he had initially distrusted and even hated the man, back when he was a slave and Chambers was the master. *Hard to believe how much the world has changed since those days*, he thought.

As he stepped up to the group, he called out, "Hey, y'all, what you thinkin'? That there's a colonel, so come to attention and give the proper respect!"

Colonel Chambers turned toward the sound, then smiled as the sergeants around him did as they were told, snapping to attention, and immediately saluting. Tony did likewise.

Nathan returned the salutes, and said, "At ease, and as you were, gentlemen. Please, continue your meal …"

Tony stepped forward and exchanged a warm smile and a handshake with Nathan.

"Good to see you, Tony," he said.

"Likewise, Colonel," Tony answered. "To what do we owe the pleasure, sir?"

"Please, take a seat, Tony. I have some news I wish to share with you and the men."

Tony did as he was bid, and Nathan stepped up to a position in front of the seated men so all could hear him.

"Men … I wanted to be the first to share some great news with you, before it spreads through the camp like wildfire. And believe me when I say, it is my great pleasure and honor to be able to do so."

Other passing freemen who'd heard the officer addressing the sergeants began to stop and listen, and now there were several dozen soldiers gathered respectfully to hear the news.

"Y'all will recall when President Lincoln issued the Emancipation Proclamation, freeing all the slaves in the rebel states," Nathan began. "Well, that was a *great* thing, there can be no doubt, and it inspired us to fight all the harder in order to ensure those people could indeed gain the freedom that famous document promised. However, the president's order was limited; it didn't mention those slaves in other states, nor what might happen in new, future states and territories.

"Well, men … moments ago, I received a telegram from Washington City, that the Congress has just passed a law, a very special kind of law called a constitutional amendment. What that means is it's a law that can't easily be changed later, so it will likely last forever.

"Gentlemen, allow me to congratulate you on this most happy of days—this law, called the Thirteenth Amendment, has just outlawed slavery, in every state and every territory of these United States."

Shocked, wide-eyed expressions, quickly turned to grins and laughter, as men leapt to their feet, tossing hats in the air, shouting, and embracing each other as the implications of the news began to sink in and to spread, as men raced around telling those who'd not yet heard.

Tony exchanged a smile with Colonel Chambers, who reached into his pocket, pulled out a cigar, stuck it into his mouth, and lit it. Then he tipped his hat to Tony, and still smiling, turned and strolled away.

Tuesday February 7, 1865 – Union Camp outside Petersburg, Virginia:

Union Captain Gareth Hughes of the Nineteenth Massachusetts Volunteer Infantry Regiment peeled off his leather riding gloves and tossed them on the camp table in front of him as he groaned and sat heavily in the folding chair next to it.

It'd been a long, exhausting several days in the saddle, and to add insult to injury, it had all been to no avail once again. After a promising start to a Union offensive action intended to cut off critical rebel rail traffic near a place called Hatcher's Run, the battle had devolved into a stalemate that accomplished little but left plenty of men dead and wounded.

As he'd done many times in the recent past, Gareth said a quick, silent prayer: first, giving thanks for the survival of himself and his men—they'd been mostly held in reserve and had suffered relatively few casualties—and second, asking for some kind of breakthrough in the siege of Petersburg that had now lasted for more than nine months with no end in sight. Last of all, but most importantly, in his mind, he said a prayer for the continued safety of his father and mother, Jonathan and Angeline Hughes, the pro-Union spy ringleaders in Richmond, knowing that their activities placed them in constant threat of arrest by the Confederate government.

When he raised his bowed head, and sat up in his chair, he marveled at the irony of it all when he considered all the times he and his family had traveled with impunity to and from Richmond in the years before the war. And how he himself had been snuck into the city with relative ease in order to celebrate the New Year with his folks. So far, though, the best efforts of General Grant and the Union Army had proven fruitless against the stubborn, dug-in Confederate defenders. Petersburg was the gateway to Richmond—they simply had to punch through it to gain the victory. And that seemed to be the one thing they could not do, no matter what they tried.

Gareth's dark reverie was interrupted when the tent flap was opened and Sergeant Gaines stuck his head in.

"Beggin' the captain's pardon, but I've got a dispatch for you, sir."

"Ah, thank you kindly, Sergeant. Please … enter and be at your ease."

"Thank you, sir."

"Do we know who it's from?" Gareth asked as the sergeant stepped forward and handed across a sheet of paper sealed with a blob of wax.

"Well … that's the odd part, sir …" Gaines answered with a frown.

"Odd? How so?"

"Well, the private who brung it said it was from Colonel Rice, but I ain't never seen the fellow before, and o' course I know all o' the colonel's couriers. Said he was fillin' in for a regular who'd taken ill, but couldn't tell me who. Seemed suspicious to me."

"I see …"

"And, it don't look like our regular dispatches …" the sergeant added, pointing at the sheet Gareth held.

Gareth turned the paper over and shrugged. Normally, the inter-regimental orders weren't sealed, but this one was. And the paper itself seemed somehow … *nicer?*

"So, Captain … if'n it contains orders, well, I'll be happy to trot on over to the colonel's command tent to verify 'em for you."

"Thank you, Sergeant. Let's just have a look, shall we?"

Gareth broke the wax seal, unfolded the paper, and gazed at the neatly written message within. And though he could not read a word of it, he immediately knew what it meant.

"Ah … all is well, Sergeant. No orders here … More of a … hmm … personal note. Nothing to be concerned with. Thank you for bringing it."

The sergeant saluted, then left the tent.

Gareth laid the sheet of paper out flat on the camp table, pulled the oil lamp over next to it, and gazed down at the note. He began deciphering the encoded message in his head, recognizing it as the code his father had invented, in his role as the secretive figure known as the Employer. But to Gareth's surprise, the very first line indicated that the message was *not* from his father, but rather from his mother.

Well, that's a first, Momma. Wonder what this is all about …

He continued translating the message in his head, not daring to write any of it down for fear that someone might find it and learn the code. When he'd finished, he reread it to make sure he'd got it correct the first time.

Then he stood, walked over to grab his hat off a hook attached to the tent pole, and headed out the door. *Now … where in this massive Union camp might I find one Colonel Nathaniel Chambers of the Twelfth West Virginia?* he wondered.

❧❧❧❧❧❧❧❧❧

"Excuse me, Colonel Chambers … may I enter, sir?"

Nathan looked up from the usual stack of papers in front of him on the camp table to see a Union captain he didn't recognize poking his head in at the tent flap. Harry the Dog stirred from his nap, lifting his great shaggy head to inspect the newcomer.

"Yes, yes … of course, Captain. Please enter …"

The captain pushed the flap the rest of the way open and stepped up to the table, even as Nathan rose to greet him. The captain stopped, stood to attention, and saluted, which Nathan returned before gesturing for the captain to have a seat. As the man moved to a chair, he glanced at Harry and smiled. The dog plopped his head back down, seeming to approve of the newcomer.

"Sorry to just poke my head into your tent like that, sir, but … I was surprised you had no guard at the door to announce me," the captain said, removing his hat as he sat. Nathan saw that the man had dark hair, a neatly trimmed beard, and a handsome face that reflected a happy demeanor—a man of much the same age as himself.

Nathan waved his hand dismissively. "I've no use for a guard. What have I to fear in a camp filled with several hundred thousand Union soldiers? A rebel assassin?" he chuckled. "Firstly, it'd be nearly impossible for one to get in here. And secondly, why bother? In the grand scheme, I'm of little importance. And thirdly, it's an extremely tedious task to require of one of my soldiers; why subject them to such undeserved, monotonous punishment?"

The captain smiled, and tilted his head thoughtfully. "Good points. Never thought about it much before … It's just *normal* for regimental commanders, much less brigade commanders, to have a man at the door of their HQ." He shrugged, "Good for you, colonel, for recognizing the tedium and needlessness of it."

Nathan returned the smile. He decided he already liked this man, despite not knowing the purpose of his visit. "We have not yet properly met, captain. You are …?"

"Captain Hughes, sir. *Gareth* Hughes, Nineteenth Massachusetts."

"Captain, pleased to meet you," Nathan said, reaching across the table to shake hands with his visitor. "But … *Massachusetts*? If I'm not mistaken, yours is *not* a New England accent, certainly. More like my own Virginian accent, I should think."

"Very perceptive of you, sir. And you are correct, I am indeed a fellow Virginian, born and raised in Richmond. Our family is originally from Boston, however. My father grew up there, and most of my relatives still live in the vicinity. So, when the secession happened, my folks, being pro-Union and anti-slavery, shipped me off to the North, along with my brother Edward, so we'd not be forced to fight for the wrong side."

"Ah, I see … Now it makes more sense. Similar to my own story, though mine involved a bit more … *difficulty* getting out of Virginia. So, Captain Hughes, what can I do for you, sir?"

"Colonel, my visit is more about what *I* can do for *you*."

"Oh? How so?"

Gareth's smile suddenly turned serious, as he gazed into Nathan's eyes. "Colonel … I must first state that what I am about to tell you is of the most sensitive nature … involving top-secret, pro-Union activities behind enemy lines. I must have your word that you won't divulge anything of what passes between us to another living soul, save those individuals specifically mentioned."

Nathan's eyes widened, but he nodded. "That I will do, Captain, with one exception: my second in command, Lieutenant Colonel Thomas Clark, now commander of the Twelfth West Virginia. Tom is like a brother to me, and there are no secrets between us. And you can rest assured, he is the very model of discretion."

Gareth was thoughtful for a moment before nodding. "Yes, Colonel Clark can also know … I have heard his name mentioned previously in our family's … *activities* … He is also a man who is trusted in our circle."

"All right … now you clearly have me at a disadvantage, sir," Nathan said, sitting up a little straighter, and leaning forward. "How is it you know of Tom, and what is this top-secret thing you propose to tell me about, or … to *do* for me?"

"Colonel … I have just returned from spending the holidays with my folks in Richmond—having been secretly smuggled in and back out again. As I said, they are pro-Union, and more than just that, they are very actively and *secretly* pro-Union. In fact, my father, *Jonathan* Hughes, had been supporting abolitionist causes in Virginia for years before the war ever started, secretly *employing* dozens of people, both black and white, in his clandestine activities. If you get my drift …"

Nathan sat back in his chair, rubbed the whiskers on his chin, while slowly nodding his head. "Yes, I think I do. If I'm not mistaken, this … *employer* father of yours has also helped *me* from time to time, though always from a distance."

"Yes, quite so," Gareth smiled.

"Well then, I can honestly say it is an honor and a pleasure to meet you, Captain. And … to finally put a name to my anonymous benefactor. That being said, what is the purpose of your visit, sir?"

"Yes, *that*. So, I have been tasked with bringing you some unpleasant news, I'm afraid, though to alleviate any unfounded fears, nothing terrible has happened to any of our *mutual friends* … yet."

"Go on … I take it your father has sent you to tell me this news?"

"No, my *mother*, Angeline, actually. My father is an unabashed optimist, always believing everything will work out for the best — meaning, the way he'd like it to," Gareth chuckled. "So he would've seen little point in it. Momma, on the other hand, is a bit more of a realist, so she believes in taking certain precautions."

Nathan nodded his understanding, but didn't want to interrupt, so that Gareth would get to the news he'd come to share.

"First, I do have a little *good* news … your sister Margaret is in good health and spirits, and is now living with my parents at their home in Richmond. I actually sat with her during the New Year's celebration, and she sends her greetings and warmest wishes to you and the rest of your men, especially Captain Jenkins. Since I won't be meeting with the captain, I trust you will relay her greetings, though of course, you'll not be able to divulge how you came by them …"

Nathan frowned. "Yes, of course, certainly. On the surface that *seems* good news, except for the part about her living with your folks. I have previously been led to understand she was living with … a *friend* of mine … Miss Evelyn Hanson. Has something happened?"

"Well, yes … that is the *bad* news. You see, from what I understand, Miss Evelyn has, for some time, been under the suspicion of the Confederate Signal Corps, but had managed to deflect their gaze, so to speak, until recently."

"And then?"

"They managed to convince her mother, Miss Harriet, to testify against her."

"*Damn her!*" Nathan pounded his fist on the table. To his credit, Gareth neither flinched, nor seemed put out by it.

"Yes, sir. *Damn* indeed."

"Did they arrest Evelyn?"

"They tried to, but she slipped away with the help of our man, Joseph. She is now in hiding, living at a warehouse owned by my father, along with a group of freemen and a few of my father's men."

"I see. And what is it your momma expects me to do with this information? Why did she wish for you to tell it to me?"

"I must confess to a bit of reticence in relaying her wishes to you, Colonel Chambers, as it likely goes against your orders from our superiors."

Nathan just shrugged and gestured for Gareth to continue.

"Worst case, she wishes for you to know where Evelyn is, so that, when the inevitable happens and the Union army breaks through the siege, you will be able to immediately seek her out and secure her safety."

"Hmm ... Seems prudent, and I will certainly do that. And the *best* case?"

Gareth sighed, and said, "Momma would like you to sneak into Richmond and convince Evelyn to come away with you. Now."

“◦◦◦◦◦◦◦◦◦◦◦◦◦◦◦”

Nathan sent a messenger to Tom, asking him to come meet Gareth before the latter departed for his own regiment. Once Tom arrived, Nathan repeated all of Gareth's news. Tom was, as expected, wide-eyed with interest.

Finally, when it was time for Gareth to take his leave, with Nathan promising to give him an answer to his mother's request once he and Tom had discussed the matter, they all stood. Nathan said, "I am in your debt, Captain Hughes. If there is anything I can do for you ... anything at all ... please don't hesitate to ask."

Gareth looked thoughtful for a moment, then smiled. "Nothing I can think of at the moment, Colonel, though ... there *is* something you can do for me *after* the war."

"Oh? What's that?"

"Invite me to the wedding, sir. I've heard so much about Miss Evelyn from my folks, but I've never met her. They call her the daughter they never had." He chuckled, "Guess that makes her the *sister* I never had. I think I'd like to meet this new sister of mine, before all is said and done."

Gareth and Nathan shared a smile and another handshake, "Done," Nathan answered, "it would be an honor and a privilege to have you there. Along with the rest of your family, of course."

Wednesday February 8, 1865 – Richmond, Virginia:

"What news have you for me, Jacob?" Evelyn asked as she stepped up to her major-domo where he sat at a rough-wood table in his corner of the warehouse. He had a sheet of paper in front of him and the stub of a pencil in his hand.

He looked up at her and frowned. "Nothing good, I'm afraid. I was just tabulating our remaining food supplies … Here, have a look for yourself," he answered, turning the paper around and sliding it across the table toward her.

She glanced down at the list. "So little …" She shook her head. "And has there been any word from the Employer?"

"Not much. Only that he dares not send supplies at the moment. Any wagon he might send would certainly be searched and either confiscated by the army or plundered by starving civilians. In either case, suspicions would be raised by the attempt."

"Well, it'll not be long before we too are starving civilians on the lookout for a wagonload of food to steal," she answered.

"Agreed. However, the food shortage may not be the worst of it. Tad tells me the Signal Corps is combing the warehouse district now, asking after a 'pretty blonde woman.' They're offering a substantial reward for your capture."

"How substantial?"

"Food," he answered.

She snorted a laugh. "That ought to do it, all right. Well, at least I am no longer blonde," she said, tugging at a long, curling lock of hair, now as black as coal thanks to a regular dousing of hair dye. "And with the complete lack of hygiene and fashion, likely no longer pretty."

He smiled, but shook his head. "Oh … I'd not say *that*, Miss Eve. Never in life."

She returned the smile. "Thank you for saying so, Jacob, though I've never felt so wretched for so long a time as this in my life."

"Likewise," he answered, pointedly glancing down at his worn and stained shirt.

"Sorry, Jacob. Here I am feeling sorry for myself, when everyone around me suffers this situation just as much as I do, or more so."

"Maybe so, Miss Eve, though they do appreciate that you are willing to suffer through it with them. Few people of your station would be willing to do so."

"You mean few people, such as yourself, Jacob."

He smiled again. "Yes, like myself," he agreed. Before the conflict, Jacob had been head operations manager of the Hughes's shipping company in Richmond. Now, with the Union blockade in full force, he'd found himself with little or nothing to do, so he had volunteered to help Evelyn in her clandestine pro-Union activities.

She pulled up a chair and sat across from him. "Now … let's talk about what we can do about the food situation … and about the Confederate Signal Corps, shall we?"

෴෴෴෴෴෴

Thursday February 25, 1865 – Richmond, Virginia:

Confederate Signal Corps Major Charles White sat at his desk in the War Department, once again examining all the notes and documents Colonel Grayson had left behind after his apparent assassination by Union spies. White had spent the last four hours on the exercise and was now down to the last page. He finished reading it, then set it aside with a sigh.

Nothing new, he decided. *The man was so obsessed with this Employer person, he'd never even entertained my theory of the spy queen, Evelyn Hanson. And his paperwork bears it out … Hundreds of pages of evidence, and theories about who this mysterious figure might be, but nothing concrete. And not a single page devoted to Miss Hanson.*

He leaned back in his chair and gazed up at the ceiling for a long moment. White had even considered that perhaps Evelyn Hanson and the Employer were one and the same—a woman cleverly posing as a man. However, all the evidence in Grayson's files, though inconclusive as to a specific identity, made it clear that the Employer was, in fact, male. And, though he was no expert on women, beautiful or otherwise, even Major White had to admit there was no way one could mistake Miss Evelyn for a man.

Damn it, Grayson. Why were you so obsessed with this Employer notion? We could've worked together and perhaps solved one or the other of these conundrums, rather than engaging in this pointless rivalry.

And then suddenly a thought hit him that made his eyes widen: *Obsessed, I say? But … haven't I too been obsessed? So obsessed with this spy queen that I've never considered that he too might've been right. That we both might've been right?*

He pushed the colonel's pile of paperwork to the right side of his desk, then opened a drawer and pulled out another stack of papers. This set of files were his own, dedicated to the hunt for the Richmond spy queen, whom he now knew to be Evelyn Hanson.

What if there's a connection here? Someone in common between these two lists …

He laid the file stacks side by side, and began going back through, looking for common names. He quickly found a number of them, which was not surprising; Miss Hanson was a well-known socialite, after all, and the Employer likely ran in the same social circles. An hour later, a pattern had begun to emerge. Three hours after he'd begun comparing notes, he pushed his chair back, looked up at the ceiling, and thought, *Thank you, Colonel Grayson. I now know who your infamous Employer is. And I shall have him! And when I do, I shall squeeze him until he gives me the location of Miss Evelyn Hanson.*

☙❧☙❧☙❧☙❧☙❧

"Damn it, Tony! Them rebs got us pinned down good this time," George said, as bullets impacted against the crude log wall they hunkered behind, sending splinters raining down on them.

"Yeah, gettin' mighty tired of it," Tony agreed, though he didn't bother looking over at his fellow sergeant, instead focusing on working the Minni ball down his rifle barrel with the ramrod. "Wonder if there'd be any way to get around that right side there and try'n flank 'em."

"Maybe …" George replied, lifting up to take a quick look before ducking back down again in time to avoid a face full of mud and splinters.

The Twenty-Third had been part of an attack against a rebel defensive works that'd started at dawn. They had made good progress at first, overrunning several entrenchments including the one Tony, George, and their two rifle companies were currently sheltering in. But the last several hours, the attack had stalled, and they'd done nothing but trade rifle fire with the enemy while keeping their heads down whenever the rebs fired off their artillery.

Tony had eaten nothing since breakfast, having no appetite for hardtack this time, and he could feel his stomach complaining. And then, as if in answer to his unspoken request, a messenger crawled up behind them and shouted, "Sergeants … the colonel says to fall back … that we're done for the day."

Tony felt some relief at this, but Big George scowled. "Pull back? When we done all this work to get here? What we wanna pull back for?"

The courier, a young black corporal, just shrugged. "Colonel ain't shared his plans with me. He just says 'fall back,' and so I tells it to y'all."

Tony reached over and pulled on George's sleeve. "C'mon, let's go. Just another day in the war. No doin' anything about it. Complainin' sure don't help."

"Well, it don't hurt, either," George answered, then grinned, "And it makes me feel better!"

Tony returned the grin and said, "Cheer up … If it's like last time, we'll go back an' sit on our backside for the next week or so while ol' Grant figures out what's next."

"Yeah, reckon so. All right, all right … I'm comin'," George said, and they whistled and signaled their men to crawl back out of the entrenchment.

Chapter 2. The Home Front

"There is one front and one battle
where every man, woman, and child
is in action.
That front is right here at home,
in our daily lives."
- Franklin D. Roosevelt

Saturday February 25, 1865 – Wheeling, West Virginia:

A frigid February wind rattled the canvas of the sturdily framed tent, seeming to suck the scant heat from the small woodstove out through every seam and crack. Toby and Anna sat huddled together on their small bed that they'd pulled up next to the stove. And though they wore their heaviest winter jackets, and sat with a blanket wrapped around their shoulders, still they shivered.

Out the two small windows, they could see tiny snowflakes swirling frantically in the winter breeze, darkening the sky such that the few short hours of daylight seem little different from the night.

"Reckon those old cabins back at Mountain Meadows was warmer'n this here?" Toby asked.

"Oh, I don't know," she answered. "Seem to recall some mighty cold days there, too."

He shrugged. "Maybe it just feels worse on account o' gettin' older it bites harder," he said.

"Yep. Reckon so … *old man,*" she responded, and gave him a playful elbow in the ribs.

"Ha. Good thing you're still a spring chicken," he answered.

She snorted a laugh.

And then, to their surprise, there came a banging, rattling knock on the wood-framed door.

"Well … who'd be foolish enough to be out in this here storm, I wonder?" Toby said, as he slipped out from under the blanket, and shuffled to the door, yanking it open and enduring the blast of frigid air and snow that pelted him in the face. Someone quickly stepped past him and into the room. He slammed the door shut again and latched it.

"*Brrr!* Not a fit day out for man nor beast," a woman said, while shaking snow off a hooded jacket.

When the newcomer threw back her hood, Anna immediately came to her feet. "Miss Abbey! What you wanna be out in this terrible weather for? Have you lost your wits, ma'am? Oh, meaning no disrespect."

Abbey laughed. "Apparently, I have. Nearly blew me away."

"Please, have a seat, ma'am," Toby offered, gesturing to one of the simple wooden chairs next to the one small table.

Rather than accept his offer, Abbey said, "Good gracious, it's cold in here, just as I expected. C'mon, now, gather whatever you might need for a few days and come up to the house with me. We can fetch the rest of your things later."

"Up to the house, ma'am? Why?" Anna asked.

Abbey frowned and put her hands on her hips. "Cause I'm tired of worrying over y'all; that's why. Out here practically freezing to death. It's bad enough for the younger people, but they can endure it better'n those of us who … well, have a few years on us, you could say. So, come on … I'll brook no arguments. From now on, you two will live in the farmhouse. No more tents for you. Come on, now."

"Well, if you insist," Toby said, shaking his head. "Though it don't quite seem right … after all these years."

"Well, as a matter of fact, it *is* right … and way overdue after all the years you've looked after our farm. The times are changing, Toby … and I mean to make sure at least the parts I can control will be changing for the better. So, c'mon … *please.* I'm getting cold …"

They laughed, and all three now exchanged smiles. "Thank you, Miss Abbey. Thank you very kindly," Anna said.

Abbey reached out and took Anna's cold hands in hers. "Never mention it, Anna, dear. Promise me you will never mention it again."

"Yes, ma'am," she said, then turned to pack up her few articles of clothing into a burlap bag she kept for the purpose.

ℰℭℬℰℭℬℰℭℬ

Sunday February 26, 1865 – Wheeling, West Virginia:

Abbey and Megs sat side by side in the front row of the Episcopal Methodist Church in downtown Wheeling, with Adilida and little Nathaniel to their right. Uncle Edouard sat on the other side of the boy, doing his best to keep the child from fidgeting while the Reverend Steven Holing gave his sermon. On the other side, next to Abbey, sat Belinda, the newest member of the Chambers extended family; Evelyn's best friend from Richmond was now living in the North after her husband Ollie's defection to the Union side.

Phinney was the only other Belle Meade resident at the church today, as he'd served as the wagon driver on the outing. Normally, he preferred to wait outside with the other drivers, but, though the weather had thankfully begun to moderate and the sun was finally shining on the sparkling snow, it was still too cold out for that. So he sat in the aisle seat on the left, next to Belinda.

Today, Abbey was finding it difficult to concentrate on the sermon, and the sight of Phinney's missing arm had sent her mind reeling, worrying over Nathaniel and their other men out in the war. Then, gazing about the room, she had to suppress a shudder. In the small congregation of no more than fifty, she noted six young men who'd suffered horrific wounds, two with missing legs, three with missing arms, and one with a terrible scar across one side of his face, the eye covered by an eyepatch. And she knew of over a dozen families whose sons would never return home, five of whom she knew personally.

We too have had our share of loss, she decided, thinking of Cobb, Georgie, Jamie, Amos, Will, Jimbo, and Eli, who'd died in the fighting in the East. And then there was the letter from Ned, with the news that they'd lost Jack and Sid out west. She said a quick prayer for the safety of the rest of their men, and then, with an effort of will, refocused on the sermon.

After the service, Abbey pulled the reverend aside and asked him what she could do to help.

"Help? How do you mean, Abbey?" he asked.

"You know … with those in need. Those who've lost so much in the war …"

"But Abbey … you too have lost much—several of your men, as I understand it. Not to mention your beloved home down in Greenbrier."

"Yes, that's true … and yet, we are still alive and getting by. While I fear others are suffering greatly. I feel so helpless. Just sitting in my house … waiting … every day just waiting for some sort of news. Hoping for the best but dreading the worst. And knowing that many of my neighbors have it much worse. When I look around the church, I see the terrible cost of the war. And such downcast faces." She shook her head sadly. "And am I imagining things, or are many looking emaciated for want of enough food?"

He slowly nodded. "You are not imagining things; many are suffering. But … Abbey, I have it on good authority that your own farm sustains and houses dozens of men, women, and children who would otherwise be cast adrift on the cold, hard tide of the world. Perhaps you should take solace in the fact you are already helping so many—"

Abbey shook her head. "I can do more, Reverend. And I intend to. Those who are the most desperate in their need, and have no food or shelter … bring them to me, will you please? I would help them if I can. It's not much, but I do have several sturdy tents with stoves that are presently vacant from the men out in the war. And there's more room still out in the barn if need be. And we've put up enough food to last the winter and then some …"

He gazed at her for a long moment, then said, "Very well. I will do as you wish. And … God bless you, Abbey."

"He already has, Reverend … He already has. That's the whole point."

True to his word, over the next week, Pastor Holing sent the most desperate cases to Belle Meade for aid: six families in all, including young children and their mothers whose husbands were either off fighting or had died in the war, and two families whose men couldn't work due to lost limbs.

Abbey, Megs, and the other women worked to make the newcomers as comfortable as possible in the tents. Thankfully, the weather had warmed somewhat, so the chill was tolerable, once the woodstoves were fully stoked.

Two weeks after Abbey's meeting with Pastor Holing, she invited him to visit the farm after church for a celebration. When he asked her what they were celebrating, she answered simply, "Life."

When Reverend Holing arrived at Mountain Meadows, the entire population was bundled up and gathered around a great bonfire out in the pasture near the farmhouse. Simple but warm food and drink was served out, and all enjoyed the boisterous music played on homemade instruments, accompanied by the singing of all assembled. In honor of Big George, his wife Babs and his two young daughters, Annie and Lucy, now aged eight and nine, banged enthusiastically on drums made of hide stretched over small kegs, while belting out various humorous lyrics.

The small children laughed and played, circling the fire in some game of their imagining, while the adults chatted merrily. One of the wounded soldiers laughed when little Nathaniel came up to him and asked, "Mister … where'd your leg go to, anyway? Did you lose it somewhere in the snow?"

To which the soldier answered, "Well, yes, as a matter of fact; that's right, my good fellow. Will you help me look for it later?"

Nathaniel grinned enthusiastically. "'Kay," he answered, then went back to his game.

Pastor Holing shared a smile with Abbey as they sat side by side next to the fire, sipping a warmed brandy, the last she had in the house. "You are doing good work here, Abbey. God is pleased with this; I am certain of it."

"I hope so," she answered. "Though that's not why I'm doing it."

"I know," he agreed. "And that makes it all the better."

25

Chapter 3. Incognito

"We meet ourselves time and again
in a thousand disguises
on the path of life."
- Carl Jung

Tuesday February 28, 1865 – Petersburg, Virginia:

The path is clear ahead, Captain," Billy reported. "I have made it across to where Captain Hughes' men wait for you."

The small group of Union men crouched down behind a battered hedge row in the dim light of dusk a few dozen yards beyond the federal picket lines.

"Thank you, Billy," Nathan answered, then turned to Captain Hughes. "Gareth … thank you for all your help." He reached out, and the two men shook hands firmly.

"Never mention it, Colonel. My father's men will get you in behind the rebel lines … After that, you'll be on your own. Good luck and Godspeed, sir," Gareth answered, then turned and scurried back toward the picket line, keeping his head down to avoid being targeted by possible enemy snipers.

Nathan then turned and shook hands with Billy, and then Stan.

"Colonel, I know you have ordered us to stay put … but Billy and I have already agreed, so there is no use in the arguing … if you and Colonel Clark aren't back in week or so, we *will* come get you out … even if you are being in the Libby Prison," Stan responded with a scowl, folding his arms across his chest, challenging his commander to disagree.

Nathan just smiled, and patted Stan on the shoulder. "I'd be shocked if you didn't, Stan."

Stan snorted a chuckle, and returned Nathan's smile. "You know us too well, Colonel," he answered.

Then Nathan knelt down in front of Harry the Dog, and the two gazed into each other's eyes for a long moment as Nathan reached out and scratched Harry under the ears.

"You have to stay here, my friend," Nathan finally said, then stood up. "You *STAY* … with Stan," he commanded, pointing at the big Russian.

Harry looked over at Stan, and then back at Nathan. Then he paced over next to Stan and sat, leaning up against the man's right leg.

"Good boy," Nathan said. "I'll be back soon, I promise."

Finally, he turned to Tom, "Ready?"

Tom returned a wan smile. "*No* … but if you're still determined to do this, then we may as well get on with it."

"That's the spirit," Nathan responded facetiously, then turned and headed up the path—a trail that had been secured by the Employer's men for just long enough to get across no-man's-land and past the rebel pickets.

Nathan had intended to go it alone, but he wasn't at all surprised that Tom had refused to be left behind, even jokingly threatening to have Nathan thrown in the brig for a deserter. The other men had also begged to go along, but Nathan had refused them, offering a reasonable explanation to each.

Jim, with his missing foot was obvious; despite the artificial limb William had designed, he simply couldn't walk any great distance. Besides, with Tom gone, he'd need to assume temporary command of the Twelfth.

William, being the regimental surgeon, was needed to help Jim enforce their cover story for being AWOL, that they'd both come down with a highly contagious disease and needed to be quarantined for a week or two. Nathan, however, didn't tell William that he also didn't want him along because he suspected the temptation to try to meet up with Margaret might be too great for William to resist, and nothing good could come of that. By all accounts Margaret was safer being left alone, at this point.

Ollie, who'd spent his entire life immersed in Richmond high society was simply too well known to risk attempting to enter the city incognito.

And Zeke still suffered nightmares recounting his time in Libby Prison and his subsequent harrowing escape. The last thing Nathan wanted to do was risk making that condition worse by injecting him back into a similar scenario.

Finally, Stan and Billy could not come along because they were too conspicuous. And from recent Confederate prisoners, they'd learned that the pair's reputation had grown amongst the rebels, especially with their scouts and pickets, as stories — some wildly exaggerated, others true — had spread of the murderous exploits of the Union's notorious "Giant and Indian" duo.

On top of all the individual reasons, the Twelfth simply couldn't have so many officers missing all at once; there was still a war on, after all, stalled as it might be at the moment.

Nathan and Tom were dressed as common Confederate soldiers: ragged, dirty, and smelly, intentionally not bathing or shaving for the two weeks leading up to the event. Fortunately, with all the rebel deserters coming across Union lines, there was no shortage of authentic and thoroughly wretched uniforms to choose from. They'd discussed various options concerning what rank to adopt in the Confederate Army, and had decided to dress as lieutenants. It was a rank that would allow them to bluff their way past most common soldiers assigned picket duty, but would not be so high up that they'd attract too much scrutiny, with common soldiers expecting to have heard of them. They also chose a cover story regarding their assigned Confederate regiment, choosing one that had recently been nearly annihilated in a Union ambush, resulting in a large number of prisoners. They would explain to anyone who asked that they'd managed to escape their captors and had made it back to Confederate lines. And since there'd be no one of their supposed regiment there to contradict them, the ruse ought to work — at least long enough for them to carry out their mission.

It also helped that Nathan was a native Virginian, so he didn't have to fear that he'd be given away by a "northern" accent. And Tom had spent years out in Texas with the army, so could speak a Texas drawl just as well as the native-born Texan, Jim Wiggins.

Nathan had only two concerns regarding their appearance, the first being that they were too well fed. Though, as with their personal hygiene, they'd intentionally cut their rations in the last couple of weeks, it couldn't make up for their previously healthy appearance. The Confederate soldiers they'd seen lately were nothing if not emaciated—it was, after all, the main reason most of them gave for deserting. They were simply starving.

His second concern was his own personal notoriety. He had, after all, been a state senator for Virginia before the war, and during the secession crisis he had made numerous public appearances and given any number of pro-Union speeches. As with Ollie, the chances of someone recognizing him in Richmond, despite his intentionally disheveled appearance, had to be considered high.

But he shrugged off his fears as they moved slowly and quietly down the twisting path, a shallow gully that would likely be full of water come spring but at the moment was cold and dusty. A little more than a quarter hour after they'd set out, and just as the darkness was nearly complete, they heard the pre-arranged signal: a bird whistle, two short tweets, followed by one longer one. They stopped, and Nathan responded in kind.

A man stepped out of the shadows, and whispered, "Welcome, Colonel Chambers … Colonel Clark. My name's Adam."

"Thanks, Adam … but from now on I am Lieutenant Ethan Chamberlain, and this is Lieutenant Robert Clarkson," Nathan answered, as the two shook hands.

"Very good, sir," he answered. "We've no time to waste, best follow me now." He turned and continued down the path they were on. Two other men fell in behind them, and another joined Adam out front. All held rifles in their hands, and Nathan noted they were carried at the half-cock, ready for immediate action if necessary. He and Tom were unarmed. Though they wore pistol holsters at their hips, these were intentionally left empty; officers escaping captivity would not have been able to retain their sidearms, nor could they have easily obtained new ones.

A few minutes later, the first group of men passed them off to two other men, this time in complete silence. The first group turned back the way they'd come, disappearing into the darkness. The two new men led them a short distance further, then through a portal carved into a thick, dirt wall that appeared to be reinforced with heavy logs. It seemed to Nathan that the sentry standing to one side of the portal was also in on the ruse, as he asked no questions of the newcomers, simply allowing them to pass through unchallenged.

The two men in front seemed to relax at this point, and the one on the left turned to Nathan and said in low tones, "We should be good now. Just act like you belong, and all will be well."

"Thank you," Nathan answered, switching from his previously cautious movements to a more confident, officer-like stride. Tom did likewise, such that anyone watching would simply see a couple of Confederate officers on a routine mission.

They passed several soldiers, who paid them little mind, as they were led through a series of twisting passageways, built using the same type of wood-and-earth construction, down plank stairs and up again, until they arrived at a small room underground—what soldiers called a "bombproof." The door was covered by a rough-spun sheet of dark cloth and the interior was warmed—though barely—by a small stove, which smoldered fitfully in the center of the low ceilinged enclosure.

The one man who'd spoken earlier came inside with Nathan and Tom, while the other stood outside, presumably to guard against any eavesdropping.

"Welcome to our humble abode, sirs," the man said. "My name is Silas. I bring greetings from my *employer*, though, of course I'll not name him."

"Seems prudent. What now, Silas?"

"Now, I'd suggest you get some sleep, and then depart at first light for Richmond," he answered.

"Wouldn't it be better to travel at night?" Tom asked.

"No." The man shook his head. "Traveling at night, unless you're leading a company of men, would attract suspicion—as if you have something to hide, which in this case, you do. The Signal

Corps is on high alert for Union spies, and confronts anyone moving along the roads between here and the city, especially if they seem in any way out of the ordinary. To give you an idea of how bad it's gotten, our mutual friend Joseph is no longer able to come here, despite his expertise in disguises and subterfuge, for fear of being caught. Communication for our people has become increasingly difficult and dangerous. That's why it took several weeks to arrange your arrival here."

"Makes sense," Tom answered, nodding.

"Speaking of communication … I am instructed to ask if you have changed your mind concerning notifying Miss Eve of your imminent arrival." He raised a questioning eyebrow.

"Thank you, but no, I have not. Firstly, I'd not want her suffering the worry over me if something bad were to happen preventing me from reaching her, which seems highly likely," he answered, to which Silas nodded his understanding.

"The second reason is more … selfish, I suppose," Nathan smiled. "Three times now, over the course of the conflict, she has surprised me by showing up at the most unexpected moment, nearly shocking the life out of me. I think it's time I returned the favor."

Silas laughed. "Fair enough. I shall relay your answer to my employer."

Nathan had also considered visiting Margaret, with the thought of getting her out as well. In the end, he had decided against it. The Employer was looking after Margaret directly, and would protect her come what may; trying to smuggle her out now would put her in more danger than leaving her where she was. So he'd also declined to inform his sister of his imminent arrival, assuming that would be for the best. Once the war was over, he could make his apologies.

Silas gestured at the bare walls of the hovel. "I'd offer you something to eat, if I had anything. Sorry to say, I haven't." The man grinned wryly and shrugged.

"Oh. Never mind that; we ate before we departed our camp. Here …" Nathan reached inside his shirt and pulled out a piece of hard tack wrapped in a sheet of parchment that he'd intended for his breakfast in the morning. "Take this," he said, offering Silas the hard, dry, tasteless biscuit.

The man gazed at it a moment, then reached out and took it. "Propriety would say I should refuse your offer … but I likely need it more than you do. So I'll not deny your generosity. Thank you, kindly."

Then Tom handed over his own chunk of hard tack, "Here … for your comrade." It was all they'd brought with them, assuming carrying a pack of provisions would look highly suspicious.

The man thanked Tom as well, then departed after wishing them: "Good luck and Godspeed."

Though they'd not had an especially long day, they decided to bed down, as there was little else to do. They dared not talk, for fear of being overheard with only cloth for a door with any number of Confederate soldiers passing by outside. And besides, the next few days would probably be more strenuous, and they'd likely need to be rested up for it. So they said their goodnights and laid down on the hard floor next to the stove, though it provided little heat.

Nathan soon found himself drifting off into a dream-filled sleep. When he awoke in the morning, he could remember little beyond fleeting images of a beautiful, blonde woman who seemed to have dominated his nighttime visions.

₧₧₧

As it was a twenty-five-mile walk from Petersburg to Richmond, Nathan and Tom had decided to do it in two days, following Silas' advice so that they'd need not travel at night. And though it was the dead of winter, it was thankfully not nearly as frigid as it had been the previous year, when William, Zeke, and Ollie had trekked across this same country through the snow and ice. Though still cold, it was not freezing, and they suffered neither snow nor rain.

Still, it was a long slog, due to their lack of anything to eat. They'd figured even if their "fellow soldiers" had nothing to spare, they could at least beg a meal off some sympathetic civilians. However, as they left the rebel entrenchments and headed north, they discovered that downtown Petersburg was entirely denuded of civilians due to the ongoing siege and its requisite bombardment by the Union artillery. The town was basically an armed camp: a wretched shambles of destroyed buildings and burned-out houses, occupied only by Confederate soldiers. So they crossed the bridge over the Appomattox River and headed out into the countryside on the main road to Richmond.

As the miles went by, they had about given up on the idea of eating; every farmhouse they checked was abandoned. They even forced their way into several by breaking the locks, only to discover that the cupboards were bare.

They were also surprised by the lack of traffic along the road. Other than the occasional courier, trotting quickly past on his horse, they saw no movement all morning. Nathan had expected to encounter a steady stream of soldiers marching to the front lines, but it was as if every soldier the Confederacy had was already manning their fortifications and they simply had no more to send.

It wasn't until mid-afternoon that they observed their first sign of troop movement. They'd stopped beside the road for a brief rest and a sip from their canteens—what Nathan facetiously referred to as "supper"—when they saw in the near distance a mounted cavalry company moving slowly down the roadway coming from Richmond, obviously on their way to Petersburg.

After a brief glance, Nathan paid them little mind, though Tom continued to gaze in their direction, more out of the mind's habit of following any sort of movement than any real intent.

Suddenly, Nathan heard a sharp intake of breath from Tom, who hissed, "Turn away from the road, and don't look up until they're past."

Nathan's eyes widened, but he did as he was bid, assuming Tom had seen someone who might recognize him, the one thing they'd most feared on their present mission. "Who is it, Tom?" he asked.

"*Walters*," Tom answered in a low voice.

Nathan scowled. "It's probably for the best that I'm not armed, or I'd have to shoot him. That would very likely ruin our day," he answered.

Tom nodded. They were quiet for a moment as the riders approached. When they'd come to within a few dozen yards, Nathan said, "We should have a conversation, not too loudly, but with plenty of hand gestures … as if we are deep into it. Otherwise, it will seem odd if we don't look up at them and shout a greeting."

"All right," Tom agreed. "What shall we discuss?"

"Hmm … we should discuss something that would interest two rebel officers …" Nathan answered, rubbing his chin whiskers.

"I have it," Tom said. "You're a biblical scholar—give me a lecture on something from the scriptures. That may have the added benefit that no one will dare to interrupt, as if it were a sermon," Tom said.

"Ah, good suggestion," Nathan answered, then thought for a moment. Under the stress of the present circumstance, his mind drew a blank. And then it suddenly came to him, and he smiled. *The prodigal son*, he thought, remembering Reverend Blackburn using that very sermon to berate him upon his return to Mountain Meadows after his twenty-year absence. *And it seems somehow appropriate to this occasion as well, given that I am in fact Virginia's prodigal son, returning to an uncertain reception*, he decided.

"In the Bible there's a very interesting story," Nathan began, "called the parable of the prodigal son, as told by our Lord Jesus Christ, in Luke, chapter fifteen. It goes like this …"

Nathan proceeded to recite the passage word for word, and then went on to explain its various generally accepted meanings.

Tom feigned deep contemplation, gazing down at his boots with the broad brim of his hat covering his face from the passing riders. After a few minutes he said, "You can stop now … They're out of earshot."

"But … I'm just getting to the good parts," Nathan answered, in a mock pouting tone.

Tom chuckled. "Perhaps you can finish another day."

They were quiet for a moment, then Nathan said, "So …
Walters is now here—in Petersburg."

"Yes, so it would seem," Tom answered. "I'm a little
surprised … a siege doesn't seem like his kind of fight."

"Agreed. Likely not by choice; was probably forced into it,"
Nathan answered.

"True. I'm sure they need every man they can get at this point
in the war."

"Yes, very likely so," Nathan agreed. "Still, it will give me
more motivation when it comes time for the attack."

"Not that you need any extra on that score," Tom replied.

Nathan nodded thoughtfully, then scowled. "*Hell is empty, and
all the devils are here.*"

"The Bible?" Tom asked.

"No, Shakespeare, actually. *The Tempest.*"

"Ah … seems somehow apropos, nonetheless," Tom said.

"Quite."

ॐ✿❀ॐ❀✿ॐ❀✿ॐ❀✿ॐ

They reached the small town of Chester, about halfway
between Petersburg and Richmond, just as the sun was setting.
Like most of their journey, the place was devoid of traffic. They
saw no civilians, other than the half dozen men manning the rail
station office, and the only soldiers they encountered were two
privates who'd pitched a small pup tent a few yards from the rail
yard.

The evening was rapidly cooling, and the small campfire the
soldiers had lit looked extremely inviting, prompting Tom to look
over at Nathan and raise an eyebrow. "Shall we, do you think?"

"Yes, why not? We've brought no tent, and it would be a great
bother to start a fire of our own. Besides, it'd seem odd if we didn't
ask to join them."

"Seems reasonable. And warm," Tom answered, rubbing his
arms to emphasize the point.

And though they would've been obliged to share their fire
with two officers in any event, the privates seemed genuinely
pleased to see them, and were friendly and welcoming.

After introductions were made, Nathan asked, "So, what brings you men out here into the cold all by yourselves, may I ask?"

"Oh, yes, certainly you may, sir," the one named Warren answered. "We've been laid up in hospital this past month and more. Hit by the same damned Yankee bomb, we was. I took a piece o' lead to the shoulder," he said as he pointed to the spot.

"And Milton, here," he chuckled, "well, let's just say he ain't been able to sit too good for a spell."

Milton reached across and slapped Warren on the arm in mock reproach. "Now, Warren, there ain't no call to go'n tell these fine gents about my ... backside troubles ..." But he grinned good-naturedly as he said it.

"Headin' back to the front to rejoin our regiment. Fifty-Fourth North Carolina."

"Yeah," the other private agreed. "It'll be good to see the boys again, though ... Don't take me wrong, sirs ... I mean to do my duty, come what may. It's just ... well, it sure would be nice if it were over. Ain't excited to crawl back into them trenches."

"That's quite all right, Private," Nathan answered. "Perfectly understandable to be tired of the fighting and privation. Especially for those, such as yourselves, who've already been wounded in the battles."

"Thank you, sir," Warren responded. "And what mission brings you sirs out here on the road, if it ain't above my station to ask?"

"Not at all," Nathan answered. "We're with the Thirty-Second Virginia. Had a bit of an unfortunate event with the Yankees a couple days ago. Lost a lot of good men ..." He looked down and slowly shook his head. "Rest of us were captured. But as we were being marched away, Lieutenant Clarkson and I found ourselves with the opportunity to escape, and slipped away in the darkness, crawling on our hands and knees through a field. Managed to make it back to our lines. Since the rest of our regiment is gone, we're headed back to the War Department for reassignment. Reckon someone will want us," he shrugged, and grinned.

"Oh, yes. Most certainly, sirs. You look like fine, fighting officers, if you don't mind my saying so. I'm sure one o' the other regiments'll be more'n happy to have y'all."

Nathan felt pleased that their pre-determined and rehearsed cover story seemed to be accepted at face value. He assumed that was a good sign for their mission ahead.

⁂

The next day, they were on the road again at first light. Thinking back on the evening they'd spent with the two Confederate privates, Nathan reflected on how much he'd enjoyed their simple comradery, though they were technically the enemy. It was a sharp reminder of a fact he already knew: that the vast majority of the men he was fighting against were not evil, just ordinary men doing what they thought was their duty. Only their cause was unjust, not their hearts. It was one more reason to get the war over with: that he'd not be forced to kill any more men such as those they'd just spent a pleasant evening conversing with.

As on the previous day, the road was nearly empty, with only a few soldiers and civilians passing them, heading toward Petersburg, and two times lone soldiers riding past toward Richmond, clearly messengers coming back from the front.

At mid-afternoon, they once again heard the sound of horse hooves coming up behind them and stepped to the side of the road to allow the rider to pass. This time there were three riders, and they did not continue on their way, but pulled up to a stop next to Nathan and Tom.

The man in the lead was a captain, the other two were privates. Nathan and Tom immediately stood to attention and saluted the captain, who returned it smartly.

"I am Captain Snyder of the Signal Corps," the officer announced. He was a young man about Tom's age with dark hair and a neatly trimmed beard. Nathan decided he would've deduced that the man was from the War Department by his crisp, clean uniform; nobody serving at the front would look like that for long. And the captain represented the one thing they had least wished to encounter on their journey: a Confederate Signal Corps officer—a man whose unit was charged with rooting out spies and capturing deserters.

Nathan introduced himself and Tom, giving their cover names.

"And why, may I ask, Lieutenant Chamberlain, are you and Lieutenant Clarkson heading toward Richmond?" the captain asked. He held a stern, serious expression, and did not radiate any warm feelings toward his fellow Confederate officers, if he had any.

"Certainly, sir," Nathan answered, then gave the prepared alibi.

The man seemed to contemplate this for a moment, then said, "Ah, yes, the Thirty-Second. Heard about that. Nasty business …" Then he gazed at Nathan for a long moment. "Have we met before, Lieutenant? You seem somehow … *familiar* …"

"Could be, sir … I'm from Richmond, as I guess you are as well? Perhaps we spoke with one another at some social function before the war?"

The man slowly nodded, "Maybe, maybe … Well, anyway, lucky break, you two escaping. Tell me again how you managed it …"

This time, Tom told the story, but in greater detail than Nathan had given. They'd rehearsed it many times so that he and Nathan would be sure to say the exact same things. They'd also discussed this very scenario, and had decided their first telling would be a quick overview. If they were quizzed further, they would provide greater detail, making it appear all the more real.

When Tom had finished, Captain Snyder seemed satisfied. "Gentlemen, if I had extra horses I would provide you with a ride. But we are due back at headquarters straightaway, so I fear you will have to walk, for the time being. I will, however, send back an escort for you once I arrive at Richmond."

"Thank you, sir. Much obliged," Nathan answered, but what he thought was, *And so you can make sure we really do report to the War Department, as we stated, and aren't just deserting.*

After the encounter with the Signal Corps captain, they were even more eager to slip into Richmond incognito. And the very last thing the needed was the "escort" to the War Department that the captain had offered. If they were forced to go to Confederate Army headquarters, their ruse would quickly unravel, as the authorities would discover that there were no such lieutenants commissioned in the Thirty-Second regiment.

So, after the Signal Corps men departed, Nathan and Tom remained on the lookout for riders approaching from the direction of the city. Two times they spotted horsemen and were able to duck off to the side of the road and stay hidden until the riders passed.

Toward the middle of the afternoon, they came to the point they'd been dreading: Mayo's Bridge. The bridge was the only way to cross the James River into Richmond for many miles in either direction. They had little choice but to cross it. And if anyone was looking for them, they would know that too.

Ironically, it was the very same pinch point they'd been forced to cross in the opposite direction when escaping from Richmond after the Secession crisis, now nearly four years ago. That time, they'd been forced to shoot their way through. This time, gunfire was not an option, since they were unarmed. The good news was that Nathan had all his wits about him, rather than his condition on that earlier occasion, having suffered a severe blow to the skull.

When they reached the bridgehead, Nathan and Tom paused and gazed across. They could see no one on the bridge deck, or close by on the street beyond. They turned to each other, exchanged a look and a shrug, then forged ahead.

They stepped up onto the bridge and started across, and still they saw no one. When they passed the halfway point, and were nearing the Richmond end, three soldiers stepped up onto the bridge from where they'd been hidden on the righthand side of the roadway. The man in front was a Confederate officer, and the two men behind were privates. Most telling was that the privates held rifles at the ready across their chests.

Nathan groaned when he recognized the leader, "Signal Corps Captain Snyder," he hissed.

Tom nodded.

They were too far across the bridge to attempt to turn back, so there was nothing to do but continue on and hope to bluff their way out.

When the two groups met, they all stopped, and Nathan and Tom immediately saluted the captain as they'd done at their first meeting.

This time he did not return the salute. Instead, he grinned, but not in a friendly way, to Nathan's thinking.

"I wouldn't bother with that, if I were you … *Colonel Nathaniel Chambers*," he said with a smirk.

Nathan just stared at him, at a loss as to what to say.

"You see, *Colonel*, as I rode toward Richmond, it came to me … where I had seen you before. At the Secession Convention … giving a speech. A *pro-Union* speech. And then I remembered the name, *not* Ethan Chamberlain, but rather Nathaniel Chambers. And when I made the requisite inquiries, I discovered that Nathaniel Chambers, late of the Richmond legislature, had gone over to the Yankee side, and is now a traitor."

Nathan scowled at him. "Call me what you will, *sir*, but I'll not suffer being called a traitor, by *you* or any other man."

Snyder scoffed and folded his arms across his chest. "Well, under the circumstances, I don't see as how you have much say in the matter," he said, and turned to glance at one of his armed privates to emphasize the point.

As Snyder's head was turned, Nathan reached out, yanked the officer's pistol from its holster, pulled back the hammer and fired. The shot was not aimed at the captain, rather at the private to his right who suddenly crumpled over, grasping his chest and dropping his rifle, slumping to the deck. Before the other private could react, Nathan turned and fired a second shot, hitting the soldier mid-chest, toppling him backward.

Captain Snyder backed away, eyes wide, beginning to raise his hands. "Don't shoot," he pleaded, "I'll—"

Nathan stepped forward, raised the pistol, and shot the man between the eyes. The Signal Corps captain was dead before his body hit the bridge deck.

Tom looked at Nathan wide-eyed. "I guess you *really* didn't like him calling you a traitor."

Nathan just shrugged. "If he turned us in, we'd be hanged."

Tom, already kneeling down to scoop up one of the dead men's rifles and ammunition pouch, responded, "Hey, that's almost exactly what *I* said when I shot one of your captors back when we were trying to escape from here. Seem to recall you chastising me for it back then."

Nathan knelt down and searched the captain's body for the pistol ammunition as he answered, "All right, I stand corrected for that, and beg your pardon."

"Pardon granted," Tom answered.

Nathan stood and holstered the pistol, then shoved the ammunition pouch into his belt, before picking up the other rifle and its ammunition. "Let's move," he said.

Tom didn't have to ask in which direction, knowing his friend well enough to know there would be no going back. They sprinted the rest of the way across the bridge, then immediately left the roadway toward the right, down an embankment, and into some bushes along the waterfront. Even before they were off the bridge deck, they could see men with rifles racing down Eighth Street toward them, and they could hear shouts of alarm.

They'd gone no more than fifty yards when Nathan stopped and turned back to face the bridge deck, raising his rifle. "Let's give them something to think about, Tom," he said.

Tom raised his own rifle. A group of soldiers approached the edge of the roadway where Nathan and Tom had left it and started to work their way down the slope.

"Now!" Nathan said, and the two of them opened fire, downing two of the rebel soldiers. The others scrambled for cover. Nathan and Tom turned and raced down a dirt path that led between several warehouses.

When they reached an intersection between two buildings, they turned to the side and sat down to catch their breath, their backs against the wall of one building. Tom risked a look back the way they'd come and said, "They're coming, but more cautiously now. Still, they won't be long."

Nathan said nothing, focused on reloading the rifle. Tom did the same, and also re-filled the empty pistol cylinders.

"Ready?" Nathan asked, but Tom surprised him by shaking his head.

"No."

"No? Are you hurt, Tom?" Nathan asked, looking his friend over closely.

"It's not *that* … It's just … this isn't the way to do it. We can't keep going like this. They'll eventually catch us."

"All right; what, then?"

"We must split up. You carry on with the original mission, while I lead them astray," Tom answered.

"Oh, no … I can't let you do that, Tom," Nathan shook his head.

"Why not?"

"Because … it's suicidal."

"No, it's not. You forget, I've done it before … up at Paint Bank. I led the enemy away from you and William. Got them lost in the woods, then circled back to rejoin you. I can do it better than anyone. Trust me."

"I hadn't forgotten, Tom. But this isn't the deep woods. It's a modern city. It's not the same."

Then Tom grinned, "I know … here when I shoot, I might actually hit someone!"

Then Tom's countenance and tone turned serious, "Think about it, Nathan … they've already recognized you and likely spread the word to be on the lookout for you. But nobody knows me. Once I evade them, I'll be fine. Besides … if the shoe was on the other foot, you'd do the same for me."

Nathan knew that Tom spoke the simple truth. "All right, all right," he said. "You win. Here, may as well take my rifle also."

Tom took the gun and slung it over his shoulder by its strap.

"You know the location of Evelyn's warehouse," Nathan continued. "We'll split up and rendezvous there later. Tonight, after it's dark. I'll come outside and look for you."

"Okay. And if I can't get there tonight, repeat the rendezvous each night thereafter," Tom added.

"Until when?" Nathan asked.

"Until you know I'm not coming."

The two met eyes for a long moment, then exchanged a nod before taking off in different directions.

A few moments after their parting, Nathan heard gunfire in the distance. He said a quick prayer for Tom's safety. But despite his concern for his best friend, he couldn't help feeling a welling of excitement at the prospect of seeing Evelyn again, for the first time in more than two years. He had to discipline himself to keep a steady pace and resist a strong desire to run to her.

⁂⁂⁂

Lieutenant Colonel Elijah Walters stepped down from his horse and handed the reins to one of his privates. He rubbed at the pain in his lower back for a moment while gazing about at their new surroundings, such as they were. They were on the edge of a corral, of sorts, which was nothing more than a broad pit dug into the earth, surrounded by walls of logs and piled dirt—an attempt to protect their horses from incoming Yankee artillery fire, though clearly it would do little good if they managed a direct hit. The noisome pit was full of oozing mud and horse manure, but he resisted the urge to plug his nose at the stench.

The rest of his men of the Thirty-Sixth Virginia Cavalry Battalion were actively dismounting and unsaddling their horses, with no need of any orders from him, thankfully. His second in command, Captain Roberts, had already gone in search of someone who could tell them where they were to be housed.

Walters scowled at the sight of his surroundings—a place he never wanted nor intended to be. His company's happy, extended leave back at Walters Farm in Greenbrier County had been summarily interrupted by the arrival of a Signal Corps officer with orders to report to the siege works at Petersburg without delay. The orders had come with a thinly veiled threat of court martial for desertion and dereliction of duty if not obeyed.

Walters had momentarily considered murdering the haughty fellow and burying him out in the woods, but had thought better of it. They'd just send another, and this time he'd have an armed escort. So Walters had been forced to once again close up his farm and head back to the war. That had been two weeks earlier, and despite his best efforts at foot-dragging, the day of their arrival at their dreary destination had finally arrived.

For the most part, Walters had enjoyed the war—being in command of a fighting force, killing anyone he pleased with few repercussions. And he'd gotten very good at sensing when things were about to go badly for the Southern side, then using the cavalry's mobility to quickly remove himself and his men from harm's way.

But now, even as the war was clearly winding down, he found himself forced into a grinding stalemate, where he'd likely be charged with manning a section of the Confederate fortifications. And he could think of no way out of it other than outright desertion. He'd considered that as well, but feared being caught and humiliated … or worse.

Walters' mind had just shifted to wondering whether they'd be able to find a decent meal when a young captain stepped up to him and saluted.

He returned the salute in a manner indicating his sincere lack of enthusiasm for the gesture. "Captain … is there something I can do for you?" he asked.

"My name is Captain Jubal Collins of the Twenty-Seventh Virginia, though when last we met, I was still a lieutenant. Do you remember me, Colonel Walters?" the young man said.

Walters stared at him a moment, but drew a blank. "Should I?" he asked.

"No … I suppose not. But I remember *you*, sir. Last time I saw you, you'd just shot one of my prisoners, a Yankee sergeant … right after the second Battle of Winchester."

Walters thought back, and then made the connection. "Yes … I do recall the incident. I took care of the first Yank, but you got in my way before I could shoot the officer with him."

"Yes, that I did, I'm happy to say."

Walters narrowed his eyes and glared at the captain. "Is there some point to this discussion, Captain? Otherwise, I have a battalion to get settled."

"Just this, sir: I wanted you to know that I did file an official report on the matter. If you received some punishment, it was at my behest."

"Hah. I do recall the general mentioning a formal letter of complaint … just before he tore it up. Have you come to apologize, or to gloat, Captain? Because either way, I have no interest in it."

"Neither. Just to serve notice, that you'll not get away with such mischief here at Petersburg," Jubal answered with a scowl.

Walters shrugged, turned away, and walked off, having already lost interest in the conversation, which in his mind had no relevance whatsoever.

☙

"Miss Eve, we've caught a man," Jacob announced, poking his head around the rough, wooden screen that delineated her little corner of the warehouse. "We reckon he's a Signal Corps agent, though he's dressed as a regular frontline lieutenant. He's Virginian, by his accent, and definitely military by his bearing, but though his uniform is ragged, he's too healthy looking to have spent any time at the front. Also, he won't give us his name, despite … well, let's just say we've been none too gentle with him."

"Oh! Where did you capture him?"

"He was just outside, behind some bushes. Seems like he followed you here, somehow. He definitely knows who you are … keeps asking for you. It's pretty much the only thing he'll say. He keeps repeating, 'Where's Evelyn, and who are you? Let me talk to her.' It's all we can get out of him, despite our determined persuasion. Like I said, clearly he has military training, or he'd not be able to resist our best efforts.

"The good news is we seem to have caught him before he could report back on our location. What shall we do with him, do you think?"

"Well, if he's with the Signal Corps, and has tracked me here … clearly we can't allow him to ever leave and report this location; we have nowhere else to go that will accommodate all of us." She looked down at the floor and was quiet for a long moment. Then she sighed, and looked back up. "We haven't the means to keep a captive here, and we are desperately short of food as it is …"

"Miss Eve," Jacob gave her a stern look, "I know it goes against your beliefs, and will cause you much heartache, but I believe we must do what is necessary in this case, despite our distaste for it."

She turned away from him and gazed across the room for another long time before turning back toward him.

"I guess … I guess we shall have to make an end to him."

"Yes, ma'am, I agree. We have him well tied, so it will be a simple matter; a sharp knife, and the job will be done, quickly and quietly. Very little pain or suffering. Then we can bury him deep … down in the basement. No one will ever know where he went, or why he disappeared."

"Yes … yes, I suppose that is what we *must* do. All right, go ahead with it then."

"Yes, ma'am."

Jacob turned and headed for the door.

Then a tiny voice seemed to speak in the back of Evelyn's mind. It was a voice she knew well, and often hated, but she had to admit it was usually right. This time it said simply, *But … what if I'm wrong?*

"Wait!" she said.

Jacob paused and turned toward her.

"Yes, Miss Eve?"

"If I'm going to pronounce a death sentence on a man, I should at least hear what he has to say. Otherwise, I'm no more than a hypocritical coward. If I'm going to order a man killed, I should have the moral courage to look him in the eye first, and then … I should have the stomach to perform the act myself, not ask another to do it for me."

She took a deep breath, "Take me to him."

"Yes, ma'am. He's in the basement. Hank is watching him."

When she walked into the room, she could see a man tied to a chair in the center of the room. His head was slumped against his chest, as if he had passed out. She winced as she noted the blood splatter on the top half of his shirt. Given the harsh treatment her men had meted out, it was not surprising.

Hank stood back from the man, leaning against the wall, his arms folded across his chest. He nodded at Evelyn as she entered.

It occurred to her that her men, who'd been normal, peaceable fellows before the war, had become hardened and ruthless from everything they'd been forced to endure. Now they'd not hesitate to resort to extreme, violent measures, if called for.

She stepped further into the room and walked over to where the man sat. There was a chair just opposite him; obviously where Jacob had been sitting during the interrogation. She sat down in the chair and looked over at the man.

"Excuse me, sir … Can you hear me?"

He stirred at the sound of her voice, as if awakening. He shook his head, and several drops of blood dripped to the floor; then he looked up. The face was battered, with a swollen and bloody lip, one eye showing a purplish bruising, and a stream of blood running down from one nostril, but even so, it was a face she knew instantly. She gasped.

Despite his injuries, the man smiled a broad, genuine—if bloody—smile, and said, "Hello, Evelyn."

Her heart nearly stopped from the shock. "Oh! Oh, my God! *Oh, my dear God!*"

She lurched from her chair, and threw her arms around the man, holding him tight, tucking her head into the crook of his neck.

Jacob and Hank looked at each other in complete amazement. Clearly, she knew the man, and … after a moment, it was also clear her body was rocked by heavy sobs.

"Nathan … Oh, my God, Nathan! Oh … oh, thank God … thank God, I have not killed you … Oh, my God, what have I nearly done? … Oh, I can't believe it …"

"Whatever do you mean, Evelyn? I'm all right … just a little bloodied, but otherwise unharmed … don't cry … it's all right."

She continued to sob for several more minutes, to the confusion and consternation of the men in the room. Finally, she sat up and wiped the tears from her eyes. She turned to Jacob, and said, "Cut this man's bonds, immediately!"

"Well … I now understand that you know this man, but …"

"This is Colonel Chambers, my very dear … *friend*. Untie him immediately!"

"But, Miss Eve … if he's a colonel in the army, he will certainly be obliged to tell what he knows of our activities and location, despite your obvious friendship."

"Jacob, this is Colonel *Nathaniel* Chambers—of the *Union* Army!"

"Oh! Oh, *that* Colonel Chambers. Now I see. Yes, ma'am!"

Jacob pulled out a knife and cut through Nathan's bonds, releasing him from the chair.

Evelyn once again wrapped her arms around him, and now he was able to embrace her as well. Then she pulled back and kissed him passionately on the lips, despite his bleeding injuries.

"Oh, Nathan … I can't believe you're here … thank God … thank my blessed, precious God! You are here … here at last … after … after all this time! Oh, my love … oh, my dear, sweet love …"

He returned her kisses affectionately, ignoring the pain of his recent rough handling by her men.

"Evelyn … how I have dreamed of holding you … these last two years apart," he murmured into her ear.

Jacob and Hank exchanged a knowing look and quickly departed, closing the basement door behind them as they headed up the stairs.

After a few more minutes, Nathan and Evelyn pulled apart.

"But Nathan … how is it you're here, and … why?"

"I would've come earlier, but I feared giving you away if I was caught," he answered.

"Then what has changed your mind?"

"An unexpected visitor, Gareth Hughes."

"Oh."

"He told me about your present *difficulties*," Nathan answered.

"I suppose Jonathan sent him," she said with a frown. "He worries so … has his men watching me like a hawk, as you discovered the hard way."

"Yes … they were quite *hard*," he agreed, rubbing at his bruised jaw for emphasis. "But Gareth said it wasn't his daddy who sent him, rather his momma."

"Angeline?"

"Yes. Apparently, she thinks you are in imminent danger of being caught by the Confederates. Based on the fearful reaction of your men, seems like she may be right. I've come here to get you out."

"Oh. Now that you say it, I can see her doing that. She has advocated for me to quit Richmond in the past, but I've always refused to leave. I guess she thought I could use a bit more persuasion …"

He smiled and said, "Come away with me then, back behind Union lines, where you'll be safe. The war will surely be over soon. Then we can be married, return to Mountain Meadows, and start our very own 'happily ever after.'"

"Nathan, darling … I would love nothing more, but …"

"*But?*"

"Can't you see it for yourself? There are more than a dozen freemen and runaway slaves here who need me. I am their leader … like you are with your soldiers. While the war yet rages, I can no more abandon them than you can the men in your regiment."

"Yes … I can see that. You are, above all else, truly honorable. Still, I would take you back with me to keep you safe … even against your will, if necessary."

"All right, Nathan. I will come away with you, right now, this instant … on one condition."

"Yes?"

"That you are also willing to resign your commission, quit the war, and let others end it for you; while you and I begin our 'happily ever after' together, starting today."

He was silent, and thoughtful for a minute, then smiled, shook his head, and looked up at her.

"You know perfectly well I can't do that."

"Of course, dear. Just like you know I can't leave those who depend on me. So … go back to your army. Saddle up your horse and ride forth … *finish this war!*

"Then, we will be married, as should have been done five years ago. And yes, I know … that's my fault.

"Now it is time for you to make an end, so we may finally make a beginning."

"Yes, ma'am. That I will do, if it is within my power."

He smiled at her, and she leaned in and kissed him once again.

After a few more moments, she rose, took his hand and said, "Come, darling … I would introduce you to my men."

"Oh, I believe we've already met," he replied with a wan smile.

She scowled, and said, "Yes, I know. I would have you settle *that* grievance straightaway; after all, we're all friends here, fighting for the same side. We can't let a little … *misunderstanding* come between us."

Nathan rubbed at his sore jaw. "Little misunderstanding?" He chuckled, "Easy for you to say."

She smiled and slapped his shoulder playfully.

"Ouch," he said, feigning further injury.

They headed toward the front door. Jacob and Hank were standing just outside.

Evelyn formally introduced them, then Jacob said, "I cannot tell you how sorry I am, Colonel Chambers, for … injuring you. I beg your pardon, and sincerely hope you will understand it was for good reason: for the protection of Miss Eve. I would never have done it had I known who you really were; that you were her friend and a Union officer, at that."

Nathan locked eyes with him. "Pardon granted, and all is forgiven, Jacob. As you say, I appreciate your diligence in protecting Miss *Eve*. But … allow me to give you some … friendly advice … 'words of wisdom,' as they say."

"Sir?"

"If I'd been a real enemy agent, you'd be dead, Jacob. I allowed you to 'capture' me earlier because I was unsure whether you were a friend of Evelyn's; I reckon it'd be bad manners to kill her allies before first talking with her.

"When you took me, you placed your gun to my head. It would've been a simple matter for me to disarm you when you're standing that close. When capturing an enemy, always stand a good six feet away and aim your gun at the center of his chest. You can't miss from there, and he can't possibly cover that distance before you can pull the trigger. If you stand any closer, you're at his mercy; he can disarm you before you can react."

"I … I can see that now; thank you, Colonel. I will remember … and I'll be sure to tell the others. We'll be more careful, should the occasion arise again."

"See that you are. Oh … and Jacob?"

"Yes, Colonel?"

"Don't ever hit me again," he said, rubbing his sore jaw and frowning. Then he broke into a grin, "I'd hate to have to kill you."

Jacob chuckled and shook his head. "Sorry about that, sir … It won't happen again."

❧❦❧❦❧❦❧❦❧❦

After a quick tour of the warehouse, Evelyn and Nathan sat in her little "bedroom," which consisted of two chairs, a small table, and a padded pallet on the floor in a corner of a large, low-ceilinged room, screened off for a modicum of privacy.

After asking if he'd eaten recently, and learning that he had not, she fetched him something to eat. Then, as he ate, they took turns telling each other everything of importance they could think of that had happened since last they'd parted. Several hours went by before Nathan noticed the room was becoming darker. He pulled out his pocket watch to check the time.

"Oh, Tom! I must go meet him," he said, repocketing the watch.

"Where were you to meet?" she asked.

"Here. Outside. Pray that he has evaded our pursuers and is even now waiting for me. I must go get him … alone, or he will assume something is wrong."

"Oh, all right. I will warn off my guardians and tell them to expect your return with another man dressed as a rebel officer."

After waiting for Evelyn to spread the word, Nathan went outside and took a quick look around. Seeing no one on the street, he stepped across and into an alleyway. There he paused, put his fingers to his mouth, and made a bird whistle. For a moment, there was nothing but silence, and he began to fear the worst. Then he heard it: the very same whistle in reply. In moments, he saw the silhouette of a man coming up the alley toward him, and when they met, the two men embraced with enthusiasm.

"You made it," Nathan said in low tones.

"Of course. I told you I would," Tom answered in the same manner.

"Hmm … why do I suspect it was not as easy as you put on?" Nathan asked.

Tom chuckled softly, "Probably because you know me too well."

"Come inside … then you can tell me the tale," Nathan said, then led the way back into the warehouse.

They found Evelyn waiting anxiously just inside the door. When she saw Tom, she smiled brightly and said, "Tom … thank God you've made it safely." Then she too hugged him affectionately.

"Good to see you too, Evelyn," he answered, when she stepped back. "You're looking well, despite your current rough circumstances. And the black hair … hmm … Not a bad look on you."

"Thank you, Tom," she grinned, tugging unconsciously on a long, curly black lock. "You're looking well too, though both of you are quite the filthy sight."

Tom glanced down at his rumpled and mud-splattered uniform. He brushed ineffectually at the tunic, then shrugged. "Our cleaners haven't been doing a good job lately."

She laughed. "Oh, and neither have your cooks, I understand. Please, be at home, such as it is. Nathan will show you to my little room while I find you something to eat."

"Thank you, Evelyn," Tom said. "Yes, food would be most welcomed."

Nathan resisted the urge to quiz Tom on his escape after their parting, knowing Evelyn would also want to hear the story. So, he filled the time telling his own tale, though it had been entirely uneventful, other than the fact that his future bride had nearly ordered him executed. Tom just shook his head and rolled his eyes when he heard that part.

After Evelyn had returned, and Tom had downed a few bites of the proffered supper—a cold meal of salted pork and chopped sweet potatoes, which seemed a feast to a man who'd not eaten in two days—Nathan could resist no longer. "All right, Tom … your tale now, if you please."

Tom smiled and swallowed the food in his mouth. "Yes, sir!" he said, and snapped a mock salute.

"Not much to tell," he began. "After we parted, I ran on to the next corner, then turned and waited. Fortunately, with the Union blockade cutting off all ship traffic up the James, the warehouse district is basically empty, so there were no civilians around to give away my location.

"As expected, the rebels came straight up the street, no strategy, no subterfuge … I hit one as he strode down the middle of the street, as if he hadn't a care in the world, if you can believe it. And after we'd already shot a couple of them only a few moments earlier," he snorted derisively, then shook his head. "Child's play.

"After that, they were more careful."

"I should think so," Evelyn replied, nodding.

"Of course, I immediately moved again," Tom continued. "This time, down a side alley. When they crept past the opening to the alley, thinking I'd kept on in the original direction, I picked off another. Then I moved again.

"They got smarter after that; sent some men around a block on either side, trying to flank me, but I kept moving in different directions, and they could never close their trap.

"Finally worked my way over to Main Street, figuring I was a few blocks ahead of them by that point, them having to move more cautiously. I peered out and saw a column of soldiers marching along, headed west. So I stuffed the rifles under a bush, stood up, and casually walked out, falling in behind them as if I was one of their officers. When they reached Eight Street, they turned left towards the bridge, so I followed. I finally peeled off in almost the exact same spot we'd gotten off the bridge before. Figured that would be the last place they'd think to look. By then, it was nearly dark, so I just strode down Byrd Street like I owned the place. When I was a block away from here, I hid again to wait for your signal. And now … here I am."

Evelyn was impressed by Tom's escape, and told him so in glowing terms. "Once again, you prove why Nathan holds you in such high esteem," she said.

"Thank you, but it was really nothing," Tom answered.

"The fact that you say so, proves my point," she retorted, smiling brightly, a gesture Tom could not resist returning.

Nathan was not at all surprised, knowing that Tom's superior soldiering skills, honed out west fighting Indians, were more than a match for any man stationed in the city on routine garrison duty. But something Tom had said earlier, concerning their uniforms, had triggered an idea he was now mulling over.

Evelyn noticed Nathan had become quiet and appeared thoughtful. "What is it, my dear?" she asked.

"Hmm … something Tom said earlier … about the cleaners. Evelyn, do you have someone who could clean up these uniforms, and mend the worn patches … maybe even have them pressed?"

"Yes, certainly. Several of our ladies were previously domestic slaves in fine households. Such tasks were among their normal duties. Why? Are you suddenly self-conscious of your disheveled appearance? I can assure you, my good sir, it matters not at all to me," she smiled.

He chuckled. "No, not *that*. I was thinking that they will now be on the lookout for two men—Union spies—dressed as frontline lieutenants in dirty, ragged uniforms. At first, I was thinking that we should change into something more like what a private would wear, that we might slip away unnoticed. However, as enlisted men, we'd be subject to questioning by every soldier we passed, under suspicion we were deserters, or were shirking our duties, at the least. Also, privates can hardly go where they wish, and we need to be able to get back to the point where we crossed the rebel lines so that we can return to our own men.

"Then a thought struck me: the only kind of Confederate soldier other than a high-ranking general that I've seen or heard of who can go wherever they want, whenever they want, without being questioned by anyone is—"

"A Signal Corps officer." Tom finished his sentence for him.

"Yes, of course," Evelyn agreed. "And spending most of their time at a warm, comfortable desk in the War Department, they almost always wear crisp, clean uniforms."

"Precisely," Nathan answered.

Evelyn then stepped up and eyed Nathan's uniform, tugging at a few places where seams had separated or holes had been worn. "Hmm ... shouldn't be too difficult. And fortunately—or not—the *Confederate* Signal Corps officers wear no identifying insignia on their uniforms. So, I suppose a crisp uniform is an indicator. And after that ... well, I suppose a haughty attitude will be proof enough!" she scoffed, having had plenty of unpleasant interaction with such officers, especially the dreaded Major White.

"Nathan ... I was just now thinking about what you said: that they were looking for two *lieutenants*. With a little needlework, I can add more yellow stitching to the collar and sleeves of your tunic, making you a captain."

"My dear Evelyn, I didn't know you had the power to hand out army promotions," Nathan answered teasingly.

She smiled, "You have no idea what I am capable of, my darling ... no idea."

Nathan returned her smile, then laughed, looking forward to one day finding out the entirety of what she might have meant by that.

"We'll also need horses," Nathan added. "Signal Corps officers would hardly be expected to hike between Richmond and Petersburg.

"Hmm," Evelyn replied. "That will be more difficult to arrange. It'll take a few days … Horses are in short supply, as you can imagine. We'll likely have to steal them. That will raise suspicion, so we dare not bring them here. We'll have to arrange a secret place for you to obtain them. Let me get started working on that …"

"But, Evelyn," Tom interjected, "how shall we explain *your* presence when we return to the front to cross the lines? We can hardly put a Signal Corps uniform on *you*."

It was Nathan who answered for her: "She's not coming with us, Tom. Despite the danger, she feels obliged to stay here and watch over her flock."

Tom turned to Evelyn and tipped his hat. "Very admirable of you, Evelyn. Can't say I'm surprised."

"Thank you, Tom. But I feel so awful that you two have risked your lives on my behalf … and for nothing, it turns out," she answered.

"Oh, never mind about that," Tom said, smiling. "Nathan was becoming impossible to live with for worrying over you and missing you. It was worth coming here just to calm him down a little."

Nathan rolled his eyes but couldn't deny the truth of what Tom was saying.

Evelyn gazed thoughtfully at Tom for a long moment, then over at Nathan. "Something has changed between you two since we were last together. You're more … *informal* with each other, though that's not quite the right word for it, I think. More like *equals* now, dare I say?"

Nathan nodded, "Yes, you have the right of it. Together, Tom and I have been through … well, 'hell,' might be too cliché, but something like it. At some point, I realized that we were more like brothers, and I no longer felt like I wanted to be his superior officer, if you understand my meaning."

Nathan looked over at Tom, who just shrugged.

"Oh. I think that's just *wonderful*," Evelyn answered. "Though I expected something of the kind would happen one day … I'm just happy to see that day has come."

And to emphasize her point, she stepped up to Tom, embraced him gently, then stepped back and said, "Welcome to the family — *brother*."

He smiled brightly in return.

✦✦✦✦✦✦✦

In the end, it took three days to get the uniforms, boots, and other accessories cleaned, repaired, and polished to the point they were passable, and then another full day to finish making the necessary arrangements for the horses they required—meaning theft. But to Nathan, the time flew by far too quickly. He and Evelyn spent hours talking about everything that'd happened since they'd last met. And per her insistence, they didn't just tell what happened, but also how they had *felt* about what had happened. She told him all about her ongoing troubles with Major White and the Confederate Signal Corps, and he shared his battle experiences, and the off again, on again confrontations with Walters.

They spent every possible moment together, with only two exceptions: the first was whenever Evelyn had to sneak out for a clandestine meeting with one of the Employer's men to arrange for the horses and discuss other espionage activities.

The second was at night, when it was time for bed. She and Nathan had discussed it and mutually agreed not to sleep in the same space, knowing all too well what was very likely to happen if they did. It wasn't just that it was improper before their wedding, there was a pragmatic reason as well: if Evelyn were to become pregnant under the present circumstances, it would make her life much more difficult and dangerous. It was an additional complication she simply didn't need at the moment. Nathan found it a sore test, knowing she was just a few feet away as he tried to get some sleep with nothing but a tuft of straw in between him and the cold, hard floor of the warehouse.

When the morning of their departure arrived, Nathan and Evelyn kept their parting brief, resisting the temptation to linger; both knew it would only make it more painful. So after a quick embrace and kiss, Nathan and Tom said goodbye, crossed the street to the alleyway across from the warehouse entrance, and were gone. Evelyn immediately returned to her little, semi-private warehouse bedroom and was not seen for the rest of the day.

Chapter 4. The Employer

"Spies cannot be usefully employed
without a certain intuitive sagacity."
- Sun Tzu

Sunday March 5, 1865 – Richmond, Virginia:

Nathan and Tom spoke little on the ride back to Petersburg. Nathan suffered a gloomy disposition that Tom found more than understandable under the circumstances. Not only was Nathan parting from the woman he loved, that he'd seen only for the last few days after more than two years apart, but he was leaving her in a precarious, potentially deadly situation, which he could do nothing about. So Tom left him alone with his thoughts, deciding that was likely the best course of action.

The good news was that their current disguise appeared to be working beautifully. Not only were they never waylaid by pickets or sentries, but the regular soldiers seemed to go out of their way to avoid them. Apparently, the reputation of the Signal Corps had grown to a point that nobody—from the lowliest private to the highest-ranking general officer—wanted to fall under their suspicious, watchful eyes. And fortunately, so far, they'd not encountered any *real* Signal Corps members, which might prove sticky, though with Evelyn's help, they had invented a cover story about being War Department officers, newly recruited to the Signal Corps—if anyone asked. She'd even provided them with details on several actual Corps officers to name drop if needed.

In the end, they made their way to the bridge across the Appomattox and on into Petersburg without incident.

As they reached the northern edge of the town, Nathan surprised Tom by turning left, toward the east, rather than right, toward the place where they'd originally crossed enemy lines and where they'd need to go to cross back over.

Nathan pulled his horse to a halt and looked over at Tom. "I know you're wondering why I turned this way," he said.

"Well, yes … oughtn't we go the other way to where our 'friends' can assist us once again?"

"Normally, I'd say yes," Nathan answered. "However, I've been thinking … how the Employer's associates, including Evelyn, have been frustrated in recent weeks in their efforts to gather intelligence on the enemy's troop dispositions around Petersburg. That the Signal Corps' activities have made it increasingly difficult and dangerous."

"Yes, *and* …?" Tom responded, having a feeling he knew where this was likely headed.

"And … I've been thinking that it'd be a shame to waste these nice, clean uniforms. Especially after seeing how much the regular army soldiers defer to us when we're wearing them. Seems like anyone short of General Lee himself would likely give us anything we asked for."

"Ah. So you're proposing we two do what the Employer's people have been unable to do? To spy out the enemy's fortifications?"

"Well, yes … that's what I was considering. But, if you don't wish to do it, then we won't, Tom. When I said I would no longer order you to do anything, I meant it. We're in this together, so if you'd rather just go back to our lines, I won't argue the matter."

Without hesitation Tom answered, "Hell, Nathan, I just came along to watch your back, knowing if we were caught we'd hang. To be honest, I never held out much hope that Evelyn would actually agree to leave with us. So, if I was willing to take that risk on a mission with little chance of success, I figure, why not continue on with the possibility of actually accomplishing something useful?"

Nathan grinned for the first time since parting from Evelyn. "Good man, Tom. And thank you. In that case, I'll lead on." He turned and kicked his horse into a trot.

Tom followed, silently musing that having something else "useful" to do was exactly what Nathan needed at the moment. Tom was willing to risk his own neck to make sure he got it.

❧ ❧ ❧ ❧ ❧ ❧

Confederate Signal Corps officer, Major White, could not suppress a growing excitement at the prospect of personally laying hands on, and arresting—or if necessary, executing—the nefarious Union spy ringleader known as "The Employer." White's predecessor, Colonel Grayson, had toiled unsuccessfully for years trying to put an actual name to the pseudonym, but White had solved the riddle himself in just a few short hours. That had been a great source of satisfaction, especially when he reported his findings to Secretary of Defense James Seddon.

Now, as White jogged along on his horse up the cobbled streets of downtown Richmond, headed for the mansion owned by shipping magnate Jonathan Hughes, the only potential dark cloud on his otherwise sunny horizon was a nagging concern that he was undermanned for the operation. Directly behind him rode only three Signal Corps soldiers, two lieutenants and a sergeant, along with an extra horse that would be used to transport their prisoner.

When he'd informed Seddon that Hughes was their man, he'd once again, as with Evelyn Hanson, been warned against any undue notice. Hughes was too high-profile and too highly connected to just arrest and put on trial. The man's treason would be a scandal involving the highest levels of the government, including the President himself, at a time when the Confederacy desperately needed loyalty and unwavering support from its citizens and soldiers.

So White had been ordered to only take his most trusted and discreet men with him. The fact that they were all four armed to the teeth—his men with rifles and pistols, and he himself strapping on an extra revolver before heading out—was little consolation. White knew the Employer and his spies were dangerous, especially when desperate: the proof being their brazen assassination of Colonel Grayson in broad daylight on the streets of Richmond.

He was certain he had the element of surprise going for him: no one other than himself and Seddon knew that he had solved the riddle and was about to take action. If they moved in quickly and decisively, the enemy should have no opportunity to react and counter them.

He'd told his men that if all went smoothly, they would simply arrest the man they'd come for. Once they entered the house, if there was any hint whatsoever of armed resistance, they were under strict orders to kill everyone in the residence, including the Employer and his wife, maids, butlers, and guests. No one must be left alive to report what had happened and who had been there.

As White contemplated these thoughts, one of his men called out, "Major, there's a rider coming up. Looks like one of ours."

White pulled his horse to a halt and turned back, immediately seeing what his man had reported: a rider coming up at the gallop, and by his neat uniform, very likely a Signal Corps officer.

When the man pulled up, White recognized him as Lieutenant Barnes. After exchanging a quick salute, Barnes handed White a folded sheet of paper. "From the Secretary, sir," he said.

White unfolded the paper, and read:

Major White,

We have a crisis that demands your immediate attention. Accompany Lt. Barnes to the front at Petersburg on the instant. He will lead you to where two spies have been operating for some weeks, posing as our S.C. officers. They must be taken, alive or dead, as their intel would be devastating to our cause. Have your men continue present assignment without you. Report directly to me when both missions are concluded.

- J. Seddon

White inwardly groaned at the frustrating, last-minute change in his plans, but he knew if what Seddon said was true, his presence at the front was more important than his presence at the capture of the Employer. Although this would make the raid on the spy chief's house even more shorthanded, he knew the real muscle would be his men. Other than the satisfaction of seeing it done personally, his presence was likely unnecessary—not even to identify Jonathan Hughes, who was well known in Richmond, even to the two lieutenants.

So he issued orders for his men to continue the mission, as previously planned, then turned to Lieutenant Barnes and said, "All right. Let's go … Take me to these spies' last reported location."

❧❧❧❧❧❧❧❧❧❧❧❧

Margaret blew on her steaming cup of tea before taking a sip. She'd just sat down for afternoon tea with Angeline, who sat across from her reading something on a sheet of paper, absently stirring her cup with a small, silver spoon.

Margaret felt a small twinge of guilt when it occurred to her that this particular daily routine—which she enjoyed very much, she had to admit—had been a favorite of Evelyn's while she'd lived here. Margaret had quite literally taken Evelyn's place in the luxurious household, including her bedroom, while Evelyn now lived in wretched, impoverished conditions in a drafty old warehouse near the river. Margaret knew it wasn't fair, but she also knew there was nothing anyone could do about it at the moment.

She had just opened her mouth to share her thoughts about Evelyn with Angeline when she felt a tremendous shock and heard a terrible crash out in the foyer, followed immediately by a woman's scream, and men shouting, *"Hands in the air! Hands in the air! Nobody move! Where's Hughes? Where's Mr. Hughes?"*

Margaret shared a look of shock with Angeline and sprang to her feet so violently her teacup fell to the floor and shattered, splattering tea across the marble.

We're being robbed! was Margaret's first thought. However, her mind drew a blank when she considered, *What shall we do?*

Angeline had not lost her composure; ignoring the spilled tea, she strode briskly to the library desk, reached around the left side, where she clicked something, causing a small, slender drawer to slide out just below the surface of the desk. She immediately reached in and withdrew a tiny revolver, like the one Margaret had seen Evelyn carrying. Angeline slipped the weapon up her sleeve, then turned and gave Margaret a stern look. She motioned for her to stay put before moving to the doorway and peering out into the foyer.

⁂

From her vantage point at the edge of the library doorway, Angeline could now see there were three Confederate soldiers who'd kicked in the door: two lieutenants and a sergeant, all carrying rifles in their hands with pistol holsters at their waists. They wore crisp, clean uniforms, which Angeline knew almost certainly meant these men were from the dreaded Confederate Signal Corps.

Sam the butler stood in front of them, bowing politely, as if they were invited guests. A young black woman, a freeman maid, stood to the side, eyes wide, with hand covering her mouth.

"*Where is Mr. Hughes?*" the lieutenant demanded once again.

"Mr. Hughes is not at home presently," Sam answered.

"Liar," the lieutenant responded, and punched Sam in the face, knocking him to his knees.

Angeline suppressed a gasp and immediately stepped out into the foyer to confront the intruders. "I am Mrs. Hughes. What is the *meaning* of this?" she demanded sternly.

"The *meaning* is, we've come to arrest your husband for high treason against the state," the lieutenant said. "And if he doesn't appear forthwith, we will begin shooting your servants, followed by *you*," he answered with a scowl, waving his rifle at her for emphasis.

Angeline could feel her anger rising at their mistreatment of Sam and their threats against her household. "How *dare* you accuse my husband of such slanderous lies, and how dare you threaten my servants and my person!" she demanded, wagging her finger at them and turning red in the face in her wrath.

"Don't play the innocent with us, ma'am," the man answered. "We know all about your den of spies. Well, that's all over with. Bring out your husband … *now*. Or it'll go ill on you and your entire household."

"We've told you, my husband is *not* at home," she insisted, crossing her arms across her chest and frowning.

"You're a lying whore," the man sneered. "We've had this house watched for days, so we know he's here. *Hughes! Come out, or your wife dies!*" he shouted.

"I'm gonna count to three. *One ... two ...*" the man continued.

"All right. All right," a voice answered. "I'm coming. Don't shoot. I'll give myself up."

Angeline looked back toward the stairway and saw Jonathan coming slowly down the broad, curving staircase, his hands held up, palms outward in sign of surrender. "Don't shoot," he repeated.

The soldiers turned their rifles toward him as he descended the stairs.

When he reached the bottom of the stairs, Jonathan stepped slowly forward and cautiously lowered his hands, stretching them forward so they might be shackled. "I'll not resist ... Just don't hurt my wife, or any of my servants."

"We've no orders to take anyone but you," the man answered. "Unless you resist ... then we have orders to kill them all."

"I understand. I shall not resist," he answered, nodding emphatically.

"Oh, Jonathan," Angeline sobbed, beginning to tear up as recognition of the disaster that was unfolding began to take hold of her.

"Don't worry, my dear," he said, forcing a smile. "I'm sure it's all just some big mistake, and it'll be cleared up in due time."

The lieutenant scoffed. "Not likely, Hughes. Your number is up. Sergeant, put the shackles on him."

Even as the sergeant reached behind his back and pulled out a set of steel wrist shackles connected by a short chain, a new voice said, "Sorry, missus. Old Ed is so sorry, ma'am, for bein' late with the tea. Not as spry as I once was, and done spilled the pot and had to start over. But I'm comin' now."

Angeline looked down the hallway that led to the great room and kitchen. An old white man—stooped, gray-haired, and bespectacled, but neatly dressed in the dark suit and white ruffled shirt of a butler—moved slowly down the hall carrying a large, silver tea tray. Angeline was confused; they had no butler named Ed … had Jonathan hired him without telling her? But then, as the man came closer, she thought he looked somehow familiar, but she couldn't quite place him.

The tray the old man carried was weighed down precariously by a large silver teapot, several teacups, a sugar bowl, and all the accouterments. He glanced up as he approached, "Oh, I see we have guests. Why doesn't anyone ever tell old Ed these things," he muttered as he shuffled along.

"Stay where you are, old man," the lieutenant ordered.

But the butler continued on as if he hadn't heard, muttering to himself as he came. When he was within a few steps of the foyer, the lieutenant turned toward him, threatening him with his rifle. "I said, stay still, old man!" he commanded.

The butler glanced up at the sound and gasped in surprise, apparently noticing the rifle for the first time. In his shock, he lost his grip on the tray, and its contents clattered noisily to the floor, spilling the tea and shattering the cups.

"You damned old foo—"

The lieutenant's curse was cut short by a bullet punching through the center of his face, splattering the man behind him with blood. At the same moment, the room shook with an ear-concussing *boom!*

Angeline jumped at the sudden noise, but before she could grasp what was happening, the butler turned his revolver to the sergeant and fired again, hitting him in the center of the chest, knocking him backward to the floor; gun smoke swirled in the air. Then, to her horror, Angeline saw the third soldier aim his rifle at the old man, and in that moment, she knew he was a dead man even as recognition dawned. She reached up her sleeve for the tiny revolver she'd secreted there.

A shot rang out and the butler flinched.

For an instant, nobody moved or spoke, until the third soldier collapsed, his rifle clattering to the floor, released from a lifeless grasp. The soldier now had neat hole in the side of his head, from which a dark, red liquid slowly pooled onto the marble floor where he lay.

The old butler looked over at Angeline, who held her still-smoking revolver outstretched in her hand.

"Thank you for *that*, my dear," the butler said with a quick grin, which Angeline had finally recognized as belonging to the master spy, Joseph. "I figured I could get two of them, but reckoned the third would be a near thing, which it clearly was."

Angeline stepped up and hugged Joseph. "Thank you, thank you, thank you," she said, then leaned in and kissed him on both cheeks. "You have saved us from almost certain pain and death."

"You're welcome, my good lady. But … we really must be going now. If they have men watching the house, it won't take long for others to come."

"Yes, of course," Jonathan agreed. "Quickly, everyone … into the tunnel. Leave everything behind, just come *now*, even as you are," he ordered, and everyone moved to obey.

Margaret, who'd been watching from the library, stepped out to join them as they gathered all the servants, then raced down into the basement. There, Jonathan opened a door disguised as a normal, paneled wall. After pausing a moment to light several lanterns stashed inside, Jonathan closed the door and led them briskly away into the darkness.

🙣🙢🙣🙢🙣🙢🙣🙢🙣🙢🙣🙢

Tuesday March 21, 1865 – Petersburg, Virginia:

"All right, Captain Smith," Confederate Brigadier General William Terry said, unknowingly addressing Union Colonel Nathan Chambers in disguise. "What is it you require of me?"

Though it was a cool afternoon, the sky was clear, and there was little wind, so the general had ordered a campfire lit in a small outdoor alcove in the rebel fortifications, presumably to give himself a little fresh air, after weeks of being forced into the cramped, stuffy quarters of a bombproof. Nathan sat opposite the general on a sawed-off section of log.

Tom, who'd been suffering a cramping of his bowels since early morning—not surprising considering the odd and poor quality of food they'd been forced to consume lately—had excused himself to seek the latrine.

Nearby stood two privates, who were currently serving as guards and aides to the general. Nathan noted that the two men had a relaxed posture and did not carry their rifles, having leaned them against one of the walls.

The false "Captain Smith" frowned as he reached into his tunic and pulled out a pencil and folded sheet of paper. "General, I am tasked with reporting back to the Secretary of War concerning the disposition of all military forces currently deployed in the defense of Petersburg. The secretary believes the reports he's been receiving may not be entirely accurate. So, he sent me to personally collect the information he requires: numbers of officers and men, count of functioning artillery, small arms, ammunition, food stocks, fodder, fuel for heat, and other various and sundry supplies. He is also becoming quite alarmed by reports of a high number of desertions, and wishes to hear your opinion on the morale of your troops, and any thoughts you may have on ways to improve on the matter."

It was the same line he had now repeated to several dozen frontline commanders in the past two weeks. Nathan and Tom had worked out their approach and had refined it as they went along, such that it was now surprisingly effective. It had the advantage of sounding sternly authoritarian and authentic—using the Signal Corps' growing reputation against them—but at the same time, offered a conciliatory element, which the officers seemed all too happy to jump at. It had even fooled several *actual* Signal Corps officers they'd come across during their mission, and their story of being newly assigned to the corps had been taken at face value. That Nathan had an intimidating presence and natural air of authority likely aided their cause. Their main concern was that they might accidentally stumble upon Walters, or someone else who recognized Nathan, but so far, that hadn't happened.

And happily for Nathan and Tom, this particular command post was the last they planned to visit, as they were now very near the place where they'd originally crossed over into enemy territory, after having traversed nearly the entirety of the rebels' fortifications surrounding Petersburg. After leaving this place, they planned to once again connect with the Employer's men so that they could arrange for their return to Union lines.

"Ah. Seems reasonable, Captain," the general answered, slowly nodding his head.

"I do implore you to be as precise and accurate as possible, General," Nathan emphasized. "Anything less would be a disservice to our cause."

"Of course, Captain, of course. I am more than happy to provide you with the information you seek. And, as it turns out, I do have several suggestions for the secretary concerning the wellbeing of my men ..."

"Excellent, General. Shall we begin, then?" Nathan asked, though it was clearly more of a command. He laid the sheet of paper across his knee and prepared to take notes with the pencil.

"I'm in command of a roughly two-mile wide section of the fortifications," the general began, "with a brigade ostensibly made up of three regiments, though they are so sorely undermanned that they hardly merit the title; the Twenty-Third is down to just 322 effectives, the remnants of the old Stonewall Brigade with 229, and the Forty Fifth with 423—"

"Don't answer any more of this man's questions!" a voice commanded. Nathan and the colonel looked up to see an officer striding toward the campfire. Nathan's heart sunk when he noted the man carried a pistol in his hand, and it was leveled at him. He also recognized the lieutenant as one of the legitimate Signal Corps officers they'd encountered during their clandestine mission.

"What is the meaning of this, Lieutenant?" the general asked, rising to his feet. Nathan also rose, letting the pencil and paper drop to the ground. He was tempted to reach for his sidearm, but the newcomer was eyeing him carefully, so he dared not.

Without taking his eyes off Nathan, the lieutenant answered, "This man is not what he appears to be. I am Signal Corps Lieutenant Ira Barnes, and I have just returned from the War

Department where I discovered that there is no such officer Captain Cyrus Smith in the Signal Corps, nor anyone else tasked with the mission of gathering troop information that he claims. This man is a spy!" He scowled as he glared at Nathan, but his pistol hand remained steady. Two privates stood behind him, the hammers back on their rifles, which were also aimed at Nathan.

Nathan and the lieutenant locked eyes, then another voice said, "Drop your weapon, Lieutenant, and order your men to do the same, or you're a dead man."

Nathan looked over and wasn't surprised to see Tom standing a few feet to one side, his revolver aimed at the lieutenant.

The lieutenant quickly recovered from the shock of his mistake in not accounting for the *second* spy officer. "I think *not*, sir. If you shoot me, my guards with kill you both," the lieutenant responded.

"Ah, but you see, I have nothing to lose," Tom answered evenly. "If you take us captive, we'll be tortured for information, then hanged or shot for spies. *You*, on the other hand, may live to see the end of this war, if you simply do as I say. Drop your weapons, men, unless you want to see your lieutenant's brains spread across the ground."

After a brief pause, the lieutenant lowered the hammer on his pistol and tossed it to the ground. "Do as he says, men," he said, and the two privates slowly laid their rifles on the ground at their feet.

By this time, Nathan's pistol was also in his hand, but fortunately, the general's guards were currently unarmed. All the rebel soldiers raised their hands in surrender.

Nathan turned his pistol toward the general. "Your sidearm, sir … if you please," he said.

The general slowly reached down, unbuttoned the flap on the holster, and withdrew the pistol with two fingers, handing it across to Nathan handle first. Nathan reached out and snatched it away, then tucked the weapon into his belt, even as Tom stepped forward and gathered up the lieutenant's revolver. Then, while still eyeing the enemy, he reached down and removed the percussion caps from the two rifles, then tossed them away. He then moved over and did the same to the guards' rifles over against the wall.

"All you men, move over here, and lay face down on the ground, pointing away from us," Nathan said. "You too, General," he continued, directing the men away from their discarded weapons.

"But, sir!" the general protested. "The ground is muddy, surely you'll not have me spoil my uniform by lying on the ground?"

Nathan smiled, but shook his head; "Sorry, General. Take it up with your laundress."

The general grumbled, but did as he was ordered.

"Slowly count to a thousand before rising," Tom ordered. "Assume we will be standing hard by, and will shoot anyone who gets up sooner."

Then Tom and Nathan slowly backed away, moving toward where they'd tied their horses. Tom knelt down and untied their leads, handing Nathan his horse's reins. But when Tom went to mount, Nathan grabbed his arm, gave him a look, and shook his head. Tom raised an eyebrow in response, then nodded, leading his horse instead. After one last look back at the rebel soldiers on the ground to make sure no one was peeking, they slipped away into a tunnel leading in the direction of the place they'd originally crossed the rebel lines.

Once they were out of earshot, Nathan extracted his rifle from the sheath tied to his saddle, then grabbed his canteen and ammunition pouch. Tom did likewise, then they let loose the reins, and swatted the horses on their flanks, sending them trotting off down another tunnel. The two men then turned and moved off in a different direction, loaded rifles in hand, hammers at the half cock.

"Horses won't help us at this point; they'd make it much harder to hide, and to sneak across their lines," Nathan said.

"And the rebs may yet waste some time following our riderless horses," Tom replied.

Nathan then led them through the labyrinthine rebel entrenchments on a twisting path so they'd not be as easy to follow. There were plenty of rebel soldiers, either individually or in small companies, coming and going, so their movement through the siege lines went unnoticed.

Either through good fortune or good memory, Nathan led them to the very same small bombproof they'd sheltered in the night they'd first crossed over into the rebel siege works. Their plan, such as it was, had been to stay hidden in that tiny room until the Employer's men returned from their other duties, and could then help them to escape.

The place was empty, and the stove was cold. They shared a look. "Clearly we can't wait long," Nathan said. "And we don't know if our allies will return anytime soon, if at all."

"Makes sense. But we should at least rest our legs for a spell; we may need them later," Tom answered.

"Yes, and we might as well wait until sunset, at this point, and then we can attempt to sneak past the pickets," Nathan said.

So the two sat down on the dirt floor with their backs against the log and mud walls, had a sip from their canteens, then closed their eyes to rest.

❦❧☙❧❦❧☙❧❦❧☙

"So, Lieutenant, you're telling me you allowed them to escape? Likely the two most dangerous spies we've ever had within our grasp?" Major White asked, in low, even tones, in what sounded like a simple inquiry but carried strong undertones of chastisement.

"Sorry, sir," the Signal Corps lieutenant responded, gazing down at his own boots, unable to make eye contact with the intimidating stare of the major.

"Hmm … we shall discuss *that* matter later. For the moment, we must focus our attention on recapturing them," White responded.

Then he turned to General Terry, who stood with them. "General, though we may have had a difference of opinion in the past," White said, recalling the time General Terry had threatened to shoot him if he didn't desist from trying to arrest Captain Jubal Collins for his possible connection to the Union spy queen, Evelyn

Hanson. "And, though I clearly haven't the rank to give you orders," he continued, "I would appeal to your sense of duty to lend me your men to hunt down these nefarious villains. From what I have learned, these infiltrators have gathered a great amount of intelligence on our defenses over the past several weeks. I cannot emphasize strongly enough the potential disaster that information represents should it be delivered into the enemy's hands."

"Of course, Major. Whatever you need, just ask," the general responded. "Aside from the obvious military consequences, as you point out, I have a personal bone to pick with those ... *gentlemen*," he glanced down at his badly soiled uniform, wiping ineffectually at the dried mud all down the front to emphasize his point.

"In fact, I will go so far as to lend you my very best veterans, the remnants of the original Stonewall Brigade, to assist you."

"That would be excellent, and much appreciated, General," Major White responded, though it did cross his mind to wonder if Captain Jubal Collins, one of the Stonewall Brigade commanders, was also a traitor who might actually be a liability rather than an asset. However, he did not wish to open old wounds with the general, so he said nothing on that matter.

☙❧☙❧☙❧☙❧☙❧☙❧

"Hello, Jubal," Captain Bob Hill said, as he fell in beside the jogging Jubal Collins, matching his pace.

"Oh, Captain Hill, good to see you," Jubal answered.

"What's this all about, do you know?" Bob asked.

"We're ordered to hunt down a couple of spies dressed as our officers, is what I was told," Jubal answered. The two captains were followed by nearly a hundred soldiers, rifles in hand, quick-marching down a pathway inside the rebel fortifications.

"All this, for a couple of spies? Seems odd," Bob responded.

"Signal Corps," Jubal said, rolling his eyes.

"Ah! That explains it. Need us to do their dirty work for them, I suppose."

"Seems so. Anyway, General Terry was all in a lather over it, so I reckon it's a serious matter. Likely stole someone's battle plans or something. He suspects they'll try to cross over to Yankee lines now that they've been discovered. We're heading out east at the double-quick to try to get ahead of them and then circle back and cut them off. Captain Garrett is leading his men over to our right, as close as he can get to the front in hopes we can catch them in a pincer."

"Makes sense," Bob agreed, as they continued to jog along. Bob's own rifle company had fallen in behind Jubal's, as they'd been last to be notified of the sudden assignment. "I'll fall back with my men then, and we'll follow your lead on it, Jubal. Godspeed."

"Thanks, Captain Hill. Likewise," Jubal said, not quite able to bring himself to address his old mentor by his given name, despite the fact they now held the same rank.

For the next hour, Jubal led them through the labyrinth of tunnels, walls, and trenches that made up the Confederate siege works surrounding Petersburg until he reached the easternmost position he'd had in mind for the point from which they'd launch their pincer movement. He then turned to the right and led the column directly toward the front of the fortifications until they reached the entrance to a tunnel leading to a sally port and the outside. There he paused, and sent back one of his men for Captain Hill.

"What's the plan, Jubal?" Bob asked as he arrived at the front of the column.

"The sun is just setting, so in minutes, it'll be safe for us to be outside the wall, at least as far as the outer picket line. I'm thinking I'll lead my men along the outside of the wall heading back west toward where Captain Garrett ought to be, leaving men to guard each sally port along the way, and you stay inside the wall and do the same. Reckon those spies have been waiting for nightfall to slip through the lines, and this way we ought to catch them between us."

"Sounds like a good plan. Well done, Jubal," Bob answered.

Jubal responded with a grin, which Bob returned.

"All right, let's go," Jubal said. Then he led his men into the tunnel and out into the growing darkness.

He'd not gone more than a few hundred yards when he saw flashes of light ahead and off to his left. The flashes were immediately followed by the unmistakable sound of gunfire.

Nathan knew he and Tom were in a desperate situation, growing worse by the moment. Their hoped-for allies, the Employer's men, who'd helped them cross the lines previously, were nowhere to be found, and it was now clear that the enemy had launched a large-scale operation to kill or capture them.

They'd slipped out the unguarded sally door just after sunset, but hadn't gone more than a hundred yards when they heard shouting behind them, followed almost immediately by the impact of multiple bullets in the dirt near them and the loud report of gunshots. Rather than returning fire, they tossed aside their heavy rifles and broke into a zig-zagging sprint intended to make for a more difficult target, aided by the growing darkness.

Somewhere up ahead, Nathan knew they'd have to pass by the dug-in, well-hidden outer line of rebel pickets. If these rose up to cut them off …

Nathan shook off that thought—nothing he could do at the moment but keep moving. He figured they had about five hundred yards of ground to cross, as the crow flies, to reach the Union lines—much farther than that, given the meandering course they were forced to follow through the dry stream bed.

Only moments after they'd been fired upon from behind, they heard gunshots coming from their left—another large company of enemy riflemen. They ducked their heads and kept running as bullets zipped by overhead or tore through the low grass and brush around them.

And then, as they rounded a corner of the twisting path, Nathan saw a few dozen yards ahead, the thing he had dreaded and had hoped would not appear: the silhouette of a dozen or more men with rifles, cutting them off from escape.

"Halt and be recognized, or we'll open fire!" one of these men called out.

Without pausing in his stride, Nathan pulled a revolver from his belt and began firing. Tom did likewise.

❧❧❧❧❧❧❧❧❧

"C'mon men, we've got them now," Jubal called out, as he led his men in a sprint across the undulating ground of no-man's-land. "Our sentries have cut them off."

He was now within two hundred yards of the spies and could see flashes of gunshots being exchanged between two groups of men.

He could see little in the distance in the darkness, though it seemed to him for a few moments the gunfire suddenly intensified. And then, incongruously, he heard a man scream, then the gunfire ceased. He assumed it meant the spies had been subdued, but he picked up his pace until he and his men reached the place where the small, intense gun fight had taken place.

What he found there was entirely unexpected.

❧❧❧❧❧❧❧❧❧

Though their initial pistol barrage had taken the rebel sentries by surprise, and had downed several of them, Tom and Nathan had been forced to duck down into the sparse cover of the dry ditch as the enemy sentries returned fire. The wily veterans from Texas knew not to stay in one spot, but continually moved from side to side on their bellies, then popped up to get off a shot, before ducking back down and moving again.

With a growing sense of desperation, Nathan knew there was no way out this time. They were cut off and outnumbered, with likely hundreds more rebels coming up fast behind.

As Nathan popped up to squeeze off a shot at a rifleman in front of him, the man suddenly flinched, and the front of his face oddly seemed to explode outward, replaced by a sharp, metallic object. And then, before his mind could register what he'd just seen, a great shout and thunderous volley of rifle fire rang out, causing Nathan to duck his head. When he looked back up, he

76

realized that the gunfire had not been directed at him or Tom this time. The entire row of sentries had simply vanished, all save one, who now faced in the opposite direction.

And even as the rebel raised his rifle to fire, something large hit the man, knocking him backward. Nathan heard a snarling, growling sound, and a scream. Then silence.

"Colonel Chambers! Do not be shooting me, I am coming over," he heard a voice call out. With a sigh of relief, he recognized the voice of Stan. In moments, the big Russian was reaching down to give him a hand up, but before he could accept the help, a large furry creature pounced on him, knocking him back to the earth.

"Hello, Harry," he said. As he stroked the big hound's jowls, his hands came away bloody.

Nathan looked up at Stan, who just shrugged. "Not his," he said with a grin.

Another officer was suddenly kneeling down next to Nathan, gazing into his eyes. "Are you wounded, sir?" he asked.

"William! Good to see you. No, I'm fine, thanks for asking." Then Nathan turned toward where Tom lay on the ground a few yards away. "Tom, are you hit?"

"No … I'm unscathed," Tom responded.

Nathan then noticed Billy, with a bow in his hands, crouching next to Tom, gazing out at the advancing enemy column. A hundred Union riflemen had accompanied them, spread out on either side, actively checking to make sure all the rebel pickets were down and reloading their rifles, preparing to face the oncoming enemy.

"Neighbors don't look too friendly, Colonel," Stan said, gazing out at the approaching column of rebel riflemen. "Shall we?" He gestured back toward the Union lines.

"Yes, please. Lead on, Mr. Volkov."

∞∞∞∞∞∞∞∞∞

Major White felt a mixture of frustration and incredulity at the escape of both the Union spies at Petersburg and the Employer with his entire household. And though he was not especially sensitive about such things, he considered that it had also not done his record any favors that they'd had a number of soldiers killed in the process in both instances.

When he went to meet with Secretary of War Seddon, he was shocked at what he saw. The typically intense and intimidating man appeared glum and downcast, barely making eye contact with White, and answering in a low, monotone voice.

"It's a disaster, White. A complete and utter disaster," he muttered, slowly shaking his head and staring at the desktop in front of him.

"Well, it is a setback, certainly," White answered, removing his glasses to wipe away an annoying smudge. "But we will hunt down the scoundrels, I promise you. And as for the spies at Petersburg ... at least they didn't sneak away without our knowing of them and their activities. Knowing what information they were able to obtain about our defenses, we can counter their moves by switching things up, moving troops around, and so forth. In a matter of days, the intelligence they gathered could be rendered outdated and meaningless," White argued.

Seddon slowly shook his head. "You don't understand, Major ... we *have* no troops to move around. That's the point, and the most dangerous thing they learned from their espionage. We are spread thin to the point of breaking all along the line. Our men are starving and running out of ammunition, fuel, fodder, and other basic necessities. The enemy will now know that any major attack at any point along our lines will necessarily succeed. There is no clawing back from this, White. Compounding that, of course, is the escape of their spy ringleader, giving us nothing good to present to the president, save this ..."

He handed across a single sheet of paper. White took it and read:

President Jefferson Davis,

Sir, I respectfully submit my resignation as Secretary of Defense of the Confederate States of America, effective this date. It has been the greatest honor and privilege in life to serve my country in this capacity, but I believe our cause would be better served at this particular juncture by my departure.

With respect,

J. Seddon

White handed the sheet back to Seddon. "You're giving up?"

"I'm *resigning*. It's the only thing I can do now to save whatever shred of honor and dignity I have left."

White grunted noncommittally, set the paper back down on the desk, then stood, turned, and walked from Seddon's office without another word.

𝔰𝔬𝔠𝔯𝔠𝔰𝔟𝔬𝔰𝔬𝔠𝔯𝔠𝔰𝔟𝔬𝔰𝔬𝔠𝔯𝔠𝔰

Thursday March 23, 1865 – Richmond, Virginia:

"But where have they gone, Joseph?" Evelyn asked after he'd told her the news of the raid on the Hughes house and their subsequent harrowing escape.

"All I will tell you is, they have gone to one of the Underground Railroad stations … a place outside Richmond, which should be out of the way of the fighting, as it has no strategic advantage to anyone."

"*All you will tell me?* Why, you suddenly don't trust me?" she asked with a frown.

He scowled in return. "You know better than to ask me that. I'd trust you with my life without a moment's hesitation."

"Then why?"

"Because you are still a target, and they continue to close in on you, despite the war crashing down on them. If you are captured, they will … cause you pain. Best you have nothing to tell them when they do," he answered.

"Yes … yes, of course, you're right. How foolish of me. I think of myself as brave, but nobody knows how they would resist torture, when it comes right down to it." She bowed her head thoughtfully. Then she looked up, eyes wide. "Oh, present company excepted, I should say! Sorry, Joseph, I am forgetting *you* have already endured such punishment, and have never yielded."

"True, true. But it was a sore test. And all the while, I was wishing I truly knew nothing I could tell them. I feared I would break and tell them everything they wanted to know, just to make the pain stop."

"But you didn't," she responded, patting him gently on the arm.

"Yes, thanks to your timely rescue. Otherwise … who knows? In any case, that's why I don't want to tell you where the Employer and company are hiding. Better for you and better for them. Just suffice to say they are safe in a place that was planned for long ago. Angeline wanted to send you there after Major White tried to arrest you, but you refused to leave the city. So, you can assume it is as safe as any place can be in the middle of this war.

"Speaking of … it's time to get you out of Richmond as well. This area is going to quickly become untenable once the Union Army breaks through Petersburg, which could happen at any time. Likely, Lee will make a final stand here at the river's edge, forcing Grant to bombard Richmond. And, of course, even before that, the Signal Corps is an ever-present threat."

"Yes, it does seem like the walls are closing in. All right. Then why not take us to the same safe place as the Employer?"

He shook his head, "Unfortunately it's not possible to get you there now. Oh, I could possibly get *you* there, alone, or maybe with one or two others, but not with *all* your party. Too many obstacles in the way. The odds of being caught are way too high."

"Well, I'll not abandon them now. They need me."

"Yes, I assumed you would say that. As you can imagine, I have been thinking about this conundrum for some time, and I do have an idea. A place that is currently abandoned, has plenty of room for all your company, and is away from the fighting … a week's travel, or so, from Richmond, if one has horse-drawn transportation."

"That sounds ideal. Where is this place?"

Joseph grinned and tilted his head at her quizzically. "Can you not guess? You've been there yourself many times, including once with me …"

Evelyn frowned and thought on it a moment, then her eyes widened. "*Mountain Meadows!* Yes. Why, it's brilliant, Joseph! To be honest, I was fretting over how I would be able to locate Nathan if I had to flee from here. Whatever else happens, he will eventually have to return there, and then *he* will find *me*."

"My thoughts exactly. And with the Union Army concentrating all its efforts on Petersburg, the roads west should be relatively free of fighting for now. I expect no one will take much notice of a few wagonloads of refugees fleeing the war. From what I understand, there is now a steady flow of those, and I expect it will only grow heavier as the end approaches."

"Yes, that makes sense. But what about transportation?"

"Let me work on that. There is a place I know, not far from here, where I can hide horses and wagons for your use. It's owned by a reliable friend of mine. I will give you the address now, just in case."

"In case of what?"

"In case I can't return here, or you have to leave before I can."

"Oh. All right. Thank you, Joseph. You are a life saver … as usual."

Joseph grinned, "Never mention it, my dear." And then his face took on a more serious aspect. "Evelyn … if we never meet again … I want you to know that I have the greatest respect and affection for you. There isn't anything I wouldn't do for you, including killing men, as you already know."

"Likewise, Joseph. But there's no need to speak such morbid thoughts. We *will* make it through this. So, I refuse to say 'goodbye,' but rather I will say, 'see you soon.'"

"All right. See you soon, then," he answered, then scratched out the address on a piece of paper, which Evelyn promised to destroy after memorizing it. Then he departed. And despite her bold words, with the world about to come crashing down around them, Evelyn did briefly wonder if they would ever meet again.

Chapter 5. The General

"It's war that makes generals."
- Seth Godin

Thursday March 30, 1865 – Union Camp, Siege of Petersburg, Virginia:

Nathan stepped into the sparse farmhouse kitchen that currently served as the command office of the Independent Division of XXIV Corps of the Army of the James. He stepped up to the table, stood to attention, and snapped a salute. He was now bathed, shaved, and dressed once again as a proper Union colonel in the best uniform he could muster. "Sir! You wished to see me?"

"Ah, Chambers … yes, come in and sit." Brigadier General John Turner, division commander, stayed seated and gave a quick return salute with his right hand as he gestured toward the empty chair.

"Thank you, sir," Nathan answered, as he removed his hat and took the proffered seat.

"Chambers … I'm sure you're anxious to learn what fate awaits you, given your recent … *adventure*, shall we call it?"

Nathan gave a noncommittal nod and a shrug. He knew that the term "adventure" was putting it politely—he and Tom had intentionally gone AWOL, and despite Jim Wiggins' best efforts at obfuscation and subterfuge, their absence had eventually been discovered. And given Nathan's previous ties to Richmond, accusations of espionage and treason were not out of the question, and had even been openly discussed. So far, however, he'd not been arrested, which he took for a hopeful sign.

"Yes, sir … I have been *curious*, to say the least."

Turner smiled. "Yes, so I can imagine. Having spoken to you personally at length upon your return, I am inclined to believe your story … and your report concerning the enemy's current disposition and troop strength—or lack of. I have given that opinion to my superior, General Gibbon. What he did with that information is anyone's guess."

"Guess? Then you haven't any news for me on the matter, sir?"

"Just this …" He handed a sheet of paper across to Nathan. On it was a terse order commanding him to appear before Commanding General Grant at his headquarters, post haste. It was signed by Grant's adjutant, Brigadier General Seth Williams.

Nathan looked up at Turner and raised an eyebrow. "Oh!" was all he could think to say. During the course of the conflict, he'd not yet spoken to Grant in person, and had only caught glimpses of him from a distance during the present siege. But they had spoken to each other once, he recalled—a lifetime ago.

"I suspect General Grant has yet to make up his mind on the matter, and wishes to speak with you in person and judge for himself. Or perhaps he *has* come to a decision, and wishes to pronounce your fate." Turner shrugged.

Nathan shrugged in turn, folded the paper, stuck it in his breast pocket, and rose to his feet, replacing his hat.

Turner also rose and extended his hand, "Good luck, Chambers … You may need it."

Nathan shook the general's hand, then turned and strode from the room. Outside, he stepped up to the hitching post, where a private handed him Millie's reins. Harry the Dog watched intently as he saddled up and spurred the mare into motion. City Point, where General Grant had his headquarters, was eight miles away, and Grant was not a man to be kept waiting.

☙☙☙☙☙☙

"Excuse me, General. Colonel Chambers is here."

"Good, good. Send him in." General Grant waved a hand at his aide, without looking up from the map he was examining.

"Well … that's the trouble, sir. He refuses to come to your office."

"*Refuses?* What the devil are you talking about, son? A colonel doesn't refuse to meet with the commanding general!"

"Oh, it's not *that* sir; it's just … he has this … rather dangerous looking animal with him—a hound, sir, but the most gigantic beast I've ever seen. The sergeant of the guard wouldn't allow him

83

to bring it to your office, and he told Chambers to tie it up back by the horse corral. But … as I said, the colonel refuses."

"Oh, of all the ridiculous nonsense!" Grant stood, stretched, rubbed at a stiff spot in his lower back, then reached into his vest pocket, extracting a cigar and sticking it into his mouth. "Hand me my hat and coat … Need to stretch my legs anyway. I'll just go have a look at this animal for myself."

Grant marched briskly out the front door and down the front steps, pausing at the bottom just long enough to strike a match and light the cigar. He strode down the gravel drive, and at the corner, turned left where the drive wrapped around a large, red barn. He continued on another fifty yards, his aide and two privates with rifles on their shoulders following in his wake.

He could see Colonel Chambers, whom he'd only met once long ago in Mexico, standing by the corral gate talking with a sergeant. Next to Chambers sat the largest hound Grant had ever seen or imagined.

As Grant approached, Chambers and the other soldiers noticed him, and all stood to attention and saluted.

Grant strode up to Chambers and returned the salute.

"Good God, Chambers!" Grant said, and broke into a grin, slowly shaking his head. "If that ain't the biggest Goddamned dog I've ever seen, I don't know what is. I can see why my men didn't want this beast in my office. Please, explain yourself, Colonel!"

"I apologize for the trouble, sir. But whenever I tie him and leave without him, he suffers it greatly, howling like the end of creation. I have sworn an oath never to do it to him again, except in the most dire emergency."

"Sworn an oath? To a hound?!" Grant scowled, threw down the stub of his cigar, and stomped it out.

"General … the fellow has saved my life too many times to count, nearly costing him his own life on at least one of those occasions.

"And as you know from my choice of affiliations, sir, I am not a man who readily breaks sworn oaths." Chambers gave Grant a meaningful look.

Grant nodded, "Admirable, Colonel. But, still …"

Then Grant noticed a grin touching the edge of Chamber's mouth.

"Something amusing, Colonel?"

"I was just thinking," Chambers answered. "If it will make you feel better, sir … when I was still a civilian, representing the new government of West Virginia, Harry, here, accompanied me into the White House and sat at the president's feet as we met."

Grant's eyes widened, and now he returned Chamber's grin, then looked back down at Harry.

"Well, I'll be Goddamned …"

Then he looked over at his aide and scowled. "Well, what are we waiting for? If the hound is good enough for the president, he is certainly good enough for the commanding general. Bring him along, Chambers."

❧❧❧❧❧❧❧❧

A few minutes later, Nathan sat across the table from Grant, in the front room of the log cabin that served as his headquarters, as well as his family's sleeping quarters, on the Eppes family plantation. Grant had dismissed his aide, so they were now alone, except for the dog. Harry lay by Nathan's feet, panting heavily, but otherwise seeming at ease around the commanding general. Nathan wasn't surprised; Harry had always been a good judge of character, and from everything Nathan knew of the man, Grant was a straight shooter in every regard.

"Last time we spoke was in Mexico City," Grant began without preamble.

"Yes, I recall it, General. We were both young lieutenants—had just finished standing to attention as they raised the stars and stripes above the Mexican capitol building. Then you and I shook hands and shared a few words."

Grant smiled. "You left out the part where General Scott pinned a medal on you …"

Nathan shrugged. "Didn't seem material."

Grant snorted a chuckle. "Only that it was the reason I came up to you—to give my congratulations."

"And that was much appreciated, General. Though I recall at the time feeling somewhat sheepish about it; that there were many others just as deserving of recognition. Including you, if I'm not mistaken."

Now it was Grant's turn to shrug. "I did my part."

There was a moment of silence between them, until Grant finally said, "So, Chambers … going AWOL in the face of the enemy, a native Virginian sneaking into Richmond … accusations of possible espionage and treason …"

Nathan said nothing, allowing the general to continue with whatever he intended to say.

"But also," Grant continued, "General Foster has passed along to this headquarters a report written out in your own hand, containing very precise and detailed information concerning Lee's troop strength, disposition, morale, fortifications, artillery, supplies, ammunition, and so forth. If true, this is a veritable goldmine of intelligence."

Nathan then said in a quiet, even tone, "It's true. Every word of it, General."

Grant continued to stare at Nathan, as if trying to divine the truth of his statements. "Tell me why you did it, then, Chambers. Why go to Richmond without leave? Why not just tell General Foster your intentions and then go?"

Nathan gazed up at the ceiling a moment, before looking back down at the general. "Well, if I wished to be *disingenuous*, I would argue that General Foster would've refused to let me go—it being too dangerous—and if captured, I might prove a valuable source of intelligence to the other side. So, weighing the potential value of the mission versus the risks, I decided to go without permission."

Grant smiled. "But … since you are *not* planning on telling me something disingenuous … what is the *real* reason?"

Nathan snorted a chuckle. "A woman."

"*A woman?*" Grant shook his head. "That must be one helluva woman, Chambers, to risk your neck like that, not to mention your commission, and a possible noose!"

Nathan's look suddenly turned deadly serious as he answered simply, "She is. I risked my life to check on her safety, and to try to convince her to come away with me. And I'd do it again without hesitation. But she refused to leave. She's among those who've been feeding you the intelligence that you've been receiving since the beginning of the siege, and before."

"*Oh!* I see ..." Grant's eyes narrowed. Nathan thought it telling that the general didn't seem surprised by the revelation that a woman was providing him with valuable information on the enemy, nor did he deny the truth of it.

The two men sat and gazed at one another for a long moment, until Grant finally leaned back, stuck another cigar in his mouth, and lit it, taking a couple of puffs. Then he did a thing Nathan had not expected; the commanding general smiled broadly, and handed his cigar across to Nathan so he could share a puff.

"I believe you, Chambers ... and ... *by God,* we've got Lee now, haven't we, Colonel?"

Nathan returned the smile. "Yes, sir. We've got him. He's done for, this time."

"Chambers, based on your report, I'm going to order an all-out assault along the entire front, as soon as it can be organized. Your little *adventure* may very well lead directly to the end of the war."

Nathan leaned across the desk, handing the cigar back to Grant. "Let's hope so, sir. Let's hope so."

Nathan, assuming the meeting was over, began to rise. But Grant held out a hand. "Just a moment, Chambers ... There's one more matter I wish to discuss with you ..."

Nathan retook his seat, wondering if he was still to be punished for his actions, despite Grant's obvious enthusiasm for the results.

Grant reached into a desk drawer and pulled out a stack of papers, laying them in front of him on the table. Nathan assumed it was a list of the charges against him.

Grant began to read, "Graduated West Point, 1846 ... promoted to First Lieutenant during Mexican campaign ... decorated for valor by General Scott ... served with distinction against hostiles in Texas … promoted to captain … left the army upon death of father … served as part of the pro-Union contingent in Virginia that opposed secession … escaped to Wheeling as hostilities commenced, freeing more than a hundred slaves in the process … helped establish the restored government of Virginia, and then the new state of West Virginia … worked with General Rufus Saxton to help repulse Jackson's '62 attack on Harpers Ferry … enlisted as colonel commanding Twelfth West Virginia … led the regiment with distinction and valor in multiple battles … recently promoted to brigade command …"

He looked up. "And then there are various reports on you submitted by Union generals … a few negative, most positive."

Nathan shrugged. "That all seems accurate, General. Excuse me for asking, but … is there a point to this?"

Grant nodded, "The point is, Chambers … there aren't many colonels in this army who can show a record like that. None that I can think of, in fact."

He leaned back and took another long pull on the cigar, "Makes me think of the old adage, 'there but for the grace of God, go I.'

"Chambers, if things had gone only a little differently, you could easily be sitting in *this* chair, and I could be where you're sitting. Hell, other than some success I had out west early on in the war, you've had a better service record overall than I have. Not to mention helping to create a new Union state."

Grant shook his head. "It's an embarrassment for the army; a good West Point man like you, serving with distinction … A travesty, really."

"What do you mean, sir? I am well satisfied with you in your present position, if that's what you're getting at. I sincerely believe you're the right man for the job. I have no desire for your chair, as long as I can serve the country in my present one."

"Admirable of you, Chambers." Then Grant chuckled again. "You know, several months back, I became disgusted with all these brigadier generals strutting around all puffed up, acting important—with no military skills whatsoever, and nothing at all useful to do. So I put a stop to it; told the president 'No more. No more Goddamned generals—got too many already.'"

Then he chuckled, "Only broke that rule once, and that was by accident. Colonel Joshua Chamberlain, who'd been a hero at Gettysburg, was reported to me as mortally wounded in another battle later on. So, to honor his previous, heroic service, I promoted him, posthumously. Or so I thought; the damned fool went ahead and lived! Can you believe it?"

Nathan smiled, wondering where this was going.

Then Grant reached across the table, extending a closed fist. He turned his fingers up and opened them. In the palm of his hand sat a Union officer's shoulder patch, in the center of which was sewn a single gold star.

"I've decided to break my own rule for just the second time. Congratulations, *General* Chambers."

☙◊❧◊☙◊❧◊☙◊❧

When Nathan returned to the brigade's camp, he went straight to Tom's tent and entered, Harry hard on his heels.

Tom looked up from his chair. "Oh, there you are. That took a while. How did it go?"

Nathan held a serious expression, and sat heavily in the spare chair next to Tom.

"Oooo … that bad?"

Nathan shrugged. "Sorry it took so long, but I was called to the carpet by General Grant himself. Had to ride out to City Point to meet with him."

"And …"

Rather than answer, Nathan held out his hand in a fist. As Tom looked down at it, he opened the fingers, even as Grant had done for him. Tom gazed open-mouthed at the brigadier general's shoulder patch in Nathan's palm.

"*What!* Is that—"

"Yep."

Tom leapt to his feet and embraced Nathan. The movement was so sudden that Nathan's chair was spilled, and the two men fell to the floor, forcing Harry to scramble out of the way to avoid being hit. There the three of them lay, the two men laughing and hugging each other, as the dog gazed from one to the other as if they'd lost their minds.

When they were back on their feet, Nathan said, "Of course, he reminded me that it was only a brevet promotion; that if I stayed in the regular army after the war, I'd be reverted to the rank of colonel. But I told him I had no intention of staying in the army after the war; that I had a family farm to run, a good woman to marry, and a whole passel of onery children to have and raise."

Tom chuckled, "And what did the commanding general say to that?"

Nathan smiled at the memory, and in his best imitation of General Grant answered, *"Chambers ... that sounds like about the best Goddamned thing I can think of to do."*

😀

Saturday April 1, 1865 – Wheeling, West Virginia:

"'Scuse me, Megs, ma'am ..." Phinney said, as he leaned in the front door of the farmhouse. Though he had no reason to fear any reproach from those in the house, he was unused to venturing inside, so he always felt a bit reticent when doing so.

"Oh, hello, Phinney," Megs answered, looking up from sweeping. "Well, come on in ... don't be shy," she scolded. There was no venom in it, however, and her expression was friendly, so he took that as a good sign.

"Sorry to bother you, Megs, but ... I was out on my usual guard duty up at the road when a rider comes up. So, o' course we stops him and asks his business. Says he's a courier for the gov'ner with a message for Abigail Chambers—uh, his words, not mine, I'd never talk so familiar of Miss Abbey."

"Oh, never mind *that*, Phinney. Did he give you a message?"

"Yes, ma'am, a telegram he said it was. Here it is," he said, handing her a single folded sheet of paper.

He was a little surprised when Megs unfolded it and started reading—it was, after all, for Miss Abbey. Megs didn't seem concerned about that, so Phinney decided he wouldn't be either.

Megs still intimidated him a little, despite everything that'd happened, and he never wanted to cross her.

And she suddenly whooped for joy. "*Amen!*" she said, then looked at Phinney and grinned. "They done made the Captain into a general. *Hallelujah!*"

"Oh, my, Megs! That's some very good news, ain't it? Good for him … good for the Captain, God bless him."

"Yes, Phinney, that's *very* good news."

"But … Megs, does it matter do you think? In the war, I mean," he asked.

"Well, of course it does. When they make a man into a general, they give him a big ol' army to fight with. And what you figure the Captain gonna do with a thing like *that*, Phinney?"

He thought for a moment, then beamed. "I reckon he gonna go ahead and whup ol' Bobby Lee, that's what."

She smiled and patted him on the arm. "I reckon you're right, Phinney … I reckon you're right." Then she turned and headed back into the house, shouting, "Miss Abbey, Miss Abbey, we just got some great news!"

Phinney turned and left the house, trotting down the stairs, eager to spread the good news.

𝔅𝔒𝔞𝔯𝔒𝔰𝔅𝔒𝔞𝔯𝔒𝔰𝔅𝔒𝔞𝔯𝔒𝔰

Saturday April 1, 1865 – Petersburg, Virginia:

"Hey fellas … gather round … I just got a letter from the Captain. Sent it over with a courier," Tony said with excitement, as he stepped up to the area around the mess tent where the men were sitting to eat their midday dinner.

In keeping with the now established routine, Sergeant Bowen, a chubby, jolly, and popular freeman who'd been taught to read, stepped up and took the note from Tony, then turned to face the men who were now gathering in anticipation.

"It says here …"

Union Camp at Petersburg
April 1, 1865

Sergeant Mark Anthony
23rd US Colored Regiment
Union Camp, Petersburg, Va.:

Dear Tony, and company, just wanted to send my regards and tell you respectfully to make sure you and all your men are fully prepared for action, as I have a strong feeling this slow siege warfare we've all been enduring will not go on much longer. Wishing you all Godspeed, and looking forward to fighting next to you soon.

Nathaniel Chambers,
Brigadier General
Commander 2nd Brigade
XXIV Corps, Army of the James

"Wait, Bowen ... read that last part again," Tony said, frowning.

Sergeant Bowen looked back down at the paper, "Uh ... 'Wishing you all Gods—'"

"*No, no* ... after that ... the signature part," Tony shot back.

"Oh ... um ... 'Nathaniel Chambers, Brigadier General, Command—'"

"Yeah, that part! Guys ... this here telegram says that they done made the Captain into a full-blown general! How about that!"

The men gathered around were suddenly wide-eyed with surprise, and immediately shared laughter, smiles, and handshakes all around. Even those who hadn't come from Mountain Meadows had heard plenty of stories by now about the legendary "Captain Chambers," so they figured it to be good news.

Big George stepped up to Tony and said, "Well I'll be ... he a real *general*, now ... You reckon they done put the Captain in to replace old Grant?"

"Don't know, but seems like maybe," Tony answered.

"Must be true, don't you think?" Henry asked. "Like they finally figured out a fella that knows how to lick them rebs."

"Well, yeah … if anyone can do it, the Captain can," George nodded his agreement.

"I don't know 'bout any o' that, but I do know one thing for sure," Tony answered.

"What's that?" George asked.

"Now that the Captain is a general, things are gonna start happenin' 'round here, just like he says. Reckon we's finally gonna get to go after them slavers with all we got."

"Yeah, that's for sure. The Captain ain't one to sit still when there's fightin' to be done," Henry agreed. "You mark my words, boys … if today they made the Captain into a general … by *tomorrow* we'll be attackin' them damned rebs."

Tony thought about that a moment, then nodded, "I think you got the right of it, Henry. Guys … let's pass the word among the men … be ready to fight—I mean *really* fight—come tomorrow mornin'. The Captain's 'bout to start a fight with them slavers, just like he did back at Mountain Meadows. And I, for one, reckon they ain't gonna like what he gonna give 'em."

Big George and Henry nodded their agreement, and grinned in anticipation.

That evening, Lieutenant Rhodes poked his head into Tony's tent with orders to rouse the men two hours before dawn, in preparation for an all-out assault on the enemy at first light.

"*I knew it!*" Tony said with a grin and a shake of his fist, after the lieutenant left to go inform the other sergeants. *Thank you, Captain! Maybe now we can get this thing over with, and can get ourselves on to home. And I can get back to Rosa …*

Chapter 6. Rebel Fortress

"Pain plants the flag of truth
within a rebel fortress."
- C.S. Lewis

Sunday April 2, 1865 – Petersburg, Virginia:

Brigadier General Nathaniel Chambers lay on his chest, ignoring the mud while shivering in the pre-dawn chill, gazing out toward the enemy line through his brass spyglass. Though it was still too dark to see much, he looked more out of nervous habit than any real purpose; he knew all too well where the enemy line lay: the same place it'd been for the past nine months.

He also knew that the signal to attack was imminent, as the sky in the east had begun to glow, prefacing the dawn to come. Spread out on either side of him for hundreds of yards, and gathered behind him for dozens more, were the men of his brigade, nearly three thousand strong. Rifles loaded, hammers at the half cock, bayonets fixed, and nerves twitching, his men lay flat against the ground, eagerly waiting for him to give the word.

And he knew that his brigade, as numerous and strong as it might be, was but a tiny fraction of the vast host Ulysses Grant was about to unleash upon the rebel lines. For miles in both directions, more than a hundred thousand men and hundreds of artillery batteries prepared for the great onslaught that was awaiting the dawn.

He resisted a very strong urge to pull out a cigar to calm his racing nerves. Instead, he reached over and stroked Harry behind the ears. Then he took a deep breath and whispered his favorite pre-battle Bible verse, Psalm 144, the same he'd used hundreds of times before under similar circumstances.

"Blessed be the LORD my strength, which teacheth my hands to war, and my fingers to fight."

Then, without warning, a bright light flashed somewhere behind them, followed by a single loud *BOOM* that shattered the stillness and echoed across the landscape—the signal to attack.

Nathan leapt to his feet, swept out his sword, raised it high and shouted, *"Charge!"*

Three thousand chilled and shivering soldiers of the Second Brigade, XXIV Corps, Army of the James pulled themselves from the muddy earth. And with a great shout, they surged forward, following on their general's heels.

As was his habit in an all-out assault, Nathan ran in zig-zagging course, but still, he quickly crossed the gap to the rebels' earthworks. As he ran, he saw enemy soldiers lean up over their wall and fire their rifles, but as he'd hoped, there seemed but few of them to his front—no more than a hundred, he guessed. And the enemy's gunfire seemed hurried and uncoordinated, having little effect on the approaching Union lines. And before Nathan had completely covered the distance, the incoming fire seemed to let off completely.

When he reached the outer dirt wall, Nathan leapt up and scrambled to the top. But when he stood and gazed into the rebel fortification, he saw it had been entirely abandoned, its defenders streaming away in full retreat, disorganized and scattered, many throwing down their arms as they ran. He turned back toward his men and waved the saber, shouting, "Come men, the day is ours! The rebels are running!"

Aware that General Gibbon's corps, of which his brigade was a part, was on the left flank of Grant's thrust, Nathan then led his men to the right, thinking to flank any rebel formations in that direction. He glanced back and to the sides, but all he could see was a wave of blue uniforms. And the faces he saw, though still determined and ready for a fight, exuded excitement and enthusiasm; finally, something was happening … finally, the breakthrough!

The rebel frontline soldiers that'd retreated from the first onslaught raced ahead of Nathan's men, merging with other units that were likewise retreating.

And then Nathan saw ahead of them, just beyond a roadway, a crescent-shaped redoubt of earthen walls at least fifteen feet tall, reinforced with logs, overlooking a water-filled moat. *Fort Gregg,* he remembered from the maps. The fort sat on a high rise, facing southward, the land in front gently sloping down toward the roadway. On either side of the fort stretched a marshy wetland. Clearly, it'd been well designed as the second level defensive line, the fallback point, should the outer perimeter fail. *Damn … nowhere to go but through it,* Nathan decided.

He could see rebel officers atop their horses, waving sabers and shouting at the retreating soldiers, trying to turn them, get them reorganized and into the fortress. And though most of the rebels had no more stomach for the fight and continued on toward the rear, a number of them obeyed their officers' commands and moved into the fort through a sally door in the wooden rear palisade wall. By the time they secured the entrance, Nathan guessed there must've been two or three hundred armed rebels within the small redoubt, and likely several pre-positioned artillery pieces and their crews.

The other units of General Gibbon's XXIV Corps had now gathered to the right of Nathan's brigade. The sun, now risen above the field, glinted and sparkled off thousands of bayonets in a sea of blue coats. And after several minutes to regroup, during which Union artillery pounded the fort to unknown effect, these regiments were ordered forward against the fort.

Starting at about eight hundred yards out, the Union brigades advanced toward the fort at a trot. As they came within range, near the roadway, the rebels opened fire with small arms and canister fire from their artillery pieces.

The numbers were too great for the fort's defenders, and many Union soldiers soon reached the walls.

As Nathan watched through his spyglass, he could see that the moat below the walls was filled with rainwater, shoulder deep. And once the soldiers had slogged through the water, drenched, chilled, and exhausted, they still had to clamber up the slick mud walls. This they did by digging bayonets into the mud and scrambling up, or by standing on each other's shoulders, all the while taking devastating rifle fire from the enemy above.

Nathan grimaced as he watched brave men in blue dropping like flies from the walls into the cold water below, never to rise again. Others scrambled to the top of the parapet, only to be shot or stabbed before they could get inside the fort. The fighting was grim and intense—some of the fiercest fighting Nathan had witnessed in the war—hand-to-hand with bayonets, swords, and rifle butts.

Still, the stubborn defenders held, and the first wave was forced to pull back beyond the roadway, leaving the field littered with blue-clad bodies.

Nathan watched the battle with growing frustration. Another interlude of Union artillery bombardment was followed by a second infantry wave rushing forward. But as Nathan expected, the result was nearly identical. Though vastly outnumbered, the rebel defenders held a good solid defensive position, and fought with a courage and stubborn determination that proved impossible for the Union attackers to overcome.

As he watched the second attack begin to stall, Nathan knew his brigade would be next, but he was determined not to repeat the same mistakes and get his men slaughtered. So he sent for his three regimental commanders to join him in a quick council of war.

In a few minutes, Nathan's senior officers were gathered under the massive branches of an ancient oak tree: Colonel Albert Moulton of the Fifty-Fourth Pennsylvania, Lieutenant Colonel Samuel Simison of the Twenty-Third Illinois, and Lieutenant Colonel Tom Clark of the Twelfth West Virginia. Each brought with them their second in command—in Tom's case, Major Jim Wiggins. And as usual, Nathan's hulking four-legged shadow settled in next to him.

After a quick greeting, Nathan said, "Gentlemen … I'm sure you're seeing the same thing I am?"

"Yes, General," Tom answered. "Tough nut to crack there, and I'm assuming we're next. Not relishing the thought of that, sir …"

"No, neither am I," Nathan responded. "Which is why I've called this meeting ... Gentlemen, I'm not much of one for following convention: doing the same old tired thing and expecting a different outcome. I mean to crack that nut, and not to lose a large number of our men in the bargain."

"Sounds good to me, sir," Colonel Moulton replied. "What do you have in mind?"

"Well, whatever it is, you can bet it's not going to be a mindless, headlong rush into that moat and up that wall. We've seen how that turns out," he answered with a dark frown.

They all nodded, but no one spoke, waiting for him to explain his plan.

"Of course, I'm open to ideas and suggestions, but here's what I have in mind ..."

He turned and looked at Jim. "Major Wiggins, how many repeating rifles does the Twelfth have, all told?"

Jim looked up at the tree branches above and began counting on his fingers. In a moment, he looked back at Nathan and said, "I reckon we've got twenty-three. All the officers have them, and a smattering of enlisted men who've bought their own."

Nathan nodded, then turned to Moulton, "And in the Fifty-Fourth?"

"Oh ... probably a half dozen or so ..."

Nathan nodded, then turned to Colonel Simison, and simply raised an eyebrow. "We have twelve, General," Simison said.

"Hmm ... that makes the count forty-one," Nathan said, then stepped over to the tree and grabbed his own rifle from where he'd leaned it against the trunk. He stepped back to the group and tossed the rifle to Jim, who caught it smartly. "And mine makes forty-two.

"Major Wiggins, gather all those repeaters, their ammunition, and their owners from throughout the brigade, and form up a special rifle company. Then, each of you commanders provide him with an additional ... hmm ... say fifty riflemen each—your best shooters, mind. Major Wiggins, your rifles will lead the charge, but you'll stop a hundred yards out, with enough gaps between your men to allow the rest of the brigade to pass through.

Have your men take careful aim and target any rebel who dares stick his head above the wall. And also try to pin down their artillerymen—even if you can't hit them, you should be able to make it hot for them, so they'll be less able to do their job. Once the rest of the brigade has passed your position, move in closer as circumstances dictate."

"Yes, sir. It'll be done just as you say," Jim answered.

"That ought to give the rest of our men a fighting chance to reach that moat without getting slaughtered."

"But what about that moat, sir?" Moulton asked. "Seems like the men have had the devil's own time slogging across that. I imagine the bottom is pure muck and their boots are getting sucked down into it."

Nathan didn't answer for a moment, but reached into his pocket, pulled out a cigar, and lit it. After a puff he looked back at the group with a frown, then said softly, "Gentlemen … have you seen how many of our brave men have fallen into that water already today? Though it's a grim thought, the reality is, by now we'll likely be able to step right across on the bodies."

The officers assembled returned his dark look, but nobody answered. They all knew the sad truth of what he was saying.

Then Nathan gazed out toward the fort, even as the current wave of soldiers began their anticipated pull back. He raised his brass spyglass to his eye and said, "Take a look through your field glasses, gentlemen."

The assembled officers did as they were bid, and soon they all gazed out toward the fort.

"See how there's some earth piled along the left side of the fort? Like they started on another wall, entrenchment, or something, but never finished it …"

"Yes, I see it," Colonel Simison answered. The others murmured their assent.

"And I had noticed when we'd first arrived and the rebels were retreating, that the back side has a sally door through a palisade wall of logs that they used to let their men in," Nathan continued.

"Ah ... I think I see where you're going with this," Colonel Simison said, lowering his binoculars and looking back at Nathan. "If we can slip some men around to the back, using that dirt pile for cover, they can have a go at that sally door. Maybe carry a few bombs with them for good measure. Might be a lot easier to break through than that high front wall of dirt."

"My thinking exactly, Colonel."

Then Nathan turned to Tom. "Colonel Clark, let's have Captain Volkov and Billy Creek gather their men, and when we launch our main attack, have them circle around and see if they can't kick down that back door."

Tom grinned. "I can only imagine the looks on those rebs' faces when they see big Stan coming at them through that sally door."

There were smiles and nods all around. Everyone knew of and respected the capabilities of the Twelfth's fearsome—if a little odd—duo.

After a few more minutes of discussion, mostly concerning the positioning of the three regiments, the meeting broke up and the officers returned to their own formations to get everything prepared.

Nathan walked with Tom and Jim back to the Twelfth's position, and they immediately summoned Billy and Stan.

After Nathan explained the plan, Stan turned and gazed at the fort for a moment before pulling his Henry rifle from his shoulder and tossing it to Jim. Then he unsheathed his saber, as if envisioning the action to come. He looked over at Nathan, and down at his left hip. "Hmm, General ... am thinking this is going to be some good knife work ... May I borrow saber?"

At first, Nathan didn't understand what Stan was asking, then he looked down, shrugged, and unbuckled the sword sheath, handing it over. Stan buckled it onto the right side of his belt, then drew it out with his left hand, so he now held a saber in each fist. He bounced the two swords, as if gauging their weight, then shrugged, and re-sheathed them, one at a time. "Is good," he said.

Billy also handed Jim his Henry rifle, then pulled out his bow and strung it. He looked up, and in response to Tom's questioning gaze, he answered, "For some reason, rebs hate arrows ... Don't know why." He shrugged, then he and Stan trotted off to get their men ready.

Then Jim stepped up in front of Nathan with a serious look, "I wanted to thank you for this, sir."

"For what, Mr. Wiggins?"

"For giving me an assignment that I can do. Something important, to … keep my honor," he answered, and nodded toward his left boot, which they both knew contained an artificial foot. It had not escaped Nathan's earlier thinking that Jim would be unable to ford the moat or climb the wall under any circumstances, but he was too good a fighter to waste by leaving him behind.

"Nonsense, Jim … You're the best man for the job is all," Nathan answered with a smile, patting him on the shoulder.

"Thank you kindly for saying so, General," Jim replied, returning the smile.

"I need you to do me a favor, though. Something I've just thought of," Nathan said.

"Of course, sir … anything you say," Jim answered.

"When the time comes, I need you to keep Harry with you, out away from the fort. He'll not be able to climb the wall, and I fear for his safety if he should flounder in the moat.

"Oh. Well, I'm happy to do it, of course, but do you think he'll stay with me when he sees you run off?"

"He will … I've been working with him on that. He'll stay if I order him to, and if it's with one of you men he's known forever. Doubt he'd stay with a stranger, but if you also tell him to stay with you, he'll do it. He won't like it, but he'll do it."

"All right, I'll take care of him, sir."

"Thanks, Jim."

Then Jim moved off to organize his special rifle company, only limping slightly, carrying an armload of Henry rifles with him.

A half hour later, as expected, orders came down to prepare for the third attack. This time, it would be made up of a brigade commanded by Colonel Andrew Potter, composed of the 116th Ohio and 34th Massachusetts, and Nathan's own brigade. Potter's brigade would be on the right, and Nathan's on the left.

And as the time to launch the attack drew nearer, Nathan wasn't especially surprised to see Major General John Gibbon, the tall, dark, serious-looking commander of XXIV Corps, approaching on his horse with his staff officers. Nathan was, however, surprised by the man who accompanied them: General Grant himself.

After a quick exchange of salutes, Gibbon said, "Chambers, in a few moments I'll give the order to start an artillery bombardment of approximately forty minutes. Then immediately after, you and Colonel Potter will launch your advance."

"Understood, General. We'll be ready. But … will you do me a favor, sir?"

"What's that?" Gibbon responded.

"Ask your artillery batteries to target that front wall, rather than the interior, and use solid shot rather than high explosives," Nathan answered.

Gibbon looked puzzled, "But, General Chambers … we know from long experience that bombarding that type of thick earthen wall, reinforced with timbers, is a useless exercise, unless you have weeks to do it. And even then, the rebels will just repair the damage at night. It's best to target the men inside with high explosives, hoping to thin their ranks, or at least to rattle their nerves. Solid shot will simply punch dents in the wall, to no great effect."

"I'm counting on it, General," Nathan said with a grin. "We've been bombarding that fort all morning, and as you well know, it has benefitted us but little. On the other hand, if our artillery punches small holes in their wall, it'll afford our men handholds with which to climb—much easier than trying to scramble up the slick walls by digging in our bayonets …"

Gibbon was thoughtful for a moment, then said, "Hmm … an interesting notion … All right, Chambers, I'll order it."

Then Grant said, "Chambers … guess this is where you earn that star. We *need* to take this fort. *Now.* Time's a' wasting … every hour they hold us back here is an hour they buy Lee to escape our grasp. And I want him!" he said, making a grasping gesture with his fist.

"Understood, sir. We won't let you down," Nathan answered.

"See that you don't," Grant answered, then turned his horse and trotted off, Gibbon and several staff officers hard on his heels.

Nathan and Tom exchanged a look. *I sure hope this works*, Nathan thought.

When the designated time arrived, the Union artillery ceased their barrage, and Nathan led his brigade forward. To their right, Colonel Potter also started his brigade moving, so the two groups moved forward as one. As the Twelfth West Virginia was in the center of Nathan's three regiments, he and Tom moved forward side by side, with Harry the Dog directly behind them. Nathan decided it felt a little odd to be leading without the saber, so he pulled the great Bowie knife from its sheath behind his back and led with that instead.

When they came to within rifle range of the fort's defenders, Jim Wiggins' 200 riflemen moved forward at the faster double-quick march for a couple hundred more yards until they reached the roadway. There they stopped in a broad line, each man spread a dozen or so yards from the next, as they opened fire on the fort. Nathan, who had trotted forward with Jim, paused just long enough to drop off Harry, ordering the great hound to stay. He then raised his knife high, and shouted, *"Charge!"*

Nathan raced across the remaining distance, reaching the muddy moat at a run and leaping out across the water. As he'd predicted, the water trap was now choked with blue-coated bodies, and he landed with a sickening thud, but in water only up to his knees. Ignoring the ghastly sensation of walking across the bodies of his dead brothers in arms, he slogged forward to the wall and began climbing. As he'd hoped, the artillery fire had cratered the wall so that it afforded plenty of good handholds and footing for the climb. He was not surprised when he glanced to his right to see Tom climbing up next to him. He looked back up just in time to duck as a gray-clad body fell past him, splashing into the water below. *Nice work, Jim*, he thought, and then continued his climb.

Blue-coated soldiers splashed through the water and swarmed up the wall as gunfire rang out all around them in a deafening cacophony and a blinding swirl of gun smoke.

Finally, Nathan reached the top of the wall and pulled himself up over the crest onto the battlements. What met his eyes there was a scene of utter chaos, even for a man who'd seen many years of war.

When Tom scrambled up with Nathan to gain the top, he found that the regiment's color bearer, Private J. R. Logsdon, of Company C, had just been shot dead trying to plant the regiment's flag atop the wall. And even as Tom watched, Lieutenant Joseph Caldwell took up the colors and was immediately killed as well, tumbling into the rebel fortress with the colors still gripped in his hand.

Tom had little time to think, having to dodge a bayonet thrust from a rebel, whom he shot with his pistol before immediately knocking aside another rifle butt with his saber, this one aimed at his head.

The screaming and howling of the men around him seemed at times even louder than the continuous gunfire, as men fought with a ferocity and savagery unmatched by wild beasts. In the midst of the chaos, Tom noted that two men had stepped up next to him, shoulder to shoulder. A quick glance told him it was Zeke and Ollie, both of whom fired a pistol from each hand to deadly effect. Zeke shouted in Tom's ear, "Hey, Colonel … you gonna let them rebs have *your* flag?"

And when Zeke said "*your* flag," it made Tom realize for the first time that it was *his* flag. He was the commander of the Twelfth, and this was the Twelfth's flag, and the rebels now had it. Losing your flag to the enemy in battle was as close to an unforgivable sin as it got in the military.

Tom glanced at Zeke, and said, "No, by God. Let's get it back!" And with little conscious thought, he leapt down off the wall where the flag had fallen, even into the midst of their enemies. Zeke and Ollie followed him, along with a half dozen other Union soldiers from the Twelfth. They were quickly surrounded and fighting for their lives. Tom scooped up the flag and turned to toss it back up the wall to a sergeant from the regiment, who grinned as he caught it and thrust it into the dirt at the top of the wall.

Then Tom turned back to the fight just in time to witness his own death coming straight at him. A rebel sergeant thrust a bayonet hard at his stomach. Tom flinched, anticipating the blow, but the blade stopped just inches short. Tom looked up to see the man's eyes wide with shock, and six inches of knife blade protruding from his chest. The knife was yanked free, and the soldier slumped to the ground, revealing Nathan standing behind.

"Thanks," Tom gasped.

Nathan had no time to respond, turning to fire his pistol left-handed at another rebel, even while deflecting a rifle blow with the Bowie knife in his right.

A Union soldier next to Tom went down, and then another, and he suffered a sudden vision of what it must've felt like for Georgie and Jamie in their final fatal moments of battle back at New Market. He decided this was the end, but figured to go down fighting hard, and redoubled his efforts.

Then he heard a great noise, like an explosion, though the rebels had long since run out of artillery ammunition. He looked toward the back of the fort and saw that the sally port had been blown open, and Union soldiers were pouring through. Stan and Billy had finally arrived. The giant Russian came charging forward, attacking anyone who stood before him, howling like a madman, slashing with a saber in each hand. And right beside him, Billy used his bow to devastating effect, each shot a sure kill. Their men, armed with bayonets, drove the rebels back from the wall, even as more Union soldiers poured down over the front.

To Tom, the next twenty minutes were a blur of the most desperate, ferocious fighting imaginable. Then, suddenly, it was over, and the remaining rebels threw down their weapons and raised their hands. So fired up were Stan and the soldiers with him, that they continued to stab and shoot the Confederates that were trying to surrender until Nathan stepped in front of Stan and yelled, "Stand down, Captain Volkov. It's done. They've surrendered."

Stan gazed at him, uncomprehending for a moment before lowering his blades and nodding. "Oh. All right, General. If you say so."

Tom looked around and took in a scene he would never forget: bodies lay strewn across the ground in pools of blood. The wounded lay everywhere, groaning, screaming, and writhing in agony.

William, who'd fought as fiercely as anyone during the battle, now holstered his pistols and took charge of tending the wounded of both sides.

An hour later, after they'd taken stock of the battle, Tom received the final body count. Of the nearly three hundred defenders of Fort Gregg, only thirty-three had not been killed or severely wounded. He could only shake his head in wonder at the courage and determination of the rebels, fighting for a cause that was clearly now in its death throes.

✶✦✧✶✦✧✶✦✧✶✦✧✶✦✧✶✦✧

Sunday April 2, 1865 – Petersburg, Virginia:

Captain James Hawkins lead his rifle company of the Seventh West Virginia forward with a shout, saber upraised as he rushed toward the rebels' redoubt—a wall of dirt and logs. The company's color bearer followed him, flag aloft, and on both sides of him the men of the Seventh, bayonets fixed, flowed toward the enemy like a wave rushing to the shore.

Hawkins couldn't remember how many times they'd performed actions nearly identical to this one. Always the same heady feeling at the start, but like the proverbial wave, their momentum would eventually stall, and then the fight would bog down until they were inexorably forced back, usually to a point somewhere near where they'd started. And usually with the loss of yet more good men.

This time, to Hawkins' astonishment, as he crested the rise and looked down into the defensive works, he saw only the backs of the rebel soldiers, already retreating out of the other side of the redoubt: thousands of them, finally giving up the fight and relinquishing the field of battle to the Union side.

Hawkins inhaled a deep breath of satisfaction. This, he thought, is going to be a great day!

He turned back toward the advancing regiment, and waved his saber, shouting, "We've broken through, boys … the victory is ours!"

The men of the Seventh gave a cheer as they rushed up over the wall and moved to occupy the position the rebels had just abandoned.

Then off to his left, Hawkins saw other Union soldiers also pouring over the defensive works unopposed, the Nineteenth Massachusetts he recalled from the morning's action briefing, also led by a captain. So he trotted over to have a celebratory word with the fellow.

As he approached, the captain turned to him, then smiled broadly. "Great day, eh, Captain?" the man said. "Gareth Hughes, Nineteenth Massachusetts."

"James Hawkins, Seventh West Virginia. Good to meet you, Hughes." The two shook hands with enthusiasm.

"Shall we coordinate our advance—make sure we're not caught in a counterattack or a flanking maneuver?" Hawkins asked.

"Agreed. Let's push through this redoubt and see if we can't take all the ground over to the Claiborne Road," Gareth answered.

Hawkins laughed, "You sound like you actually know where that is …"

"Oh, yes, sorry—born and raised in Richmond, so, yes, I know where it is. About a quarter mile distant, running parallel to our current position. We can use the raised roadway there for cover, if need be."

"All right. And what if we reach the road and the rebels are gone?" Hawkins asked.

Gareth shrugged, then grinned, "Then we keep going."

"That'll work. Shall we?" Hawkins asked, gesturing toward the far side of the defensive works.

"See you down at the road, Hawkins," Gareth answered, then hopped down and raced toward the far wall, his men falling in behind him.

Sunday April 2, 1865 – Petersburg, Virginia:

For Tony and the other men of the Twenty-Third Colored Regiment, it'd been a heady day of charging, fighting, watching the enemy fall back in disarray, taking over their trenchworks, then rising up out of those to charge and fight some more.

Now, with afternoon winding down into evening, all fighting had ceased, as it appeared that the enemy had entirely abandoned their defenses around Petersburg. Apparently, the rebs were now on the move, retreating out west somewhere. So that was where the Union Army was headed as well.

As they marched toward the setting sun, Tony turned and caught Henry's eye, where he led his rifle company a few yards back. "Hey, Henry—what'd I say about the Captain takin' charge? I told you he'd be puttin' a whuppin' on them rebs."

Henry smiled and shouted back, "Yeah, you said it, Tony. You said it. Just don't go gettin' all high and mighty on us, now. This here ain't over yet—not 'til it's *all* the way over ..."

Tony laughed, then turned back to the front and said to himself, "Oh, it's over, all right ... This damn thing's all but over now ... I can feel it!"

Sunday April 2, 1865 – Petersburg, Virginia:

As he jogged along, headed west with the remains of General Terry's brigade, Jubal couldn't bring himself to feel downtrodden, even though their side had just suffered a terrible strategic defeat.

First of all, for once, his regiment had not suffered any casualties in the battle, as the brunt of the fighting had been elsewhere along the line; they'd only been ordered to withdraw after the federals had broken through at several other points, making holding their brigade's position untenable.

And this particular defeat, he reflected, had finally ended the terrible siege of Petersburg that had been going on now for more than nine months, though, thankfully, his regiment had only had to endure four months of that.

It also, he had to assume, was the beginning of the end for the Confederate Army and the war in general. Even if they could somehow slip away from Grant's forces, and by some miracle meet up with the remainder of the Confederate Army under Joseph Johnston down in North Carolina, what then? From all reports, Johnston was already hard pressed by Yankee General Sherman. What would happen when Sherman and Grant joined forces against them? *Nothing good*, he thought.

And then, as if to put the exclamation point to Jubal's thoroughly mixed emotions on the day's events, a cavalry unit rode past them, also headed west. Jubal scowled as he recognized the despicable Lieutenant Colonel Walters in the lead. Other than Evelyn's unknown betrothed, which he did feel somewhat guilty about, Jubal had never wished for another man in his own army to meet his untimely end. But *this* fellow …

Chapter 7. Conflagration

"One has to speak out and
stand up for one's convictions.
Inaction at a time of
conflagration is inexcusable."
*- **Mahatma Gandhi***

Sunday April 2, 1865 – Richmond, Virginia:

Confederate President Jefferson Davis sat to the right of Virginia Governor Frank Lubbock in the front row pew of St. Paul's Church for morning services. Normally, Davis's wife Varina would be on his left side, but he'd put her and the children on a train bound for Georgia two days earlier. *Hard to believe things have gotten so bad—that it has come to this*, he thought.

Then he chastised himself for not paying any attention to the long, droning sermon, and tried to refocus on the preacher's message.

"In this hour of darkness and doubt, I am reminded of the words of Moses, in Deuteronomy chapter thirty-one, verse six," the pastor said. *"Be strong and of a good courage, fear not, nor be afraid of them: for the LORD thy God, he it is that doth go with thee; he will not fail thee, nor forsake thee."*

To Davis, the words somehow fell flat, and he felt no upwelling of hope or inspiration, only gloom. And then a movement to his right caught his eye, and he looked to see a man kneeling next to him in the pew. He recognized the Confederate postmaster general, John Reagan, whose downcast visage seemed to mirror his own dark thoughts.

"Sorry to disturb you, sir," Reagan whispered. "But I have an urgent message from General Lee." He handed across a folded sheet of paper.

Davis took the telegram, unfolded it, and read:

Petersburg, April 2, 1865 — 11:25 a.m.

C.S.A. President Jeff. Davis:

As our position at Petersburg is no longer tenable, I think it absolutely necessary that we should abandon our defenses tonight and have given the orders of same to the troops. The operation, though difficult, I expect to be performed successfully. I intend to move all forces, including those at present garrisoning Richmond, to Amelia Court House, there to rendezvous and replenish supplies before moving on. Recommend the immediate evacuation of the government from the city, but request you communicate your future location to this command as exigencies allow.

R.E. Lee,
Commanding General

Davis folded the paper, slipped it into his coat pocket, then nodded to Reagan before rising and slowly exiting the pew into the center aisle. He did not have to gaze about to know that all eyes were now on him, and that little mind was being paid to the ongoing sermon.

He'd not gone a dozen steps toward the door when he heard a growing murmuring among the congregation, and by the time he was halfway to the door, the preacher had ceased speaking, and Davis could hear a large number of people moving about behind him.

By the time he reached the door to the foyer, he could sense that he was being followed by a multitude. As he strode out onto the street, turning down Ninth Street toward his office in the War Department, people began streaming out of St. Paul's.

❧❧❦❧❧❧❦❧❧❧❦❧

For Evelyn, a quiet, humdrum Sunday morning with little to do, and even less to look forward to, had suddenly changed into an afternoon of ... *what? Something else entirely*, she decided, though she couldn't yet tell what was happening.

111

Her first indication of something momentous was a great noise that she felt as much as heard: as if thousands of feet were in motion, and thousands of voices were shouting.

From her tiny window on one side of the warehouse, she could just make out a small stretch of the roadway running up the hill from the warehouse district. Its casual, slow pace had erupted into a frantic scramble of people, horses, wagons, and carts; as if the entire city were suddenly moving.

Something has happened, she concluded, and thought on what that might be. In only a moment, it came to her like a lightning bolt from the blue: *The Union Army has broken through at last! Petersburg has fallen! Oh, praise the Lord!*

Even as she was absorbing these glorious thoughts, she saw a thing that brought a knot of dread to her stomach: flames, shooting high in the air above the rooftops of the warehouses, just blocks away, though she'd heard no artillery fire. And then it occurred to her that it was not the Union Army that'd started the fires, but their own guardians, the Confederate Army. *Oh, no, they have intentionally burned the warehouses to destroy the supplies! Our building will be consumed. We must prepare to flee!*

She turned and ran through the building, shouting, "Everyone get ready to leave now! Fire approaches … fire! Gather your things, quickly!"

As she passed by the main entrance, the door popped open and Jacob rushed in.

"What is happening, Jacob?" she shouted at him, but he raised his hand, and leaned down with his hands on his knees, gasping for breath, as he'd clearly run a long distance at great speed.

"They … they've broken through at Petersburg … Lee has fled to the west …" he got out between deep breaths.

"Yes, yes, of course, what else could it be? Now catch your breath, then tell me what you've seen. I must know what is going on in the surrounding neighborhood, so we can plan our escape."

Jacob took several more deep breaths before standing up straight and looking her in the eye.

"Shortly after noon, rumors began to be repeated of something big happening—that people reported seeing government clerks hurriedly loading boxes onto wagons and piling others in the street outside their offices and setting them alight. One even told me he saw them dump unsigned Confederate dollars into a bonfire and burn them!

"And then I began to see things for myself, loaded wagons heading out of town; piled high with goods and people, everyone suddenly in motion, both rich and poor alike.

"Then I heard the government had opened the doors to the supply depots and encouraged people to take everything they could. After all these months of deprivation and near starvation, I saw people carrying off armloads of food: hams, bags of coffee, sugar and flour, sides of bacon … so I took my men and went to see if we could procure some for us.

"By the time we got there, the rebel army had already showed up with orders to burn everything. The depots were set on fire, and the flames were quickly spreading. Like many others, we risked the flames and went inside, grabbing whatever we could that'd not yet been consumed by the growing blaze.

"We ended up on an upper floor, where we'd each gathered an armload of goods and were preparing to get out when I glanced out a window and saw a crowd of starving women and children on the street below. So we broke out the windows and started tossing food out to the people below. Soon others joined us, and we did as much as we could before the flames became too hot and we were forced to flee. We have brought some food stocks with us, but … well, I'm sorry, we could've brought more if we hadn't stopped to help the others."

"You did rightly, Jacob," she said, reaching out to pat him on the arm.

"I heard they also opened the jails," he continued, "and the wounded soldiers have been turned out of their sick beds and lead out of the hospitals. I don't know how much of *that* is true." He shrugged.

"We saw some soldiers hauling off barrels of liquor, while others smashed them and lit them on fire. Eerie blue flames burn in the gutters on several of the streets. A few blocks from here everything is ablaze, and the fires are spreading. I fear they will soon reach us."

"Yes, I've seen them in the near distance. I have already ordered everyone to get ready."

"Evelyn … There's one more thing I want to make sure you understand …"

"Yes?"

"The army is preparing to evacuate, and clearly the government is as well. We must assume there is no longer any law and order in Richmond. Our once-fair city has just become a very dangerous place. We must be prepared," he said, and to emphasize the point, he drew out his pistol from its hiding place tucked into his belt under his shirt. He spun the cylinder, inspecting the percussion caps.

"Agreed. Now let's get moving," she answered, then turned as Mary came running up.

"What's happening, Miss Eve?" she said, wide-eyed and gasping for breath from her run across the warehouse.

"General Grant has broken through at Petersburg, and the Confederates have set fire to the town," she answered. "We must leave at once; the flames are quickly spreading, and may be here in moments. There's no time to lose, so I need you to take charge as we've discussed, starting with making sure we take all the food with us, such as it is," she said with a wry shake of her head. In the past few weeks, they had been down to nothing but cornbread and boiled dried beans with salt or brown sugar added to give it a modicum of flavor. It was a Godsend that Jacob and his men had been able to rescue a few items from the flames at the army supply depot.

"Then, make sure everyone takes only one blanket each," she continued, "and have them wear their warmest clothing. We must leave everything else."

"All right, Miss Eve, I will see to it. But what will *you* be doing?" Mary asked.

"To escape the city, I must forgo my longtime disguise as a dirty, unkempt street waif—clean myself up, and don the best traveling clothes I have, so that I can pass for an upper-class lady while traveling. If we encounter any Confederate roadblocks along the way—I must play the role of a Richmond aristocrat, fleeing the hated Union Army advance, taking her loyal slaves with her."

Mary nodded thoughtfully. "Yes, that makes sense, Miss Eve. I will see to it that everyone is ready," she said, then hurried off to supervise the preparations.

Evelyn retreated to her corner of the warehouse to clean up and change, while Jacob went back outside to join the two other white men, Hugh and Adam, who'd been provided to Evelyn by the Employer, plus Hank, the escaped former butler of Confederate President Jefferson Davis. The four of them kept a watch on the growing conflagration as well as the stream of people passing by.

As she hurriedly wiped dirt from her face and stripped off her filthy, ragged clothes, Evelyn reflected on how she had planned for an emergency evacuation, knowing it was inevitable, though whether that might be from war, some action by the enemy, or other causes, she'd had no way of knowing. So she'd not been caught entirely unprepared, though in the end, it had happened shockingly fast. One moment everything was normal, and the next people choked the streets, fleeing through the city in every direction, with the army lighting warehouses and other storage buildings on fire as they went.

Though Evelyn could understand, in general, the military reasoning for destroying anything that might be useful to the advancing enemy, in this case she considered it inexcusable and unconscionable; the Union Army by all accounts had more than enough food, equipment, and ammunition to finish out the war. They had no need for any stockpiled rebel supplies, so destroying it was unnecessary, and only put the civilian population at great risk.

It angered her to think of the innocents that would likely be killed or left destitute by this thoughtless act of desperation by the Confederates, which in the end, would only harm their own people.

Once she was ready, Evelyn grabbed her small carpet bag and moved toward the door. But before she could reach it, Jacob poked his head in: "Gotta go *now*, Evelyn. The fire has reached the south end of the building."

"Mary … we must go!" she called out, and in moments the freemen were queued up behind her at the door, their meager goods in hand, the men with packs on their backs holding their remaining food supply.

"Jacob, you guard the rear with Hugh, I'll take the lead with Adam and Hank, since I know where we need to go," Evelyn ordered. Jacob nodded, then waved to Hugh to join him at the back of the queue.

Evelyn stepped out the door into a world she no longer recognized. Smoke filled the air and fires raged across the skyline of the once beautiful city. The roaring of the fires, along with shouting and screaming of men and horses, was nearly deafening.

Evelyn turned and strode briskly up the street, glancing back to make sure everyone was following. Adam walked next to her, pistol in hand, while Hank walked directly behind her, followed by Mary and the rest of the freemen. As ordered, Jacob and Hugh guarded the rear.

Evelyn led them through the back alleys and side roads, avoiding the main avenues. She used this route for two reasons: first, that they were not clogged with the retreating army, and second, though dressing as an upper-class lady was generally a good plan, the downside was she was now at greater risk of being spotted by the ever-lurking Signal Corps. However, with the chaos enveloping the city, she considered the risk of the enemy still concerning itself with capturing her had to be extremely low.

As she rounded a corner, she noticed a disheveled, dirty looking man standing across the street in an alleyway. He gazed at her intently for a few moments, then looked away. She thought it odd that he was just standing there, watching, when everyone else in town was moving. However, she kept going and quickly forgot all about it.

The man waited until all of Evelyn's party had passed, then turned and raced down the alleyway in the opposite direction.

"Describe the woman again," Major White demanded of the decrepit-looking man before him. The fellow was dirty, his clothes ragged, and he walked with a stoop. It was all White could do to stand near enough to the man to speak with him, given the stench emanating from him. But the fellow said he had seen the woman they were seeking.

"Dressed nice-like … darned near the purtiest thing I ever seen. Was leading a dozen or more slaves, and three white men with guns," the man answered.

"Men with guns? Soldiers, you mean?"

"No, sir. Regular fellas. Like me. Just pistols, no rifles like a soldier'd be like to carry."

"Ah, I see. What else about the woman? Hair color? Eye color?"

"Couldn't make out no eye color, but long dark hair under a fine, blue bonnet."

"Dark hair? Are you certain?"

"Yes, sir. Black as night."

White exchanged a look with Sergeant Maxwell standing next to him, who shrugged. "Not our target after all, sir?" Maxwell asked. The private standing by Maxwell looked on but said nothing.

"Not necessarily, Sergeant. Everything else fits. Easy enough to dye one's hair, I believe. That may help to explain how she has evaded us for so long. If it *is* her, it seems as if things are working as I had hoped—that the fires and chaos have finally forced her out of her hiding hole. If all goes well, we may finally nab her."

The sergeant said nothing, taking a quick glance over his shoulder toward where the raging fires lit the skyline.

White turned back to the vagrant. "Take us to where you last saw this woman," he commanded.

"What about the reward?" the man said in a whiny tone, frowning and holding out a grimy, twisted hand. "Twenty dollars in greenbacks," he insisted, referring to the much more valuable United States issued dollars.

"Oh, yes, certainly," White responded, reaching into his jacket and pulling out a leather wallet. He reached in and pulled out a single ten-dollar note, handing it across to the man. "Ten now, and another ten when we have her in captivity."

The man looked down at the bill he'd been handed. "Hey, this here ain't no greenback, it's Confederate. Damned thing's pert' near worthless. The man said it'd be paid in greenbacks."

"Then he said it *wrong*," White answered. "But if it'll make you feel better, I will also give you a fine basket of food when we're finished. A ham, bread, butter, and so on."

The man's eyes widened. "All right, Captain."

"It's *Major*," White responded. "Now, lead us to where you last saw this woman."

"This way, *Major*," he answered, and shuffled off. The three Signal Corp men followed closely in his wake.

⚜ ⚜ ⚜ ⚜ ⚜ ⚜

Evelyn led them down a dark alleyway that opened onto a broad avenue. She paused at the end of the alley and gazed out, looking down the street in both directions. To the south, she could see fires raging, but they'd now put several blocks between themselves and the growing inferno. Looking to the north, she was not especially surprised that this street was almost empty at the moment; it was not a major through road, so there was no reason for the retreating rebel army to use it as they headed through town and out into the surrounding countryside, and all but a few straggling civilians had long since fled from the advancing conflagration.

She started across the street, and had nearly reached the other side, when a voice called out, "Halt, in the name of the Confederate Signal Corps!"

She stopped and turned toward the sound, which was behind and to her left. Though it was now nearly dark, she could see three uniformed men, pistols in hand, standing in the street, facing in her direction.

She flinched at the sudden concussive *boom* of a pistol shot emanating from the back of her own column. *Jacob*, she thought.

Then Adam standing next to her also fired his pistol, making her ears ring. Suddenly, the air was filled with the harsh noise of multiple gunshots as the Confederates returned fire.

Even as Evelyn reached up her sleeve to extract her own small Smith and Wesson revolver, she felt a strong arm grab her around the shoulders and pull her to the ground. The strength of the arm was too great for her to resist, and she was forced to her knees and then facedown onto the hard stones of the street.

"Let me go! Let me go!" she shouted in desperation.

Then she heard Hank's strong deep voice say, "Keep your head down, Miss Evelyn ... You too, Mary!"

She struggled to extract herself from his firm grip, but he refused to relent.

"Hank! You *must* let me go!" she shouted as she finally squirmed from his grasp and rose to her feet, pistol in hand. When she looked out toward where the Signal Corps soldiers had been, she saw only Major White standing, just a few feet away, a large revolver aimed directly at her chest. Smoke curled up slowly from its barrel. In that moment, she first realized that all the gunfire had ceased.

"Drop the weapon, Miss Hanson," White ordered. "All your men are dead, and unless you wish to join them, I'd suggest you do as I say."

She gazed about, and saw he spoke the truth. In the short, furious gunfight, only Major White had survived unscathed. Both of his men, and three of hers lay unmoving on the ground. She felt choked up at the thought that her brave men, who'd served her so faithfully, had likely been killed trying to defend her. Especially Jacob, who'd been her right-hand man ever since the war started.

She didn't wish to show any weakness in front of this hated enemy, so she answered back, "Yours are dead too, Major."

He shrugged, "These things happen in war. *Drop ... your ... weapon,*" he demanded once again.

She sighed, then lowered the hammer, and tossed the tiny pistol to the ground.

White stepped up closer, kicked her gun away, then spoke to her in a formal, projecting tone, "Evelyn Hanson, you are under arrest for high treason against the government of the Confederate States of America, and for espionage against its military forces."

As he made this official pronouncement, she felt an anger welling up inside her. A deep-seated rage born of all the pain, suffering, and injustice that'd been heaped upon her and the people she'd been trying to help since the beginning of the war. And now, they'd been forced from their home, such as it was, by their mindless destruction of their own capital city.

"Treason?" she answered. *"Treason?!* Oh, you mean treason against a government and its military who'd burn down their own city rather than protecting its citizens? A government who would willingly leave the people who have supported it, and whom it has sworn to protect, starving and destitute? A government that has willingly enslaved more than half its population for the sake of greed? How is it even possible, I ask you, Major, for a person to commit treason against a government that behaves so treasonously against its own people?"

Evelyn could feel her face burning in her wrath, but White remained unmoved.

"None of that is my concern, Miss Hanson. It is only my duty to arrest you, and then take you to the proper authorities for lawful execution."

"Major … look around you! The war is over … Richmond is in flames. The army is in full retreat, and likely the government has already fled the city. Exactly which 'authorities' do you intend to turn me over to?"

White shrugged. "General Lee's army is still in the field. We will ride out to wherever they are bivouacked. I'm certain the general can arrange for a proper hanging."

"No!" a strong, deep voice said.

Both Major White and Evelyn looked to see that it was Hank who'd spoken, even as he stepped up next to her.

"You're not gonna take her," Hank said.

White tilted his head, as if confused. "I don't believe I was speaking to you, *slave.*"

"Yeah, but I'm speaking to you, *soldier*. I said *no*, you're not taking Miss Evelyn anywhere. She stays with us."

Major White stared at him a moment, then switched his aim from Evelyn to Hank. "You don't seem to understand … I will simply shoot you, and then take her wherever I please."

"Yeah, you can shoot me, all right. But I watched the gunfight; you already fired three shots. That means you only got three left. There's *nine* of us black men."

Hank glanced back, even as the other eight men stepped up behind him, all glowering at the major.

"You can shoot me and two others, then there'll still be six left. And though they're not armed, they'll kill you just the same. Oh, not quick—like with a bullet or knife. I reckon it'll be all the more painful, what with only fists, feet, fingernails, and teeth. Eyes gouged out … groined kicked in … A very painful way to go, I reckon."

White glanced back at the glowering black men who'd stepped up to support Hank and to keep Mary and the other black women safely behind them.

"So, what'll it be, Major?" Hank spread his arms wide, "Go ahead and shoot me first. I'm ready. Then pick two more—don't much matter which. Then you'll go ahead and get beat to death."

White and Hank stared at each other for a long moment, neither one moving.

Then White lowered the hammer on his pistol and holstered it.

"I have to hand it to you, your logic is impeccable," he said to Hank, with a curt nod.

Then he turned to Evelyn and said, "Miss Hanson. I've never before had much respect for a woman until you came along. Hunting you down has been … quite interesting, challenging— even rewarding. For that, I thank you. But this is *not* over … I *will* track you down—no matter where you go, no matter where you hide. And when I find you, I will bring you to the justice you so richly deserve."

Then he tipped his hat to her. "Good day," he said, then turned and strode away into the darkness.

Evelyn let out her breath, which she realized she'd been holding ever since Hank stepped up and said his piece. She immediately knelt by Adam, who'd been standing next to her when the gunfight started. He lay face down, and she could see that he was dead, two large bullet holes in his chest, leaving large, gory exit wounds in his back. She next went to where Hugh had fallen, and he too was clearly dead, a bullet having hit him in the face. Finally, she came to Jacob. At first, she felt hopeful that he yet lived, as he lay on his back with his eyes wide open. However, when she bent down to look at his face, she saw that it was not so. The eyes were glazed over and lifeless. She reached out and gently closed his eyelids, then bent down and kissed him softly on the forehead, whispering, "Goodbye, dear friend. I shall miss you so … always."

Tears streamed down her face, and she yet again felt a strong twinge of guilt, as the old familiar accusing voice in the back of her mind scolded, *Another good man has died for your sake, Evelyn.*

Yet she still retained enough righteous indignation at Major White and the Confederacy to argue back this time, *No! Not for my sake. He died fighting for what he believed in—for what we all believe in. So, just shut up for once!*

She stood, then walked over to retrieve her Smith and Wesson, slipping it back into its hidden holster up her sleeve.

Seeing what she was doing, Hank asked, "Should we pick up the other weapons, do you think?"

Evelyn thought a moment, then shook her head. "No. For one, you men aren't trained in their use, and there could be a tragic accident. More importantly, if we're stopped by Confederate soldiers, and you men are armed …" She gave him a severe look but left the sentence unfinished.

Then she gazed once again at her three fallen comrades and sighed. "I am truly sorry. They deserve better, but we must leave them and continue on for the sake of the living. Come, let's go," she said, and headed off into the night.

৩৩৩৩৩৩৩৩৩৩

Evelyn led them to the address Joseph had given her, where she hoped to find the wagons and horses they needed in order to flee Richmond. She prayed when she arrived that it would be so, but she'd neither seen nor heard a word from Joseph since he'd informed her of his plan and promised to make the necessary arrangements. She fought down a growing anxiety that something had happened to him, and that he'd not been able to follow through. Then she reminded herself of how resourceful and resilient the man was, always showing up when least expected, and coming through when things seemed the most hopeless.

Their destination was another large warehouse, very similar to the one they'd just vacated. It featured two sizeable barn doors on the side, but these were secured with a heavy iron padlock.

She shared a look with Hank, but he shrugged, "We got no tools that can break that one, Miss Evelyn."

She nodded her agreement. So they traversed the outside of the building until they located a small, solid, single door on one side. She knocked several times, but there was no answer. Then she tried the doorknob, but found it locked. Once again, she shared a look with Hank, but this time he just stepped up, planted his boot in the middle of the door, and it crashed inward.

He stepped into the room with Evelyn right behind him. To her surprise, the room was illuminated by a small oil lamp on a sconce, high on one wall. To her further surprise, Hank immediately raised his hands above his head.

"You done made a *big* mistake, mister," a voice said. "You picked the wrong place to rob."

Evelyn stepped to one side of Hank, raising her own hands as she did. She saw a thickly built, middle-aged man sitting in a chair at a desk. He held a double-barreled shotgun leveled at Hank.

"We're not here to rob you, sir," she said.

"Oh! Didn't see you there, miss," he answered, seeming to relax a little but still pointing the shotgun at Hank. "You Miss Eve?"

"Yes. You are Joseph's friend, I presume?" she responded.

He lowered the gun, and stood. "I am. Have knowed him since … well, forever, I reckon. My name's Dodge. Frank Dodge. Sorry about the greeting, but things've been a bit chaotic these last few hours, and I've been fearing the worst. I'd thought *you* weren't coming after all, since I'd heard no word from Joseph. So when you kicked in the door … well, I figured it was either thieves looking to loot the place or soldiers looking to burn it down."

"Sorry 'bout the door," Hank said.

Dodge waved his hand dismissively. "Don't worry, my friend. It's been busted before. It's the least of my worries. Hell, if the whole place ain't burned down come morning, I'll be greatly surprised."

"May we come in, sir?" Evelyn asked, beginning to feel anxious about those left out on the street. "I have more than a dozen people waiting outside," she said.

"Oh, yes, of course. Bring 'em in, bring 'em in."

The freemen were quickly ushered into the warehouse, and Dodge stepped outside and had a brief look around before coming back in and pushing the broken door closed.

"Where's Jacob and your other men? Joseph said you'd have armed guards," Dodge asked.

"Dead. We were accosted by the Signal Corps only moments ago, and there was a gunfight. Though those of us you see here were able to escape, our guardians were killed, along with several of our assailants," she answered, while fighting to keep her bottled-up emotions from choking her voice.

"Oh. Sorry to hear *that*. Jacob was a good man. Very reliable type," Dodge said.

"Yes … he will be greatly missed," she answered, in barely a whisper.

"Come," Dodge said, gesturing toward a door in the back of the small room, "the fires burn the next block over. Time to go."

He led them into a spacious room with a dirt floor, which, to Evelyn's relief, contained two large open-bed wagons, each with a horse hitched to it. Three extra horses were tied to the back of the wagons by long leads.

Two young men, Evelyn guessed to be only in their teens, stood by the wagons. Each had a rifle slung over his shoulder and a pistol tucked into his belt.

"My boys," Dodge announced. "Mathew and Abner. Though we been hopin' the wind would change direction and our place would be spared, we been fixin' to leave as soon as the fires drew near. Now that y'all are here, we may as well head out. Don't suppose any o' your men are armed?" he asked, to which Evelyn shook her head.

"Do *you* know how to shoot, Miss Evelyn?" he then asked.

"Yes, certainly. I grew up on a farm outside Richmond, and my daddy taught me from a young age. Why?"

Rather than answer, Dodge strode back toward his office and returned shortly with a revolver in his hand. He still carried the shotgun, and she noted he had another revolver tucked into his belt.

"Here, Miss Evelyn, take this. With the town coming apart at the seams, it's like to get a bit lawless out there."

She reached out and took the gun, immediately inspecting to see that the cylinders were fully loaded, with percussion caps in place. "Thanks," she answered. Though she still had her tiny Smith and Wesson revolver up her sleeve, she knew it would be woefully inadequate if it came to an actual gunfight. The solid weight of the heavy revolver felt reassuring in her hand, though it would be burdensome to have to carry it the entire way. Dodge solved that problem as well when he held out a leather gun belt and holster. "Here, though it don't much look ladylike, this here'll make it easier to carry," he said.

She thanked him, then strapped it on around her waist and holstered the gun.

The freemen were quickly loaded into the beds of the wagons, squeezing themselves in amongst various boxes and barrels, which, they were happy to learn from Dodge, contained food supplies.

Evelyn sat up front with Dodge in one wagon, and Hank sat next to one of Dodge's boys on the other. The second boy mounted one of the spare horses, taking the other two animals in tow.

"Wasn't thinking to go with you," Dodge said. "But seein's how y'all have lost your protection, it wouldn't be prudent."

"Thank you very kindly for that, Mr. Dodge. It is most gallant of you," she answered.

"Not at all, Miss Evelyn. Just lookin' after my property," he said with a grin and a wink. She returned his grin with a smile of her own, accompanied by a sudden profound feeling of relief that they might just survive the horrific events of this day after all.

❧ ❧ ❧ ❧ ❧

Utter chaos met Evelyn's eyes as they exited Dodge's warehouse and went back out onto the streets of Richmond. As they made their way beyond the fires, heading north through town, the roads quickly became clogged with wagons, carts, and drays loaded to the beams with goods of every description, and people clinging to anything they could. Those on foot, with no transportation, thronged amongst the vehicles, carrying whatever they were able upon their backs.

It was also clear that all semblance of lawfulness and decorum had been abandoned; fights were commonplace as people battled each other for food, or robbed one another of horses and other forms of transportation. Dodge and his boys held their weapons in hand and threatened anyone who approached their wagons. The freemen had armed themselves with stout sticks or even rocks. Evelyn anxiously rested her hand on the handle of the big revolver, but resisted the urge to unholster it.

Thankfully, either by divine providence or for fear of their bristling defense, their little caravan eventually made it out onto the rural roads leading away from Richmond.

Though she could feel a heavy exhaustion, Evelyn gazed ahead upon the countryside with renewed hope; they'd escaped the nightmare, and she knew that somewhere ahead in the darkness, though a week or so away, sat the great, sparkling white Big House of Mountain Meadows Farm. She could picture it clearly in her mind, and could almost feel its inviting presence calling to her, *Come to me … Come home to me, my child. Here you will be warm, safe, and loved …* The thought gave her chills, and she was forced to wipe joyful tears from her eyes. *Not much longer now, and then all will be well*, she thought, even as her chin leaned against her breast and she nodded off to sleep.

And then she was started from her brief slumber by a great rumbling in the earth, followed by a tremendous *boom* in the distance, an earsplitting noise such as she'd never heard in life. It was as if every artillery piece ever forged had all been fired at once.

She glanced back and saw a great ball of flame and smoke rise high into the sky above the city.

She turned to Dodge wide eyed. "What in God's creation was that?" she asked.

He shook his head sadly. "Reckon they done lit off the powder magazine—thousands of barrels of gunpowder all at one go. Like the very thunder of God, ain't it? Likely whatever was left of the old city is gone now. Never seen the like, and I pray I never do again," he concluded, shaking his head sadly.

"Amen to that," Evelyn replied, then looked back one last time at her once beautiful, beloved hometown, now a lawless, uninhabitable, hellish nightmare engulfed in flames. *An inferno caused by the very men who'd sworn to protect it. Damn them all!*

☙❧☙❧☙❧☙❧☙❧

After leaving the scene of his confrontation with Evelyn Hanson, Major White hurried up the street to where he'd left his horse tied. When he arrived, he encountered two scruffy looking men who had untied the three Signal Corps horses and were preparing to lead them away. He unholstered his pistol and threatened them with it as he shook his head, frowning. "No, you don't. Retie those animals, immediately. Then pray I don't put a permanent end to your thievery," he ordered.

"No need for violence, General," one of them said, "we're tying 'em, don't worry."

"Thought they was abandoned," the other said, nodding and grinning tentatively. "Not meaning any trouble, sir," he concluded, bowing and nodding.

"It's *Major*," White replied. "And please do just leave off with your pathetic lies. I've no time nor patience for them," White answered. "Hurry up!" he demanded.

"Yes, sir," the first man answered, and soon the horses were refastened to the hitching post where they'd previously been tied.

"Now, go!" White shouted, waving his pistol at them.

The two men turned and sprinted away.

White holstered his pistol, retrieved his own horse, mounted and rode off, caring nothing for the other two mounts—after all, their riders were now dead.

He raced to the War Department intending to round up more men and return to take up Evelyn's trail once again. He also held out some hope that he might meet some members of the Signal Corps along the way, but the few soldiers he encountered were either drunken, actively involved in burning and looting, or quickly heading in the other direction, out of town. All ignored his entreaties to render him assistance, even when threatened at gunpoint. So he rode on. *Useless creatures*, he thought with disgust.

When he arrived at the War Department offices, he was met with a shocking scene: great piles of boxes and papers littered the streets, many on fire. Loose sheets of paper were strewn everywhere, blowing around on the fiery breeze like snow in a blizzard.

He saw that the door was thrown open, so rather than tying his horse outside and risking having it stolen again, he dismounted and led the animal indoors. He immediately called out, asking if anyone was in the building. Only echoey silence answered his queries. As he walked down the hallway, he saw that the inside mirrored the outside in its disarray: papers were strewn everywhere, tables were overturned, personal items were smashed, and inkwells had been dumped on the floors. He shook his head in disbelief; it was as if the men who'd worked here so studiously and professionally for so long had suddenly gone mad.

When he reached the stairs leading up to his own desk, he tied the animal to the banister and quickly climbed the stairs. He called out again but received no answer, and once again searched the floor for any sign of inhabitation.

Finding no one, he went to his desk and sat heavily in his chair. He was pleased to see that it had been left unmolested, and everything was still in its proper place. Whether this had been due to fear of his reputation or just plain dumb luck, he had no idea. But he was grateful, for it allowed him to retrieve his precious files and notes. These he quickly gathered, stacking them neatly before placing them into a saddle bag.

This is not over yet, Miss Evelyn Hanson. I may not have the manpower to capture you today, but that will not be true for long. I'll be coming for you soon … this I promise you.

And then he felt the oddest sensation he'd ever experienced in life. The entire building shook and heaved with a great rumbling vibration, followed immediately by a tremendous *boom* that rocked the structure, shattering all the windows and knocking down everything left on its shelves.

Good Lord, what the …? he wondered. And then he realized it must be the army's powder magazine going off, and in that same instant, the realization dawned on him, *I must leave this city … now!*

He jumped up, threw the saddle bag over his shoulder, and rushed down the stairs.

ॐ

Monday April 3, 1865 – Tree Hill, Virginia:

Union Major General Godfrey Weitzel, commander of XXV Corps, gazed into the distance with his spyglass, trying to make sense of what he was seeing. Though he stood on a small rise, Richmond was frustratingly shielded from direct view by the heavily forested, undulating earth. All he could see were occasional red and yellow flashes of light in the pre-dawn darkness, like large flames reflecting off the clouds in the sky. Oddly there were no sounds of artillery nor of battle in general coming from that direction, so he could not divine what was happening.

Likewise, though he could not see Petersburg in the distance, the unmistakable sounds of a great battle had echoed across the land from that direction starting at first light the previous day, continuing through the noon hour before abruptly ceasing in midafternoon, and all had been quiet since.

He could not recall ever feeling more frustrated and impotent. Being in command of the area north of the James, and east of the city, he was cut off from timely communication with General Grant's headquarters on the opposite side of the river. So he'd received no word all the long, fretful previous day. And as he had no orders to advance, all he could do was to wait and watch, in ever-growing anxiety and frustration.

He slowly lowered the spyglass and breathed a heavy sigh, even as he heard someone step up behind him.

"Excuse me, sir." He recognized the voice of Major Eugene Graves, so he turned to greet him. Weitzel was surprised to see that Graves was accompanied by a very elderly civilian: a gentleman who was neatly dressed, but appeared careworn and weary. The man respectfully removed his hat.

"Sorry to disturb you, sir, but this gentleman just arrived on a horse, and … well, I believe you will wish to hear what he has to say."

"Very well," Weitzel answered, turning to meet eyes with the gentleman.

"Thank you for speaking with me, General. Allow me to introduce myself, sir. My name is Joseph Mayo," he said, and then paused, as if expecting the general to recognize the name. Weitzel gave him a blank look, so he continued. "Well, as it turns out, I am the mayor of Richmond."

"*Oh!* I see. Pleased to meet you, Mr. Mayo. I am Major General Godfrey Weitzel," he answered, extending his hand, which Mayo took and shook firmly.

"And what is it I can do for you, Mr. Mayo?" Weitzel asked.

"Well, sir, to get straight to the point, I've ridden out here in order to surrender the city to you, sir."

"Surrender the city? *Richmond?* Why ever would you do a thing like that, sir? We've been fighting to take Richmond for four long years … and now you are just going to ride out here and *give* it to me?"

The mayor gazed at General Weitzel, opened-mouthed. "But … you mean … *you don't know?*" he asked in obvious astonishment.

"Don't know *what?* Please speak plainly, sir. We've been sitting since yesterday, wondering what in creation is happening in both Petersburg and Richmond. Plenty of noise and smoke, but nary a word whatsoever. So, if you have some news for us, please do share."

"*Oh!* Oh, my goodness, yes sir. It seems your General Grant has smashed through at Petersburg, and General Lee is on the run. Jeff Davis and the whole gul-durned Confederate government has fled the city, and good riddance to 'em, I say!" he scowled.

Now it was Weitzel's turn to be wide-eyed and open mouthed in shock. "Truly? Richmond is wide open to me? What of its garrison?"

"Abandoning the city, after setting everything ablaze, curse them. General Ewell is in command, and I reckon by the time we get there, they'll be completely gone. It's part of why I came here seeking a Union commander. General, I come on bended knee, begging you to save my city. Please, sir, come as quickly as you may, and I will give you the very keys to the city. Whatever glory comes with that shall be yours for all time. In return, I beg of you, please have your men come put out the fires while there is still something left to save."

And then, as if to emphasize the mayor's words, they heard a great, rumbling boom in the distance, and looked over to see a large ball of flame rise high above the city.

"They've set off the powder magazine," the general said.

Then he looked the mayor hard in the eyes. "Sir, I accept your surrender and agree to put out your fires. But first, I can't resist pointing out to you the very great irony of the moment … *poetic justice* one might even call it—almost Shakespearean, in fact. Please, sir, if you would … turn and gaze upon my soldiers." He gestured toward where his troops were camped.

The mayor did as he was bid, and at first saw nothing out of the ordinary: thousands of blue-clad soldiers, going about the normal routine of a large army camp. Then he saw their faces,

reflected in their many campfires. He gasped, "Why they're …
they're all—"

"Black men," the general finished the statement for him and
smiled. "Mayor Mayo, the XXV Corps, of which I am the
commander, aside from its officers, is made up entirely of black
soldiers of the United States Colored Regiments. And I, for one,
find it quite satisfying to think that the capital city of the
government that fought so hard to keep them enslaved will be
conquered in the end by the very men who were once its slaves.
And then, to beat all, they will also be the men who will save your
city from utter destruction."

Mayo groaned and slowly shook his head, but found nothing
to say in answer.

"Major Graves, please pass the word: Today we march to
Richmond!" General Weitzel commanded, arms folded across his
chest, beaming brightly.

⚜⚜⚜

Monday April 3, 1865 – Petersburg, Virginia:

Nathan and Tom strode through the midst of the brigade an
hour before dawn, Harry hard on their heels, checking on the
wounded and getting a report of their numbers and condition
from William, as those still effective ate breakfast and began
breaking camp, preparing to take up the chase after the retreating
rebel army.

They'd reached the far edge of the camp when Billy came
riding up at the gallop, pulling to a hard stop and snapping a
salute. "Captain, the rebels have abandoned Richmond after
torching it. I saw no enemy soldiers from here to the city."

"The city burns?"

"There is a great burning. Many buildings destroyed, and
more in flames. With none of their soldiers left to put out the fires,
I expect it will be completely destroyed. Even the bridge is afire,
so I dared not enter the city."

"Damn them!" Nathan responded.

"Burning their supplies so we'd not have the benefit of them, I suppose," Tom said.

"But they should've known we've no shortage of supplies, and have no need of theirs," he frowned, shaking his head. "Tom, I must go; Evelyn is in the midst of that conflagration. I must get her out of there!"

"I'm coming with you," Tom immediately answered.

"No, not this time, Tom. Lee's not done yet, and you must lead the brigade to the west in my stead. I will ride like the wind to Richmond, and then will catch up to you, with Evelyn in tow."

Tom thought a moment, then said, "All right. But take Stan and Billy with you, at least. I'll not have you unguarded, and Billy will ensure you can find us again in all the chaos."

"Agreed," Nathan said, "and thank you, Tom."

"For what?"

"For not arguing about it, and for doing my job for me," Nathan answered, reaching out and gripping Tom hard on the arm. The two shared a hard look.

"Godspeed, Nathan," Tom said.

"You too, Tom," Nathan answered. Then, turning to Billy, he said, "Please fetch Stan, and meet me back here while I go grab my gear and saddle up Millie." Then he looked down at Harry the Dog and said, "Yes, you too, Harry."

"Yes, Captain," Billy answered, and spurred off into the camp.

⊱⋅☙❧⋅⊰

Monday April 3, 1865 – Richmond, Virginia:

When Major White exited the War Department and remounted his horse, he was shocked at the sudden difference that greeted him. For one, the sun had risen, though thick, swirling smoke reduced visibility to less than a few dozen yards.

And though he'd had to force his way through the crowds thronging the streets to get to the army's offices, the streets were now virtually empty. Looking around, he realized with a shock that the hotel just across the street from the War Department was already ablaze, and it was likely only moments before his own long-time workplace would also be engulfed.

Deciding his best course of action would be to follow the retreating army, he knew he needed to head south through town and then cross Mayo's Bridge. However, southward everything was ablaze, so he backtracked uphill and across the capitol building grounds, which was as yet untouched by the flames. He crossed the sprawling, sloping lawn at a gallop, heading east, knowing now he must get around the spreading fires in order to get across the James before all was consumed.

And when he'd crossed the capitol grounds, his plan seemed to be bearing fruit, as the buildings on both sides of Franklin Street were still intact. After two blocks, he turned right down Fourteenth Street, which headed straight out onto the bridge. After only a block, he was stymied by a great swirling fire, and was forced to move further east before once again attempting to move southward.

When he finally was able to skirt the fires along the waterfront, his heart sank. He saw the bridge ahead had been set afire in the center of the span. But he continued on, climbing the embankment up to the roadway leading onto the bridge deck. He approached the bridge at a trot, then dismounted, leading his horse out onto the decking until he was within a few yards of the fires.

And though the boards of the bridge deck were blackened, and the beams above and below were still aflame, the structure had not yet collapsed, and the roadway appeared to be intact, with only about fifty feet of the deck affected. He couldn't guess why the army hadn't done a more thorough job of it, such as setting off explosives to ensure the job was done. *Probably the general panic of the moment*, he guessed.

Reaching into his coat, he pulled out a bandana and wrapped it about his face against the blowing smoke, then stepped out cautiously onto the blackened decking, carefully testing its weight before moving ahead. As he felt no give, he pulled his reluctant mount after him, fearing the worst, and ready to spring away if the horse fell through. The boards held, and he made it across, then remounted and moved off at a trot.

He reckoned he'd catch up to the rearguard of the army in a few hours; after all, most of the footsore, weary soldiers would be marching on clogged roadways, while he'd be riding, nearly alone.

Even as he came to the outer edge of the small town of Manson, occupying the south shore of the James, and moved into the wooded rural countryside beyond, White had a sudden sense that he was no longer alone on the roadway. He glanced back and gasped; a Union soldier trotted along just behind him, a pistol in his grip. And to his amazement, when he gazed at the soldier's face, he realized the man was an Indian.

⁂

Despite his assurances to Tom, Nathan did not "ride like the wind" to Richmond, though he greatly desired to. For one, it was a distance of some twenty miles, and the horses simply couldn't keep up a gallop that long. And for another, it was unwise in the extreme to blindly trust that there were no enemy combatants present, despite Billy's earlier reconnoiter.

So, though it galled him, Nathan allowed Billy to range out ahead while he and Stan moved at a slower, steadier pace. Even so, by mid-morning he and Stan had nearly reached the outskirts of Manson.

They could now see a great cloud of smoke rising above Richmond in the distance, and Nathan had to fight down a growing sense of dread. *No, I will not give in to despair*, he argued with himself, *Evelyn is alive. I know it … I can feel it. My heart still beats, so my love yet lives. No power on this earth could keep us apart.*

And then, as they rounded a corner, Nathan saw two men approaching on horseback. One he recognized immediately as Billy, the other appeared to be a Confederate officer. Billy held the man at gunpoint.

As the two groups met and came to a halt a few yards apart, Billy said, "Hello, Captain. Found this fellow along the road. Thought you might want to question him."

"Well done, Billy," Nathan said. Then, turning to the man, he said, "I am General Chambers. Please give me your name, Major.

And please kindly explain to me why you were out on the road alone, given that the rest of your army has apparently departed Richmond."

The man sat up straight on his horse and saluted, which Nathan returned sharply. "General, I am Major Charles White, of the Confederate Signal Corps. As for why I am alone ... I had certain duties that detained me in the capital, even while the evacuation was underway."

Nathan frowned. "What duties would those be, Major, if you don't mind my asking?"

The man tilted his head thoughtfully for a moment, then answered, "Why not. As you are no doubt aware, General, the Signal Corps is tasked with counter-espionage activities, among other duties. And I am, if nothing else, diligent in carrying out my assignments. I was conducting an important operation in the capital even as the evacuation was ordered. I considered it my solemn duty to complete that assignment before quitting the city."

"Very admirable of you, Major," Nathan answered. "And were you successful in your mission? If you don't mind satisfying my curiosity."

"I don't mind at all, General. I can see no reason not to discuss the matter in *general* terms with you. To answer your question, *no*, sadly I was unsuccessful. But I am most persistent, and still intend to apprehend the wom — uh ... the *individual*, and bring the person to justice," White answered.

Nathan stared at White for a long moment before reaching into his jacket, pulling out a cigar, and lighting it.

"But, Major, since you are clearly now my prisoner, and therefore one must presume will remain incarcerated for the duration of the conflict, surely you must now admit defeat and forgo any further action against this ... *person* you seek?"

"Ah. It's an interesting question, General," White said, and removed his glasses, giving them a quick wipe down before replacing them on his face. "I believe spies and traitors are the very worst sort of nefarious criminal, for it must be assumed that their treachery has cost the lives of countless Southern soldiers. As such, I believe it is the duty of men, such as myself, to pursue them to justice—in the form of a swift hanging—even should hostilities cease. Do you disagree, General?"

Nathan gazed at White for a long moment, then took a long drag on the cigar, blowing the smoke out slowly before answering.

"Major ... does the name Evelyn Hanson mean something to you?" Nathan asked.

White's eyes widened for an instant, but he quickly regained his composure. "Um ... hmm ... yes, I do recall hearing the name before ... she's a Richmond socialite, is she not? A friend of the First Lady, perhaps? Why do you ask, sir?"

"Because, Major, I am close ... *very* close with Miss Evelyn."

White slowly nodded. "I see. That's ... *interesting*, General. And now that you mention it, I do detect that you speak with an accent that could place you from Virginia. So I suppose you must know her from the time before the war. But ... why do you mention her now, may I ask?"

Nathan slowly nodded. "Let's cut straight to the heart of the matter, Major, shall we? I have heard your name before. From *her*. In fact, Evelyn has told me all about your relentless campaign to incarcerate her."

"Ah, I see," White replied, then shrugged. "Very good ... I prefer to speak plainly, General. Miss Hanson is a traitor and a spy, and I have but done my duty, attempting to bring her to justice."

Nathan scowled. "A spy, maybe, but she is no traitor. She has remained loyal to the rightful government of this land, which is the United States of America and no other," Nathan answered.

White just shrugged, "That is a debate which is of no concern to me. I am simply doing my duty."

"And now ... I'm doing mine," Nathan growled, then pulled his pistol from its holster, aimed at White's head, and fired. Before the smoke swirled away, White slumped from the saddle onto the ground of the roadway. Harry stepped over, sniffed at the body, then turned away.

Billy trotted up and neatly snatched the horse's reins before it could shy away. "I was thinking we might need this animal later, to carry the woman," he said.

Stan just gazed at his leader for a long moment until Nathan turned, and they met eyes. Then Stan grinned, and said, "Billy ... how many enemy men you reckon the general would shoot for Miss Evelyn?"

Billy snorted a laugh, then shrugged. "Hard to say ... Don't know how many there are," he answered, returning Stan's grin.

Nathan just shook his head, let out a long breath, then holstered his pistol. "Let's go," he said.

❧❧❧❧❧❧❧❧❧❧❧❧

By the time that Nathan, Stan, and Billy reached Evelyn's warehouse, the fire was out, but the entire structure had been burned to the ground, with only smoldering rubble remaining.

Nathan had little fear that Evelyn had been caught up in the blaze; she was too clever and her protectors were too watchful for that to have happened. But where had she gone?

He was gratified and hopeful to see the streets were now swarming with Union troops, though he was disappointed to learn that the Twenty-Third Regiment, which included Tony and the other freemen from Mountain Meadows, was not present with the other colored regiments, and was instead amidst the action in Petersburg.

He also appreciated how diligently the soldiers worked to contain and put out the fires in the city that was the very epicenter of the Slave Power that had kept their people in bondage for more than a hundred years. It was as honorable as it was ironic, he decided.

Though Nathan questioned everyone they encountered, black soldiers, white officers, and even the occasional civilian who'd braved the inferno, nobody reported seeing a civilian of Evelyn's description.

Then they heard a voice call out, "Colonel Chambers ... is that you, sir?" as a horse trotted up.

"Gareth! Well met," Nathan said, as Captain Hughes pulled his horse to a halt and snapped a salute.

"Oh, I see it's *General* Chambers now. Congrats on that, sir. Well-deserved, no doubt," Gareth said as Nathan returned the salute.

"Thanks. Any news, Gareth? Do you know where Evelyn is? And Margaret, for that matter."

Gareth frowned. "No, I'm afraid not. I was hoping you knew something. I have been to my parents' home, but it has apparently been abandoned for some time. And though it has been looted, thankfully it has been spared from the flames. I have also been to Evelyn's warehouse, as I assume have you."

"Yes, and no one seems to have seen her. The good news is that we captured and interrogated Major White, so we know she has *not* been arrested."

Gareth nodded thoughtfully. "Good to be freed from that nuisance, finally," he said. "He's been a thorn in my father's side for several years now. Turned him over to the Union officers here in Richmond, did you?"

"Not exactly," Nathan answered, frowning.

Stan snorted a laugh. "The general decided Major White needed new hole in head." He made a gun with his finger and comically mimed shooting himself in the head.

"Ah," Gareth chuckled. "Good riddance, is all I have to say about that."

"You seem calm, considering you haven't been able to locate your parents in all this chaos," Nathan said.

Gareth shrugged, "I know them well enough to assume they had an escape plan, and that they've now executed it. Unfortunately, I don't know exactly where they've gone. But I choose to assume they are safe and well. I believe the same is likely true of Evelyn. That she too had an escape plan and has gotten safely away by now."

Nathan nodded, but said nothing, so Gareth continued, "And I believe we must assume, now that the city is in Union hands, their safety is assured once they do come out from hiding."

Then he caught Nathan's eye and grinned. "Especially as we no longer need to fear Major White causing mischief, thanks to you, sir."

Nathan smiled for the first time, and shrugged.

"If I may suggest, General," Gareth said, "there is little more we can do here for the moment, and we ought to make haste to join the chase for Lee's army. It is my firm belief that we can do more good there than we can here."

Nathan sighed, and answered, "Yes, I know you're right, Gareth, though it galls me. Billy … Stan, let's go find our brigade. Captain Hughes, you are welcome to join us in our pursuit."

"It would be an honor, sir," Gareth answered.

The four of them turned and headed back toward the bridge. By the time they got there, it was no longer smoking and already under repair by Union engineers.

∞❦⨳❧∞❦⨳❧∞❦⨳❧

Tuesday April 4, 1865 – Richmond, Virginia:

"Why have we stopped, Admiral?" President Lincoln asked, as he stepped up to Rear Admiral David Porter on the quarterdeck of the *USS Malvern*. They'd been making good time up the James, and the president had high hopes of arriving at Richmond within the hour. Since he first received the telegram from General Wietzel announcing the liberation of the rebel capital after four long years of hellish warfare, he'd felt an upwelling of joy that threatened to pull him up out of the dark, constant, sleep-robbing malaise that had plagued him for much of that time.

Suddenly, their heady progress had come to a complete stop.

"I'm sorry, Mr. President. The closer we get to Richmond's docks the more choked the river becomes. What with sunken ships, and debris of all descriptions, including even unexploded naval torpedoes floating amongst the flotsam and jetsam, I dare not proceed further.

"I know you are eager to make landfall, but under the circumstances, you may have to wait until the engineers can be brought in to clear the waterway."

Lincoln stepped over to the railing and gazed at the water below confirming the admiral's bad news; there was simply no way for the large vessel to safely work its way any further through the dangerous mire of debris.

He turned back toward the admiral, "Then we shall simply have to take your rowboat. A 'tender,' I believe you mariners call such a vessel."

"Oh, *no*, we should not do that, Mr. President. The tender would only carry the two of us, plus a dozen or so sailors, at the most. I've brought along two full rifle companies of soldiers to give you a proper escort in the enemy capital city, sir. Anything less would not be a fitting honor suitable to your high station, sir, nor would it be safe, I daresay."

"Admiral, I appreciate your concern, but the city is already under the control of our army, so there is little to fear. And I'm not here to gloat. I need not arrive at the head of some great army like a conquering Caesar. No."

He slowly shook his head and chuckled, "I am only here to declare peace, and to offer hope and reconciliation. With due respect, my good sir, *that* does not require an army."

"Yes, sir; as you say. I will make the arrangements straightaway."

"Thank you, Admiral."

Fifty minutes later, following an arduous journey, which Admiral Porter navigated with a high-level of anxiety only matched by his obvious expertise, the tender reached the docks at the riverfront in Richmond. And though Porter would've preferred a quiet, anonymous debarkation for the president, those on the tiny boat could see it was not to be. Lincoln's grizzled, bearded face, great lanky frame, and tall top hat had been clearly visible aboard the tiny craft ever since leaving the gunboat.

Word of the president's arrival had spread through Richmond like a wildfire in August-dry grass on a breezy day. By the time the tender was secured, a large crowd had begun to form on the dock, with more people streaming in by the moment.

Lincoln was pleased but not surprised to see that most of those in the crowd had black faces, and their enthusiasm at his arrival touched him to the very depth of his soul. Women wept, men laughed aloud, and children shouted and sang.

As he stepped onto the land, he was surrounded by the people of Richmond, many bowing to the ground in his presence, or reaching out to touch the hem of his pants or his coat tails, to kiss his boots, or to touch the fingertips of his long hands.

The president called out to them, "Do not kneel to me! I am but a man; you must kneel only to God. Thank *Him* for the liberty you will now enjoy!"

The joyous crowd now pressed in so closely that Admiral Porter ordered his sailors to surround the president and keep the civilians back with the threat of their bayonets as they attempted to move him up the street. Lincoln had ordered them to make for the Confederate White House, the former home of Confederate President Jefferson Davis, now occupied by General Weitzel as his command headquarters. The ever-growing crowd, however, made movement nearly impossible, and the procession was in danger of coming to a complete standstill in the midst of the impromptu celebration.

Finally, a Union army captain, observing the situation from up the street, jumped into action, leading a rifle company to come to the president's rescue. Lincoln decided that the blue-clad soldiers having black faces, like most of those in the crowd, had likely helped to prevent any animosity between the soldiers and the civilians. The president was now able to move casually up the street as if on parade, smiling, waving, and calling out well wishes to the surrounding throng.

When they finally arrived at the Confederate White House, General Weitzel welcomed the president with great enthusiasm before ushering him into Jefferson Davis's office. There, Lincoln sat down in a thickly padded chair with a deep sigh of satisfaction, stating, "This, my good general, is a moment worth savoring."

A few hours later, as Weitzel hosted Lincoln on a carriage ride tour of the city, the general broached the subject that had been foremost on his mind: "Sir, how do you think I should best deal with the local residents, former Confederate officials, and former soldiers still in the city, now that we are firmly in control?"

Lincoln was thoughtful for a moment before replying, "If I were you, General, I should let 'em up easy. Just … let 'em back up easy."

"Yes, sir. That I can do. Thank you, sir."

Chapter 8. The Chase

"Lee's army will be
your objective point.
Wherever Lee goes,
there you will go also."
- General Ulysses S. Grant

Wednesday April 5, 1865 – Staunton, Virginia:

By afternoon of their third day out from Richmond, Evelyn was relieved that they'd finally escaped the great jam of traffic that'd crowded the roadway ever since they'd left the city. It'd made for frustratingly slow going, continually forced to halt and wait for broken-down wagons and horses somewhere ahead on the narrow roadway.

To her delight, Dodge turned out to be a highly skilled wagoner, with just the right touches of caution and aggressiveness when it came to driving, and just the right amount of kindliness and forcefulness when dealing with their trying fellow travelers. As a result, after two days of determined effort, he'd managed to get their little caravan ahead of the crush of other evacuees, for which Evelyn felt a great sense of relief and gratitude.

As they neared the town of Staunton, she learned the downside of being alone and out ahead of the crowd: the old adage about "safety in numbers" bore out when a group of six ragged-looking armed riders came trotting up the trail and overtook them from behind, then turned and forced them to a stop.

Dodge and his sons had not been completely taken by surprise, and Evelyn decided they had likely practiced against such an eventuality. Dodge and Mathew quickly turned the wagons in opposite directions and halted, while Abner rode between them with the spare horses. There they stopped, guns pointed outward as the strangers slowly circled them, rifles in hand.

From their lean, hard looks and ragged scraps of uniform, Evelyn decided these must be Confederate soldiers, likely recently deserted.

One man slowly stepped his horse forward, rifle in hand, but with its barrel pointed upward.

"Where y'all headed?" he asked in tones that were cold and unfriendly.

"Well, I reckon that's our business, and none o' y'all's," Dodge answered back with a scowl, his shotgun leveled at the men surrounding them, but not aimed directly at the leader.

The man continued slowly forward, then paused only a few feet away.

"You got food in there?" he asked, ignoring Dodge's response.

"Again … I say, that ain't none o' your concern, mister," Dodge answered.

The man just stared at him blankly. Evelyn looked in his eyes, and felt a sudden, eerie chill; it seemed to her there was almost nothing behind those eyes, as if the war had drained the man of his very soul.

"We'll be taking those wagons and horses now," he finally said.

To everyone's surprise, it was Evelyn who answered. She stood to her feet, pulled the revolver from the holster at her hip, and aimed it straight at the man's face, pulling back the hammer with a *click*. "No, you will *not*. I've already killed men in this war, and one more is of little difference. And in case you have any doubts, my daddy taught me to shoot when I was barely old enough to walk. So I assure you, *sir*, I will *not* miss from here."

He turned his blank gaze on her, and said, "We have you outnumbered and outgunned. You can't win this fight."

"That may be so," she answered, "but I promise I *will* kill *you*, no matter what else happens. Are you prepared to die today, *sir*? Because I know if I give up my wagons, horses, and food, we will surely starve out here on this road."

He stared at her a long moment, then said, "You're only bluffing."

"Try me," she answered evenly.

They stared at each other for several tense moments, the only movement a slight twitch under the man's left eye.

"C'mon, Hiram," one of the other men finally called out, "There's plenty o' other easier meat out on the road. Ain't worth gettin' kilt over this'n here."

Several other voices chimed in their assent.

And still the man stared at Evelyn. She stared back.

Finally, he slowly reached up with his left hand, took ahold of his hat and tipped it to her. "Ma'am," he said, then pulled his reins over, and rode off, his men thundering after him.

"Let's move," Dodge called out. "But keep an eye out, boys, case them scoundrels decide to come back," he concluded.

Evelyn let out her breath, then sat heavily as the wagon lurched back into motion.

⊗⊘⊗⊘⊗⊘⊗⊘⊗⊘⊗⊘⊗⊘

Wednesday April 5, 1865 – Amelia Court House, Virginia:

C.S.A. Lieutenant Colonel Elijah Walters strode between the tents of the Confederate camp after deciding to take matters into his own hands—a testament to how desperate the situation had become. His men hadn't eaten in three days, ever since the forced retreat from Petersburg. The speed of the Yankee breakthrough had forced them to withdraw with nothing but the supplies in their traveling packs. And now, with the bulk of Lee's army encamped outside the small town of Amelia Court House, foraging was out of the question—anything worth having had already been had.

An hour or so ago, they'd seen a train arriving on the Richmond and Danville Railroad line, from the direction of the city: the desperately needed supply train, at last! He'd immediately decided to go himself to secure the supplies, rather than sending any of his men. He figured even with a trainload of food, it would be a scarce commodity with such a large army gathered, and he meant to secure enough to keep his cavalry battalion supplied. And a colonel had a better chance of doing that than a lesser rank.

When he arrived at the place where the train had come to a stop, he was confused to see soldiers tossing sheets of paper into the air from boxes that'd been pulled from the freight cars of the train.

Then he noticed a stern-looking Brigadier General with graying hair striding toward him with a scowl that could curdle milk. Walters thought the man looked familiar, though he couldn't immediately put a name to the face. As the general drew closer, Walters stopped and snapped a salute, which the general returned in a half-hearted manner without stopping.

"General … what is happening, sir? Why are these men unloading stacks of papers from the supply train?" Walters asked before the general could pass by.

The general stopped and frowned at Walters. "Supply train? I only wish it were so. *That*, my good colonel, is a worthless piece of idiocy. Our government at Richmond, in its infinite wisdom, has chosen to send us a trainload of precious official documents, rather than something as useless as food, or even ammunition."

"*Documents?*" Walters asked, not sure he'd heard correctly.

"Yes, Colonel … reams and reams of forms, contracts, requisitions, wills, orders … you name it. All properly filled in, signed, and countersigned, no doubt."

Walters slowly shook his head, and growled, "Someone ought to get a bullet for this, General …"

The general tilted his head and eyed Walters as if really noticing him for the first time. "Well said, Colonel … well said," the general agreed. "Hmm … do I know you, sir?" he asked. "From before the war, I mean. Your face looks familiar."

"I was thinking the same, General …" Walters responded.

This comment elicited a smirk from the General. "Ah, how quickly fame fades," he responded. "I am Henry Wise, formerly governor of the Commonwealth of Virginia."

Walters eyes widened as recognition dawned. "Oh! My apologies, sir. It has been several years since we met in person, and of course you weren't wearing a general's uniform at the time. I am Elijah Walters from Greenbrier County. I helped promote your election in the county when you initially ran for governor."

"Ah, yes. Walters, now I recall. And no apology necessary, sir. As you say, it was a different time, and we were perhaps different men then. Certainly not in uniform, as you say."

"True, Governor. At any rate, it is good to see you again, sir. And I am sorry about the train. That is … a bitter pill."

"Indeed, Colonel. Hmm … your mention of Greenbrier County just brought to mind another fellow I knew from that area. Perhaps you know him: Nathaniel Chambers?"

Walters frowned. "Yes, I know him. He was my neighbor before the war."

"Ah. And do I rightly deduce from your expression, sir, that you two were *not* on the friendliest terms?" Wise asked.

"I despise the man, Governor. Not only is he a shameless abolitionist and Yankee, but he did *this* to me," Walters said, holding up the stump of his left arm.

"Oh! I see. Then you and I have something in common, it seems. I too have a fondness for hating the man. He got himself elected to the Secession Convention under false pretenses, allowing us to assume he was on *our* side of the debate—and so, we used our considerable influence in support of his cause. Then, after he was elected, he stabbed us in the back by switching sides."

"Sounds like the man," Walters agreed.

Wise smiled, a wicked leer. "I *did* try my best to have the scoundrel murdered right after the Secession. But he's crafty— and has some even craftier men. Managed to slip the noose, so to speak."

Walters nodded, "I've also tried to kill him on numerous occasions. And I agree, the man has proven damnably hard to kill. And his men are a band of trained killers from Texas, which makes it harder still."

"True, true," Wise said, nodding thoughtfully.

"I still mean to kill the man," Walters said, "either during the war … or after, if it comes to it."

Wise smiled at this. "Truly? How interesting. I would love to hear how you intend to do it, if you wouldn't mind indulging me, my good sir."

"Not at all, Governor. His home in Greenbrier County is currently vacant. I know, because I was there just before reporting to Petersburg in February. I nearly torched the place, but then thought better of it, thinking to instead use it as bait for a trap."

"Oh? And how do you propose doing that? Just wait for him to show up after the war? That could take months, even after a general surrender—assuming that comes soon, which I think highly likely given the current dire circumstances. It takes time to muster out all the troops and make arrangements to send them home, I presume."

"Agreed. And no, I don't intend to just wait for him. I know where his mother lives, up in Wheeling, along with my whore of a wife—another reason to hate Chambers, by the way—fornicating with my wife, a properly married woman, though she's clearly scandalously disloyal."

"I should say," Wise agreed, nodding.

"I mean to convince his mother to come south to the vacant house and then take her hostage, and hold her in exchange for him—one life for another. My wife is a different matter … I'll not trade her life … I've a different plan for that faithless witch."

"I would imagine so. Still, I think your plan for Chambers is very clever. But how do you think to persuade her to come to the house, if may I ask?"

"I don't know yet. Haven't figured that part out. I'm thinking a phony telegram, sent from the Union-held telegraph office in Lewisburg, pretending to be Chambers. But I haven't come up with a plausible reason that she'd need to come to the old house in a hurry, which is critical I think, to make sure things are still in an unsettled state while I carry out my plan."

"*Oh!* I think I may be able to help you there," Wise said with enthusiasm. "I have heard, from certain trustworthy sources, that the Yankees mean to seize any vacant property owned by Confederate soldiers or government officials, then auction them off straightaway to the highest bidder, to help defray the costs of the war. You can simply tell her—pretending to be Chambers, of course—that you fear that the federals in their haste may assume the officer who owned the house was a Confederate, based on its location alone. And that it could take months, if not years, to straighten it all back out again. If she were there, however, already in possession of the house, then that calamity could be entirely averted."

Walters thought about this suggestion, then said, "Yes … yes, that sounds like it might work. Thank you kindly for the idea, Governor. You've been most helpful."

"Never mention it, my good fellow. I'm pleased to have the opportunity to strike a blow against my old adversary. Happy hunting, sir," he said, then tipped his hat and strode off, now grinning wickedly.

Thursday April 6, 1865 – High Bridge, Virginia:

Elijah Walters and his men of the Thirty-Sixth Virginia Cavalry Battalion were finally able to get down from their horses and stretch their legs after a long day in the saddle—a day that featured a desperate battle defending the southern end of High Bridge against a federal raiding party intent on burning it down, and thus depriving Lee's retreating army of a feasible method of crossing the Appomattox River.

It had been an intense, hard-fought battle between Confederate cavalry and Union infantry, such that Walters had been unable to keep his men out of the thick of it, as he usually endeavored to do. They'd suffered over thirty percent casualties as a result, leaving him with only forty or so effectives remaining.

And worse yet, several officers had been killed on both sides, include Walters' current superior, brigade commander Colonel Reuben Boston. In the end, the Confederate cavalry had prevailed, and so they still held the bridge, capturing several hundred Yankees in the process.

Now, as darkness began to descend over the battlefield, Walters and the Thirty-Sixth found themselves alone on the north side of the bridge, starring out at open countryside in that direction. Walters took a drink from his canteen—the difficult one-armed task now routine—re-stoppering it with his teeth as he gazed out into the rolling hills to the north. And then it occurred to him that, with Colonel Boston dead, the command would be in a state of disorder for several hours while the new officer took stock of the situation and regrouped the battered men under his command. *An opportunity?* Walters pondered.

He walked over to Captain Roberts, and said, "Saddle up the men, Roberts. We're moving out."

"New orders, sir?" Roberts asked.

"You could say that … *my* orders. We're getting out of here. The federals will soon have the entire army surrounded, and I, for one, want to be outside that noose when it closes. We'll head for the hills, and cross back over to Greenbrier. What say you, Roberts?"

"I say *yes* to that, Colonel. I'll get the men going, sir."

❧❧❧❧❧❧❧❧❧

Thursday April 6, 1865 – Sailor's Creek, Virginia:

"What is the situation, General Mahone?" Robert E. Lee demanded. He pulled his horse, Traveler, to a halt on the bluff overlooking the little valley, through which two streams flowed, called Big Sailor's Creek and Little Sailor's Creek.

Major General William Mahone saluted Lee, then answered, "Not good, General … the two small bridges over the creeks have proven too great a bottleneck. Much of my division has stalled on the far side and been cut up by the federals."

Lee pulled up his binoculars and scanned the field below. He turned back to Mahone with eyes wide, "My God, General … thousands of our men are marching away … prisoners under guard of the federals." He raised the binoculars again and continued to scan the field. "And even those that've crossed the bridges seem downtrodden and disorganized … streaming away from the battle … tossing down their rifles as they come …"

He lowered the field glasses and looked back at Mahone. "My God, has the army dissolved?" he asked.

"No, General," Mahone replied, shaking his head and gesturing toward the greater portion of his division that was still

151

intact, holding the near bank. "Here are troops ready to do their duty."

Lee followed Mahone's gaze, and nodded. "Yes, I see there are still some true men left. General Mahone, will you please keep those federals back?"

"Sir!" Mahone snapped a salute, and trotted off to take charge of the rear guard action.

⁂

Thursday April 6, 1865 – Rice's Station, Virginia:

"Did you find the rebels, Billy?" Nathan asked, after his brigade had been sent forward from Burkeville Junction, Virginia by Major General John Gibbon to reconnoiter a rebel force reportedly occupying the small town of Rice's Station.

"Rebels dug in all along the tracks there," Billy answered. "Our skirmishers engaged them briefly, and killed several. One lived long enough to tell us it's a force of rebel General Longstreet, but how many men he has with him he didn't say. Not knowing if we faced a regiment or an entire army corps, I thought it best not to push our attack, so I came back to report."

"Well done, Billy. I'll report back to General Gibbon on what you've found." He looked up at the sky, already turning a dark-orange shade, and added, "Likely too late tonight for further action. The general will likely want to hit them hard in the morning. Come, let's get the brigade organized for an attack at first light."

When morning dawned, Billy reported back that the rebels had fled during the night, leaving their entrenchments empty. So Nathan's brigade formed up and marched after them.

⁂

Saturday April 8, 1865 – Appomattox Court House, Virginia:

"General … may I have a moment, sir?" Brigadier General George Sharpe asked, as he leaned under the flap of Grant's command tent.

152

"Oh, hello, Sharpe. Of course, of course ... come on in," Grant answered, before taking a long drag on his cigar and letting it out slowly. At the moment, he was leaned back in his chair with his feet up on the camp table, taking a much-needed respite from reviewing the reports and maps laid out in front of him. It had been a long day in the saddle, and he'd sent his aides away only moments earlier, hoping to rest his eyes a spell. But a visit from Sharpe, commander of the Union Bureau of Military Information, or BMI—the Union's spy corps—was usually important as well as relatively uncommon, so he always figured it was a good idea to listen to the man.

General Sharpe entered the tent and doffed his hat, though he did not salute, per Grant's standing orders to his headquarters staff.

"Sir, I do apologize for disturbing you at this late hour, and given all you already have to concern yourself with. I debated whether or not to bring this matter to your attention, but in the end, I decided it *might* be important."

"All right, you have my attention, Sharpe. Go on," Grant answered, waving toward the folding chair across the table from him.

"Thank you, sir," Sharpe said as he sat. "This morning, a Confederate lieutenant rode into the camp and gave himself up to the sentries. At first, they figured him for just another of the steady stream of starving deserters who've been arriving at their lines since the fall of Petersburg. But this fellow was most insistent that he speak with you, sir, and only you. He claims he is a Union spy, only *disguised* as a Confederate officer, and that he bears important information. Of course, I have attempted to interrogate him, but he refuses to speak to anyone other than you personally, sir. The only thing I can tell you for sure is, he's *not* one of ours, meaning the BMI, of course."

"Hmm ... any reason to believe he might be telling the truth?" Grant asked, taking another puff on the cigar.

"Well, he did offer that one of our officers can vouch for him, a Colonel Chambers, commander of the Twelfth West Virginia. Do you know him, sir?"

"Yes, I know him, though he's now *General* Chambers, and in command of a brigade. Hmm … easy enough to drop a name, I suppose. Chambers being a Virginian, and well known in Richmond before the war, his name would be one a Confederate officer might know off the top of his head. And he'd likely know that it might take a while to locate Chambers at the moment."

"Agreed, sir," Sharpe answered.

"Did he say anything else?"

"Well, yes … but I must confess, I found it quite odd."

Grant raised an eyebrow expectantly, but allowed Sharpe to continue.

"He said, 'Please tell General Grant *the Employer* sent me.'"

"*Oh!*" Grant responded, stubbing out the remains of the cigar on the table, before tossing it into the dirt, and sitting up straight in his chair.

"Do you know what it means, sir?"

"Yes, as a matter of fact, I do. Send the man in straightaway, Sharpe. If he turns out to be what he claims, I'll brief you on the details later."

"Very good, sir!" Sharpe rose to his feet, pivoted and strode from the tent.

Moments later, Sharpe returned with the Confederate lieutenant in tow. The rebel officer, claiming to be a Union spy, appeared middle aged, but lean, hard, and vigorous. He removed his hat respectfully as he stepped into the tent, meeting eyes with the commanding general.

"General, the prisoner we spoke of," Sharpe announced. "I would introduce him, but … he refuses to give me his full name."

The Confederate lieutenant bowed his head slightly, "My apologies for *that*, General, but I didn't wish to insult you or your men by giving you the pseudonym I've been using in the rebels' camp. And in my line of work, I never give out my *real* name. But please just call me Joseph."

"Understood, Joseph," Grant answered. The general then turned to Sharpe, and said, "You may leave us now, General Sharpe. Thank you."

"Yes, sir," Sharpe replied, then turned and exited the tent.

Joseph stepped up to Grant's table and said, "Sir, I must confess to a very strong urge to salute you, but I refrain from doing so for propriety's sake, since I am not, strictly speaking, a soldier on either side."

"And yet, if I guess correctly, you've been fighting on our side from the outset of the conflict," Grant answered, slowly rising to his feet and extending his hand.

Joseph reached out and took it, and the two exchanged a firm handshake, and a slight smile, as Joseph nodded.

"Please, be seated, Joseph, and tell me what it is you came here to tell me."

"Thank you, sir. Do I assume correctly, since I am here now, alone in your presence, that you believe I am who I say I am? Or, I should say, I am *what* I say I am ..."

"You mentioned two names to my officers ... tell me them," Grant responded.

"Ah, yes. The first name I mentioned is Colonel Nathaniel Chambers of the Twelfth West Virginia. I have known Colonel Chambers personally since the beginning of the conflict, having helped him and his men to escape from Richmond when Henry Wise tried to have him murdered for not going along with the secession. Since then, I have seen him and his associates from time to time during the conflict. We have developed a strong trust of one another, you could say."

"Interesting ... though he is now *General* Chambers," Grant answered.

"Is he? That's very gratifying to hear, and well deserved, I believe. The people I work with have always considered him to be one of the very finest Union officers, though he clearly hasn't received that sort of recognition to date."

"I don't disagree with you," Grant said. "But speaking of the people you work with ..."

"Yes, the *other* name I mentioned—*the Employer*. He is one of the wealthiest and best-connected men in Virginia, and he has also run a pro-Union spy ring since before the war started. I have worked for him for years, first in the Underground Railroad, of which he was a major sponsor, and later in spying on the rebel government and its armies. It is my understanding that you have received regular updates from him and his agents since you began your campaign against General Lee."

"It's an interesting tale … but it just now occurred to me that a member of the Confederate Signal Corps might be able to come up with the same story, hoping I might verify their guesses."

"Ah, good point, sir. Hmm … would it help if I were to tell you something the Signal Corps would *not* be likely to know? Something, I assume, known only to you and the Union spy ring in Richmond?"

Grant gestured for Joseph to continue.

"I know this, because I have witnessed the preparations on the Richmond end with my own eyes: that often times the reports from our agents are delivered to you with a handwritten note from a woman who signs with the letter *E*, and often this note is accompanied by the most current Richmond newspaper, or sometimes even fresh-cut flowers."

Grant smiled, this time more broadly. "All right, I believe you. I can't think of how the enemy would know *that*, unless they'd broken the spy ring, which clearly they haven't, since I have received such messages even up to the day before Petersburg fell. That being the case, what intelligence have you brought me?"

Joseph looked down at the table for a long moment, then looked back up. "It's good that you now trust me, because what I am about to ask of you is … well, I hate to admit it, but it is exactly what a rebel spy might say."

"Go on," Grant ordered.

"Just this, General: at great personal risk, I have embedded myself into Lee's camp, getting as close to him as I dared. Even so, everything I'm about to tell you is second-hand. I've not been able to attend any meetings involving General Lee himself or his senior officers."

"I expect a rebel spy would tell me he *had* been at a meeting with Lee," Grant said.

Joseph chuckled, "Maybe so, maybe so. Anyway, to the point. From what I have overheard from reliable officers who *were* in those meetings, there is a split among their senior officers as to what comes next."

"A split?"

"Yes, sir. Between those who wish to surrender and end the war, and those who want to continue the fight."

"Oh, well, that's perfectly normal. There's almost always that debate at the bitter end," Grant said.

"No … you misunderstand me, sir. When I say 'continue the fight,' I'm not talking about here, on the battlefield. I'm talking about *after*."

"After?"

"Yes, there's a strong contingent that wants to continue fighting after the Army of Northern Virginia is officially finished and disbanded. They want to instigate a war of bushwhacking — a *guerilla* war, as it's sometimes called. To never give up their so-called 'cause.' To continue on for years, or even decades in a never-ending, senseless war."

"Oh, I see. And which side of the debate is Lee on?"

"From what I heard, he is leaning toward a complete end to the war."

"That seems hopeful. A moment ago, you said you had something to ask of me?"

"Yes, General. It is my belief that you will soon have Lee's army completely surrounded and cut off from escape or resupply."

Grant nodded, "This afternoon, General Custer's cavalry division seized a supply train and twenty-five big guns, cutting off Lee's path to Appomattox Station just west of here and depriving him of desperately needed food. By tomorrow morning, Sheridan's cavalry and two full infantry corps will completely sever his path to the west."

"His situation is clearly hopeless, General," Joseph replied. "An all-out attack on the morrow will surely finish him. What I am asking of you is to *not* finish off Lee tomorrow."

"Not to finish him? Why?"

"Because, if you destroy his army, and crush him in battle, he will lose the debate. He will no longer command his men nor garner their loyalty and respect; he will lose his voice concerning what comes next, both here and throughout the South. Though his army may disintegrate, and you may proclaim a great victory, the war will continue on, perhaps indefinitely.

"General, I'm asking you to give Lee a chance to save face and be able to order the peace on their side. Likely he will try one last effort to break your lines first light tomorrow, after which he must conclude the inevitable. Rather than counterattack and crush him, I beseech you allow him time to come to the honorable, inexorable conclusion: that their cause is lost, and that he must formally surrender his army in order to end needless bloodshed."

Grant gazed down at the tabletop for a long moment. He slowly reached into his pocket for another cigar, which he proceeded to light.

He leaned back in his chair and took several puffs before sitting back up to once again meet eyes with Joseph.

"All right. The president has already authorized me to offer Lee generous surrender terms, should the opportunity arise. Seems like this may be the time. I'll pen a letter and have it delivered to Lee this evening under flag of parley.

"I'll order my officers to hold the line in the morning, but not to aggressively counterattack, giving Lee the remainder of the day tomorrow to surrender. But if he still refuses to relent, I *will* crush him."

"Thank you, sir. And one more thing, if I may be so bold: though I have as much reason as any to hate the enemy, and to wish to see them humiliated in defeat, I ask you to forbear doing so, for the reasons I just mentioned. I have given this a lot of thought, and I believe if you treat their defeated soldiers with honor and respect, later attempts to recruit them into nefarious activities will prove unsuccessful."

Grant nodded. "You and I are of the same mind on that score, Joseph. I have developed a great deal of respect for the enemy's common soldier; I believe there have rarely in history been more resolute and courageous fighters under such grueling conditions. Damned shame they've wasted their greatness fighting for a dishonorable government. Though, I suppose that's a common enough occurrence throughout history. So, yes, I will treat them with honor, and even if the president hadn't ordered it, I would forbear any sort of harsh punishment after a general surrender."

"I am very pleased to hear it, General. I believe you will not regret this."

"Maybe, but it could be that *you* will regret it. I am ordering that you be kept in custody until this matter is resolved. If I'm wrong about you, Joseph, and you prove to be a false double-agent … I will shoot you myself."

Joseph smiled. "As it should be, General. And may I say, it somehow feels like it would be an honor to be shot by the great General Grant himself."

Grant snorted a laugh and grinned. "Being shot dead's never an honor, Joseph," he answered.

❧❦❧❦❧❦❧❦❧❦❧

Saturday April 8, 1865 – Greenbrier County, West Virginia:

Seeing the glorious Big House at Mountain Meadows, gleaming white against the brilliant green of its surroundings, as they crested the road leading through the farm had been thrilling enough, but when Evelyn opened the door and stepped inside, she was nearly overcome by the flood of memories that came unbidden to her mind. Her breath caught, and she had to pause with her hand over her heart for a moment as she gazed about the grand foyer.

More than just a magnificent house, this was where she'd first fallen in love, the source of her very fondest memories in life, where she'd briefly lived with the man who continued to be the love of her life, despite their long, forced separation. More than any other place on earth, this was *home*.

It was also, she had to admit, a place of great, aching sadness and regret. And not just because of its long neglect and emptiness; memories of the emotional crisis that had sent her scurrying back to Richmond and away from Nathan still haunted her. With a force of will, she shut out the bad memories and focused on the good. *After all*, she thought, *I no longer need wonder who I am. Now I know. I am me, Evelyn, and that is, and always has been, quite enough.*

And though the house was thick with dust, bugs, and spider webs, and devoid of any furnishings, she fought down a strong urge to immediately start cleaning. They were all exhausted from ten days of travel in the back of hard wagons on heavily rutted, pothole-filled roads that alternated between dusty and muddy, depending on the weather.

They were also hungry, despite the food Dodge had supplied them; Evelyn had insisted on severe rationing, not knowing what they might find at their destination, nor how long it might take to acquire additional foodstuffs.

So she gave everyone a quick tour of the house, and then, once back outside, gave a general description of where things were on the farm: the barns, toolsheds, and so on. And, of course, the former slave cabins. Then she announced that they could choose where they would prefer to sleep, save only one room, which she claimed for herself: Nathan's room.

And though there were no beds, by now they'd become accustomed to sleeping on the hard ground under the wagons, with only a blanket and shared body heat to warm them. After that experience, sleeping indoors, even on a hard wooden floor, seemed a great luxury.

Evelyn was not surprised that Dodge chose a large room in the Big House for himself and his sons. And she was amused when Hank and Mary chose separate but adjacent rooms. A few of the women, who'd been domestic slaves, chose to share a room in the house.

She was surprised, however, that the remainder of the freemen settled into the half-dozen or so slave cabins nearest to the Big House. But when she went to speak with the ladies in the first cabin, to remind them that they were no longer slaves and were welcome to stay in the house, they declined, saying they were more comfortable in the cabins, as it was what they were accustomed to.

Evelyn pondered this for a time, but then remembered that Nathan's soldiers from Texas had said much the same thing when they stayed at Mountain Meadows: that the Big House was much too grand and fancy for their simple tastes, and they felt more comfortable and at ease in simpler accommodations. *All things in good time*, she decided with a mental shrug.

The day after their arrival, Dodge and his sons hitched up the wagons, determined to return to Richmond.

"Are you sure you'll not stay?" Evelyn asked. "Richmond is likely nothing but a lawless, burned-out shell at the moment. Why not stay and be safe for a time?"

Dodge shook his head, "Burned out or not, it's our home. We must go see what's left of it, and likely start rebuilding. The longer that waits, the longer it'll take."

Evelyn had to admit, she'd come to rely on Dodge's strong presence on the dangerous trek, and his absence would make her feel much less safe and secure.

"I do have a bit o' good news for you, Miss Evelyn," Dodge announced. "I'm leaving one of the spare horses with you. A little gift from Joseph. He said you might need it when you reached Mountain Meadows."

"Oh! How very thoughtful of him. Yes, that should certainly be a boon to us. Please do thank him for me, if you should see him before I do."

"That I will, Miss Evelyn."

"And … also, if you should run into Union Colonel Nathaniel Chambers, of the Twelfth West Virginia, please tell him where I have gone."

"Yes, ma'am. I certainly will do that."

CHAPTER 9. APPOMATTOX

"There is nothing left
for me to do but to go
and see General Grant
and I would rather
die a thousand deaths."
*- **General Robert E. Lee***

Sunday April 9, 1865 – Appomattox Court House, Virginia:

The entire Union XXIV Corps of Major General Ord's Army of the James, including Brigadier General Nathaniel Chambers' Second Brigade, trotted at the double-quick over rolling grassland in the dim light of pre-dawn. They'd marched all night in an effort to get ahead of Lee's army to cut them off from moving any further west.

Nathan knew they were nearing exhaustion, having been on limited rations since overrunning the Petersburg defenses a week earlier, and being on forced marches or fighting ever since. The good news was they were also nearing their destination, after which they would turn due north and join up with General Humphrey's II Corps of the Army of the Potomac, completely cutting off Lee's army.

As the sky lighted in the East, Nathan heard the sound of pounding hooves behind him. And above that sound he heard a familiar voice shouting, and he smiled. He'd briefly served under Major General Philip Sheridan out in the Shenandoah Valley, and he knew that nothing on earth could dampen the man's boundless enthusiasm.

"C'mon men, keep up the pace! Damn, what fine specimens of manhood you are," Sheridan shouted as he slowly trotted up the line of marching soldiers. "You're gonna give them rebs the devil's own whuppin'. Stomp them sorry sons of bitches right into the dirt … Keep it up, boys, don't lag now … you're almost there …" And on and on in his usual manner.

Nathan laughed. Though he had his horse Millie with him, of course, he'd chosen to march with the men, understanding the positive effect on the morale of exhausted men to see their commanding officer suffering alongside them.

So when General Sheridan trotted close, Nathan couldn't resist throwing a tease at his old commander, and called out, "Easy for you horse soldiers to be jolly, General, when you get to ride all the way!"

Sheridan raised his fist, and slowed his horse to a walk, looking down to see who'd been impudent enough to shout insults at a major general.

When Nathan looked up at him and grinned, Sheridan snorted a laugh. "*Chambers!* Still up to your old mischief, I see. Never could resist berating your senior commanders, could you?"

"No, sir … but only when they deserved it," he answered, still smiling.

Sheridan chortled, sweeping his odd, flat-topped hat from his head and slapping it against his thigh. "Well said, sir. Well said. Oh, and by the way, that star on your shoulder suits you … though there probably ought to be *two* of those."

"Thank you for saying so, General. But I think it's a little late for that now."

"True, Chambers, true. Today is the day … the day we bag old Bobby Lee. See you at the surrender!" he called out as he kicked his horse into a gallop and thundered off, followed by his cavalry division.

A half hour later, just as the sun peeked over the eastern horizon, the march came to a halt, and the XXIV Corps formed up facing east. Just to their north, on their left, the V Corps was doing the same. An impenetrable thicket of bayonets awaited the arrival of Robert E. Lee. The rebels had nowhere left to go.

৪৩৫৫৪৩৫৫৪৩৫৫

Panting with exhaustion from the all-night march—the last several miles at the double-quick—but wide-eyed with anticipation, the eight hundred some members of the Twenty-Third Colored Regiment lined up with bayonets fixed, the warm light of the rising sun upon their faces, awaiting the last battle they knew must come with the dawn.

Tony could feel it to the depth of his soul; after a lifetime of slavery and bitter war, today was finally the day of reckoning. Today was the day it all ended. Today the Confederacy would die, and freedom would live. *Today is the day*, he decided, then said a quick prayer that he, and all those men he knew, would live to see tomorrow.

❧❦❧❦❧❦❧❦❧❦

Sunday April 9, 1865 – Appomattox Court House, Virginia:

At dawn, the Confederate Second Corps under Major General John B. Gordon, including Captain Jubal Collins and the remnants of the old Stonewall Brigade, launched an all-out attack against a division of Union cavalry to their west. Jubal understood that they need only break through the relatively thin line of cavalry to open the path for the rest of Lee's army to reach the rail hub at Lynchburg. There, they would be resupplied, and then transported south to join up with General Johnston in North Carolina.

Major General Fitzhugh Lee's cavalry spearheaded the attack, followed by Gordon's infantry corps. Together, they quickly forced back the Union cavalry line. And though they were fighting uphill toward a ridgeline, the federals gave ground without great resistance, leaving Jubal hopeful that their efforts this day would prove successful.

Jubal's men charged through the Union lines, shouting the rebel yell and taking the crest of the hill. But when he looked down into the valley beyond, Jubal's heart sank. There spread before him, rank upon rank, stood Union infantry—uncountable thousands of rifles, bristling with bayonets spread in a broad arc as far as the eye could see, cutting off all possibility of escape.

As if of a single mind, with no orders relayed, the entire Confederate army came to a stop. Jubal gazed down at what he assumed was his own death. When that vast army launched its inevitable attack, the entire Confederate army would simply be slaughtered, as surely as the sun rising in the east. But to his surprise, the Union army did *not* attack, seemingly content to simply prevent the Southerners from retreating any further.

Five minutes passed, and then another five, and still nobody moved, and no shot was fired. Then Jubal saw a Confederate officer riding toward the Union lines with a white flag, and he knew the battle was over. Hungry and exhausted, rebel soldiers began to sit down in the grass where they'd stood. First a trickle, then a handful, and soon all were seated on the grass, awaiting whatever fate had in store for them.

⁂

Jubal looked over at Bob Hill, and could see that his old captain and mentor was exhausted, barely able to hold his eyes open as he sat in the grass, leaning on his rifle. In that moment, two things came into Jubal's mind at almost the same instant: the first was that the two hundred some men now sitting alone in this field—all that remained of the once-proud Stonewall Brigade—by odd circumstances of the march, were currently slightly separated from the main body of the regiment. The second was that he was now the de facto commander of the unit, as Bob deferred to him on practically every decision, and the two of them were the highest-ranking officers left from the old brigade.

As he gazed around at his exhausted, dejected men, he made his final command decision. Standing up, he stepped out in front of the company, then waited a moment until he had most of their eyes upon him.

"Men … y'all know I'm not one for making speeches, but I reckon I'm gonna make one now. To the end of our days, we can stand proud to have been a part of this, the Stonewall Brigade. We've fought longer, harder, and better than any other unit in the war, on either side. We've marched into the enemy's territory and back again three times, and have never shirked our duty when called upon. We've been in the thick of the most hellish firefights on earth, and those of us sitting here have lived to tell the tales, though most of our comrades have not.

"It has been the honor of my life to serve with you men. You've been hard as iron, but the best comrades a man could ever hope to have."

He paused and looked about, and was pleased to see that all eyes were now upon him, though he was surprised to see that many had tears in them.

"Men … the Bible says to everything there is a season … a time for war and a time for peace. We've done all we could do, to the very last ounce of our energy and courage. We've earned our rest. The good book also says, 'they shall beat their swords into plowshares.' I reckon it's time we did just that. Men … it's time we went home.

"I know we've been ordered to stand by our arms, that this ceasefire is only temporary, but I know in my heart, as do all of you, that our long, hard war is finally over.

"So, if you will allow me to issue one last command as your captain … *Company will stack arms!*" he called out. Then in a softer voice he added, "And then be at peace."

For a moment, nobody moved. Then Bob Hill stood and walked over to Jubal. The two met eyes, then shared a smile. Bob reached out and took Jubal's rifle, then set it on the ground, butt-first, leaning it against his own by the bayonets. Another man trotted up and leaned his next to the other two to make a tripod that would stand on its own. Soon, the entire company was doing the same.

ↂↂↂↂↂↂↂↂↂ

Tom raised his binoculars and gazed out at the enemy position, only a hundred yards away. He lowered them and looked over at Nathan. "Do you see that?" he asked.

"Yes, I see it. They've stacked arms on the battlefield. That's as sure a sign of surrender as you're ever going to see," Nathan answered.

"But … the ceasefire is only temporary. It's due to expire in …" Tom reached into his pocket and pulled out his pocket watch, "an hour and forty minutes. We've standing orders to re-commence hostilities if there is no formal word by then."

"Yes, that's true," Nathan agreed.

"When the time comes, will you obey those orders, and open fire on those men?"

Nathan turned to Tom, "Certainly *not!* Look at them … they're finished. Orders or no, I'd never fire upon them; it'd be just plain murder."

"Glad to hear that, but not surprised … but I wonder what our other officers will do," Tom said.

"Hopefully the same, but all we can do is order our own brigade. Speaking of … please pass the word not to re-engage the enemy unless I give explicit orders to do so. Even if some other Union hothead decides to restart the fighting, that doesn't mean we need to join in."

"Gladly," Tom said, and trotted off to do as he'd been asked.

Nathan turned his gaze back toward the enemy line, and raised his spyglass to have another look at them. This time, he noticed a man walking toward them, his arms raised above his head. Nathan waited until the man was halfway to their position, then ordered one of the sergeants to grab a couple of privates and go out to escort the man the rest of the way in.

Tom returned to stand next to Nathan, "The word has been given. There'll be no more action from this command without your explicit say so."

"Good. Thank you, Tom."

"What's this?" Tom asked, noticing the incoming rebel officer for the first time.

"Appears the fellow wants to have a talk. Can't say I'm surprised. I expect he wants to surrender."

"Seems reasonable."

They waited until the young officer was brought before them. He stopped and stood with his hands still upraised as the sergeant and privates stepped to the side. Nathan saw that the man's pistol holster was empty, as was his sword scabbard. He also noted that the man was youthful, though he was lean and hard looking. Nathan suppressed a grin when he noted the man's startlement when he caught sight of Harry the Dog, sitting just behind Nathan. The hound just gazed at the newcomer with disinterest while resting contentedly in the grass, so Nathan figured the man was likely a decent enough fellow.

"You may lower your hands, Captain …"

"Collins, sir. Jubal Collins, Twenty-Seventh Virginia. Sorry, nobody had a white cloth for me to wave, so I figured raised hands would have to do," he answered as he relaxed his arms.

"I'm General Nathaniel Chambers, Twelfth West Virginia. Good to meet you, Collins," Nathan announced, as he extended his hand, which Jubal accepted in a firm handshake.

"Twenty-Seventh?" Nathan asked. "Stonewall Brigade, isn't it?"

"Yes, sir. What you see over yonder is all that's left of the brigade. Just over two hundred men," Jubal answered, gesturing back toward his company.

"*But* … Captain Collins … there must've been three or four thousand in the Stonewall Brigade at the outset of the war," Nathan said, in a tone of astonishment.

"Yes, sir—3,874, to be exact. And many more recruits were added over time. All told, we've had much higher than one hundred percent casualties in the brigade through the duration of the war, though I doubt anyone's ever done the math on it."

"*My God,*" Nathan whispered, slowly shaking his head. "What have we done, Captain?" he asked, slowly shaking his head.

Jubal shrugged, "Killed a lot of good men, I reckon. And for what … I'm sure I don't know."

Nathan just shrugged, then said, "So … what is it I can do for you, Captain?"

"Sir … though they say that this ceasefire is only temporary, my men and I are finished. I've come here to formally surrender my command to you. We won't fight any more."

"Seems prudent, Captain. And there is certainly no shame in it. By all accounts, your brigade has fought more valiantly than any other. You've been a great thorn in our side from the outset, and I for one will be happy never to see you on the battlefield again," Nathan answered.

"Thank you for saying so, sir. There is one more thing I would ask of you, sir, if possible. I would not ask it for *myself*, you understand, but … my men are starving, sir. We've not eaten since we left Petersburg a week ago, and little enough for weeks before that. If you could find it in your heart to issue some provisions to my men, we'd be most grateful. And I'm certain the other nearby Confederate regiments are likewise in great need."

Nathan turned to his second in command. "Tom … what is the brigade's food situation at the moment?" he asked, though he already knew the answer.

Tom shook his head, "Not good … our men also have barely eaten since Petersburg, on account of the supply wagons have been unable to keep pace with the forced march. The men have been living off hardtack and other personal rations they've carried in their packs. So far, there's been no word as to when we might expect any relief in that regard. Could be days yet."

Nathan nodded, then turned back toward Jubal.

"I understand, sir. Thank you, anyway, for looking into it," Jubal answered.

Rather than answer Jubal, Nathan turned to Tom and said, "Colonel Clark … kindly order the men to split whatever rations they carry into two halves, then take half out to the Stonewall Brigade and other Confederate units to our front, under a flag of truce."

Tom smiled, "Yes, sir!" He pivoted and went to issue the orders.

"Thank you very kindly, sir!" Jubal said. "That was handsomely done, and speaks volumes as to your honor and decency."

"You're welcome," Nathan answered. "As President Lincoln famously said, 'it is time to bind up the nation's wounds.' This seems to me as good a place to start as any."

∞∞∞∞∞∞∞∞∞

To Nathan's relief, before the hour arrived for the ceasefire to expire, orders came to stand down, and that Lee was expected to meet with Grant sometime that day to discuss a general surrender.

Nathan sent for William, thinking to have him take charge of the Confederate wounded and arrange for their transport to the Union field hospital.

In the meantime, Nathan decided to go speak once again with the young captain of the Stonewall Brigade to assess any additional needs they might have, and to arrange details of the surrender.

He walked across the field to the rebel position escorted by a sergeant and six privates—Tom had insisted, though Nathan thought it unnecessary. In his mind, there was no fight left in the rebels, so there was little danger. But he deferred to Tom on it, thinking it wasn't worth the argument. And, as expected, Harry the Dog plodded along behind Nathan, keeping a close watch over his master.

When he arrived at the rebels' field, Captain Jubal Collins rose to greet them, stepping up in front of Nathan, and this time standing to attention and saluting. Nathan returned the salute with a grin. "You're looking a little more alive, Captain," he said.

Jubal returned the grin, and answered, "Amazing what even a small bite of food will do for a man's demeanor, sir. Thank you very much again for that."

"Never mention it," Nathan answered, just as another Confederate captain stepped up next to Jubal.

Nathan gazed at the newcomer for a moment, then frowned and said, "I know *you*, Captain. I never forget a face; you're from Greenbrier County ... one of Elijah Walters' men."

"Yes, and I know you too, General Chambers," the captain answered. "Though I'm ashamed to admit it, I am among those who willfully wronged you and your family before the war. It is a thing I am not proud of, and for which I am greatly sorry. I have since attempted to repent and to make amends."

Nathan continued to gaze at the man for a long moment, slowly nodding his head. "And exactly what is it you've done to 'make amends,' as you say?"

"I … well, now that you ask, I suppose it rings hollow to say that I have served my country faithfully and selflessly in time of war," the captain answered with a shrug.

"If you'd served on the *Union* side, I might say that all is forgiven. But given the circumstances …" Nathan answered cooly, and shrugged.

Jubal looked from one man to the other, not comprehending what had transpired to put them at odds before the war. But hoping to defuse the tense situation, he said, "General Chambers … whatever happened between you two before the conflict, I can assure you, sir, that Captain Hill has been the very model of decency and heroism throughout the conflict. He is a man I admire and respect, and would vouch for without a moment's hesitation."

Nathan raised an eyebrow at this statement, "*Hill*, did you say? *Bob* Hill?"

The man nodded, "Yes, that's correct. I am Bob Hill."

Nathan's frown turned to a grin, and he stepped forward, extending his hand. With a puzzled expression, Bob accepted the proffered hand and shook it.

"My good sir, Margaret has told me all about how you helped her escape from Walters. And William … uh, that is, Captain William Jenkins, has told me about all you did for her when she was wounded later in Richmond," Nathan said.

"So, yes, you have certainly made amends. More than made amends, you have won my undying gratitude, sir."

"Well … I am very gratified to hear it, General. But I … wasn't aware that you were close with Margaret, though now that you mention it, I suppose her being friends with your man William …"

"*Close?* Yes, you could say *close*; Margaret has become my adoptive sister. She has lived in my household in Wheeling since escaping Walters, up until the time she returned to Richmond to help break William out of Libby Prison."

"Well, how about that? I never knew it," Bob answered, now returning Nathan's warm smile.

And just at that moment, William stepped up, accompanied by two assistant surgeons. "General, you asked me to come see about the rebel wounded—*oh!* Captain Hill, good to see you again, sir!" he said, extending his hand to Bob, who shook it in turn.

"Captain Jenkins … likewise. You are looking fit; much more so than when I last saw you at Libby, I daresay," Bob answered.

William chuckled. "Well, that's not saying much; I expect I had lost more than twenty pounds during my incarceration there. Captain Hill, I never really had the chance to thank you for what you did for Margaret …"

"Never mention it, Captain Jenkins. It was the least I could do after all that Walters put her through. I'm pleased that she is doing well. Speaking of … I trust she is now safely back in the North?"

At this question, both Nathan and William's features darkened. "She has remained in Richmond," William finally answered. "And with the chaos in that city, we're not sure of her *exact* whereabouts at the moment, though …" he again shared a look with Nathan, "the general assures me she is somewhere safe."

"Ah!" Bob answered, looking from one man to the other, as if trying to figure out what they might *not* be telling him. "Well, I will pray for her continued safety," he said.

"As will we. Thank you, Captain," William answered.

Jubal then escorted William to where the Confederate wounded were being tended, leaving Nathan alone with Bob.

"Well, it was good to finally put the name to a face, Bob," Nathan said, "and again, I thank you, on behalf of Margaret. Oh, and I had a thought just now … It seems like once the war is done for good, I'm going to have two farms to run, and it's yet to be seen how many of our freeman may wish to stay on. So, if you find yourself in need of a job after the war, do come see me at Mountain Meadows."

"Thank you very kindly, sir. I may just do that," Bob answered, returning Nathan's smile.

⁂

Nathan pulled Millie up to a bouncing stop, causing Tom to scowl at the fresh splatter of mud on an already soiled uniform.

"Sorry, Tom … but grab your horse and come," Nathan said.

Moments later, the two rode at a canter back through Union lines toward the little village of Appomattox Court House, with Harry the Dog trotting along behind, as usual.

"I intercepted a courier who said Lee has arrived at a house in town and that Grant is to meet him there. This is *it*, Tom, the surrender! I wish to be there, at least outside."

"Oh, do you think it'll be okay for us to be there?"

Nathan grinned, then stuck an unlit cigar into his mouth.

"Well … nobody said we couldn't."

Tom chuckled. "All right … what's the worst that could happen, anyway. That they might fire us?"

Nathan returned Tom's smile, but then his visage turned more serious. "I would speak with my old mentor, if I may."

"Lee?"

"Yes. I feel we have unfinished business between us, and I would resolve it before the end."

Tom nodded, but said nothing.

When they arrived at the small village, they quickly ascertained where the meeting of the two great men was taking place—at a private home owned by the McLean family—so they quickly made their way there. When they arrived, they found another brigadier general and several other Union officers waiting outside by the hitching post. So Nathan and Tom dismounted, tied their horses, and approached the other officers.

Nathan stepped up to the general and introduced himself, extending his hand.

"Joshua Chamberlain," the other answered. "Good to meet you, General Chambers," he said.

Nathan grinned, immediately recognizing the name of the Gettysburg hero, and the only other general that Grant had promoted recently, though he'd done so assuming Chamberlain was dying.

"A pleasure and an honor to meet you," Nathan said. And then he shared the story of General Grant mentioning

Chamberlain when he'd received his own recent promotion. However, he left out the part about Chamberlain being mortally wounded at the time, not knowing if it was a touchy subject.

Chamberlain grinned. "Yes … apparently Grant thought I was dead already and wanted to award me a posthumous honor. Messed up his plans by going ahead and living."

The two shared a laugh.

"Well, if it makes you feel any better," Nathan said, "when he promoted me, he was torn between that and having me executed for a traitor and a spy. Guess I won him over."

The subject then turned to the moment at hand, and Chamberlain described the arrival of the two generals. "I was sitting my horse, watching over my men, when a rider came through the lines, accompanied by a single staff officer. I realized in a shock that it was Robert E. Lee himself, though I'd never seen him before in person—a commanding presence, superbly mounted, and richly accoutered. A man of imposing bearing and noble countenance. But it seemed to me he bore a great sadness, mastered by a deep inner strength."

"Yes, that fairly describes my old commander from Texas," Nathan replied. "But you certainly describe him with a flourish, sir."

Chamberlain smiled, and shrugged, "I was a college professor before the war … Stringing the proper words together was my vocation."

"Ah, that explains it," Nathan replied. "I was guessing you were an author."

Chamberlain nodded, then continued his narrative, "A short while later, General Grant arrived. Him I instantly recognized, and though he wore plain, unassuming, simple attire, with mud-splattered boots, he was somehow no less imposing. A man sure of his own greatness and might … he rides with the smooth confidence of a man who is the master of all he surveys."

Nathan nodded. "Yes, I agree. I have always believed he was the best choice the president could've made to lead us to the final victory. And speaking of … apparently, here we are."

"Yes … so it would seem, General Chambers."

They hadn't long to wait; less than an hour later, the door of the house opened and General Lee stepped out, followed closely by another Confederate officer. Though he appeared even as Chamberlain had just described, to Nathan he looked to have aged more than a dozen years in the four years since they'd last spoken, and seemed downcast and careworn, but he still held his head high.

When Lee approached, General Chamberlain stood to attention and snapped a salute. Lee returned the salute without pausing, seemingly more out of habit than from any great courtesy. Then he looked at Nathan, seeming to notice him for the first time, and he stopped.

"Nathaniel. I see you are finally a general. Pity it took so long … You would've long since been a lieutenant general in the Southern army, second in command only to myself … if that."

"With all due respect, General, I'd rather be the lowliest private on the righteous side of history, than the supreme commander on the other."

Lee nodded, but didn't answer. The two gazed at each other in silence for a long moment.

Finally, Lee broke the silence, "Nathaniel … I wonder how many brave young men would still be alive and well today if I would've accepted your offer to put down the rebellion at the very start; when we last met on that long-ago day on the streets of Richmond …"

Nathan didn't immediately answer and gazed skyward for a long moment. When he looked down again, he answered in a quiet voice touched with emotion. "All of them, General Lee. Most likely *all* of them."

Nathan and Lee continued to lock eyes. Then, Nathan stood to attention and snapped a salute.

Lee returned the salute, then turned and walked slowly away.

❧❧❧❧❧❧❧❧❧

Lee's staff officer, a brigadier general, who'd lagged behind presumably taking care of details, came striding out. And though he looked older, thinner, and more haggard than when they'd last met, Nathan immediately recognized him.

"Henry Wise," he said, as the general stepped up to where they stood.

Wise looked up at the sound of his name, and at first didn't seem to recognize Nathan; it had been four years since they'd last met. Then recognition dawned, and he seemed to perk up.

"Chambers. Once again on the winning side, I see. Come to gloat?"

"No ... I haven't the heart for it; too many good men have fallen—on both sides. I feel only tired and ... sad ... though with an abiding gratitude it's finally over."

Wise nodded.

"Not to rub salt into the wound, Mr. Wise, but could you satisfy my curiosity about something?"

"What, pray, would that be, sir?"

"I am wondering what you now think of Virginia's secession, after all that's happened since we last debated the subject in Richmond."

Wise didn't immediately answer, but looked at his shoes as if considering his response. When he looked back at Nathan he had a serious expression; almost sad. He said, "I will now freely admit you were right about it, Chambers. As I recall, you said, 'nothing but death and destruction will come of it.' Should have trusted a military man to know his business in that regard. I thought I knew, but ...

"In the end, I have helped cause the destruction of everything I held dear."

"Yes, and you've destroyed much of what I held dear in the process."

"Well, at least there's some consolation in that."

Nathan scowled. He gazed over at the house. "You know, the last time I was in this town, I was wounded and fleeing for my life from your hired killers."

"Hmm ... yes. That seems eons ago now. Believe it or not, Chambers, though I tried my best to murder you at the beginning of the conflict, I now find I'm happy you're still alive."

"Oh? That seems a great change of heart for you, Wise. I am almost touched by it."

"Don't be; I've no angelic motivations in that regard. I'm happy you're still alive so you can suffer along with the rest of us."

Nathan chuckled. "But, sir, though I have lost dear friends in the conflict, still I am not among the vanquished. I don't see how you think I am suffering over much."

"I'm impressed with your fortitude, Chambers! I would have expected a man whose family has been murdered and his childhood home destroyed would be more downcast and reticent. Apparently, you are made of sterner stuff!"

"But … my family is *not* dead, sir, but is safely in the North, away from the conflict. And I have it on good authority my home in Greenbrier has survived the war with only minor damage, though all the furnishings have apparently been looted."

"Oh? Say you so? Well then, my congratulations on that." He gave Nathan an odd look, with just the hint of a smile, which seemed incongruous. "Apparently, I have been … *misinformed* … in that case."

Nathan did not respond, but now felt an odd anxiety; did the man know something he wasn't sharing? Had there been some plot against him that had either failed or had not yet come to fruition?

Wise tipped his hat. "Well, good day to you, sir." Then he looked over at General Chamberlain and nodded. "General."

"General," Chamberlain responded, tipping his hat.

After Wise was out of earshot, General Chamberlain turned to Nathan, "Henry Wise, former Governor of Virginia?"

"The same."

"Ah … I see his reputation is not exaggerated, then. Charming to the last."

"Yes … so it would seem."

On their ride back to camp, Tom asked, "What was all that with Wise about? What an odd thing for him to say …"

"Yes, wasn't it? And it has just reminded me to wonder … where is Walters?"

Tuesday April 11, 1865 – Appomattox Court House, Virginia:

Jubal was as surprised as the rest of his men when it was announced that General Grant had signed the document of surrender granting all former Confederate soldiers amnesty, and allowing them to immediately return home when they'd expected to be sent straight to a prison camp. Officers would even be allowed to keep their sidearms—pistols and swords—as well as their personal horses, though Jubal didn't have one of those.

They were also given food and spare clothing from the Union supply wagons, some of which, he understood, had been acquired from captured Confederate supply trains by the Union cavalry. And most amazing of all, Jubal and his comrades were treated with honor and respect by the Union officers and soldiers, even granting them a formal surrender ceremony where they were saluted as they stacked their arms for the last time.

If he'd had any lingering doubts about how he'd be treated by his former enemies, now fellow countrymen, after his kindly treatment by General Chambers, they'd been completely dispelled. General Grant proved to be every bit as gracious a winner as he'd been a tenacious fighter, for which Jubal was grateful.

Now, three days after the surrender, Jubal had packed his things, said his goodbyes, and was finally headed home. It seemed unbelievably odd to be walking alone, at his own pace, under no orders, nor any imminent threat of violence for the first time in nearly four years. *Almost seems unreal*, he realized.

Also odd was that he was walking past row upon row of Union tents, teeming with Union soldiers, most of whom gave him a friendly smile or nod of the head as he passed. All he could do was shake his head in disbelief.

As he passed a larger tent that he assumed belonged to an officer, a Union Captain stepped out, and the two met eyes for a moment.

"Hey!" the Captain said, holding up his hand as if he wished to speak. So Jubal paused and turned toward him as the man approached.

"Hey," the Union Captain repeated, "weren't you up at the Antietam battle?" he asked.

For a moment, Jubal couldn't think of what to say, as it seemed the strangest question imaginable, coming from a Union officer. Then he decided there was something familiar about the man's face. "Yes … I was there …" he answered.

"Damn! I knew it. When I saw you just now, I *knew* it was you. I'm Captain James Hawkins, Seventh West Virginia—'The Bloody Seventh.' You remember … we tried to kill each other down in the 'bloody lane' at Antietam, but we'd run out of ammo …"

Jubal thought for a moment, and then the memories flooded back in … the terrible slaughter … waking from being knocked unconscious … a Union officer leaning over him … pulling his pistol and … both men's pistols clicking on empty chambers. So they'd talked instead.

"*Oh!* Of course, Captain Hawkins. I do remember you. I remember being surprised that a Union officer seemed a nice enough fellow after everything we'd been through."

Hawkins laughed, "I recall you were pretty decent too, for an officer of the 'Bloody Twenty-Seventh.' Sorry, but I'm bad with names …"

"Collins … Jubal Collins."

The two shook hands.

"Hey, Collins … if you're not in a hurry, I'd appreciate hearing your story after Antietam. I know you boys were in the thick of just about every battle, most of which we were in as well."

Jubal hesitated, so Hawkins upped the ante: "I've got fresh food in my tent, straight off the supply wagons … likely better'n what they've been giving you boys …" he gestured back toward his tent invitingly.

Jubal shrugged, "I been gone from home for the better part o' four years, so I reckon another hour or so won't make much difference. Thanks."

Once they'd settled into camp chairs and shared out the food, which seemed a great feast to Jubal, Hawkins said, "I was surprised to see you alive today, Collins. I figured you for dead back at the Spotsylvania Court House Battle—what we took to calling the 'mule shoe,' on account of the shape of your salient." He slowly shook his head, "What a horrible sight … we buried hundreds of your men that day. Right there in the defensive trenches they'd dug themselves and then died in."

Jubal nodded, remembering that terrible day, though he'd received such a hard blow to the head that it remained a bit fuzzy. "I thought I was dead too. I think I tripped and fell on my face in the mud just as your men opened fire on us. Reckon the bullets must've passed right over top of me. Then one of my men grabbed me by the back of the shirt and got me moving again. I just ran and never looked back until I was safely away from the battlefield."

Hawkins listened and nodded, bearing a serious expression, until something triggered a related memory. "*Hey!* I just remembered … I have something of yours."

"Something of mine? How can that be?" Jubal asked.

"Just a minute …" Hawkins said, as he jumped from his chair and moved over by his cot, next to which lay a small black trunk. "Luckily, the wagons with our personal gear finally arrived today," he said as he rummaged through the trunk, which contained clothing, letters from home, and a few odd personal items. "Now where …? Ah! There it is."

He pulled something from the trunk, held reverently between his two hands, and carried it over to Jubal. He held out what appeared to be a tightly folded piece of cloth of red, white, and blue colors.

Jubal looked Hawkins in the eye, and said, "*What …?*"

"Take it … see if you recognize it," Hawkins prompted, unable to suppress a grin.

"All right," Jubal said, taking the thing and carefully unfolding it. He could immediately see that it was a typical Confederate battle flag: square, with a red background and a blue X filled with white stars. And then with a sudden intake of breath, recognition set in, and he laid it out on the camp table next to him, flattening the cloth where the folds had been. He could now see that it was a regimental flag, and though it was badly stained, he could still read the names of all the unit's battles stenciled neatly in black across the four red sections: Manassas, Kernstown, Winchester, Port Republic, Manassas No. 2, Chantilly, Fredericksburg, Cold Harbor, Malvern Hill, Cedar Run, Chancellorsville, Winchester No. 2, and at the very bottom, Gettysburg. The entire flag was trimmed in white, and upon the white border at the bottom was written the most important and telling inscription of all: "27th Va. Regt. – Stonewall Brigade."

"Our battle flag ..." Jubal said in a voice choked with emotion. *"How?* How did you come by it?" he asked, wiping tears from his eyes.

"I found it after the battle, trampled into the mud. I pulled it out and decided to keep it as a souvenir. Have had it in my kit ever since, though I'd nearly forgotten it until just now. What a pleasure it is that I can return it to you," he said and beamed.

"I ... I don't know how to thank you, Captain Hawkins," Jubal said, continuing to gaze at the flag.

"Please, call me James, now that we are no longer enemies," Hawkins said, holding out his hand.

"Then you must call me Jubal," Jubal answered, and they shook on it.

And Jubal's delay of "an hour or so" on his journey home, stretched into the rest of the day, and well into the night, as the two shared stories of their numerous battles and other adventures during the war. Finally, Hawkins had another cot brought in, so Jubal could spend the night in the tent.

As they settled down into the cots, Hawkins asked one last question, one that he'd assumed would be fairly straightforward and not in the least controversial: "Jubal ... what do you think you'll do now that the war's over? Go back to being a policeman?"

Jubal didn't immediately answer, pausing so long that Hawkins assumed he'd nodded off. Finally, he answered, "I'm not sure, but ... there's this lady ... back in Richmond. We've written letters throughout the war. Just as friends, you understand … but …"

"But you'd like to see if something more may come of it?" Hawkins prompted.

"Yes. But she has told me she's betrothed to another man … an officer, though she wouldn't tell me his name." Then Jubal chuckled mirthlessly. "I'm ashamed to say it, but I found myself hoping the man would end up killed in the fighting, as so many others have been."

"Understandable," Hawkins said. "I don't think you should feel too badly about that. It's not like wishing for a thing can make it happen. Whatever happens to him happens, and it wouldn't be your fault." Then Hawkins chuckled. "Unless you shot him yourself, of course."

Jubal smiled, and then a vision of Evelyn came into his mind, clear and sharp: her dazzling smile, her warmth and charm. *"Evelyn …"* he whispered, not intending to say it aloud. Now that he had, he continued, "She's the sweetest, most beautiful lady in all of Richmond."

Then, inexplicably, Hawkins asked, "Uh … Jubal … what is your Evelyn's last name?"

"Hanson. Evelyn Hanson. Why? Do you know her?"

Hawkins stared up at the ceiling and sighed. "I know *of* her, though I've never met her," he answered cryptically.

"What do you mean … how do you know of her?" Jubal asked, sitting up in the cot and gazing over at Hawkins.

"Because … I know the man who is her betrothed," he answered.

"What? How?"

Hawkins took a deep breath. "Because he is a *Union* officer, not a Confederate," he answered.

Jubal's eyes widened as he absorbed this news. "Oh … oh, now that you say it, it makes sense. That's why she wouldn't tell me his name. And … who is this Union officer?"

"Before I answer that, let me tell you, Jubal, that he is the finest officer and the finest *man* I've ever met. Nothing personal, you understand, but Evelyn could not have possibly chosen better."

"All right … who is he?"

"His name is Brigadier General Nathaniel Chambers, commander of the Twelfth West Virginia," Hawkins answered.

"General Chambers?" Jubal said in wonder, laying back down in his cot. "I've met him. He is the very officer that I surrendered the remains of the Stonewall Brigade to. We were starving, so he gave us half his meager supply of food, though his own men were also hungry."

"That's him, all right. He is a truly great leader of men. Someone I greatly admire. But I am sorry, Jubal. Truly."

Jubal was quiet and thoughtful for a long time, then finally said, "Well, I suppose if I must lose out to another man, it may as well be to someone like him. I think you must be right, James … she has chosen the right man. It's just too bad for me."

Hawkins reached across and gripped his new friend on the shoulder.

In the morning, before Jubal departed, the two exchanged addresses and promised to write, and then to visit each other once things had returned to normal.

As he strode down the road, once again headed toward Richmond, Jubal decided he still wished to speak with Evelyn one more time, despite Hawkins's heartrending news about the man she was to marry. Then he suffered a dark, dreadful thought … the last time he'd been in Richmond, he'd been unable to find her, and he knew she'd been under the suspicion of the disreputable Confederate Signal Corps. What if … what if something had happened to her? Something terrible? He shuddered at the thought and picked up his pace.

Chapter 10. Evil Yet Lives

"The fear of the LORD
is to hate evil:
pride, and arrogancy,
and the evil way…"
- **Proverbs 8:13**

Sunday April 9, 1865 – Greenbrier County, West Virginia:

Evelyn stood on the grass gazing up in wonder and delight at the glorious sight of the great magnolia tree growing in the middle of the Big House's lawn. It was in full bloom, covered in uncountable thousands of light lavender-colored blossoms. She sighed, feeling a deep sense of satisfaction just staring up at it.

She heard a footstep behind her and turned to see who it was. Her sense of peace and happiness was instantly swept away when she saw the hard expression on Hank's face. Sweat ran down his face and he was breathing heavily, as if he'd just been running.

"What is it, Hank?"

"Riders, coming down the driveway, Miss Evelyn. Confederate soldiers, by their uniforms. Though they are walking their horses slowly, they will be here in minutes."

"*Oh!* How many are they?" she asked.

"Must be thirty or more," he answered, then frowned. "And that's not the worst of it."

"Oh? What could be worse than that?"

"The officer leading them … I've heard him described, though I've never seen him before. Mean-looking fellow, strongly built and … missing his left hand."

"*Walters …*" she hissed.

"I fear so," he said.

"*Damn it!* All right, just as we discussed, I'm your mistress, Miss Eve Smith, escaping from the fall of Richmond with her loyal household slaves."

He nodded, "But doesn't he already know you, Miss Evelyn?"

She thought about that a moment, then shook her head, "I don't think so … he's only seen me once or twice, four years ago, and he was very distracted by a confrontation with Nathan at the time. With my hair now dyed black, he may not recognize me at all. But if he does think I look familiar to him, he'll likely assume it was from meeting me at some social function in Richmond. And I shall endeavor to convince him of that very thing."

"All right, that seems hopeful. I'll make sure the others remember what to do."

"Thank you, Hank."

"You be careful, now, Miss Evelyn," he said, sharing a concerned look with her.

"I will. You too, Hank."

As Hank headed for the back door of the house, Evelyn turned and walked toward the drive. She decided it would be best if she greeted Walters at the front door, and at least attempted to steer things in her favor, perhaps shaming him into behaving decently in front of all his men. It was worth a try, anyway.

So when she reached the front of the house, she climbed the stairs to the veranda and stood in front of the door. She looked up the drive, but could not yet see anything of the riders. The great oak tree that she'd often sat under with Nathan presently blocked the view further up the road.

In moments, the enemy soldiers came into view, and just as Hank had described, they were led by a burly looking fellow who was missing his left hand, and there could be no doubt who he was—her worst nightmare scenario in the flesh, Elijah Walters.

Evelyn took a deep breath to calm her mind and settle her nerves, then focused on summoning up her very best Southern aristocratic lady persona: a woman of the slave power class, genteel and charming, the very picture of femininity, and yet at the same time expecting to be obeyed without question by all lesser beings. Though she was also a fighter, she knew this was her best weapon, and she meant to wield it with as much grace and ruthlessness as she could manage, knowing that her life, and the lives of everyone around her, were very much dependent on it.

When the riders finally reached the hitching post, she stepped forward to the top of the stairs and curtseyed, looking straight at Walters. And though he gazed at her with the odd, unreadable expression he was so famous for, she thought he betrayed just a hint of surprise.

Good, she thought, *not at all what he was expecting to find here. I must turn that against him before he can recover his wits.*

"Good afternoon, gentlemen," she said, beaming brightly. "Thank God you've arrived. Have you ridden far this day, Colonel? I am so sorry and ashamed that I can't offer you brave gentlemen refreshments, as I have only just arrived yesterday, and this house, though pretty enough, we've found almost entirely empty," she laughed lightly, sweeping her hand as if to dismiss her embarrassment at her failure to properly entertain guests, despite the circumstances. While she was talking, she'd made eye contact with Walters and then the other men near him, intending to draw them into the irresistible web of her charms. Several of the men returned her smile, while others quickly looked away, seemingly embarrassed and unable to meet her gaze.

"Lieutenant Colonel Walters, ma'am," their leader said, reaching up to tip his hat. "Thirty-sixth Virginia Cavalry Battalion."

"Colonel, it's a great pleasure and honor to meet you, sir. I am Miss Eve Smith, late of our beloved city of Richmond—forced to flee my dear home in the face of those dreadful Yankee invaders. My husband, Brigadier General Elias Smith, sadly was killed in the conflict, back at the Battle of Shiloh. He served under General Beauregard. Did you know him, by chance, sir?"

"I am sorry for your loss, Miss Eve. But no, I never met General Smith. You said, 'we' just now … who else is here with you?" Walters asked.

"Oh, just a few of my most loyal slaves. Though I am ashamed to admit it, some of my slaves simply ran away when the chance presented itself, the scoundrels, though I have always treated them with great kindness and forbearance. But the rest, happily, have continued to serve me. You'll find them now settled in around this farm, such as it is."

Walters nodded, then turned to the man next to him, a captain, and said, "Roberts, have the men dismount and see to the horses. Then they can bivouac in the old slave cabins." He looked back at Evelyn and said, "Those cabins not already occupied by Miss Eve's slaves."

She returned Walters' look with a smile.

"Very good, sir," the man answered, then immediately gave the order for the men to dismount. While they were doing so, Evelyn made a quick count of their numbers.

Thirty-eight, she concluded. *Thirty-nine, counting Walters.* She filed the number away for future reference, and reflexively felt the hard lump of the pistol hidden up her left sleeve. *So many*, she lamented. *Too many to fight, even if we had enough weapons*, she decided.

Walters also dismounted, handing his reins to Captain Roberts, then stepped up the stairs to stand in front of Evelyn. There, he paused and gazed at her face for a long moment. And though she'd never had any interactions with him, she'd heard all about him from Nathan and Miss Abbey, so she was not surprised by his odd lack of expression, despite pouring on her very most potent charms.

"You look somewhat familiar," he said. "Have we met before, Miss Eve?"

"I was just thinking the same, sir. Have you spent much time in Richmond? Before the war, I mean?"

"Yes … some," he answered.

"Attended many balls, or other social functions?" she asked, knowing full well from her conversations with Margaret that he had. Walters had, after all, selected her for a wife at one such function a year or so before the Secession.

"A few," he agreed.

"Well, I'm sure that was it, then," she said, nodding, "Oh, my … I must've attended a hundred of those things before finally meeting my husband. So it's almost certain we would've run into each other at some time or other."

"Yes, very likely," he agreed.

"Won't you come in, sir?" she asked, gesturing toward the door. "The house is yours, of course, sir. And though, as I said, I've little comfort to offer, you can at least take rest in the shade, and what little we have we shall provide, certainly."

"Thank you," he said, removing his hat and entering the house.

She silently took another deep breath, then followed.

⁂

Fortunately, Walters was apparently tired from his long ride, and likely from fighting along the way, though he said little about that, despite Evelyn's promptings—she being eager for any kind of news of the war, even if it came from such an untrustworthy source. So, he'd retired early, after partaking of the scant food Evelyn had to offer, then picking out an unused bedroom upstairs.

Evelyn took advantage of his absence to have a whispered conversation with Hank and Mary out on the veranda, away from any possible eavesdroppers.

"What are we gonna do now, Miss Evel … uh … Miss Eve?" Hank asked, remembering to use her pseudonym, just in case.

"I don't know what he means to do here," Evelyn answered, "But I imagine it's nothing good; otherwise, he would've just ridden on to his own place, which is just a few miles away."

Hank nodded, but waited for her to say what was on her mind.

She was quiet and thoughtful for a few moments, then said, "Hank … I must ask you to do something that may be very dangerous," she finally said.

He snorted a mirthless chuckle. "I can't think of much I've done since meeting you that *hasn't* been dangerous," he said with a wry grin.

Mary rolled her eyes and nodded her agreement, but she did not share his grin.

"Can you ride?" Evelyn asked.

"Yes, a little," he answered. "Though I'm not too practiced. Occasionally, I'd have to help the grooms bring the horses round for Mr. Davis, so I got in a little riding that way. Why?"

"I'm sorry, but I can think of nothing else to try … It seems to me Walters means to set a trap for Colonel Chambers. I need you take our horse and ride back toward Richmond. On the way, you must ask every Union soldier you meet if he knows where the Twelfth West Virginia regiment may be found, and keep going until you locate him. Then tell him what's going on here."

"All right, but won't that just make him come here, like Walters wants?" Hank asked.

"Yes, but the difference is, he'll know what to expect and will come here prepared for a fight. Otherwise, he may ride in here and be caught unawares. In the meantime, the rest of us are in grave danger. Every day that goes by with Walters around is a great risk, so the sooner Nathan gets here the better."

"But, Miss Eve," Mary said, "won't Walters' men be watching the road, even in the dead of night? How will Hank get past them?"

"Yes, you're right about that, Mary. But I've already been thinking on it, and I know a way that likely won't be watched."

She described for Hank the trail that climbed Nathan's grandaddy's mountain, where she'd spent many happy hours with Nathan on her first visit to Mountain Meadows. Then she explained about the elk trail that went down the back side, instructing him to lead the horse down the steep trail—that it was difficult, but doable, Nathan and his men having successfully traversed that route in the past.

So waiting until midnight, having said his tearful goodbyes to Mary, Hank snuck out to the barn, saddled up the spare horse, and quietly led it out into the cotton field, now nothing but a vast weed patch across from the old slave cabins. Fortunately, there was enough moonlight to make his way to the trail Evelyn had described, up the mountain and down the back side. As dawn was breaking, shining its first rays directly into his face, he kicked the horse into a trot, headed east down the main road and headed back toward Virginia, a place he'd hoped never to see again.

And ... how on earth am I going to find one soldier in the middle of this great war? he wondered. He decided it was likely a fool's errand, but then he realized it was the only hope he had of saving Mary, Evelyn, and all the others. So he stiffened his resolve and carried on, determined to succeed in his mission, or die trying. At that moment, he couldn't decide which was the more likely outcome.

⁂

Sunday April 9, 1865 – Greenbrier County, West Virginia:

"Ah, Colonel Walters ... there you are," Evelyn said, as she stepped up to Walters where he stood at the top of the front steps. The sun was just peeking up over the hills to the east, and Evelyn had just overheard the very last few words of a conversation Walters was having with one of his men, who was sitting on a horse at the bottom of the stairs. Oddly, the man, whom she recognized as Captain Roberts, was no longer wearing a soldier's uniform and looked like a common laborer or farmer.

"Don't forget, Roberts ... tell the operator you don't want the city name on the telegraph. I don't want her to know where it came from," Walters instructed.

The man saluted and answered, "Yes, sir. I'll not forget." Then he tipped his hat to Evelyn, "Mornin' ma'am," he said, then pulled on the horse's reins and headed up the drive.

Evelyn couldn't puzzle out what it meant, but she suspected Walters was up to no good, whatever it was.

Walters turned to Evelyn. "Good morning, Miss Eve." And though the words were polite, she was not surprised there was no warmth in them, nor in his expression. "You were looking for me?"

"Yes, sir. I have most distressing news to share with you, and a favor to ask," she answered. "It seems my longtime butler was not as loyal as I'd believed ..."

"Oh?"

"Yes, Colonel ... When I awoke this morning, expecting him to attend to my morning meal—such as that may be, at the moment—he was nowhere to be found. So, I sent one of my maids to look for him. She came back all fretful, saying he'd run off, stealing my only horse to make his escape! Can you believe it, sir?"

Walters nodded. "Sadly, yes, I can. These creatures have no appreciation for our largess on their behalf. Stab us in the back first chance they get."

"So it would seem," she agreed. "I was wondering if any of your men had seen him ride off, sir …"

"No. No one came or went. My men watch the road, night and day, in case a Yankee patrol comes near. If they'd seen anyone, I would've been told. He must've slipped off across the fields in the night."

"Oh. Well, that's disappointing. I don't suppose you'd be willing to send a few of your men out to look for him? I'm most distressed about losing such valuable property, both the slave and the horse."

Walters just shook his head, "No ma'am … I'll not do that. Though I am sorry for your loss, I'll not risk my men chasing after one treacherous slave. There'll soon be Yankee cavalry on the main road, no doubt, and it'll not be safe for men of our persuasion."

Evelyn frowned, but then nodded. "Well, yes … I do understand, Colonel. And you're absolutely right, of course, now that I think on it. I feel silly and ashamed for having asked it of you, after all that you brave men have already done for our country. Good morning to you, sir."

He tipped his hat to her, then she turned and walked back into the house, closing the door softly behind her. And as she walked back toward the kitchen to take her breakfast, she smiled brightly.

❧☙❧☙❧☙

Monday April 10, 1865 – Wheeling, West Virginia:

Miss Abbey was excited when Sarah brought her a telegram from Nathan that had just been delivered by a courier, this time from the main telegraph office in downtown Wheeling, rather than from the governor's office, as was the usual case.

"Megs! Megs, where are you, dear?" Abbey called out after reading through it.

"I'm here, I'm coming," a familiar voice called out from down the hallway toward the kitchen.

In a moment, Megs appeared, wiping her hands on an apron tied around her waist.

"It's a telegram from Nathan," Abbey said, beaming.

"What's he say?" Megs asked as she stepped up in front of Abbey.

"Here, read it for yourself," Abbey said, handing over the sheet of paper.

Megs read:

> *April 10, 1865—11:45 a.m.*
>
> *Abigail Chambers:*
>
> *Momma, busy with impending action, so must be brief. Lee expected to surrender shortly, so war will soon end. Word is the Union will seize and auction off all unoccupied land owned by Confederate soldiers to pay the cost of the war. I fear MM will be mistaken for such because of its location, and we may lose it. As Lee is done for, roads are now safe. Please come to MM with all haste to claim the property. Bring only yourself, Margaret, and whomever else you may need to run the house, along with supply of food and other necessities. I will meet you there when I may.*
>
> *Nathaniel Chambers,*
> *Colonel, Twelfth West Virginia*

"Oh, Megs," Abbey gushed, "we can finally return to Mountain Meadows! Isn't it wonderful news?"

Megs scowled, "Yes, I suppose so."

"What is it, dear?" Abbey asked. "You don't look pleased."

"I don't know … Somethin' don't seem right, Abbey."

"What do you mean, dear?"

"This telegram … it's … *odd*, somehow," Megs answered with a thoughtful expression.

"Odd? How so?"

"Well, for one, why does he ask for Miss Margaret? Doesn't he know she's not here? That she's still in Richmond?" Megs asked.

"Hmm … maybe he thinks she's finally returned home. It would make sense, since she's now fully recovered, from all we've heard. She really has had no reason to remain there. I've wondered myself why she hasn't already returned home," Abbey answered.

"Maybe … but then why does it say 'come to MM'? Shouldn't it be 'go to MM?' And why does he sign it 'Colonel' when he was promoted to general a week or so ago?"

"Well, likely he wrote the thing in a hurry and made a few simple mistakes. And he's surely used to signing everything as a colonel and just forgot. Or perhaps the telegram operator made a mistake, since the promotion was so new."

Megs folded her arms. "But he never mentioned *me* coming along."

Abbey frowned. "I'm sorry, dear. I'm sure that hurts your feelings. But as I said, he was in haste, and likely meant nothing by it—a simple oversight. You should try not to take it personally. After all, you know how much he loves you. It's not like he hasn't said so on many occasions. Come on now, dear, we must pack and load up a wagon so we can leave first thing in the morning. Oh! I'm so excited! We're finally going home!"

Abbey headed up the stairs, but Megs stood where she was, unable to shake an uneasy feeling about the whole thing.

"Megs! Aren't you coming?" Abbey called from upstairs.

Finally, Megs shrugged, then called out, "Yes, I'm coming."

❧❦❧❦❧❦❧❦❧❦

"Edouard … Edouard! Oh, there you are," Abbey said, as she stepped into the small sitting room that was somewhat ironically referred to as the library, though it contained very few books.

He looked up from the newspaper he was reading, smiled and said, "Yes, I'm here, Abbey. What can I do for you, my dear?"

"Edouard, I just received a telegram from Nathaniel ... now that the war is over, he needs me to return to our old home at Mountain Meadows to reclaim it so the government doesn't auction it off as a Confederate property."

"Oh! And you wish for me to accompany you?" he asked, setting the paper to the side and beginning to rise.

"Uh ... no, that's not what I was thinking," she said, suddenly realizing she might hurt his feelings if she told him the truth—that she wouldn't trust him to protect her on the road, and she'd rather take a couple of the freemen. But what she said was, "I need you to stay here and be in charge of the farm."

"Oh," he said, settling back down into his seat. "Well, of course I will do anything you ask, Abbey, dear. But ... I haven't the slightest idea of how to run a farm."

She smiled, "Oh, don't you worry about that, Edouard. Just defer to Toby on anything to do with farming. The times being what they are, it's still best to have a white man seen as being in charge of a big place like this. It will avoid any sort of trouble that might otherwise arise."

"Ah, I see. So ... I shall *play* the king, while the parliament has all the *real* power?" he asked, with a grin that showed he did not feel insulted by it.

"Something like that," she answered, returning his smile. "Though, of course, I wouldn't ask it of you if I didn't have complete confidence in you in every regard," she added, to which he nodded in acknowledgment.

"Well, of course, certainly, I will do whatever you wish," he said. "But who then will you be taking with you?"

"Only the bare minimum to take charge of the house. We don't know how safe the roads may be, nor what supplies will be available for purchase once we arrive. So, I'm thinking just myself, Megs, and two armed freemen to drive a couple of wagons and provide protection. Hmm ... probably Phinney and Moses."

"Ah, yes ... that seems prudent to me," he agreed.

But when word spread throughout the farm, Rosa approached Abbey and said, "I'm coming too."

"Oh, I don't think so, dear—" Abbey began to answer, but paused, as Rosa's look said she was not going to take no for an answer.

"Miss Abbey ... whatever you may think of me, I am now family. Nathan is my brother, and Mountain Meadows is my home. I won't be left behind." She crossed her arms and frowned.

Abbey chuckled and smiled, reaching over to pat her on the arm. "You're right, Rosa," she answered.

"I am?" Rosa's frown turned to a look of surprise.

"Yes ... You *are* family now, my dear. So, of course you may come if you wish. But hurry up and pack. I wish to depart straightaway."

"Thank you, Miss Abbey!" she beamed, then hurried off to get ready.

⁂

Wednesday April 12, 1865 – Greenbrier County, West Virginia:

Evelyn sat on the veranda opposite Walters, sipping tea and trying to carry on a conversation, which was challenging with the man. She found he was extremely intelligent and knowledgeable on a broad range of subjects, but was anything but gregarious, making it difficult to keep the situation from devolving into an uncomfortable silence. However, she knew it was important, for all of their sakes, to keep up a good relationship with him in order to prevent him from finding any reason to harm them.

She was happy to finally be able to sit on a chair at a table. And she did have Walters to thank for that, as he had ordered some of his men to fashion the rough furniture from wood they'd scavenged around the farm.

Though she never quite felt comfortable around him—and she shuddered to think what might happen if none of his men were around—she had to admit that he had behaved respectfully since his arrival. If he were anyone else, she might've tried to win him over with her charm, and then attempted to talk him into surrendering and ending his war effort. But she knew better. She knew he intended to wait for Nathan and then to try to murder him.

And she had decided that if it came right down to it, and she had no other choice, she would do anything to stop him, including giving up her own life in the process.

"So, Colonel … out of curiosity—though, if you say it is none of my concern, I shall certainly understand—what are your plans for you and your men, sir? From the rumors I heard before fleeing the city, it seems the war has taken a turn for the worse … do you intend to keep fighting? Or is this simply a place to rest for a time before returning to your homes?"

Walters gazed at her thoughtfully for a moment, then said, "I expect the war is nearly over, as you say, and sadly not in our favor. As for my own plans … let's just say I intend to wait here for a spell. This place belonged to an old *friend* of mine, before the war. I plan to wait for his return, that we may … reconnect … and then settle some unfinished business. After that …" he shrugged. "Likely, I'll disband the unit, and we'll all return to our homes."

"Oh, how lovely and so very admirable of you to wait to see your old friend again. I am so gratified to hear it," she said, and smiled, though he only nodded in return.

Then he gave her an odd look, and said, "What about you, Miss Eve? What are your plans once the war is over?"

"Oh, well, I shall return to Richmond, I suppose. Though I can't imagine what I shall do, since my husband has been killed in the war, my home has been burned to the ground, and—assuming the Yankees will have won—I'll no longer be able to retain my slaves."

He nodded slowly, then said, "Well, I do own a considerable estate, not far from here. And … it just so happens that I too have lost a spouse during the course of the conflict."

"Oh, truly? I am so sorry for your loss," Evelyn answered, resisting a strong urge to shudder at the thought of where Walters was clearly heading with this conversation. She was now regretting telling him her husband had been killed in the conflict. She'd initially said it to evoke sympathy from Walters' men, but now she was thinking the potential threat of a living husband who was a general might've better served her.

She looked away from Walters's gaze, out toward the lawn, resting her eyes on the magnificent flowering magnolia out in the center of it.

Then, in an attempt to change the uncomfortable subject, she said a thing she immediately regretted: "Oh, Colonel Walters … have you ever seen a more beautiful sight. Why, that must be the most glorious magnolia I've ever beheld."

Walters looked over at it and nodded. "Yes … it is impressive. I can only imagine how greatly my old friend admires and treasures it."

Evelyn felt a sudden dread; Nathan loved that tree more than just about anything else on the farm, and she had just brought it to Walters' attention.

When she awoke the next morning and stepped out onto the veranda, her heart sank: the great magnolia lay across the lawn, its flowers scattered like snowflakes on the grass. It'd been chopped to the ground.

෨෦෬෪෨෦෬෪෨෦෬

Thursday April 13, 1865 – Appomattox, Virginia:

Nathan leaned back in his chair, smiling as he blew a puff of cigar smoke toward the ceiling of his tent. He found he was greatly enjoying the company of Captain Gareth Hughes of the Nineteenth Massachusetts, who'd stopped in to pay his respects.

Though they'd seen each other recently in Richmond and Petersburg, this was the first time they'd been able to relax and just talk about their various adventures during the war. Gareth also shared stories about his parents and their family up in Boston, and Nathan's tales served to satisfy Gareth's curiosity concerning Evelyn, whom he had never met, despite the obvious family connection. The two men were of a similar age, belonged to the same upper class of society, and were fellow Virginians. And clearly, they were of the same mind concerning the current conflict and the evils of slavery, so they had much in common.

197

Their pleasurable interlude was suddenly interrupted when Tony poked his head in at the tent flap, and said, "Hello, Captain … Oh, sorry, didn't know you had company, sir."

"Tony, come on in," Nathan said, standing to greet him.

"*Captain?*" Gareth asked, looking at Nathan.

Nathan grinned, and said, "Tony's one of my men from the old days at Mountain Meadows. Everyone just called me 'Captain' back then, and now it feels odd for them to call me anything else."

"Ah," Gareth said, then stood to shake Tony's hand and introduce himself.

Tony smiled, "Well, if I was a *proper* sergeant, I would always call you 'general,' sir," he said as he took a proffered seat.

Nathan waved the comment off. "Tony is also my future brother-in-law, as he is betrothed to my half-sister Rosa."

"Oh, well, congratulations on that, Tony. I suppose now that the war's over, the wedding will be imminent?" Gareth asked.

But Tony shrugged. "Reckon so," he answered, then looked at Nathan and grinned. "Likely whenever Rosa says, that's when it'll be."

Nathan snorted a laugh. "I know the feeling."

Sergeant Nichols poked his head in at the tent flap. "Sorry to disturb you, sirs," he said. "But … well, General, I don't know if it's important, but there's a fellow out here … a civilian freeman, sir … says he must speak with you straightaway. Claims it's most urgent."

"Oh? Did he say what it was concerning?"

"No, not really … Something about a lady … hmm … I forget the name he mentioned … Ethel? Emma? *Eva?*"

Nathan's eyes widened and he sat up straight, "*Evelyn?*"

"Yes … that's it!" the sergeant said, scratching at his chin whiskers.

Nathan leapt to his feet. "Where is this fellow?"

"Uh, just outside, sir, uh—"

Nathan was out the tent door before the sergeant could finish his sentence, with Gareth and Tony fast on his heels. Harry the Dog, who'd been asleep under the table, jumped up and followed.

Just outside, they found a tall, handsome, strong-looking black man, whose only indication of his age was a slight graying at the temples. He was dressed in simple traveling clothes and held a horse by its lead.

Nathan knew the man instantly, from his recent visit to Evelyn's hideout in Richmond.

"*Hank!* Well met … but what are you doing here?" Nathan asked, extending his hand and exchanging a firm handshake, then quickly making introductions to the other two men.

"Colonel Chambers … you have no idea how happy I am to see *you* again, sir … Though I see by the star on your sleeve, you're now a general."

"Yes, that only happened a short time ago. How is it you're here, Hank, and what news have you of Evelyn?"

"She is presently at your old farm, sir. A place just over the hills in West Virginia, that she called 'Mountain Meadows.' We fled there with a dozen other former slaves when Richmond was in flames. She sent me out from there to find you, sir."

"Oh! Well, that's good news, I—" Nathan trailed off as he noticed Hank held a dark frown. "What is it, Hank? Is ought amiss?"

"Yes, sir, you could say that. We'd only been at your place a couple days when a troop of Confederate soldiers rode up, led by a stern looking fellow in a colonel's uniform."

Nathan frowned at this news, but the next words from Hank froze his heart.

"The man was missing his left hand …" Hank said, gazing intently at Nathan for a reaction.

"*Walters* …" Nathan said in barely more than a whisper.

Tony scowled, and said, "*Damn.*"

"Yes, sir. I suspected it was so when I first laid eyes on him, from stories I'd heard from Miss Evelyn," Hank continued. "Then, once he'd arrived at the house, she confirmed it. She sent me to find you so's I could warn you. She believes he means to ambush you whenever you return home."

"Walters holds Evelyn captive, then?" Nathan asked.

"Well, not exactly. Seems he doesn't rightly recognize her, with her hair dyed black, and all. He thought she looked familiar, but couldn't quite place her, so she's convinced him they met at some ball or other over to Richmond."

"Ah. Well, that's hopeful, anyway. Though the man certainly can't be trusted to behave as any sort of gentleman."

Nathan turned to Nichols, "Sergeant, has Colonel Clark returned yet from Richmond with the supply wagons?"

"Well, no, sir. I heard he ain't expected until day after tomorrow … at the earliest. Could be longer …"

"*Damn it!* I can't wait for him … hmm. Sergeant, run on over to the Twelfth's camp and fetch all the other officers … Tell them I need them at my command tent post haste … that it's a most dire emergency. Tell them to come mounted, with guns, ammunition, and food for a two-day ride. And have them bring a dozen or so of their best riders, fully armed and ready for a fight."

"Sir!" Nichols saluted, then sprinted off to do as he was bid.

"I'm going with you, if you'll have me," Gareth said, unholstering his pistol, and examining its cylinders to confirm it was fully loaded.

"Count me in," Tony said. He too carried a pistol at his hip. "Though, I ain't got a horse."

"Thanks, men. I appreciate that," Nathan said. "I'll send someone over to your camps to let your commanders know that I've borrowed you. And I'll get you a horse, Tony. Do you still remember how to ride?"

"Yes, sir," he answered. "You recall we did plenty of riding that time down in the Kanawha Valley when them rebs invaded. Don't expect my backside will soon forget …" He rolled his eyes and mimed rubbing a sore buttock.

Nathan nodded, but was in no mood for levity.

Then, looking back at Hank, he noticed for the first time the weariness in the man's eyes.

"You're exhausted. That must've been one hell of a ride to find me. Have you slept or eaten?"

Hanks shrugged. "Not much. Started out three days ago with a few hard tack biscuits in my pocket. Have only stopped to rest when there wasn't even enough moonlight to ride. Thought I'd have to ride all the way to Richmond or beyond to find you, but some soldiers steered me here. Though they knew nothing of you or the Twelfth, they said most of the Union Army was here, so I figured it was worth a look."

"Well, come on into my tent and rest a spell," Nathan said. "I'll have someone fetch you a meal while we get organized. Will you ride back with us, or would you prefer to stay here and recuperate?"

Hank scowled. "You'd have to tie me to a tree to keep me from coming with you, General—they've got Mary. Besides, I owe Miss Evelyn for my freedom, so there ain't much I can think of I wouldn't do on her account."

Nathan nodded. "Good man."

"I would borrow a pistol from you, if I could," Hank added. "Miss Evelyn trained me up on how to use one, though I've not had much practice, I have to confess. Still, better to have something to fight with, if it comes to it."

"Agreed," Nathan replied. "We'll get you a side arm and ammunition. Don't get too comfortable, then; we ride within the hour."

A half-hour of anxious pacing later, Nathan's men arrived bristling with weapons and ready for battle: Jim Wiggins, William, Stan, Billy, Zeke, and Ollie Boyd. And they'd brought with them fifteen of Billy's skirmishers and scouts from the Twelfth.

When he saw them arrive, Nathan groaned inwardly, knowing he had a problem to deal with that he hadn't anticipated.

He immediately drew Jim aside, and said, "Jim … I don't know how to say this other than to just say it: you can't come on this one."

"What!? You can't leave me out o' this fight, sir!"

"Look, Jim, I don't have time to argue. Evelyn's life is at stake, and every minute we spend here puts her at greater risk."

"But, Captain—"

"Jim … you're one of the best fighters I've ever known, but you're no longer the best *rider*. I would fight beside you anytime … but not this time; this isn't your fight. We've got to ride fast and hard … all day and all night, if there's any light at all to see by. And at the end of the ride, it's going to be a fight at the farm: in and out of buildings, up and down stairways …"

Jim scowled, but slowly nodded.

"Look, if it helps, Tom can't come either … He's not back from Richmond yet, and I can't wait for him. So you stay and tell him what happened. Then you two can just sit this one out together."

"Ah … well, that'll at least make it more tolerable," Jim groused.

"Come, my old friend … wish me good hunting, and hold down the fort while I'm gone. I hear the telegraph at Lewisburg is now working … I'll send word as soon as I may," Nathan said.

"All right … all right, fine. I'll stay. But, *Nathan* …"

The two met eyes, and it was not lost on Nathan that Jim had just used his given name for the first time in all the years they'd known each other.

"Godspeed to you … and do me a favor … Just go ahead and *blow that son of a bitch's head clean off!*" Jim swore, then spit to the side to emphasize his point.

Nathan reached out and patted Jim on the shoulder. "I will," he answered.

When Hank realized they were about to start out from Appomattox with just twenty armed men, knowing that Walters had almost forty, he turned to Nathan and said, "General Chambers … not that it's my place to tell you your business, but … is it wise to take so few men? Walters has nearly twice your numbers."

Before Nathan could pull the unlit cigar from his mouth to answer, the gigantic man named Stan snorted a laugh and answered for him: "Is no matter number of lambs, wolf still wins fight."

Hank knew that Walters' men were also experienced fighters, hardly lambs. But now, watching the general's men prepare for action, in their stern, businesslike manner, he began to believe the big man might be right.

Saturday April 15, 1865 – Greenbrier County, West Virginia:

Abbey's heart soared as the wagon crested the hill and she saw her beloved home for the first time in four years. She squealed with delight, gripping Megs' arm and sharing a bright smile.

She immediately turned and looked back over her shoulder at the wagon following and caught Rosa's eye, where she sat up next to young Moses, who was driving. Rosa too was beaming, and waved at Abbey.

As they moved down into the valley and passed the first of the old slave cabins, their happiness turned to concern, as two mounted men, who'd been concealed behind one of the buildings, suddenly rode out onto the drive behind them and began to follow. And not just any men … these men had pistols at their hips and wore Confederate uniforms.

Abbey and Megs shared a concerned look, and Phinney, who was driving their wagon, said in low tones, "Don't like the look o' this, Miss Abbey …"

She could not disagree with his assessment, but could think of nothing to say, so she just nodded. Clearly, they had no choice but to continue on to the house. Abbey was hopeful that there was an officer in charge of these men, whom she might be able to reason with. After all, Nathan said the war was basically over, but it might be that some scattered units hadn't yet received the word.

When the wagons came to a stop at the front of the house, and the door opened, all Abbey's earlier hopes were dashed. Elijah Walters stepped out and stood at the head of the stairs, gazing at her with his eerie blank expression.

Though she found him personally detestable, and wished to be a thousand miles from the man, Evelyn was determined to keep as close a watch on Walters as possible. Her most immediate concern was that he might mistreat one of the former slaves, or order it done, and she wanted to be able to intervene as necessary. And then, there was her fear that Hank would be unable to locate

Nathan, and so he might just show up suddenly, falling victim to an ambush by his old enemy. She was determined to prevent that from happening, if she could.

So when she saw Walters gazing out the window for several minutes, then suddenly stride out the front door, she immediately stood up from where she sat in the library and followed. When she stepped up behind him, she had to suppress a gasp of shock. Two wagons had pulled up next to the hitching post, surrounded by a half dozen of Walters' men on horseback, pistols drawn.

Two black men who'd been driving the wagons sat with their hands in the air as soldiers on foot stepped up to the wagons and disarmed them. Evelyn recognized one of the drivers, who was missing his right arm, as Phinney. The other was a very young man—a teenager, most likely, she decided—but Evelyn didn't remember him. He'd likely been but a child when she'd briefly lived at Mountain Meadows four years earlier.

The thing that made her heart feel like lead was seeing Miss Abbey and Megs in the first wagon and Rosa in the second. Abbey's face was a mask of fear and shock as she sat staring at Walters. No one spoke, but one of Walters' men did assist Abbey down from her wagon. The two black women were left to their own devices, not surprisingly.

Abbey walked toward the house like a person in a trance, staring at Walters as she came. Megs followed closely behind her. When Abbey reached the bottom of the stairs, she paused, then slowly climbed up to the veranda until she stood directly in front of Walters, only a few feet from him. Even so, neither spoke. Evelyn hoped to catch Abbey's eye and somehow communicate that she should feign non-acquaintance.

Then Abbey suddenly looked at Evelyn, seeming to notice her for the first time. She cried, "*Evelyn!* Oh, no—not you too!" Abbey covered her mouth in shock.

Walters slowly turned toward Evelyn, a curious expression on his face. "*Evelyn?*" he said. He gazed at her for a long moment, looking thoughtful. Then the barest hint of a smile seemed to touch the corners of his eyes. "Ah … now I remember … only you had *blonde* hair, then." He chuckled mirthlessly. "Not Miss *Eve* at all … but Miss *Evelyn*, Chambers' mistress. Oh, this is rich … good fortune beyond my wildest imagining — to bag the mother and the whore at the same time."

Then he turned back to Abbey as another thought seemingly occurred to him. "And where is Margaret, Abigail?"

"Margaret? Whatever do you mean, Mr. Walters?" she answered with a puzzled expression.

"Don't play games with me, witch. I know Margaret was living at your farm in Wheeling. I saw her there with my own eyes, so don't bother to deny it. I ask you again … Where is she?"

"Safely away from you," Abbey shot back.

Without warning, Walters lashed out and backhanded her across the face, knocking her a step backward. Megs stepped up and caught her before she could stumble. Abbey glared at Walters as she rubbed her face.

"There is nowhere that is safe from me. Tell me where she is, or I will not bother to hit *you* next, I'll hit that old hag slave that's with you. And not so gently, I promise you that …"

"Miss Margaret went back to Richmond, master," Megs said, bowing her head respectfully, gazing at the boards of the veranda. "Master Chambers … he said he'd grown tired of her. So … he sent her away, master."

"Ah … there, you see, Abigail. The slave has more sense than you have. Hmm … so, he grew bored of using the faithless wench. Well, one can hardly blame him for that. She was not much of a woman to speak of. Still, one must claim one's own or people will think they can step all over you. Don't you agree, Abigail?"

She shrugged, "You don't care what I think on it anyway."

"True enough," he responded.

"So, it was your telegram that lured us here," Abbey said. "What do you mean to do with us? Murder us for some kind of revenge against Nathan? You must know he'll just hunt you down and kill you for it."

"I'm counting on it … In fact, I intend to send him a telegram this very day, inviting him to come. But he won't be coming here to kill me. He'll be coming to make a trade. His life, for yours … and now his mistress, too, I suppose," he said, glancing over at

Evelyn. "Though, that may cost him more … The lives of several of his men from Texas?" Then he held up the stub of his left arm, "Perhaps the ones who did *this* to me …"

Evelyn could see that Abbey was wide-eyed with fear, but to her credit, she continued to stand up to Walters. "You don't have to do this, Elijah," she said, still rubbing at her face, which now bore a red mark where Walters had struck her.

"Do *what*?" Walters asked, tilting his head quizzically as he gazed at her.

"This … this *thing* with Nathan … the two of you determined to kill each other," she answered. "You don't have to do it. The war is over, for all practical purposes. So many horrible things have happened the last four years … if you were to just ride out of here and go home … send your men home, too … then whatever has happened before will be forgiven, if not forgotten entirely. Swept away with the passage of the war. You can start anew, rebuild your farm as we rebuild ours. You don't have to keep killing. It can finally be over."

Walters didn't immediately answer, gazing up into the sky above Abbey's head. For a brief moment, Evelyn thought his features softened, and she held out a sliver of hope that he might do as Abbey suggested and just leave them in peace.

Then he looked back down at Abbey and his features hardened again as he slowly shook his head. "Abigail, I've done so much killing these last four years, I wouldn't know how to stop. Chambers and I … we are alike in that … this has to end with one of us dead. There's no other way."

Then he looked over at his men and said, "Roberts, take charge of these slaves, and distribute their food and other supplies to the men. I will personally deal with these white witches. Then, round up the other slaves that belong to Miss Evelyn. I'll not have them running around loose causing mischief."

"Yes, sir. And what shall we do with them?"

Walters thought for a moment, then nodded. "Hmm … put the women in one of the barns and place a guard on them. They may yet give us service once our business here is concluded. Especially that pretty one over there," he said, leering at Rosa, who wisely stared straight at the ground with no expression.

"Very good, sir. And the slave *men?*"

"Take them out in the field under heavy guard. Have them dig a very large hole."

Roberts raised an eyebrow, but then nodded and said, "Yes, sir."

❧❧❧❧❧❧❧❧❧

Ten black men dug in the knee-deep hole as the Confederate soldiers kept watch. And though Phinney had offered to take a turn, the soldiers had laughed at him, on account of his disability, making him sit to the side, saying he would only slow things down.

Which is likely true, he thought glumly, as he reached up with his remaining left arm to wipe a bead of sweat that streamed down his face and into his eyes. Even though he knew they were literally digging their own graves, he still felt bad for not being able to do his part. The hole was now six or seven feet long and about ten feet wide, so Phinney figured they were nearly half done with it.

Any thought the black men had of extending their lives by digging more slowly was strongly discouraged by the sour expressions of their stern overseers: ten armed soldiers, two of whom had brought out bull whips, which so far had not been used.

And though Phinney had briefly considered somehow trying to overpower their guards and take their weapons, he knew it would only get them killed sooner, and likely whipped as well for their efforts. These were experienced soldiers, and they were prepared for any trouble, with loaded weapons held at the ready.

Surprisingly, Phinney found that he wasn't afraid, and that he didn't feel sorry for himself. He decided he was likely the oldest of this bunch, at something over thirty years, and figured he'd lived long enough to experience being a free man, something he'd never thought possible when he was younger. And though he'd lost an arm in the process, he felt pride in having also fought for his own freedom, so he reckoned he'd actually earned it.

He did feel sorry for the younger men, however. They had more life ahead of them, especially Moses, who was still a teen. That was a bitter pill, he decided.

Phinney thought back to the day when he'd lost his arm, when Doctor William had removed it. Then he smiled at the memory of William talking him into going through with the painful procedure by making Phinney envision a future where he'd get to bounce grandchildren on his knee while gazing across at his loving wife. And then a surge of hope welled up in his breast, and for some inexplicable reason, he suddenly felt that he wasn't going to die this day after all, and he said a quick prayer of thanks to God for his salvation, and that of the other black men with him.

And then, as if in answer to his prayer, he heard the sound of pounding hooves and a man shouting.

He looked up just as a rider, one of the rebel soldiers, pulled up to a hard stop, shouting, "Sarge! Yankee soldiers come—a mounted cavalry patrol led by a Brigadier General. Captain Roberts says to come now!"

"All right, what about these fellas?" the sergeant asked. "Shall we go ahead and shoot 'em now?"

The man shook his head. "Up to you, Sarge, but I wouldn't. We may need all the ammo we got. We can deal with 'em after we deal with the Yankees."

The sergeant glanced over at the black men, who'd wisely kept shoveling, as if nothing at all unusual was happening. The sergeant turned back to his men. "Barnes, you keep watch over 'em 'til we get back. The rest of you, come with me," he shouted. All but Private Barnes trotted off toward the house, rifles at the ready.

Barnes, who had a pistol at his hip, a rifle in his hands, and sour look on his face, said, "Y'all just keep on a diggin' … don't matter none what's happenin' back up at the house." He sat down a few yards back from the hole where he could keep a good watch over the proceedings, but not so close that the men might take a chance on rushing him. Phinney stood a few feet away trying to be inconspicuous, not daring to sit, for fear of invoking the man's wrath.

It crossed Phinney's mind that between the rifle and the pistol, Barnes had only seven shots, and there were eleven black men. But still, it'd be a desperate thing to attack him, and many of them would die. But at the thought of assaulting their guard, he realized that the man was paying him very little mind. To the rebels, Phinney was, after all, just a crippled black man, so not much of a threat nor worthy of any concern. Then he noticed several extra shovels laying on the ground behind Barnes, and it gave him an idea.

The only one of the men Phinney knew was Moses, so he stared at the boy until Moses noticed and glanced back, though he wisely continued to shovel without pause. Phinney mimed setting the shovel down and then rolled his eyes.

Moses nodded slightly. Then he stopped digging, set the blade of his shovel on the ground and leaned on the handle, wiping his brow as he did.

"Hey … what you think you're doin' there, boy," Barnes snarled.

Moses just scowled at him. "What difference it gonna make, *master*," he said, in a sarcastic tone. "Y'all's gonna kill us all anyways."

Barnes jumped to his feet and took a step closer to the hole, leveling his rifle at Moses, "Yeah, well maybe I'll just kill you right now, boy!"

But at that moment, something crashed down on the top of Barnes's head and he crumpled to the ground, lifeless. Phinney stood behind him, scowling fiercely, a blood-covered shovel held tightly in his left hand.

He tossed down the shovel, then knelt down and grabbed the rifle, immediately tossing it over to Moses. Then Phinney unbuckled the man's gun belt and took it, strapping it around his own waist before unholstering the revolver and spinning the cylinder to make sure it was fully loaded.

Then he said, "C'mon fellas … and just bring them shovels; at least they's some kinda weapon. We gotta do what we can …"

"But what's it mean, Phin … them Union soldiers comin'?" Moses asked.

Phinney smiled. "It means the Captain has returned, and you can bet he gonna kill him some rebs."

And then, as they sprinted toward the house, they heard gunshots ring out in the near distance.

Chapter 11. Battle of Mountain Meadows

"Whenever you are offered violence, fight back!
The aggressor does not fear the law,
so he must be taught to fear you.
Whatever the risk,
and at whatever the cost, fight back!"
- Lt. Colonel Jeff Cooper, USMC

Saturday April 15, 1865 – Greenbrier County, West Virginia:

"All right, Sergeant, the telegram's ready. Go find Captain Roberts and tell him, 'same drill as before.' He'll need to put civilian clothes on, then ride over to the telegraph office in Lewisburg," Walters said, folding the sheet of paper and handing it across to Sergeant Slater.

"Yes, sir," Slater said, taking the note with a nod, then turning and exiting the library, heading for the front door. As he stepped up to grasp the handle, the door suddenly flung wide and he nearly collided with Captain Roberts, who was just coming in.

"Oh! Beg pardon, sir," Slater said, stepping aside as Roberts rushed past, not bothering to acknowledge him.

Roberts went straight to the library where Walters sat, now looking up expectantly. "Colonel, sir ... Riders approach!" Roberts gasped while trying to catch his breath. "Union cavalry ... twenty, we counted. Led by a brigadier. They'll be here in minutes."

"A general? What'd he look like?" Walters asked.

"Tall ... dark haired ... mean-looking fellow."

"*Chambers* ..." Walters muttered. Then he looked back up at Roberts.

"Yes, sir ... I reckon so, on account o' he's got an Indian and a giant man with him, even as you've described," Roberts responded.

Walters stood up, "Damn him … Why is he here so soon? No time to even set up an ambush … not that it would've done much good against *his* men."

He was thoughtful for a moment, then said, "Roberts, get back out there and get the men positioned to defend this house. Sergeant Slater, you stay here and help guard the prisoners. I still intend to use them to my advantage …"

Roberts saluted, then rushed back out to do as he was bid.

Walters went out into the foyer to where he could gaze out the front window at the driveway beyond. Slater followed, respectfully hanging back a few steps. *You still won't win, Chambers … Even if you get past all my men, I've still got your women,* Walters thought as he turned and walked down the hallway that led to the kitchen where he'd locked up Miss Abbey and Evelyn.

"Come, Slater," he said as he strode down the hallway.

෨ාෲ෨ාෲ෨ාෲ

Evelyn paced back and forth in the kitchen, debating with herself about what to do. She still held the tiny .22 caliber Smith and Wesson revolver up her sleeve and the stiletto strapped to her thigh, but those would only serve as a last-ditch measure under the most dire circumstances, and were of little use for breaking out of the locked room in which they currently found themselves prisoners. The outer door had been locked with a key, while the inner door had been wedged closed from the hallway side with a chunk of wood. Evelyn had already tried forcing it, but it wouldn't budge.

She stopped and gazed over at Abbey, sitting at the small kitchen table where the maids and cooks used to take their meals. "You're sure you haven't another key secreted in this room somewhere?" Evelyn asked.

"No, dear … and I haven't grown one since the last time you asked," Abbey responded with a frown.

"Sorry, Miss Abbey … nerves …"

"Yes, I feel the same, dear," Abbey responded. "Walters took the only key I had before locking us in here. I thought about trying to keep it from him, but didn't relish the thought of another hard slap across the face."

"Oh, no … of course not!" Evelyn replied. "Sorry … I didn't mean to imply you should've done anything different. It's just … being locked in here, I feel so … helpless. At the mercy of a madman. And our dear freemen out there … digging that hole. There *must* be something we can do."

"I agree with you," Abbey said, "but I can't think of *what* … If we try to somehow break the glass on the door, or force the lock, it will make way too much noise. Walters or one of his men will surely hear it. Then he may decide to bind us as well. That would be most unpleasant."

"Yes, you're right about that, I fear," Evelyn agreed.

"Please, dear … come sit," Abbey said. "Save your strength. Perhaps some opportunity will present itself."

Evelyn sighed and nodded, but before she could take a seat at the table, they heard a scraping noise behind the door, and then the handle turning. The door opened, and Walters stepped inside, followed by one of his men.

Walters stopped and gazed at Abbey for a moment, then over at Evelyn. "Take the girl," he said to his man. "We'll leave the old lady for now."

"Who're you calling *old?*" Abbey snapped.

Walters looked at her and smiled slightly. "Well, at least you've got some spunk, Abigail. Not that it'll do you any good in the end."

Then he looked at Evelyn again, stepped out of the doorway and gestured toward the hallway, "Come, unless you'd prefer to be dragged," he said.

Evelyn looked back at Abbey and gave her a smile that she meant to be reassuring, though she wasn't sure if she had pulled it off. Then she turned and stepped out into the hall, led by the sergeant. Walters followed behind.

She didn't know what Walters intended, but she feared the worst. And once again, her thoughts strayed to the pistol up her sleeve, and she mentally prepared herself for the moment she might have to use it.

Abbey sat alone at the kitchen table gazing out through the small window in the outer door, worried about what Walters was doing with Evelyn. Why had he taken her? Had something happened? She tried to think if Walters had looked worried or stressed, but the man's expression was so inscrutable that she really had no idea what he was thinking or what he was feeling, if he ever felt anything.

And as she sat, stewing about what might happen next, a loud noise made her start. *Gunfire! Multiple shots … A gunfight? Oh, what is happening?* she wondered, jumping to her feet and rushing to the window to see if there was anything to be seen. But she could see nothing from the small window but the wide lawn and the distant trees beyond.

And then her heart sank as she thought of the black men sent out to dig a large hole in the fields … their own grave. *No, not a gunfight,* she decided. *He's killed them, the monster. Poor, dear Phinney and bright, young Moses. What a horrible beast he is,* she thought, and began to tear up as she turned away from the view.

But then she heard an odd shuffling noise at the door, so she turned back to have a look, and jumped in startlement: a face appeared in the window, staring back at her. It was a black man's face, and one she knew well: *Phinney!*

She heard the doorknob rattle, and then Phinney said, "Stand back from the door, Miss Abbey. We gonna get you outta there."

She did as she was bid and stood back by the table as she heard a grinding, squealing sound at the door. Suddenly, with a metallic *bang,* the door popped outward. Phinney poked his head in, "Come, Miss Abbey. I'm sure they done heard *that.* We gots t'get movin'!"

Abbey needed no convincing. Doing as she was bid, she rushed out the door, then down the short flight of steps to the lawn level where the outdoor ovens stood in their own small, low-ceilinged brick building. But Phinney led her at a sprint, along with the other black men, shovels in hand, headed out toward the woods. She realized it'd been the shovels she'd heard, prying the door open. As she ran, she heard more gunfire ring out behind her, this time much closer to hand.

Elijah Walters gazed out the front window of the Big House, watching for the arrival of Chambers and his men down the drive, but so far there was nothing to be seen.

He glanced over at Evelyn where she sat in the library. Sergeant Slater stood watch over her, pistol in hand. Walters meant to use her against Chambers in the end—her and Miss Abbey. He looked back up the drive but still could see no one.

Walters felt a sudden chill of fear. *If Chambers won't show himself, how can I use the hostages against him? If I walk outside with them, that damned Indian will put an arrow in me before I ever see him. No, I'll have to stay inside the house and wait for Chambers to come to me*, he decided.

In the meantime, he figured it was always possible his men might win the gun battle. After all, based on the numbers Chambers had reportedly brought with him, the odds were in Walters' favor almost two to one.

Then he heard a loud noise in the back of the house—not a gunshot, but more like … a door slamming? He'd made sure all the doors except the front one were locked, and even nailed shut, not wanting to take any chances on one of Chambers' men sneaking in and getting at him. What had that noise been? And then he thought of Miss Abbey locked in the kitchen; the sound he'd heard had come from that direction. Perhaps Miss Abbey was trying to break out of the room, though he thought it highly unlikely that she would succeed. Still, best to check, he decided.

So he strode down the hallway to the kitchen. The door was still wedged shut, but there was also an outer door. He opened the inner door and immediately saw that the outer door had been pried open, and Miss Abbey was gone. He rushed to the doorway and gazed out. Abbey was running across the lawn led by a one-armed black man and several other black men carrying shovels, which they'd obviously used to pry open the door.

Damn them, he thought, as he unholstered his revolver. He aimed and fired. One of the black men fell, though he'd aimed for Miss Abbey. He fired again but missed. They were nearing the woods at the edge of the lawn, so he fired four more shots in quick succession, but all missed. He re-holstered his pistol in disgust, then pushed the door closed. Though the lock was now broken, he grabbed the wooden wedge he'd used to lock the inner door, and now used it to force the outer door closed.

He returned to the front entrance of the house, noting that Evelyn was still safely held in the library. He took one last glance out the window, then stepped back, realizing he might be targeted through the glass if any of Chambers' men were lurking outside. He stepped over to the front door, opened it a crack, and called out, "Captain Roberts … to me!"

A few moments later, Captain Roberts slipped in the door, pushing it closed behind him. "They're still coming down the drive, sir," he said. "Just beyond that large oak tree before the slave cabins."

Walters nodded. "Roberts, I've been thinking … Chambers, being an academy-trained officer, is most likely to try a flanking attack. Position our men all around the house, using whatever cover there is. Or have them lay prone on the grass, if necessary. And send some out into the gardens and woods beyond the lawn. Chambers' men like to sneak around through the brush, and may try to get at us from there. We must be ready for an attack from any direction."

"Yes, sir! I'll see that it's done," Roberts said, then rushed back out the door.

And then, as if in response to Walters' fears, he heard gunfire outside … multiple gunshots from back up the drive by the slave cabins. The battle for Mountain Meadows had begun.

❧❧❧❧❧❧❧❧❧

"Here they come … Get ready …" Private Aaron Cahill whispered to his comrade, Peter Redman, as the two of them aimed their rifles at the approaching riders from their position behind a hedgerow alongside the driveway at Mountain

Meadows farm. Cahill took careful aim, targeting the big man riding in front dressed in a Union general's uniform. They hadn't discussed it, but he hoped Peter would target one of the others, so they'd not waste a shot aiming at the same rider.

Instead of an answer from Peter, Cahill heard an odd *thunk* sound, followed by something hitting the ground. He looked over toward his friend but couldn't believe what he was seeing: Peter lay slumped over on the ground, his eyes closed and the shaft of an arrow sticking out from his chest.

"Hey—" Cahill started to call out, but his breath was cut off, and he was slammed backward against the tree trunk behind him. The force of the impact caused him to yank on the trigger, and the rifle fired before he dropped it to the ground. He glanced down and saw another, even larger arrow sticking out from the middle of his chest. In that moment, he realized that he'd been pinned to the tree behind him, even as a wave of pain washed over him and his vision began to fade. The last thing he saw before all went black was an enormous man dressed in a Union officer's uniform leaning down in front of him, taking ahold of the arrow shaft, and yanking.

۞۞۞۞۞۞۞۞۞

As Stan yanked his arrow free, another gunshot rang out, this one a pistol coming from one of the cabins. A bullet impacted near his right boot, kicking gravel up onto his pant leg. He dropped the arrow, pulled his revolver, and returned fire, but his round impacted on the door frame of the cabin. He ducked behind the tree trunk where he'd killed the rebel even as another round impacted against the other side of it.

He saw a flash of motion out of the corner of his eye, then looked back out in time to see Billy rushing up to the cabin. When Billy reached the front step, he slid up next to the open window from which the shots had come, then leaned in and fired two quick shots. He turned and signaled Stan to come.

Stan sprinted over to join Billy, but was greeted by more gunfire as he ran. He returned fire, then ducked under cover even as Billy moved in the direction of the new threat. Then, while Billy

217

held the shooter's attention, Stan rushed up and crashed through the door, firing his pistols as he went, taking out another assailant.

After several more minutes of moving through the cabins in a similar leapfrog fashion, and having eliminated a half dozen enemy combatants, they concluded that the area was now secure just in time to greet Nathan and the rest of the company coming down the driveway.

ๆฆยฉยฉฉฉฎฌฌฌฆยฉยฉฉฉฎฌฌฆยฉยฉฉ

"Hello, General. While you were having nice little ride, Billy and I have been here working," he grinned, which Nathan acknowledged with a tip of his hat as he and the rest of the company dismounted and began securing the horses, tying them to bushes and trees near the cabins.

"Have killed six here by cabins," Stan said, "so, it is leaving … hmm … thirty-two still, if Hank's numbers are right. Oh, and Walters, of course, which makes thirty-three."

"The numbers are correct," Hank answered. "Miss Evelyn counted them herself, and she made sure I had it exact, knowing it might be important to y'all when you came."

Stan nodded his head respectfully in acknowledgment.

Nathan nodded. "Good work, Stan … Billy. I expect these were just a skirmish line, hoping they might pick off a few of us, but mostly so they'd know we're here. Likely Walters has got the rest of his men back guarding the Big House. Still, we should send a small reconnaissance group to check all the outbuildings, just to be sure."

"So, what is the plan, General?" Zeke asked. "Should we divide into groups, left, right, and center, then try'n flank 'em, do you think?"

Nathan stuck a cigar in his mouth and chewed on it for a moment. "No. Firstly, it's what he'll expect us to do, so he'll be ready for it. And secondly, he's got Evelyn in there, and possibly other hostages. If we try a flanking maneuver, we'll have to direct most of our gunfire inward toward the house. The risk to our own people inside is too great.

218

"But if we hit them with an all-out frontal assault instead, we can push through to the front steps, then work our way around the house from there. That way, our gunfire will be parallel to, or away from, the house after the initial push. Gentlemen, we must endeavor to avoid hitting the house with gunfire unless the enemy is actually firing at us from within. And even then, we must take careful aim at our intended targets. During that initial assault, be sure to aim low. Is that understood?"

He looked around the group and was gratified by the serious looks he received and the nods of understanding.

"Once we reach the front steps, I'll go inside to free the hostages while the rest of you clear the outside."

"I'm coming with you," Stan said.

"No. I must do *that* alone," Nathan answered with a frown.

"Alone, Captain?" Stan asked. "But why? Seems to me if we rush into the house, we will have him outnumbered by many. Maybe he just gives up, then ..."

"No. He'll never give up. He'll die first. And ... thank you, but no. I must do it alone. If anything were to happen to the hostages, it should be on my head, and mine alone. If anyone else were to cause it ..." He looked hard at Stan, until the latter nodded his understanding.

Then he looked down at Harry the Dog. "Plus, I'll need you to look after Harry, Stan. He can't come into the house either."

Then Nathan looked over at Stan's companion and said, "Billy, take five of your men and make sure the outbuildings are clear, then meet us back at the house." Billy nodded his understanding, then turned and pointed to five of his scouts before trotting off.

Nathan turned back to the rest of his men, tossed the still-unlit, badly chewed cigar onto the ground and said, "Let's move ... Godspeed, gentlemen."

ഇയ⊙ଔঙ⊙ஐயᎧ⊙ଔঙ⊙ஐயᎧ⊙ଔঙ

They moved forward, keeping close up against the cabins and out of the roadway so they'd not be exposed to gunfire coming from the direction of the Big House.

219

Nathan held up his fist for a halt as he moved in beside the cabin closest to the house. This would be the launch point for their assault, a sprint of nearly a hundred yards over mostly open ground. He had just turned toward his men to make sure they were ready, and to give them a few last-minute instructions, when he heard a sharp whistle coming from further down the line of cabins. It was a whistle he knew well, so he was not surprised when he looked in that direction and saw Billy waving at him. Then he noticed a group of ten or so black men running toward him, and to his shock, in the midst of them ran a white woman—Miss Abbey!

"Momma! What are you doing here?" he said, as she rushed forward and they embraced. He looked up and saw Phinney and Moses and gave them a puzzled look. "How is it you're here?" he asked.

"It's a long story, Nathan. Walters had me prisoner, locked in the kitchen, until Phinney and the men broke me out," she said between gasps for breath, reaching over and patting Phinney on his shoulder.

"Thank you most kindly for that, Phinney," Nathan said with great sincerity. "That was a heroic deed that will never be forgotten."

"Never mind that now, Nathan. Walters has got Megs, Rosa, and Evelyn!" Abbey said.

"Megs and Rosa, too?" Nathan shook his head in disbelief. "How has this happened, Momma?"

"He sent us a telegram, pretending to be you, to lure us here. But Evelyn was already here when we arrived. Oh, Nathan, there is no time for this now ... you must rescue them!"

Nathan scowled. "That I will do, Momma. Or die trying."

"They're holding Megs, Rosa, and the other women in the barn. I don't know how many of the rebels there are."

Nathan looked over at Billy, who'd brought his team back with the newcomers. "Billy, as you've just heard, you now have a rescue mission up at the barn."

"Understood, Captain," Billy said.

"I'm going with him—Rosa's in there!" Tony said, eyes wide with fear.

"Me too," Hank added. "They have my people from Richmond … my Mary."

"We're coming too," Phinney said, nodding to Moses, who held a rifle and a determined look. "We gots to take care of old Megs, after all!"

"All right. Just follow Billy's lead. Go on, now," Nathan ordered. Then Billy trotted off in the direction they'd come, followed by the other members of his company.

"Momma … please stay here at the cabins," Nathan said, "And you men who've only got shovels … though I have no doubt of your bravery and willingness to fight, those'll do no good in a gunfight. So please just stay here and look after Miss Abbey."

☼☽☼☽

Not Rosa. Not … Rosa! Tony had never felt so afraid before, despite all the horrors he'd faced during the war. He wasn't afraid of dying, but he could not imagine how he could go on living if Rosa didn't. And now she was being held hostage by a man who was so wicked, by all accounts, that he killed people just for sport.

Then, despite a burning desire to immediately rush into the barn and get Rosa out of there, he decided the best thing he and the other men could do was to follow Billy's lead. The Indian was one of the greatest fighters of the entire war, Tony figured. If you needed someone to pull off a rescue, you wanted him.

They moved silently between the cabins, and then the smaller outbuildings, until they approached the barn. The white Union privates that now accompanied them had served as scouts under Billy's command in the Twelfth West Virginia, so they followed his silent hand signals without question as he directed them to surround the building, assigning two to the front door and three to the back. He sent Phinney and Moses with the two, by pointing and gesturing, and Tony and Hank with the other three. Billy himself clambered silently up the outside of the barn and entered through the hay loft on the upper level.

Tony, Hank, and the three privates moved up quietly next to the back barn door, which was pulled almost completely closed, save a thin crack. Tony figured the men inside were using the crack to see what was happening in the battle outside. In the fading light of evening, he could see the glow of oil lamps through the doorway and other cracks in the barn wall, confirming there were indeed people inside. Tony noticed there was a knothole in the wall, so he peeped through it. What happened next was entirely unexpected.

Rosa, Megs, and four black women he didn't know sat on straw in the middle of the floor. Over them stood three nervous-looking rebel soldiers, pistols in their hands. It seemed to Tony that the soldiers spoke quietly amongst themselves, though he couldn't make out any of the words. He imagined they'd heard the earlier gunshots and were now feeling anxious about what was happening.

At that moment, Billy appeared in the hayloft above the rebels, aiming his Henry rifle down at them. "Hello, Confederate soldiers. I am Sergeant Creek of the Union Army. This barn is surrounded by my men from the regiment called Twelfth West Virginia. Drop your sidearms and surrender, or we will have to kill you."

The rebels, to their credit, didn't immediately panic and try to shoot him—which Tony reckoned would've been bad for all concerned. Instead, they waved their pistols toward the women, and one of them said, "Listen here … uh, Yankee … we got us some hostages here, so back out o' this here barn, or we'll have to kill 'em."

Billy just shrugged. "All I see is some runaway slave women. Nobody cares about them. Throw down your guns—now—or you will die in a pool of your own blood. Decide."

The three looked at each other, then lowered their pistols and dropped them to the floor, raising their hands. Megs immediately reached back and scooped up the pistol that'd been dropped behind her. She rose and backed away, pointing the gun at the rebels as she did. Mary, seeing what Megs had done, followed her example, and even Rosa picked up one of the pistols, though she held hers gingerly by the handle, barrel pointed downward, as if afraid it might accidentally go off if she held it too firmly.

Billy gave a whistle, then the privates threw open the doors, and came in to take charge of the prisoners.

Tony laid down his rifle and rushed forward to embrace Rosa. Phinney and Moses immediately greeted Megs with happy affection, as Hank embraced Mary and greeted the other women who'd been his companions in Richmond.

Billy climbed down the ladder from the hay loft and stepped up in front of the Confederates. The one who'd spoken previously looked over at Tony and Rosa, then back at Billy and said, "Hey … I thought you said nobody cared about them black women."

Billy snorted a laugh. "I lied," he answered.

Then Billy turned to Phinney and Moses and said, "Escort the women back up to the cabins and put them with Miss Abbey." Then he looked at the two of his soldiers who'd come in the front door: "You two, take charge of the prisoners. The rest of us will go toward the house and join in the fight as best we can. Let's go."

But as one group moved toward the front door and the other toward the back, someone tripped, stumbled, and knocked an oil lamp from its hook on the wall. It shattered against the wood, and crashed to the floor, sending flames up the wall and across the hay.

Billy gazed at the quickly spreading fire for a moment, then back at the people gathered in the barn, shrugged, and said, "The fire must burn. We have more important matters. Do as you were ordered."

☙❧☙❧☙❧☙❧☙❧

The race from the cabins down the driveway and to the front steps of the Big House had been dangerous and nerve-wracking as they sprinted a zig-zagging course, not daring to return fire until they were almost to their destination for fear of hitting the house.

As he'd advised back in Texas, what seemed another lifetime ago, Nathan had told them that if someone were to fall, not to stop

223

but to keep running. The one exception was William, of course, who would once again hang back to see to the wounded, if any.

Bullets kicked up gravel, which pelted Nathan's legs as he ran, but when he came to within a few dozen yards, he stopped, pulled up his Henry rifle, and targeted a rebel who was on the ground to the left of the stairs. The rifle spoke, and the rebel slumped to the earth. He heard another rifle fire to his right and glanced over to see Ollie there. When he turned to look forward again, another rebel had fallen. He rushed on, diving to the ground at the foot of the stairs. Now gunfire rang out all around him, but he glanced up to see Ollie, Zeke, Gareth, and Stan, along with most of their other soldiers, all snugged up against the brickwork at the base of the stairs, pointing their rifles out to either side and firing shots up towards the sides of the house. And Harry the Dog plopped down at Nathan's heels, panting heavily.

Nathan's men quickly moved along the wall, driving the rebels back to the corners and beyond. The Union men were not only more experienced and skilled, but their Henry repeating rifles were a great advantage over the single-shot rifles and six-shot pistols of their enemies.

Stan, however, stayed near Nathan, and after a few moments, they shared a look.

Then, Nathan turned to Harry and said, "You must stay here this time, Harry. Stay with Stan!" he commanded. And as usual, the dog tilted his head, sat down hard, and looked disappointed. But he did as he was told.

Nathan handed Stan his rifle and unholstered his pistol. "Good hunting, Captain," Stan said, reaching out to grip him on the arm. Nathan nodded in answer.

The sun had set and it was beginning to darken when Nathan stood up and turned toward the stairs. Then, remembering Billy's mission at the barn, he glanced over in that direction, and gasped in shock. The barn was on fire, the flames licking up out of one of the haylofts toward the roof above.

He hesitated, thinking he ought to see to the barn. *No, he scolded himself,* and turned back around. *Evelyn needs me. If the farm burns, so be it ...*

He leapt up the stairs three at a time, then stepped up to the door just as it opened.

Despite the looming danger of Walters' presence, Evelyn's heart soared. That none of Walters' men had returned to report on the action, despite the sounds of raging gunfire, meant that the rebels were clearly *not* having it their way. And besides, she still had her tiny revolver up her sleeve, not to mention the razor-sharp stiletto strapped to her right thigh under her skirts.

And, best of all, she was almost certain that Walters' pistol was empty, which he seemed to have forgotten about. When he'd rushed to the back of the house, she'd counted six shots fired. Then he'd returned to the library with his gun smoking, immediately re-holstering it without reloading, fuming and muttering something about Miss Abbey escaping.

Evelyn was confident that, with the aid of only a minor distraction, she could get the jump on the sergeant and get herself out of the mess she was presently in.

Walters paced nervously in the library, no longer daring to approach and look out the window. Finally, he turned to the sergeant and said, "Step outside and have a look. See if you can tell what's going on."

"Yes, sir," the sergeant said, but Evelyn thought she detected a hint of hesitation in his manner. Still, he did as he was told, and she watched as he exited the library.

She figured it was now her chance to pull the gun on Walters and end this thing. But before she could make her move, he said, "Come; this window is too vulnerable … we're moving to the great room," and he reached out to grab her left arm.

Her heart sank as Walters jerked her hard toward him and said, "What's this?" He gripped the fold of her sleeve and ripped, exposing the small pistol strapped there. He immediately yanked it out, then shoved her away. He gazed at the revolver a moment before looking back at her. "Very clever. But little good it'll do you now."

He slipped the pistol into the pocket of his trousers, and then grabbed her and wrapped his left arm around her throat, pulling her head back toward his face. "Don't try anything else, witch, or I will hurt you."

She nodded, but had already turned her thoughts to the stiletto, wondering if she could pull it out and stab him before he could break her neck.

By now, Sergeant Slater had crossed the foyer and cautiously reached out to open the front door, his pistol held out in front. As he began to step outside, a noise like an explosion rocked the house, and Slater fell backward onto the hard floor of the foyer, a neat red spot in the middle of his forehead and a pool of blood spreading at the back of his head.

A man stepped into the house holding a revolver that was still smoking: Nathaniel Chambers.

❦❧☙

Nathan stepped over the body of the rebel sergeant and into the foyer. "Walters ... I have come for you ..." he called out.

And then a familiar voice answered, "I'm here. Come and get me." The voice came from inside the library. So Nathan cautiously stepped in that direction, gun held out front, ready to fire — or not, as circumstances dictated.

And then, as he stepped toward the library door, the sight he'd most dreaded met his eyes: Walters stood there with Evelyn in front of him, his handless arm around her throat and the barrel of a pistol pressed against the side of her head.

Nathan cautiously entered the room, meeting eyes with Evelyn. And to his great surprise, he saw no fear there. She seemed oddly calm, though she held a serious expression. He wondered if she'd been through so much during the war that nothing could frighten her any longer.

"Nathan ..." she said in an even voice.

"Hello, Evelyn," he answered, returning her serious look.

Walters snorted a mirthless laugh. "How touching ... the young lovers, about to meet their doom, greet each other for the last time ..."

Nathan now met eyes with Walters, and what he saw there chilled him—emptiness. Like looking into a bottomless pit. If the man had ever possessed a soul, he seemed to have lost it long ago.

"Throw your weapon down, or the wench dies," Walters said.

Then to Nathan's surprise, Evelyn shook her head, "Don't do it, Nathan … his gun is empty. He's already fired all his rounds."

Nathan looked from her to Walters, who continued to stare at him. "Are you willing to gamble her life on it, Chambers? Are you certain she knows? Perhaps she miscounted my shots … Perhaps she heard other shots …"

Nathan hesitated, then lowered the hammer on his pistol, and tossed it aside, where it clattered across the hardwood floor before banging against the wall.

"Chambers … I've waited a long time for this," Walters said, then aimed the pistol at Nathan's chest and pulled the trigger.

❧❧❧❧❧❧❧❧❧

The hammer clicked on an empty chamber. Walters tried again with the same result, then tossed the weapon to the floor. But even as he did, Evelyn squirmed from under his arm, which had no hand to grasp her with. She backed away toward the wall as Walters pulled out a wicked-looking knife, with a long, slender blade.

"Guess the whore was right … I'd fired it already," he said then shrugged. "No matter. I will just have to kill you with the knife …"

Nathan reached behind his back and pulled out his Bowie knife, angling it toward his opponent, crouching into a fighting position.

Evelyn stepped back to the wall to get out of the way as the two men circled each other in the center of the room. She briefly toyed with the idea of pulling out the stiletto and joining the fight on Nathan's side, but she immediately thought better of it. She'd likely only distract Nathan, who was, after all, a highly skilled fighter and didn't need her help.

And then, as if to emphasize her thoughts, Nathan suddenly lashed out, nicking Walters' left arm, making him wince and back away. Blood ran down his left sleeve and dripped onto the floor as he stepped back.

But then, to Evelyn's surprise, Walters tossed aside his knife and reached down into his trouser pocket. Before Nathan could react, Walters held Evelyn's small pistol in his hand, aimed at his chest.

Walters chuckled. "I find it beautifully ironic that your own woman has provided the very means of your death … This was her own pistol that I took from her just moments ago. And now … die, Chambers."

A gunshot rattled the room. Nathan flinched, clutching at his chest with his empty hand. But when he pulled his hand back, there was no blood on it.

Walters slumped to the floor, a puddle of red spreading from under his head where it lay on the floor. Smoke curled up from Nathan's pistol, held in Evelyn's hand.

Evelyn lowered the gun and turned to face Nathan, fearful of his reaction to her sudden display of extreme violence. Though he'd heard about many of her clandestine activities, he'd never actually witnessed that side of her before. Would he still see her in the same way, or would he turn away and reject her in the end, unwilling to marry a woman who'd just proved herself a killer? And then she noticed that all the gunfire outside had ceased, and a complete silence now fell over the house, as if the entire world held its breath awaiting Nathan's response.

Nathan just stood where he was, mouth agape, first staring down at Walters, then staring up at Evelyn for a long moment, as if he too did not know what to think of her in that moment. Finally, he turned his gaze toward the hand still gripping the great Bowie knife.

"Well … guess I won't be needing this anymore," he said, then opened his fingers, letting the knife fall free. It dropped to the floor, where it hit point first, embedding itself several inches into the hardwood.

He looked up at Evelyn and smiled. He stepped toward her, swept her into his arms, and kissed her.

A moment later, Stan rushed into the room, pistol at the ready with Harry the Dog hard on his heels.

"Oh. Well, nothing more to do here, I see," Stan said, looking down at Walters' body and holstering the sidearm.

Just then, Megs arrived, out of breath, along with Miss Abbey, Rosa, and Tony. The two older women held pistols that had been taken from the rebels in the barn.

Megs looked over at Stan and said, "That ain't true, Mr. Stan ..."

"Oh?"

"Yes ... can't you see it? We now gonna have ourselves a wedding to plan."

"Oh! Yes, now that you say it, I am seeing *that* ..." he laughed, then reached down to scratch Harry on the head.

Chapter 12. Joy and Despair in Equal Measure

"It is because of pain that you value pleasure,
sorrow that you value joy,
despair that you value hope,
war that you value peace,
and hate that you value love."
- Matshona Dhliwayo

Sunday, April 16, 1865 – Greenbrier County, West Virginia:

When Nathan arose the day after the battle with Walters and his men, he felt exhausted right down to his bones. He realized that he'd been pushing himself and everyone around him from before sunrise to well after sunset for many days, starting before the breakout at Petersburg, through the forced march to Appomattox, and on into the fighting leading up to the rebel surrender. Then, with no respite, he'd received the terrifying news that Walters may have set a trap at Mountain Meadows. The mind-numbing tension and anxiety of *that* fear had driven him to push men and animals harder than he'd ever done before.

Then came the brief, furious Battle of Mountain Meadows, the surrender of the last nineteen members of Walters' cavalry, including one officer, Captain Roberts, and all hands then putting out the fire in the barn, which was a total loss, but fortunately never spread to any other of the outbuildings.

After the dust and smoke had settled, they'd suffered only one killed, the freeman that Walters had shot during Miss Abbey's escape, and three of the privates wounded, only one seriously, though William was hopeful he'd make a full recovery.

Nathan had ordered the prisoners to finish digging the mass grave Walters had intended for the black men, which was instead used to bury the slain Confederate soldiers. Nathan himself had the satisfaction of unceremoniously dumping Walters' body on top of the others, then shoveling dirt on top. After that, Nathan informed the prisoners of General Grant's pardon, and to their shock and amazement, he released them to return to their homes.

This morning, the day after, he had slept past dawn—an extremely unusual occurrence for him—and had been rewarded by awakening to the wonderful, musical sound of Evelyn's joyous voice and laughter echoing through the house from somewhere downstairs. As he lay there, gazing out the bedroom window at a clear, bright sky, he reveled in *that* sound, and smiled. *This will be a good day,* he decided. *A day that I get to spend entirely with her. And for once with no fear of the morrow.*

And then he threw back the covers, set his feet on the floor, and stood. *Oooo … guess you've overdone it this time, Nathan,* he thought as overwrought muscles and joints sent waves of pain through him. He reached up, stretching his arms and shoulders, trying to get some life back into his limbs.

When he was finally dressed, and managed to hobble painfully down the stairs, Evelyn's greeting was so warm and enthusiastic that all his aches and pains were instantly swept away. Her infectious happiness soon had him laughing and smiling like he hadn't a care in the world, and it recalled to his mind the thing he had always loved best about her—true, she was the most beautiful, desirable woman he'd ever known—but it was her childlike joy for life that had always lifted his soul.

After greeting the rest of the family, he and Evelyn ended up sitting side by side on the floor of the great room, made necessary by its complete dearth of furniture.

They'd been sitting there, speaking of nothing in particular, just the mundane small talk of two people who were completely comfortable in each other's presence but had long been apart when Miss Abbey and Megs stepped into the room and stood, gazing down at them.

"Hello Momma, Megs …" Nathan said, looking up expectantly at the two ladies. Clearly, they wished to discuss something; he assumed any one of an endless list of tasks that needed doing in a household that'd been entirely neglected for four years.

Miss Abbey held an unreadable look on her face, though Nathan knew her well enough to detect the faintest hint of a smile. Megs held a similar enigmatic look. *Hmm ... what are they up to?* Nathan wondered.

"The old house fared surprisingly well, given the various unwelcome guests it has no doubt housed since our departure," Abbey said, gazing about the room.

"True," Nathan answered. "Though I suspect it'll take a while to repair all the scars from its abuse and long neglect."

Abbey nodded, then said, "Too bad it's so empty ..."

Nathan thought this statement odd. Not the *words* per se, but rather the way she said it. He would've expected an aching sorrow for all the wonderful furnishings that'd been lost. A lifetime of Abbey's irreplaceable memories were contained within a household of precious items that they'd been forced to leave behind when they had escaped the rebel siege. And now, four years later, not a stick of furniture nor a scrap of velvet window covering remained.

"Well ... I suppose we shall just have to do our best to refurnish the place," he offered. "Though I fear we must be practical about it. After all, the place hasn't made a cent of income in four years, and the other farm up at Wheeling has barely, covered expenses. So money will be in short supply—for a time anyway ..." he trailed off, looking from one to the other of the two ladies, noting that his words were not having the effect he'd expected.

Rather than frowning, tearing up, or pouting ... his mother was surely smiling—he was now almost certain—though it was still subtle.

"What are you thinking, Momma?" he finally asked. "Is there something you wish to tell me?" He glanced over at Evelyn, but she just returned a puzzled look.

"No, I don't have anything to *tell* you, Nathan, dear; but we do have something to *show* you," she said, exchanging a look with Megs.

"Come … you too, Evelyn. Come!" she said, smiling brightly and holding out her hand to Evelyn, who returned the smile and took Abbey's hand to assist her onto her feet.

Nathan looked up at Megs and extended his hand, but she just scowled, "If you think I'm going to help you off the floor, you great heavy thing, you can think again!"

He snorted a laugh, then groaned as he painfully rose to his feet and followed the women, already headed down the hallway. Harry likewise heaved himself up from the corner where he'd been sleeping and plodded along after.

Abbey led them out the back door, through the flower garden, and on toward the duck pond. Turning right at the great willow tree, they circled around the pond into the field on the far side. Past the field lay a thicket of bushes that tangled the women's skirts and scratched their arms as they pushed their way through. Nathan couldn't imagine why they were doing this, but he knew better than to question his mother or Megs, so he did his best to help them push through the undergrowth. And to his keen, wilderness-trained eye, he could see someone had been here before, and very recently—branches were snapped off in places, and the grass had been recently trod upon. *Hmm, maybe I did learn a few of Billy's tricks along the way*, he thought with amusement.

After a time, Abbey stopped, and Megs stepped up next to her. The bushes had thinned out, giving way to large rocks covering the landscape in front of them. Nathan recognized this as part of the property that had no use for farming, though he'd enjoyed playing in and around the boulders when he was a little boy. The sight triggered faint memories that began trickling back into his mind for the first time in many long years.

"Come, Nathan … Evelyn … let us show you what we came to show you," Abbey said.

She led them via a twisting route around the rocks and through a few more bushes. Finally, she stopped again and gestured with her hand, "Here it is."

At first, all Nathan could see was more bushes, only these were a bit taller than the others had been. Then he noted where these, too, had recently been forced apart to make a path, behind which was … nothing. Nothing but … darkness. And then the memories came flooding back in, and he knew where he was, "It's a cave … a great, dry cave with plenty of space inside," he said.

Megs turned to him, a startled expression on her face, "You knew of this, Nathaniel?"

He slowly nodded, thinking back on the incident. "Yes … but I had nearly forgotten. I was … hmm … maybe six years old. Up to my usual mischief, no doubt," he snorted a laugh and shook his head. "I used to play out among these rocks, climbing them. Searching for pirate treasure." He looked at Megs and they shared a smile. It was the kind of story she used to read to him when he was a boy.

"Anyway, one day, I stumbled onto this cave. So, naturally, I went inside. It was large and dry, so I thought I'd found a great new place for an adventure, that would be a secret place just for me. But I saw a faint light further back, so I went further in. I was surprised to find a man sitting there on the floor. He was a black man, with some gray in his hair, I remember. I was frightened at first; I knew every black man on the farm, of course, and many others on the nearby farms, but I didn't know him. I couldn't fathom what he was doing there.

"But he had kindly eyes, and he spoke to me in a tone that eased my fears. We spoke together a little, and I remember asking him why he was there. He said he would only be there for a day or so, then he would have to leave again. That he was hiding from a bad man who wanted to hurt him, and that if anyone found out he was hiding there, the bad man would get him. He asked me not to tell anyone he was there, not even my Momma and Daddy. So I said I wouldn't tell. Then he asked another favor of me, which I didn't understand at the time, but now that I think on it, I do … He asked me never to come back to the cave. That it was a special secret place where people who were in trouble and afraid could come to be safe. That if I told anyone or if I came back and someone saw me come, then the people who used the cave would never be safe again. So I agreed … and though I was only a little boy," he smiled and shrugged, "I guess I already had a sense of honor; I did as he asked. I never told, and I never went back into the cave. As the years passed by, I forgot all about it … until now."

Megs shook her head and smiled. "Nathaniel, every time I think I know you and everything you're made of, you surprise me again with something new. That was … I don't know … a hint of what you would become, I guess. As you've now guessed, this was a hideaway for escaped slaves from other farms. The slaves of this farm would hide them here, bring them food and water, and provide them with the means to try to head north. It was a sacred secret, until you freed us and then I showed it to Abbey."

"Well, this is an interesting story and a fond memory for me, but why are we here, ladies?" he looked from one to the other, but they just grinned in answer.

Then he gave Evelyn a questioning look, but she said, "Don't look at me. I knew nothing of this."

"Megs, will you light the lamp, please?" Abbey asked, and for the first time, Nathan noticed Megs had been carrying a small kerosene lantern. She pulled out a match, struck it, and soon the lantern was burning brightly. She handed it to Abbey, who led them into the cave with Megs behind her, then Evelyn, followed by Nathan, and finally, Harry the Dog.

When they'd all gathered inside the opening, Abbey raised the lantern high to illuminate the darkness. Nathan saw that the cave was indeed as large as he remembered, maybe fifty feet across, with a ceiling more than twenty feet tall. It had a fairly level, dry, sandy floor. The thing that caught his gaze was what was on the floor. Various shapes of differing sizes filled the open space in front of them—what appeared to be objects covered with blankets and tarps, mostly covered in dust.

Nathan's eyes widened, as recognition of what he was seeing began to dawn on him. He met eyes with Abbey, who was now beaming, "Momma … is it …?"

Abbey just nodded, continuing to smile, so Nathan stepped up to the nearest and largest object. He examined it for a moment, then reached out, grabbed the tarp, and pulled.

Nathan gasped, and Evelyn squealed with delight. It was Miss Abbey's grand piano.

"My God, Momma … Megs … how? How is this possible?"

Abbey grinned. "Well, you remember how furious you were with us because we were so tardy in our evacuation of the house?"

"Yes … I remember saying, 'I sure hope you have a good reason for being late.' And I recall you saying that you did but never telling me what it was."

Abbey laughed. "It was Megs' idea, so she should really get the credit. It's all here—our entire household. So, now that you know the reason for our delay, how do you judge us, my dear?"

"I judge you … *wonderful*, Momma," he said, and then scooped her up into his arms, swung her around and kissed her. She squeaked and said, "Put me down, sir! You're like to break me!"

He set her on her feet, and then immediately swept up Megs and repeated the act. She laughed and slapped him on the arm, "You great brute!"

Evelyn laughed with delight, but she was already stepping through the room, pulling off blankets to see what was underneath. She turned back and smiled, "Why, this is better than all the Christmases put together!"

ℬↄ∝ℭℬↄ∝ℭℬↄ∝ℭℬↄ∝ℭ

Monday, April 17, 1865 – Greenbrier County, West Virginia:

Evelyn pitched in to help Megs stock foodstuffs in the kitchen, newly arrived from Lewisburg via several of Nathan's men who'd been sent on a "foraging mission"—meaning they'd gone to see if the general store had any supplies—when she heard the men discussing the news that made her heart freeze: The president had been shot and killed in Washington City two days earlier.

First to her mind was a great, heartrending sadness. Abraham Lincoln had been the heart and soul of the effort to save the Union and abolish the evil of slavery for the past four years and more. And now, when he should've been able to finally reap the fruits of his labors, he was struck down. It was senseless and maddening. She found she had to sit to absorb the news. Megs, who'd been helping her, left the room in tears—a thing Evelyn had never before seen or imagined.

After sitting for a moment to digest the tragedy, Evelyn's next thought was, *Where is Nathan? This will hit him hard. He had a great admiration—love, even—for Mr. Lincoln, and speaks often of their one meeting in the White House. I must go to him and comfort him, if I can.*

She jumped to her feet and went to find him. But after asking everyone in the house and out in the cabins, it seemed that no one knew where he was. It was Stan who finally confirmed her worst fears—that Nathan had indeed heard the devastating news, and had been visibly shaken by it. The big man had not seen Nathan after that, being busy unloading supplies.

Where would Nathan go? Evelyn sat in one of the chairs on the backside of the veranda—one of several pieces of furniture newly arrived from the cache that'd been hidden in the cave. She pondered the question. In a moment, it came to her, and she jumped to her feet, fairly running toward the place where she was almost certain she would find him.

When Evelyn approached the duck pond, she saw Nathan sitting on the swing under the big willow tree. He was staring out at the water, and she followed his gaze, noting ripples on the surface caused by its usual inhabitants, the ducks. If they'd noticed the disruption Mountain Meadows had suffered from four years of war, they showed no sign.

As she approached, she saw that Nathan held a bottle of whiskey in his left hand, resting on his lap. But she was relieved to see that it was still stoppered and appeared to be full—at least, for the moment.

She stepped up quietly behind him, but as she opened her mouth to announce her presence, he said, "I've just been sitting here holding a debate with this bottle."

She stepped up in front of the swing, then sat down next to him.

"And what is it you are debating?" she asked in a serious tone, knowing he was in no mood for levity.

"The bottle argues that life is nothing but endless, pointless pain and suffering. That even at the very height of righteous accomplishment and victory, the greatest among us can be stricken down and taken from us for no good reason or purpose.

That all our hopes, dreams, and efforts are for naught, and we may as well give in to despair, and seek the comfort and release from its contents."

Evelyn nodded and waited a moment to see if he would say more before prompting, "And how are you answering its well-reasoned arguments?"

He was quiet for a moment, then said, "At the moment, I am having difficulty countering them, I have to confess. I feel … like someone has just stabbed me in the heart …" And then, for the first time, he looked over at her and they met eyes. She could see he was fighting back tears, and her heart ached for him.

"How about arguing that despair is almost always answered by hope and joy in equal measure?" she said. "And you and I should know *that* better than anyone, after all we've been through, both when we've been together and when we've had to be apart."

He continued to gaze into her eyes, and nodded, but said nothing.

"You might also tell that bottle that you have a woman who treasures you above all else in this world, and who is so full of love and joy at the prospect of finally living with you, that no amount of pain and tragedy may penetrate her armor."

Nathan slowly nodded, and said, *"Put on the whole armor of God, that ye may be able to stand against the wiles of the devil."*

She nodded, recognizing the Bible verse often quoted by soldiers preparing for battle.

He sighed, then said, "Thank you for *that*, Evelyn. You have given me my argument. I now know what I shall say to the bottle."

"And what is that, my darling?"

"I shall say, 'despite the truth in all you say, feckless counselor, I have a weapon you cannot hope to overmatch. I have *Evelyn*, and that is all I need to resist your evil temptation.'"

Then Nathan dropped the bottle onto the ground and leaned his head into her bosom. She embraced him, then gently kicked the swing into motion.

∗ ∗ ∗

The day after the tragic news of Lincoln's death, Nathan and Evelyn stood side by side, out on the lawn, gazing at the fallen magnolia tree. It lay on the grass, the petals from its flowers thickly covering the lawn all around it, like a fall of lavender-colored snow, already turning to brown. Its green leaves wilted sadly in the sunlight.

Nathan sighed, and Evelyn's heart went out to him as she gazed at his pained expression, knowing how much he'd loved that tree, even from earliest childhood, and feeling that she'd inadvertently triggered its demise by thoughtlessly bringing it to Walters' attention.

She leaned into him, putting her arm around his midsection. "I'm *so* sorry, Nathan. It was such a beautiful thing, and its destruction is such a needless tragedy."

Nathan shook his head. "It's not your fault, Evelyn, despite what you say. Walters likely would've come up with the idea all on his own. The man was just that mean." But Evelyn saw that the hurt reflected in his eyes belied his kind words.

"Well, thank you for saying so, Nathan. But I can't help feeling guilty about it, nonetheless," she answered.

Nathan reached out and took her hand, "Come … let us not speak of it again. I would remove to a happier place. Down by the pond, perhaps?"

She looked in his eyes and graced him with a gentle smile, gave his hand a squeeze, and said, "Yes, of course, darling. That would be lovely."

❧❦❧❦❧❦❧❦❧❦

After a few minutes of silence, slowly rocking the swing, gazing out at the tranquil waters of the duck pond, Nathan decided it was as good a time as any to broach the subject he'd been dreading: "Evelyn, I must leave again in the morning."

To his surprise, she answered, "I know."

"You do?"

"Well, yes … I do know something about how armies work after spending most of my time spying on them these past four years. A general can't just ride away from his command to deal with personal matters and never come back. Though the fighting may be over, you still must return and see to your men."

He chuckled. "Yes, I should've known you'd understand that. But hopefully, if all goes well, it'll not take long. If the other rebel commanders follow Lee's lead—which I expect they will—then hostilities will cease, and the government will be eager to muster out all the men as quickly as possible to keep from having to supply their every need, not to mention paying their salaries."

"Makes sense," she agreed. "And don't feel badly, Nathan. I knew this day was coming, though I'd hoped for a little longer. But maybe the sooner you leave, the sooner you may return."

"Let's hope so. Anyway, I am already feeling sheepish about leaving Tom behind, not to mention the entire brigade. That was a hard choice, and I have been dreading having to apologize to him for it."

She chuckled, "I'm sure he'll forgive you."

Nathan shrugged, returning her smile.

They were quiet for a moment, and then she said, "Nathan … there's something I wish to discuss with you."

"Oh?"

"Yes. Um … you see … I've been thinking on this, and I … well … Oh, why is this so *difficult?!* I'm going to do as you always do, and just say it straight out: I am well aware that you and I are about four years overdue for being married and, to my point … *sleeping together* … and I freely admit *that* is all my fault. So, what I wanted to say was, if you wish to do so tonight, on our last night together for maybe several months, then I won't refuse you."

Nathan stopped the swing and turned to her with a serious expression. "Is that truly what you wish?"

She looked away and could feel the heat rising in her face. "Well, *yes* … and … *no*."

He chuckled, but she ignored his obvious amusement at her discomfort, and continued, "*Yes*, I've been wanting to, but *no*, I'd rather not tonight. I think … I think it would be best to wait for the wedding. It is not just the proper thing to do, but I believe it would make the wedding more special. But that being said, I wanted you to know that I *do* want to be with you—have dreamed of it many times, in fact—and that I *will* say yes, if you ask it of me."

He smiled and nodded his head, reaching into his pocket and pulling out a cigar before lighting it and taking a puff. Gazing at her with an amused expression.

Finally, she scowled, but then couldn't suppress a smile of her own. "Well ... are you going to answer me?"

"You haven't asked me a question," he said, and continued to puff on the cigar.

She sighed. "Very well ... do you wish to sleep with me tonight, or not?"

He chuckled, "Evelyn, you have no idea how many times I've thought of nothing else. All those lonely nights out in the wilderness in a cold tent, not knowing if I'd live to see the end of another day, let alone ever see you again."

He took another long, slow puff. "It took me more than thirty years to find you, Evelyn. And since we found each other, it has taken another four years—four long, hard years of almost constant fighting—to get to a place where we can finally be together. If I've been able to wait that long, I can wait another month or so."

She smiled, "All right. If you're sure."

"I am, my dear. And I'm certain you are worth the wait."

She smiled demurely and answered, "When the time comes, I shall endeavor to make it worth your wait."

He laughed again. "If you keep saying things like *that*, I may change my mind about tonight!"

She laughed with him.

"Tell you what," he said, "I'll make you a deal. While I'm off mustering out the men, you go ahead and get the wedding all planned out and arranged, so that when I come home, we can do it straightaway." Then he chuckled, "Lord knows you don't need my help anyway, and likely would prefer not to have it."

She grinned. "True, you men only get in the way. Yes, I will happily do that; and don't worry, I do understand that money is tight right now, so I will endeavor to keep it simple."

"I'll just write you up a list of those I wish to invite and leave the rest in your capable hands," he said.

"It's a deal," she said, and held out her hand for a handshake. He took her hand and kissed it instead, lingering a bit longer than necessary as he gazed up into her eyes.

"Deal," he said.

❧❧❧❧❧❧❧❧❧❧

The next morning, Nathan sat astride Millie just below the veranda steps where Evelyn stood gazing out at him.

Nathan's men were also mounted, waiting respectfully a few dozen yards up the drive so the couple could say their goodbyes in privacy. Likewise, everyone who was staying behind had already said their goodbyes before retreating indoors.

After a long silence, which neither wished to break, Nathan reached up and tipped his hat to her. "Ma'am, next time you see me, I promise we shall never again be parted," he said, holding a serious expression that reflected the pain he felt in this last parting, brief though they hoped it would be.

"Sir, that is the sweet dream I've been awaiting these past four years," Evelyn answered, gracing him with a formal courtesy. She too was no longer smiling, and he could see tears brimming in her eyes.

"Until then …" he tipped his hat again, then jerked Millie's reins and trotted off, never looking back.

❧❧❧❧❧❧❧❧❧❧

Thursday April 20, 1865 – Richmond, Virginia:

When Jonathan, Angeline, Margaret, and the Hugheses' household employees returned to their manor house in Richmond, they were only mildly surprised to see a man sitting in the library on a once-grand chair that was now oozing cotton stuffing from a damaged leather cushion.

And though the face was familiar, Margaret decided she wasn't used to seeing this particular man dressed as a proper gentleman, though she did note that he wore a pistol holster at his hip. "Hello, Joseph," Margaret said, as he stood and approached the party coming in across the foyer.

"Greetings, Margaret … Jonathan, Angeline, Sam, Maddie …" he proceeded to shake hands with and greet each member of the more than a dozen in the party by name, including the grooms, maids, and cooks.

After the warm greetings were exchanged, Jonathan and Angeline began to take stock of the state of the house, which had clearly been looted and vandalized. Everything of value that was portable was missing entirely: sculptures, paintings, vases, candelabra, and many other items. Every scrap of cloth was gone, including all the elegantly embroidered velvet curtains. And much of what couldn't be easily carted away had been vandalized: cushions slashed, initials and vulgar words scrawled on highly carved and enameled furniture, mirrors shattered, walls stained, and on and on.

"Would've been worse if I hadn't arrived a week or so ago," Joseph said. "I've chased off those that thought to come back for more mischief. They seemed disinclined to test the accuracy of my aim with a pistol."

"Thank you, Joseph," Angeline said.

"Yes, thank you," Jonathan agreed. "Well, Angel … at least the house is still standing, and not burned to the ground. Many have suffered much worse."

"True, true," she answered. "We should count our blessings, surely, starting with the fact that we here are all still alive after all, and the war has finally ended."

"And that Major White is apparently dead," Margaret added. They'd heard that report a week or so ago, which had been the final piece of good news that had prompted them to pack up and return to Richmond, there to reoccupy the house after spending the last month at a rustic, out-of-the-way hunting lodge up in the hills twenty miles or so outside of town.

"Yes, and I say amen to that," Joseph agreed. "He was the type of man to continue a vendetta even after the war was over. And, speaking of ... I have some *other* good news, and this time it's firsthand, so I know it's true. My old friend Frank Dodge has reported that Evelyn and her party have made it safely to Mountain Meadows. He took them there himself."

"That is wonderful news," Angeline said, then she and Margaret exchanged a hug in celebration.

"Oh ... but I am sorry to say there was some bad news concerning the whole affair," Joseph said, looking pointedly at Jonathan, who raised an eyebrow questioningly.

"Yes ... unfortunately, before they could escape Richmond, there was a confrontation with Major White and several of his soldiers. Though Evelyn and the freemen managed to get away unharmed, all three of our men who were guarding them were killed: Adam, Hugh, and of course, Jacob."

Jonathan put his hand over his heart and bowed his head as if in pain. Angeline stepped over and softly embraced him, but said nothing.

After a long moment, Jonathan looked back up, and though he was no longer smiling, he said, "Well, despite the sad news, we still have much to be thankful for. And ... also a lot of work to do. So, let's take a few minutes to get settled in, and then get to work cleaning up this place, shall we?"

⁐⁐⁐

Tuesday April 25, 1865 – Richmond, Virginia:

Though his homecoming to his parents' house had been joyful, Jubal could not shake an emptiness and a dread that gave him a constant knot in the pit of his stomach. After an initial day of celebration, rest, and recuperation, he had launched himself into the task of locating Evelyn.

Now, more than a week later, his level of frustration was growing apace with his fear for her wellbeing. He could not shake the vision of the haughty, arrogant Major White, who'd seemed determined to extract some kind of punishment from her—Jubal assumed because of her involvement with the Underground Railroad. Even seeking out White had proven another dead end — this time literally. From what he could learn, White had somehow been killed in the fighting, though Jubal had a hard time envisioning the fastidious war department major actually being involved in combat.

He visited all the places he'd known Evelyn to frequent, and talked to everyone he knew of that she'd associated with, but nobody had seen her or knew anything of her whereabouts. In fact, it seemed as if she'd disappeared from Richmond months before the Yankees had broken through. He could not puzzle out what that meant until it hit him like a bolt from the blue: *She's been arrested! Nobody has seen her because she's been in jail!*

So he switched tactics and went to visit all the jails and prisons in Richmond. This too had proven fruitless. The federals seemingly had simply emptied the prisons, letting everyone free, not just Union soldiers. Thieves, murderers, and all manner of criminals were simply turned out, under the assumption that they were being persecuted for their support of the Union cause, which Jubal considered highly unlikely in most cases. He sighed, knowing if he went back to being a policeman, he'd likely be chasing down these same men to put them right back into the very same jails.

As he trudged down Carey Street, past the burned-out shells of houses and other buildings, he passed a beggar, sitting on the street, leaning up against a tilting gas lamp post. The man glanced up at Jubal and scowled, then grimaced, showing his lack of front teeth. "You're a devil!" the man shouted, rolling his eyes, and shaking his head violently from side to side. "You and Satan lit these fires to burn the angels. Now they're all dead. All the angels are dead! And God, too. You damned devils burned them. But not me … You ain't burned old Willy … not yet, you ain't. Ha." Then he reached out, grabbed a stick and swung it at Jubal, hitting him across the shin. The man was emaciated, and the blow held no force, so Jubal just shrugged as the man cackled, and screamed, "Be gone, devil! You'll not get old Willy, you won't."

Jubal shook his head and looked down at the man with sympathy. Clearly, he'd lost his wits entirely, and if nobody came soon to take him someplace safe, he'd likely starve out here on the street. So Jubal reached into his pocket and extracted the piece of hardtack he'd intended to chew on as he walked home.

"Here," he said, extending his hand with the offering.

The man gazed at the food with wide eyes, and then reached out suddenly, snatching it away and growling as he stuck it in his mouth and chewed, slobber running down his chin as he did so.

Jubal turned and continued down the street. *Poor fellow*, he thought. *I wonder if the lunatic asylum is still functioning … Wait a minute … the lunatic asylum. That's it! That's where they've taken her … yes … it'd be away from prying eyes. None of her friends would think to look for her there, and even the Yankees wouldn't just turn those inmates loose.*

He turned and sprinted back up the hill, passing old Willy once again as he did, though this time the man was too engrossed in his scant meal to take notice.

Though he'd not been there before—thankfully—every policeman in Richmond knew exactly where the lunatic asylum was located, and Jubal wasted no time getting there, though it was more than a dozen blocks away, and most of that uphill.

Thankfully, the building was located up on Shockoe Hill, so it had been nowhere near where the fires had raged along the waterfront and in the central downtown area. When Jubal arrived, he took the dozen or so stairs two at a time, and finding the door unlocked, immediately stepped inside. Across a small foyer sat a balding, middle-aged man behind a desk. He appeared to be reading a newspaper and looked up in startlement when Jubal stepped forward.

"Oh! Hello, officer … How can I help you?" he asked. Jubal realized he'd been wearing his uniform for so long now that he'd never thought to change back into civilian clothes since his return. And most of the other soldiers he'd seen on the street hadn't either. Likely many had lost everything they owned, and had nothing else to wear.

"I'm looking for a lady," he answered.

The man smiled, "Aren't we all, son?"

Jubal scowled in response, being in no mood for humor. "She's young … about my age, with blonde hair … pretty girl. Is she here?"

"Oh! Well … uh … I'm not allowed to say who's here and who ain't. 'Cept to the proper authorities, you understand," he answered, but Jubal could tell from his initial reaction that the description he'd just given had struck a chord with the man.

"She *is* here. Take me to her, immediately!"

"Well, I ain't supposed to do that, not without the proper authority."

"Look here, Mister … uh …?"

"Fuller, Captain. Harvy Fuller."

"Look here, Mister Fuller. There is no Confederate authority left in Richmond. But I'm a commissioned army officer, so that's got to be good enough."

"Well … I'm sure you've heard, Captain … the Yankees are in charge now. They now tell me what I can do and what I can't do. So, you'll need to go see them and get the proper papers."

Jubal closed his eyes and took a deep breath, fighting down a very strong urge to just punch this man in the face and take his keys. But he knew the fellow was just trying to do his job.

"Look here, Mr. Fuller. If it helps, I was a Richmond policeman before the war, so I would've been one of those proper authorities you speak of. This lady is a friend of mine, whom I believe was falsely accused by a disreputable Signal Corps officer—one who's now dead, as I understand it. If you give her over to my custody, it'll be the same as giving her to a policeman … or an army officer, whichever you prefer. Either way, nobody could say you didn't do your duty."

The man eyed Jubal thoughtfully, but didn't immediately answer, so Jubal decided to try another tack. "Please, Mr. Fuller. I've been out fighting the war, and have been searching all over for her ever since my return. You wouldn't keep a good, honest soldier from the woman he loves on account of some orders from the Yankees, would you?"

Fuller gazed down at the table for a moment, then slowly shook his head. "All right ... I'll give her over to you, Captain. Never seemed right her being here in the first place. She's clearly not insane. Seems a nice enough lady, considering what she's been through. There's really no reason for her to be here other than orders from the War Department. Just ... don't let them federals hear about it."

"It's the last thing I intend to do, Mr. Fuller, believe me. And I thank you."

Moments later, after Fuller led them down a long hallway, through a locked door, and down two flights of stairs to a dimly lit, moldy smelling basement, and then down another corridor, they stood outside a solid, darkly stained wood door, framed with rusting iron. Only a small slit, just above the keyhole, served for a window.

"Hello in there, miss," Fuller called out. "You have a visitor."

"A ... a *visitor?*" A female voice responded. Jubal winced at the sound—raspy and weak, but pitiably hopeful.

"Yes, ma'am. Give me a moment ..." Fuller answered, pulling a ring containing several dozen keys from his pocket and flipping through them until he located the one he sought. In a moment, he'd unlocked the door and pulled it open, stepping back and gesturing Jubal forward with a curt bow. Fuller then turned away and strode back down the hall, leaving Jubal alone with the newly freed inmate.

Jubal stepped into the cell, forced to duck through the low doorway. In the dim light of a single oil lamp in a sconce on the wall, he could make out a slim figure sitting on a bed that was attached to the stone of the wall by an iron bracket. The room reeked from the contents of a bucket that served as a bedpan over in one corner. The woman wore a crude, homespun cloth dress, loosely fitted, looking more like a potato sack than an article of women's clothing. Jubal's heart skipped a beat as he noted the lady's long, curling, blond hair, hanging down past her knees. He reached up, grabbed the oil lamp, and then knelt down in front of her, holding the lamp forward.

"It's me ... *Jubal*," he said. "I've come to take you out of here, Evel—*oh!*" As the lamp lit the features of her face, he was shocked to see that she was indeed a beautiful young woman—but she was *not* Evelyn!

"Who ... who are you?" he asked.

She gazed at his face a long time before answering. "You have a good, kindly face, sir. But ... I'm certain I don't know you. *Jubal* did you say your name was?" she slowly shook her head. "No ... I'm sorry, I don't remember you, Jubal, if I knew you before. But ... you say you've come to take me away from this place? Oh, bless you, sir, bless you," she said, and tears began to well in her eyes as she reached out her arms to embrace him.

His heart melted at the sight. Though this was not Evelyn, as he'd hoped and believed, still she was clearly someone in great need. Still kneeling on the floor next to the bed, he took her in his arms and held her gently as she began to sob.

"What is your name, miss?" Jubal asked again.

"Oh ... sorry," she said, leaning back out of his embrace and wiping her eyes before looking over at him once again. "My name is Alice. Alice Spencer."

"Good to meet you, Miss Alice. I'm Jubal Collins," he answered, gracing her with what he hoped was a friendly, reassuring smile.

"*Captain* Collins, I see by your uniform," she responded.

He shook his head. "No longer, Miss Alice. I suppose you've not heard the news down here in this cell ... the war is over, at least for me. The federals are now in control here in Richmond."

"Oh!" she said, and then she seemed thoughtful. "That's good news, I suppose. You don't happen to know if my father is still alive, do you? He is Brigadier General Charles Spencer. He was serving on General Beauregard's staff out west, last I knew."

"Sorry, Miss Alice. I've not heard of him, nor do I know what has become of General Beauregard's command. Last I heard, they'd joined up with General Johnston fighting against the federal General Sherman somewhere down in North Carolina. But how they've fared in that fight, I've heard no word.

"My own regiment was among those with General Lee when he surrendered to the Yankee General Grant over to Appomattox. Grant was gracious enough to pardon all us Confederate soldiers after the surrender, and just send us on home.

"Come, Miss Alice. Let's get you out of here, shall we?"

"All right. Thank you, Captain Collins," she said, rising to her to her feet and straightening out her dress, though to his mind, the garment was so filthy and disheveled there was little point to the effort. However, he hadn't the heart to tell her so.

"Please … just call me Jubal. I've no desire to be a captain any longer, nor to ever fight again, for that matter."

For the first time, she smiled, though it was quick and seemed almost unnatural after her long incarceration. She reached out and took his offered arm. "All right, Jubal. Please, lead on. I've had such little exercise these last … however many months it's been … that I dare not trust my own two feet."

"Understandable, Miss Alice. Never fear, I'll not lead you astray."

Again she smiled, this time gazing into his eyes, "That I believe, Jubal. Thank you."

☙❧☙❧☙❧☙❧☙❧

A half hour later, Jubal was rewarded for his rescue by the pleasure of bearing witness to the joyful reunion of Alice with her mother, who likely would've collapsed from the shock right in her foyer if Jubal hadn't stepped up to catch her; until that very moment, she'd believed her long-missing daughter was surely dead.

And though Jubal had no idea what may have happened between the two women prior to Alice's long forced absence, clearly they were now making amends.

Alice was exceedingly contrite and apologetic to her mother, saying, "Momma, I am so sorry for how I treated you before. I was … acting so foolishly and with such unconscionable lack of respect. I have learned my lesson and have served my penance. Can you forgive me?"

"Oh, my dear, darling … there is nothing to forgive. I am just so grateful that you have returned to me. I couldn't possibly be happier," her mother answered, tears of joy streaming down her cheeks as the two embraced.

As Jubal made his excuses and prepared to take his leave, Alice once again took his arm and walked with him to the door. "Jubal … I have no way of thanking you for rescuing me, and I don't even know why you did it. Would you … come call on me again when I'm …" she looked down at her ragged clothes and chuckled, "a little more presentable? If it's not too forward of me to ask," she said, smiling demurely.

Jubal returned the smile and tipped his hat. "It would be an honor, Miss Alice. Yes … I would like that. Uh … to check in on how you're doing, after your recent ordeal. Say, day after tomorrow? Around two o'clock?"

"I'll be looking forward to it, sir," she answered.

And as Jubal strode down the street, headed for his parents' home, he couldn't help feeling a sense that something important may have just happened. And though he still felt a worry for Evelyn, the dark cloud of dread and despair he'd recently been living under seemed to have lifted, and the sun now threatened to shine through in all its glory after a very long absence.

And as if to complete Jubal's growing sense of wellbeing, when he reached home, his mother handed him a letter that had just arrived postmarked Lewisburg, West Virginia. It was from Evelyn.

Chapter 13. Homecoming

"Having a place to go - is a home.
Having someone to love - is a family.
Having both - is a blessing."
- Donna Hedges

Wednesday April 26, 1865 – Richmond, Virginia:

It had not yet been a week since their return, but even so, Margaret was amazed at how much things had improved at the Hughes household. The place had been thoroughly cleaned, holes patched, walls painted, and the few remaining pieces of broken furniture, repaired—some of which had even been completely refinished.

About the only signs of the home's recent abuse was the nearly complete dearth of furnishings, those being impossible to replace given the current state of upheaval in Richmond and throughout the South.

The good news on that front was that the Union blockade was now officially ended, and Jonathan was busily working on plans to restart his shipping trade. Though, that would have to wait for the Union Navy to finish clearing the James River and the Richmond harbor of artificial barriers, sunken ships, and other debris clogging the waterways. It was only a matter of time before goods would once more start flowing into Richmond from all over the globe. Of course, finding anyone who could afford to pay for those goods might be a whole other matter, Margaret considered.

This morning, Margaret was sitting in a recently patched chair, still pungent with the odor of fresh lacquer, sipping a cup of tea and enjoying a day at home after having spent the last three days back at Chimborazo Hospital assisting Head Matron Phoebe Pember take care of patients. To Phoebe's credit, she'd accepted Margaret back no questions asked, as if she'd not just been absent for a month without warning or explanation. And though there was a new government in control now, the Union Army seemed more than happy to let Phoebe continue running the hospital as she'd done throughout the war.

As Margaret ruminated about the slowly improving conditions at the hospital, now that the Union Army was providing food and medicines, Angeline poked her head in at the library door. "Ah, there you are, my dear," she said, smiling brightly.

"Good morning, Angeline. Won't you join me for some tea?" Margaret responded, returning Angeline's smile.

"Well … I was intending to do just that when I heard a knock on the door just now. Not knowing where Samuel has got to at the moment, I answered it myself."

"Yes, and?"

"Well, there was a gentleman at the door, dressed as a Union officer, and he's asking for you."

"Oh? Who is he?" Margaret set down her tea and sat up in her chair.

Angeline beamed, "Best you just come and see for yourself, dear. I'll not spoil the surprise."

Margaret jumped up and raced out the library door. She'd heard reports that Nathan had been in Richmond shortly after the fires were put out, but then he'd left again. That was before Lee had surrendered, so he still had his men to lead, she supposed. Now that the fighting was over, she was excited to see her brother again after such a long separation.

As she stepped out into the foyer, she saw the Union officer standing there in parade dress uniform, freshly laundered and neatly pressed. Though a bit older and more careworn, his was a face she knew well, and dearly loved—but it was *not* Nathan's. This man was shorter of stature and wore spectacles. He held a small bouquet of wildflowers in his fist, which he held out with a tentative smile on his face.

"*William!*" Margaret squealed, raced forward, and leapt into his arms. She clung to him, burying her face into his neck as he gently held and rocked her. She reveled in the feel of his warm, strong arms, and the familiar smell of him that she'd nearly forgotten after more than a year of separation.

And then she was overcome by a wave of emotion and began to sob. "Oh, William, when you left here, I thought I'd never see you again … and now … now … you're here. I can't *believe* it."

"Yes, I'm here, my love. And I promise, this time we will never be parted again. Never in this life."

Friday June 16, 1865 – Richmond, Virginia:

Tony, Henry, Big George, and the fifteen other freemen remaining of those who'd set out from Belle Meade farm a year and nine months earlier—what now felt more like nine *years*—marched together up the dirt road, kicking up a small cloud of dust as they went. Tony reflected on how they were now free men once again, this time free from service in the army, having just been paid and unceremoniously mustered out a few hours earlier.

They passed various groups, large and small, of other uniformed but now disarmed Union soldiers, both black and white, who'd similarly been dismissed. These were headed toward the nearest train station for transportation back to their homes, if they had any.

Tony and company had a different destination; General Chambers had sent them word that he and the other Mountain Meadows men of the Twelfth West Virginia were also mustering out today, and would then set out immediately afterward for his old farm in West Virginia. He'd invited the freemen to meet up with them so they could all travel home together.

When the freemen arrived at the Twelfth's camp, a rolling pasture on a farm a few miles north of Richmond, Tony could see that the mustering out ceremony was just beginning; several hundred uniformed soldiers were formed up, standing to attention as for an inspection, and General Chambers was slowly riding his horse to a position out in front of the assembly. Colonel Tom Clark and Major Jim Wiggins rode beside him, and of course, the great shaggy hound plodded along behind as always.

Tony turned to his companions, and said, "C'mon boys … let's step it up—I'd like to hear what the Captain has to say."

They moved into a trot and made it to the back row of the regiment just as Nathan turned his horse to address the men.

"At ease, gentlemen," he called out, prompting nearly eight hundred men to simultaneously snap to the formal at-ease stance: feet shoulder-width apart and hands behind their backs.

"I'll not keep you long, as I know y'all are eager to start on your way home. But I do believe that a momentous occasion such as this demands a few appropriate words …

"Firstly, let us remove our hats and bow our heads for a moment of silence in which to remember our dear comrades who have given all in our righteous cause, including and especially our late beloved leader, President Lincoln. These heroes have selflessly given their 'last full measure of devotion,' that we who are left behind may inherit a better world."

Then all the soldiers present, including Tony and his men, did as they were bid, following their leader's example.

After a moment, Nathan looked back up, replaced his hat, and continued. "Gentlemen, I know I speak for Colonel Clark as well when I say it has been an honor and a privilege to fight beside you proud soldiers of the Twelfth West Virginia Volunteer Infantry Regiment. Y'all have performed every duty asked of you with courage and determination unmatched by any other outfit in the army. And that is saying a lot, for you may not have realized it in the heat of the action, but you men have just been a part of the greatest fighting force ever assembled. Nothing the Caesars or Napoleon ever mustered comes close.

"And in recognition of your particular heroics at the recent Battle of Fort Gregg, I have received this," he held up a gold eagle, of the type one mounted on a flagpole. "This eagle, to be mounted on the regimental flagstaff, has been given to us by our corps commander. On the plaque at the eagle's feet are engraved the following words: *Presented by Major General John Gibbon to the 12th W. Va. Volunteer Infantry, for Gallant Conduct in the Assault upon Fort Gregg, April 2, 1865.*"

At this announcement, a cheer went up from the assembled troops that lasted for several moments, until Nathan raised his hands for silence so he could continue.

"And you have not only just achieved a monumental and glorious hard-fought triumph over a bold and tenacious enemy, but with that victory you have also won everlasting renown and the undying gratitude of your fellow countrymen. The army in which you've served has saved the great Union of these United States—the greatest nation to ever grace the face of the earth—and freed millions of innocent men, women, and children from the evil scourge of slavery in the process."

Then he paused, and it seemed to Tony that he looked over at their small group, then gestured in their direction.

"And speaking of ... I see we have been joined by some of our brothers in arms, from the Twenty-Third Colored Regiment. Let us turn and give them a hearty Twelfth cheer!"

"About, face!" Major Wiggins called out, and all eight hundred soldiers pivoted about and faced Tony's small group, who continued to stand facing forward in the at-ease stance.

"*Huzzah! Huzzah! Huzzah!*" the men of the Twelfth shouted, removing and waving their hats at Tony and his men.

When they'd finished, Tony called out, "Atten ... *SHUN!*" and the men of the Twenty-Third snapped a salute and held it until General Chambers acknowledged and returned it smartly. Tony saw that Nathan was now grinning brightly.

The men of the Twelfth were then ordered to "Face front!" and turned toward their commanding officers once again.

"Men, I couldn't be prouder of you, and I wish you all a well-deserved peace, joy, and happiness in the years to come," Nathan continued.

"And I would leave you with a verse from the Good Book: in Matthew chapter eleven, verse twenty-eight, the Lord says, '*Come unto me, all ye that labor and are heavy laden, and I will give you rest.*'

"Amen, and Godspeed to your well-deserved rest, gentlemen. Colonel Clark ..."

"Gentlemen, it has been the greatest honor and blessing of my life serving with you," Tom called out. "Allow me to be the *first* to congratulate you on becoming civilians once again. And it is my great joy and privilege to be able to say to you all, for the very *last* time ... COMPANY DISMISSED!"

To which all assembled gave a hearty cheer and threw their hats in the air. Tony and his men did likewise.

Then Tony turned to Henry and Big George and said, "Well ... reckon it's time to go home now."

❧❧❧❧❧❧❧❧❧

Nathan and Tom rode side by side at the head of the small column of riders traveling to West Virginia, including four wagons filled with Tony, Big George, Henry and the other black men from Mountain Meadows. Though Tony and a few others had done a little riding, they didn't own horses, and none of the other former slaves had ever learned to ride, so Nathan had procured the wagons so that they needn't walk the whole distance home—or suffer the pain to the backside from the unfamiliar experience of riding for the first time, or at best, the first time in years. Behind their two leaders rode the former officers of the Twelfth: Jim Wiggins, William, Stan, Zeke, and Ollie Boyd. Margaret rode next to William, and the two conversed quietly as the miles went by.

Tom glanced back at the men, then turned to Nathan and asked, "Hey, where's Billy? Surely he's not out scouting ... not now that the war is over?"

Nathan grinned and pulled a lit cigar from his mouth. "He probably would be, knowing him. But *no*, he's not out scouting. He took off at first light this morning, after a quick goodbye. Said he had some personal business to attend to for a few days. That he would meet us at Mountain Meadows after."

"Didn't even want to stick around for your speech to the men?"

"Nah, he never had much use for speeches." Nathan smiled.

"True," Tom agreed. "Did he say what it was about?"

"No, and I didn't figure it was my business to ask. I think Stan knows, though. But he won't talk about it."

"Oh?"

"I think he's a bit peevish that Billy didn't invite him to come along."

"Ah. Well, I'm sure he'll get over it. Those two have some kind of special connection that's quite extraordinary."

"As do we," Nathan said, gracing Tom with a grin.

Tom returned the smile and nodded.

They were quiet for a few moments, listening to the steady rhythm of their horses' hooves, then Nathan said, "Tom … this is about the happiest day I can recall."

"I know what you mean," Tom answered. "Like a great shadow has been lifted from the world, and the sun is suddenly shining." Then he chuckled, "And us poor souls rise up from cowering on the ground and gaze about wide-eyed, surprised and elated to find that we are still alive after all!"

Nathan grinned. "Yep. And it's all I can do not to kick Millie into a gallop and race all the way home."

"I hear you … I can't wait to see Addie's face again, and give her a big ol' kiss."

"Amen to that," Nathan agreed, thinking the same thought about Evelyn.

"And next is little Nathaniel. What a wonder he is …"

"Yes, and not so little anymore. He's four years old!"

Tom shook his head, "I can hardly believe it. I've missed too much. He's practically grown already."

"Not yet, not yet … and, yes, it will be good to see the little fellow again," Nathan said, and stuck the cigar back in his mouth, grinning brightly at the thought.

ༀ℘ℂ℘℘℘ༀ℘ℂ℘℘℘ༀ℘ℂ℘

Thursday, June 18, 1865 – Newtown, Virginia:

Billy slowly reached down to unbutton the flap of the holster on his right hip as he rode up the mountain trail. He'd been aware of two men following on horseback a short distance back for the last several miles, but had thought little of it. Now he'd noticed two more men sitting on horses behind bushes off to each side of the trail just ahead. Likely they thought to hide from him, and it might've worked on any other man. But Billy wasn't an ordinary man in that regard, so they'd not be able to take him unawares.

He casually slipped the revolver from its holster and rested it in his lap just behind the saddle horn. Although the war was officially over, he thought it likely some men wouldn't see it that way. *Better safe than sorry*, he decided, and clicked back the hammer.

When he was less than a dozen yards away, the men ahead kicked their horses into motion, moving up onto the trail in front of him to block the narrow way. They turned to face him, and in that instant, he could see they each carried a rifle and wore the gray garb of Confederate soldiers, though calling such attire a "uniform" was a bit of a stretch. Billy himself still wore the blue uniform and insignia of a Union sergeant. The war had gone on for so long now that he hadn't anything else to wear.

Billy pulled his horse to a halt and gazed at the men. He didn't need to turn around to know how close the men behind were; his finely honed scouting skills had tracked them by the noise of their horses.

"War's over," Billy said in a matter-of-fact tone. "No need for any trouble with you men."

Even as he said this, the riders behind came to a halt some twenty feet behind.

"Well, lookie here, fellas," the tall, skinny one in front to Billy's left said. "We got ourselves a blue belly sergeant. And I'll be damned if he ain't an injun to boot!"

Billy just looked at him and shrugged, "You observe correctly. What do you want?"

"What do we want? Well, for starters, your horse and your weapons and ammunition. Then we'll take any food you got. But if you're lucky, we won't also take your life."

Billy slowly nodded, then sat up straight in the saddle, and looked back over his left shoulder, as if noticing the men behind him for the first time. Then he looked back at the men in front. So confident were they of their prey that three of the four held their rifles pointed skyward in a relaxed attitude. Only the one behind and to the left pointed his weapon at Billy's back. *Fools*, he decided.

"Let me pass, and I won't have to kill you," he said.

The man laughed. "You hear that, boys? He figures t'kill all four o' us. Like we was still wet behind the ears, and not hardened veteran soldiers."

Billy just shrugged, "Hardened or not, you'll still die, when you could just go on living …"

"Oh really? And how you gonna do tha—"

The man's words were cut short by a knife handle that suddenly appeared in the center of his chest, sent with a flick of Billy's left wrist. And at the same moment, a gunshot rang out, and the man behind Billy to his left tumbled from the saddle, struck by a bullet fired backward from under Billy's left armpit.

Billy's revolver sprang forward like a snake and another round fired, taking out the second rider in front.

A loud concussion sent a rifle round screaming over Billy's head as he ducked down, and he could feel the breeze of it pass through his hair, even as he turned back and took out the fourth man with the revolver.

He sat up, gazed about to see if any of the men yet moved. Three were stone dead, but the fourth still twitched. He was the one who'd been behind and on the left, who Billy had shot without looking, purely by memory from the brief glance he'd taken back over his shoulder. So Billy stepped his horse up next to the man. He could see that the bullet had missed the heart, slightly to the right. The man's eyes were rolled back in his head, and he was gurgling on his own blood. Billy leaned down, pointed the revolver at the man's forehead and fired, ending his suffering.

He then holstered the Colt and climbed down from the saddle. Stepping over to the man who'd spoken, he knelt down and yanked his hunting knife free, wiping it off on the man's shirt before returning it to its sheath behind his back.

He looked around but could see only one of the bushwhackers' horses; it had apparently tangled its reins on a tree branch and could no longer move. The other three horses had apparently already run off, likely spooked by the sound of the gunshots and the smell of their masters' blood.

Billy stepped over to the remaining horse and removed its saddle, dropping it to the ground. Then he untangled the reins, and removed the bridle, tossing that aside as well. Then, giving the horse a swat on the flank, he shouted, "*Go on now!*" The horse bolted off, back down the trail. "Go on ... and be free," he whispered, watching until it passed out of sight around a bend in the path.

Then he returned to his own horse, swung back into the saddle and kicked her into motion, stepping past his fallen adversaries where they lay next to the trail.

He looked down at them and shrugged, "I told you the war was over ..." To this sensible statement the dead men gave no answer.

ഗ്രരദ്രരദ്രരദ്ര

Two hours later, Billy reached the place he'd been seeking: a high point covered in tall pines, overlooking a wooded terrain stretching for miles on every side.

He tied the horse to a tree limb, and then, remembering the four bushwhackers earlier, pulled the Henry rifle from its sheath at his saddle and took the time to hide it a few yards away. *Just in case*, he decided.

He knew his present mission had little chance of bearing fruit after all this time, but he felt a need to try ... to seek out his old companion, hoping against hope to find her again. Then he snorted a chuckle. *Like so many other foolish men—chasing an elusive female!* It was likely a waste of time, but it was his to waste, now that the war was over. And this was where he'd last seen her, so he figured it was worth a try.

He shrugged. Then, picking out the tallest tree on the hilltop, he reached up, he grabbed a branch, and heaved himself up. After a brief scramble, he reached the top. There he clung, swaying sickeningly on the thinnest section of tree, hundreds of feet above the ground.

He pulled up the binoculars that hung from his neck and slowly scanned the landscape in front of him, looking for any sign of movement in or above the trees.

Seeing nothing, he decided to try the thing that'd worked before; he cupped his hands to his mouth and made the distinctive, shrill call of a red-tailed hawk.

And then ... nothing happened. He repeated the call every half a minute or so, aiming in different directions, but still ... nothing.

Again he scanned the forest with the binoculars, but there was nothing to be seen other than a few distant vultures, distinguished by their odd, wobbly manner of flight.

Billy stayed up in the tree for several more hours, repeating the calling and scanning every few minutes. Eventually he tired of the sport, and decided it was time to admit defeat. So he climbed back down, retrieved the Henry, untied the horse, and remounted.

He'd originally thought to camp out in the hills for several days, if necessary, perhaps trying out different high points. Now, however, with the dead men back down the trail, it didn't seem worth the risk. After all, they may have had friends who'd likely not appreciate Billy having killed them. He decided it was best to not push his luck, and for the same reason, he planned to take a different trail back to town.

He was trotting along, chewing on a piece of hard tack, when something struck the top of his head, crumpling his hat and nearly toppling him from his saddle. The horse shied and whinnied, but Billy managed to maintain control and bring her to a stop. He sat up straight, then slowly reached up to feel the top of his head. He felt something hard and sharp clutching at the felt of his hat, and then something soft. Like ... *feathers*.

He chuckled. "Hello, Ladyhawk ... Where have you been?"

Her only answer was a loud squawk.

❧❧❧❧❧❧❧❧❧

Nathan knew from an exchange of telegrams with Miss Abbey that nearly everyone, with a few exceptions, had now relocated from Belle Meade Farm in Wheeling, West Virginia back to Mountain Meadows Farm to await the return of the men who'd fought in the war. And he'd also informed Miss Abbey of the date of the men's mustering out from the service, so she was aware of their imminent arrival.

So he was not surprised to see a large gathering in front of the Big House as their company crested the rise and looked down into the valley where the farm lay. And as the soldiers became visible to those below, he could see them react: jumping, waving hats and handkerchiefs, and embracing one another joyfully.

And though the crowd stayed back respectfully as the men made their way down the long, sloping drive, once they'd passed the old slave cabins, the floodgates opened, and everyone came streaming out to greet them.

Nathan paused and allowed the other men to pass by him in their excitement and enthusiasm. Men leapt from the saddle and from the wagons and rushed forward to meet their friends and loved ones in a passionate throng of warm greetings, embraces, and kisses.

Nathan stayed in the saddle, gazing out at the Big House … where *she* stood all alone, tall and slender in a pale colored dress, at the top of the stairs at the edge of the veranda. Her hair sparkled like gold in the sunlight—and it occurred to him then that he'd not seen it that color in years, as the last several times he'd seen her, she'd worn it dyed black in disguise.

She gazed out at him and their eyes met. And though she bore a warm, serene visage, she was not smiling. And he knew without any doubt that this was one of the greatest moments he would ever behold in his life. The moment when they would finally come together, and never again be apart.

He stepped down from the saddle and waded into the happy crowd. As if in a dream, he greeted everyone, warmly and sincerely, exchanging kind words and embraces, and drinking in the joyous reunions around him: Big George crushing Babs in his strong embrace, then gently lifting his girls, Annie and Lucy, one in each arm; Tony and Rosa, laughing and smiling while she congratulated him on not getting killed but chastised him for being away so long; Addie screaming as she rushed into Tom's arms and clung there while he reached down and scooped their son up into the embrace, even as Uncle Edouard stepped up and patted Tom on the back with great affection and enthusiasm; Henry and Lilly crying like babies as they quietly spoke together a little apart from the crowd; Ollie and Belinda, who'd been apart for the least amount of time, enjoying a more subdued, but nonetheless heartfelt reunion. And even those with no current love interest—Jim, Stan, Zeke, and many of the black soldiers—waded into the crowd laughing, joking, exchanging warm greetings, embraces, and pats on the back with everyone there.

And, of course, Nathan hugged and kissed his momma, and Megs, sharing warm, loving greetings as expected. Even Harry the Dog joined in the merriment, wandering through the crowd, wagging his tail, and suffering anyone who wished to pet him without taking offense.

All the while, no matter where he looked, and no matter who he greeted or embraced, Nathan could feel *her* presence … there on the veranda … drawing him in like an irresistible magnet. *Evelyn, my love … my life. She is waiting.*

Finally, Nathan had worked his way through the crowd. He now stepped toward the house. Evelyn stood there, gazing down at him, staring into his eyes as he approached. And then it seemed to him that the world stood still, and all was quiet around him. In that moment, nothing seemed to exist but her intense eyes and the warm glow of her presence, drawing him toward her like a moth to the flame.

He stepped up to the bottom of the stairs and removed his hat. Then he bowed to her, and said, "Well … I'm home, my lady."

Then she curtsied deeply. "Welcome home, General Chambers … *my love.*" And in that moment, he realized that *home* was not Mountain Meadows after all; home, from now on, was wherever he and Evelyn were together. And though they were not yet married, it was clear that she was now the lady of the house, and not by reason of being his betrothed, but rather by way of having earned the right.

They continued to gaze into each other's eyes for another long moment, and it seemed to Nathan as if the world held its breath. Then he smiled, and she returned his smile, and she laughed, a sweet, joyful sound. He leapt up the stairs, three in a bound, and swept her off her feet and into his arms.

And as he held her and kissed her, a loud noise behind him caused him to spin her around so he could look back toward the drive. He laughed and set Evelyn back onto her feet. Gazing out at the crowd on the drive, they saw that everyone was now watching the two of them. Perhaps sensing that something special was about to happen, they had all paused to watch. And when the Captain and Miss Evelyn had finally embraced, a resounding cheer had gone up.

Later that evening, as the entire farm gathered around the traditional celebratory bonfire, Nathan fell asleep leaned back in a chair, holding Evelyn's hand, a contented smile still lighting his face.

ॐॐ

Saturday July 1, 1865 – Fort Leavenworth, Kansas:

"Hey, there you are, I been looking for you," Lieutenant August "Auggie" Gordon said, as he stepped up and sat next to Ned on a bench outside the mess hall.

"Hello, Lieutenant … Sorry, was just restin' for a moment, 'fore I headed back to the barracks," Ned explained, as he sat up straighter.

Auggie chuckled and shook his head. Ned smiled, and said, "All right … I was slackin', you got me. Just felt nice to sit in the sun for a spell."

Auggie just slapped Ned on the knee and said, "Don't worry, I'll let it go … *this time*." The two shared a smile. It was a running joke, as the two of them had been through so many battles together and had covered each other's backsides so often that they'd become close friends. *Closer than friends*, Ned decided, *more like brothers*. It'd been years since Auggie had even said a stern word to Ned, let alone meted out any punishment. And though Ned still referred to Auggie by his rank, it was more out of habit and propriety in the ranks than out of a feeling of subservience.

"So, why you been lookin' for me?" Ned asked.

"I had a question for you."

"All right …"

"Ned ... now that the war's over and all, have you given any thought to what you're going to do once we're mustered out? Go on back to Virginia, maybe?"

Ned's expression suddenly turned serious. "Don't rightly know, Lieutenant. Part of me wants to go back, just to see all them old folks I growed up with. But ... to be honest, the thought of goin' back to farmin' ... after all we been through." He slowly shook his head. "I ... I don't know 'bout that."

"I know *exactly* how you feel," Auggie said.

"You do?"

"Oh, yeah. Ned ... we been soldiers for four years now. Frightful life-or-death adventures ... mixed with unspeakable boredom," he laughed. "Hard to go back to normal, civilian life after doing all that. It seems like it'd just be ... I don't know ... *odd*, somehow."

"Yep. 'Odd' seems the right word for it. So, you don't want to go back to being a store clerk back at Kansas City?"

Auggie shook his head. "Just can't imagine standing behind a counter serving out hard candy to toddlers or helping ladies pick out fabric for their new Sunday dresses ... not after watching men get their heads blown off by a cannon ball."

"Yeah ... I know what you mean. I feel the same about hoeing weeds," Ned said. "So ... what can we do now?"

"Ah, glad you asked," Auggie said, now grinning.

"The colonel says there's talk of recruiting a new regiment of them that wants to stay in the army rather than mustering out. A regiment to stay right out here on the frontier. And I figure a lot of the freemen like you won't want to go back to farming now that they've been trained up for soldiers and had a taste of adventure. And ... I have it on good authority that they're finally gonna let you black men be officers, now that you've proven yourselves in battle.

"Think about it, Ned ... you an' me can be officers together, leading the regiment," he concluded, eying Ned expectantly.

Ned nodded, thinking over the idea, but then he chuckled, "Hell, Lieutenant ... there ain't nothin' out here in the Kansas wilderness. Who're we gonna fight, the buffaloes?"

Auggie laughed. "No, not buffaloes, silly: hostile Indians! Now that the war is over, folks are gonna start moving out west again, and I reckon them Indians are gonna be none too happy about that. There's bound to be a big ol' fight."

"Hmm … makes sense," Ned agreed.

Then Auggie got a thoughtful expression, "But you know … you got me thinking about them buffaloes …"

"The buffaloes? What about them?"

"I was just thinking we need a catchy, romantic name for our new freeman regiment of Indian fighters, and I think you've got it. We'll call ourselves *the Buffalo Soldiers!*"

⁂

"So, back at the beginning of the year, General Sherman had proposed giving each freed slave family forty acres and a mule. But if *we* did that, given something like fifty families, you'd have no land left, even dividing up both Mountain Meadows and Belle Meade farms," Tom said, looking up from the sheet of paper he'd been scribbling on with his pencil. "Not to mention, with no income other than our army salaries and the corn crop from Belle Meade these last few years, we'd never have enough money to buy all those mules. Unless we restarted the saltpeter works."

"Well, that's a possibility," Nathan said, "And speaking of, it does look like the Confederates discovered and expanded our simple works. I notice they put in a road up to the place where we'd originally dug."

"Oh? That's interesting. I wonder how much they were able to extract. But regardless … I have to believe the price of saltpeter will plummet, now that the war is over, and gunpowder will no longer be in such high demand," Tom answered.

"True, true … Well, clearly, giving out forty acres is beyond our reach, as are mules, though I *can* give most of them a horse, thanks to the ones left behind by Walters and his cavalry," Nathan said.

"Oh, that's true … I'd nearly forgotten about those," Tom replied. "Must be around forty of them, I should think."

"Yes, forty-three," Nathan answered.

"Well, that'll help," Tom nodded.

"You know … it's one thing for the federal government to dole out that much property, it's quite another for us," Nathan continued. "Though, from what I understand, that has been something of an empty promise by the government anyway, at least so far. And with the new president, Johnson, being a Democrat, it seems to me that particular program may never happen."

Then Nathan shook his head sadly, "It's one more reason to mourn the passing of Abraham Lincoln. I think we've yet to appreciate the full ramifications of that tragedy. And ironically, it's likely to hurt the people of the South more than in the North. Already we hear rumblings of punishing the South rather than reconciling, of punitively stripping it of any remaining wealth and resources, rather than rebuilding it."

"Agreed. It felt like Lincoln would reunite us all in a spirit of forgiveness and brotherhood, while those now in charge only want their pound of flesh," Tom answered.

"All that being said, Tom … what *can* we do for the freemen?"

"Well, how about we start with five acres and a cabin? And we help them obtain or borrow equipment? That would come to 250 acres, which is about a quarter of Mountain Meadows. And what of Belle Meade up at Wheeling? What are you thinking on that?"

"Well, I've been thinking that I can't be in two places at once, so I had figured on just selling it off. But now … well, old Toby and his wife Anna have decided they want to stay there, and so have a dozen others. I don't have the heart to sell it out from under them, and I fear if I start dividing it up into small parcels, it'll be more difficult to sell later. I figure I'll just wait and see on that. So for the time being, let's focus our attention on Mountain Meadows."

"All right," Tom said. "We could see how it goes with the five acres, and if we can still maintain a profit, we could increase it to ten acres in a few years."

"Okay … that seems doable. Will you start drawing up the papers, Tom? I'd greatly appreciate it."

"Certainly. I'll get started straightaway."

They were quiet for a few moments as Tom finished scribbling down some notes. When he'd stopped, Tom looked up at Nathan and said, "There's one other thing I wished to discuss with you …"

"Oh?"

"Yes … speaking of farms … it's my understanding that Walters' farm, being abandoned and him leaving behind no heirs—and given his status as an enemy officer—his land has been confiscated by Greenbrier County and is to be auctioned off."

"Interesting …" Nathan said.

"So … I was thinking of buying it and living there, so we could be neighbors. Oh, and I could contribute some of that farm's acreage to the freemen as well, which ought to help. But, though I expect it will sell for pennies on the dollar—given that the Northerners who might afford it likely won't have heard of it yet—I was wondering if you might see your way clear to fronting me some money, if what I've saved up from my officer's pay isn't enough."

"Oh! But, Tom … I'd always assumed you'd stay here with me at Mountain Meadows. You're certainly more than welcome …" Nathan answered, frowning.

Tom didn't immediately answer, but gave Nathan a serious look.

After a moment Nathan shook his head. "You're right, you're right. Of course. You have a family now, and your own life … if you live here, you will never be the master of your own home. And that wouldn't be proper—you deserve better."

Tom just nodded and smiled, appreciating that he hadn't had to explain it.

"Tell you what … I'll front you the money, and later you can pay it back by redrawing the disputed property line in my favor."

"Done, and thank you!" Tom answered, extending his hand.

"But … there's one more condition," Nathan said, not yet taking Tom's proffered hand.

"Oh? What's that?"

"That you and I must get together regularly. At least twice a week … every Sunday for family dinner after church, and … say Wednesday after work for a whiskey and cigars."

Tom smiled, "Agreed."

Then they shook hands to seal the deal.

Chapter 14. Wedding Bells

"When I saw you, I fell in love,
and you smiled because you knew."
- Arrigo Boito

Saturday July 15, 1865 – Greenbrier County, West Virginia:

As Reverend Holing stood in front of the large gathering on the lawn in front of the Big House at Mountain Meadows and raised his hands to begin the ceremony, Nathan and Evelyn met eyes and shared a warm smile.

"Dearly beloved, we are gathered this day to invoke a most sacred and blessed event," the pastor began.

And though Nathan and Evelyn were dressed in finery fitting to the matrimonial occasion, their shared smile was not because this was their special day—which it was not—but rather in anticipation of *that* special day yet to come.

This day was another "big wedding," such as had been held at Mountain Meadows back before the war. This time, there were only three couples, Tony and Rosa, William and Margaret, and Hank and Mary. And the couples had requested a much simpler ceremony, so Evelyn had been forced to reel in her inclination toward excess, for which Nathan was grateful; unlike that earlier wedding, money at Mountain Meadows was now very much in short supply.

When the three couples had together approached Nathan and Evelyn to discuss the joint wedding, Nathan and Evelyn had immediately agreed to host the event, and had even offered to join in and make it a quadruple affair.

It was William who answered for the group, "Nathan … Evelyn … we have discussed what to say in the event you suggested such a thing, and we are all in agreement that you two should *not* join with us in this ceremony."

"Oh? Why not?" Evelyn asked.

"Though we are, of course, honored by the offer, we are all in agreement that it wouldn't be proper. You two have been the leaders of this"—he waved his hand to include not only the couples there, but the entire farm behind them—"extended family, and as such, deserve your own special day. And we think it ought to be the grandest event ever, while we three couples just want something … simpler."

So in the end, they'd agreed to hold the one triple wedding, and another, grander affair for just the two of them a month or so later.

And though Henry gave away Rosa, serving as her father, as earlier promised, Nathan served as the stand-in father for Margaret, while Tom performed the same duty for Mary.

Nathan, as usual, had left the details to the ladies, so after listening to much the same ceremony from Reverend Holing as he'd witnessed on the previous occasion, complete with the three couples repeating their vows, he was as surprised as anyone when the pastor turned to the gathering and said something unexpected.

"Dear loved ones," the minister said, smiling, "I have been asked by the couples to add something to this particular ceremony that, I must confess, I've never done before in all my years of ministry. So, please bear with me, and if I misspeak my lines, I humbly ask your understanding and forgiveness in advance. Gentlemen … ladies," he said, turning to the couples, "please hold hands and line up as we've planned."

The three couples did as they were bid, with Hank and Mary in front, Tony and Rosa behind them, and finally, William and Margaret.

And then, to Nathan's further surprise, Evelyn stepped up in front of him, where he stood next to the bridegrooms, and held out … a broom?

"What's this, Evelyn?" he asked.

"Well … it's a broom," she answered with a grin, which caused a chitter of laughter through the crowd.

"Come on, Nathan … we have a job to do here," she said, and turned toward where the couples were waiting. With a shrug, he followed.

Evelyn stood in front of Hank just out to one side, and she directed Nathan to stand to the side of Mary, but also out in front. Then she stretched the broom in front of the wedding couple, extending the handle toward Nathan. He smiled, nodding his understanding, and reached out to take the broom handle.

"Now, as many of you may know," Reverend Holing continued, "it has long been a practice among those held in bondage to perform a tradition known as 'jumping the broom' in lieu of a traditional Christian wedding that many of their masters forbade. The two freeman couples standing before you today wished to add this tradition into the formal Christian ceremony to honor those who've come before, their suffering and forbearance, and their newfound freedom.

"So, if my esteemed assistants will position the broom, please."

Evelyn and Nathan did as they were bid, lowering the broom stretched in front of Hank and Mary until it was only inches off the ground.

"And now, Henry, being the father of one of the brides, and also having participated in the ceremony himself with his lovely wife Lilly, will please come forward and officiate this part of the ceremony."

Henry stood and stepped up next to the pastor, then turned to face the congregation. "The old tradition says that jumping the broom means the couple jumps into a new life," he said. "Two parts that's separate, into one that's whole, so they say. And the broom is meant for the sweeping away of the past, 'cause after that, the two become one, forever after.

"Mary and Hank … go ahead and jump the broom now," he said, gesturing toward the implement stretched in front of them.

The two looked at each other, shared a smile, and then jumped, landing to the applause and cheering of the gathering. And if the pastor was disturbed by this boisterous interruption of the sacred ceremony, he showed no sign of it, smiling as Henry ordered Rosa and Tony to follow suit.

Then all three of the couples turned and stood before the pastor, and he said, "Now that these men and these women have given themselves to each other by solemn vows, I pronounce they are husbands and wives, in the name of the Father, and of the Son, and of the Holy Spirit. Amen."

"Evelyn, dear, do we have any more of that dark-red thread?" Abbey asked, looking up from the rose she was embroidering.

"Um … I think so … Let me see," Evelyn responded, setting down the section of cloth she'd been working on to rummage in the small basket sitting on the floor next to her.

"I have some extra, Momma," Margaret offered, reaching down to pick up a small spool, then walking it over to where Miss Abbey sat in a chair in one corner of the kitchen.

"Thank you, dear," Abbey said, as she accepted the spool and began to unwind a length of thread for her needle.

Evelyn took advantage of the interruption to gaze around the room, which brought a smile to her face. It was a true team effort, as well as a labor of love among the women here—made even more so by the object of their labors: Evelyn's wedding dress.

And not only was the wonderful comradery of the present effort a blessing, but the materials themselves were something that Evelyn had assumed she would have to forgo, settling for a simpler, less-expensive garment due to the present desperately tight money situation of the Chambers family. Without prompting, Angeline Hughes had sent Evelyn all the supplies she could desire to make pretty much any wedding gown she could envision: yards and yards of the finest white satin, roll upon roll of lace, and a veritable barrel of thread spools in every color of the rainbow, along with needles, scissors, measuring tapes, and all the other necessary accoutrements.

The gift had been delivered to Mountain Meadows along with a handwritten note:

Megs sat next to Evelyn on her left, helping her to sew lace onto the shimmering satin cloth, and after that, in addition to Miss Abbey and Margaret, around the kitchen table working on various aspects of the project with Belinda, Adilida, Rosa, and Sarah.

And on the floor in the corner sat little Nathaniel, engrossed in a hat box full of hundreds of buttons of all shapes, sizes, and colors that Miss Abbey had provided to keep him entertained. He was presently sorting and stacking them with a logic and efficiency that brought his father Tom to mind, Evelyn decided. *Guess the apple doesn't fall far from the tree,* she thought and smiled.

And then, as Evelyn's eyes continued panning the room, she came at last to the woman seated directly to her right: her mother,

Harriet. Harriet had her head down, focused on the flower she was embroidering, and Evelyn had to admit her mother performed the task with great skill. However, her presence was still conflicting.

It had been a source of contention between Evelyn and Nathan since shortly after settling back into life at Mountain Meadows. Evelyn had mentally and emotionally written off her mother, and had decided never to have anything more to do with her. Harriet's betrayal had nearly turned deadly, and Evelyn had not been able to emotionally move past it.

It was Nathan's steady, even-tempered approach to the situation that had gradually worn down her resolve. He argued that it was time to mend fences, especially where family was concerned, and even invoked the late president's desire to "bind up the nation's wounds." Finally, Evelyn had relented and written to her mother, inviting her to come back to Mountain Meadows.

When Harriet had arrived a few weeks later, they'd walked down to the pond, sat on the swing, and talked for a long time. Evelyn had vented her anger and frustration, and Harriet had tearfully apologized. In the end, Harriet had promised that she would defer to Evelyn on all matters from that moment on. And so far, she had been true to her word, Evelyn had to admit. She also knew it was going to take a long time before any warm familial feelings might be rebuilt, if ever.

Evelyn turned her attention back to the project, deciding she was pleased with the progress. She felt a sudden thrill of excitement at the thought of Nathan seeing the gown on her for the first time on their wedding day.

Hmm … guess it's about time we started planning that, she decided, smiling to herself.

❧❧❧❧❧❧❧❧❧

Thursday August 31, 1865 – White Sulphur Springs, West Virginia:

Nathan and Evelyn had originally intended to hold their wedding and the following reception on the lawn in front of the

Big House, just as the other couples had done. However, once they started compiling the list of guests to invite, it quickly became apparent that Mountain Meadows simply could not accommodate the event. There was plenty of room on the lawn, of course, and given enough time, they could fashion a sufficient quantity of chairs and benches for everyone to have a seat, but there simply weren't enough bedrooms to house all the expected guests. And given that the list of invitees included some *very* august individuals, pitching tents out in the pasture was out of the question.

To Nathan's relief, it was Tom who not only came up with the solution to the problem, but also took charge of making sure the event venue was properly prepared.

"Why not hold it at the Greenbrier Hotel at White Sulphur Springs? It can't be more than ten miles east of the turnoff to Mountain Meadows, and it's got plenty of rooms," Tom suggested.

"True, but don't you remember the shape it was in when last we saw it?" Nathan responded. "I recall how sparklingly new it looked before the war. But like everything else around here, it has suffered through the long conflict. From what I understand, the place has changed hands multiple times—been used for a barracks, hospital, quartermaster's depot, officers' headquarters, etcetera. When last we saw it, the place was looking sadly disheveled—most of its fixtures and furnishings were either damaged or missing entirely."

Tom just grinned. "Yes, I remember. But leave that to me. As we say in the army, every crisis is also an opportunity. And though we don't have much money, the one thing we do have at the moment is plenty of labor. All our original Texas and Mountain Meadows men, plus lots of other ex-soldiers wandering around looking for employment while things slowly get back to normal around here."

True to his word and in short order, Tom made a deal with the hotel owner, that he would provide the labor if the proprietor provided the materials to fix the place back up. In return for their help, Mountain Meadows would be allowed to use the event venue and guest housing for free, other than paying for the out-of-pocket expenses for food, cleaning, and so forth. It was a win for all concerned; it gave the hotel the sudden boost it needed to get restarted and back on the map, and it solved Nathan's wedding venue conundrum.

So now, the day before the wedding, Nathan and Evelyn had relocated to rooms in the hotel, along with the other family members, and busied themselves with greeting their important guests as the last of them arrived.

Nathan was standing by the door of the foyer of the hotel when two handsome, nicely dressed young gentlemen came in, accompanied by a pretty young lady with curling blonde hair flowing down from under her stylish hat. Nathan immediately greeted his old protégé, James Hawkins, with great affection, and the two shared an embrace. Hawkins turned to his companions, and said, "General, I believe you have already met my friend—"

Just then, Evelyn stepped up and threw her arms around the other young gentleman. "Jubal!" she exclaimed, as he returned her embrace, smiling, but seeming slightly embarrassed, blushing furiously. "Oh, Jubal," she continued, "I didn't know until just now if you were even still alive. Oh, thank God you're safe."

Nathan and James exchanged an amused look, and a shrug, but Nathan noticed that the young lady looked puzzled, and … *uncomfortable*, maybe?

The two separated from their embrace, and Jubal said, "But Evelyn … I answered your letter, telling you that all was well with me. I even told you I'd met your betrothed, General Chambers, on the battlefield, and that James had invited me to come with him to your wedding. Didn't you receive my letter?"

She shook her head, wiping back a tear, "No … it's the darned post, you know … still hasn't recovered from the war, apparently. I never heard anything from you, and I was so worried, and … *oh! Alice!* Alice Spencer, my dear … I … I didn't know you'd be here either. So good to see you again, and I'm so delighted you've come." She glanced at Jubal, who continued to blush, but smiled. Evelyn gave Nathan a meaningful look, which he returned with a subtle nod.

Alice then smiled for the first time, and the two women embraced.

"Speaking of …" Jubal said, extending his hand toward Nathan, "It is good to see you again, General. And I would be remiss if I didn't thank you once again for the kindness you showed me and my men after that last battle."

"Never mention it, Mr. Collins. And welcome, most welcome. I am also pleased to see you again, but I had no idea that you and Evelyn were acquainted."

Though Evelyn had never mentioned Jubal, Nathan decided not to mention that he *had* heard the name *Alice Spencer*. Evelyn had shared the story of how she'd turned the tables on the young lady who'd been an enemy double-agent, and had arranged to have her arrested by the Confederate Signal Corps. However, Alice had known nothing about Evelyn's involvement in that plot. So apparently, now that the war had been settled, all would be forgiven and forgotten.

He decided that the two women would figure that out without his help. And indeed, they were already chatting away like old friends.

And he had to admit to feeling pleased that this handsome and heroic young "friend" of Evelyn's apparently already had a lady friend of his own.

ᏚᎯᏟᎦᏩᎠᏚᎯᏟᎦᏩᎠᏚᎯᏟᎦ

At the end of the day, Nathan and Evelyn were finally able to find a few minutes to be alone, sitting at a table outside on a patio, watching the sun set over the long, sloping lawn of the hotel.

Nathan sipped a glass of whiskey as Evelyn enjoyed a glass of warmed brandy and read from a newspaper, and Harry the Dog lounged under the table.

"Listen to this, Nathan—it's from the *Wheeling Intelligencer*. Reverend Holing was kind enough to bring it along, and gave it to me this morning:"

Momentous Wedding to Be Held in Greenbrier County

The famed Greenbrier Hotel in White Sulphur Springs, West Virginia, has announced an historic wedding to be held at their location, which is celebrating its grand reopening after being used mostly as a military hospital throughout the late war.

The wedding, to be held on the first of September, will join together one of West Virginia's statehood heroes, Union Brigadier General Nathaniel Chambers, with well-known Richmond socialite Miss Evelyn Hanson.

General Chambers most recently led the Twelfth West Virginia Volunteer Infantry Regiment as well as an entire Union brigade in the victories at Petersburg and Appomattox. Prior to accepting his commission, Chambers was instrumental in assisting Governor Francis Pierpont in establishing the Restored Government of Virginia, and the new state of West Virginia, serving the dual role of chief law enforcement officer and military advisor to the governor. Chambers currently owns a large estate outside Wheeling, as well as another in Greenbrier County, recently liberated from the late Southern rebels.

Miss Hanson, for her part, is said to have been one of the most well-respected and beloved ladies in Richmond prior to the war, and has remained a loyal Unionist and avid abolitionist throughout the course of the conflict.

The wedding is touted as one of the grandest ever to be held at the Greenbrier, as it includes among its esteemed guests two governors—the honorable Francis Pierpont of Virginia, and the honorable Arthur Boreman of West Virginia—one United States senator—Mr. Waitman Willey of West Virginia—and two Union major generals—General William Rosecrans, and General Rufus Saxton. The ceremony will be conducted in the

"Well, you sound like quite the catch, Mr. Chambers," she said, looking back up and smiling, "while I sound … hmm … somewhat ordinary by compare."

He chuckled. "Perhaps because they failed to mention that you are not only charming and brilliant, but are in fact the world's most beautiful woman … and its deadliest!"

She scowled and whacked him with the newspaper in response, but then the two shared a laugh and leaned in for a long kiss.

Friday September 1, 1865 – White Sulphur Springs, West Virginia:

Nathan stood at the front of the assembly dressed in the elegant full-parade uniform of a Union brigadier general, its long navy blue frock coat with its double row of shining brass buttons secured at the waist by a gold silk sash, and a sword belt from which hung a sparkling sword sheath. On top of all, he wore his best officer's Hardee-style hat, with its signature brim pinned up on one side and an ostrich plume on the other, with brass infantry officer's bugle insignia at the front.

And though it was a bright, sunny day, there was a gentle breeze that kept the air moving so that he did not feel overly uncomfortable in the heavy clothing.

Reverend Holing stood to his right, with Tom to his left, though Harry the Dog, who sat behind them on the grass, currently had his prodigious head rested between them, to the reverend's amusement. Next to Tom stood Nathan's two groomsmen, his brothers-in-law, William and Tony. All three of Nathan's groomsmen wore their finest parade-dress uniforms, complete with sabers at their hips.

On the other side of Reverend Holing stood the bridesmaids, Belinda—the maid of honor—followed by Nathan's two sisters Rosa and Margaret, and finally Tom's wife, Adilida.

To their back stood the elegant springhouse at the Greenbrier, which had been built atop the spring of sulfurous waters from which the town took its name. The house featured a copper dome, topped by a statue of Hebe, the Greek goddess of youth, held up by a dozen white columns. The pavilion was surrounded by brightly colored, freshly planted flowers, giving the wedding scene a magnificent, colorful, classical look.

Out of the corner of one eye, Nathan saw a flash of movement up in the sky. He looked over and was not surprised to see Billy's hawk streak high across the lawn and settle into the topmost branches of a tree, presumably where she could keep watch over her constant companion.

Nathan turned to look at the congregation and noted the family members in the front row on the left side: Miss Abbey, Megs, Little Nathaniel, Uncle Edouard, and surprisingly, Harriet Hanson. Evelyn had resisted inviting her mother for the longest time, but had finally relented, to Nathan's surprise. He thought it was generally a good thing to make amends with family, though he wondered if he would live to regret pushing her on it.

On the right side in the front row were the esteemed guests of honor, even as the newspaper had mentioned: the two governors, one US senator, and two major generals, along with Jonathan and Angeline Hughes, though Nathan noticed that Jonathan was not yet in his seat, for some reason.

The last, but not least, honored guest in the front row, seated next to Angeline, was their old friend, the master spy Joseph, who had shocked everyone at the event by announcing his real name for the first time in four years: Averell Joseph Langford, a prominent Richmond attorney before the war. However, he asked that everyone continue to call him Joseph, as he'd become accustomed to it, and most of his favorite people only knew him by that name.

Nathan continued to gaze out at the audience, taking in all the other familiar faces: Jubal Collins and Alice Spencer, Gareth

Hughes in his dress captain's uniform, Hank and Mary, and many of the freemen who'd returned from Belle Meade, including Big George's wife Babs, and their two girls, now nearly full grown, Annie and Lucy. Noticeably absent were old Toby and his wife Anna. They'd decided not to undertake the long trip south, and to finish up their days at Belle Meade farm instead. Besides, Toby had argued, someone had to stay and get the corn harvest in, which Nathan couldn't argue with, knowing they would shortly be in desperate need of the money; they now had two farms to run, and Mountain Meadows would have no fall harvest, requiring a complete restart on all its crops come spring.

Busily escorting ladies to their seats were the members of the honor guard, decked out in their finest military uniforms, cleaned and polished to perfection, with sparkling swords at their hips: Jim Wiggins, Zeke, Stan, Billy, Henry, Big George, James Hawkins, and Ollie Boyd.

Evelyn had once again arranged for a small orchestra, but this time from Wheeling rather than Richmond, as had been the case for the Mountain Meadows "Big Wedding" of four years earlier.

It had come as no surprise to him that Evelyn had planned the whole thing with the help of Miss Abbey and Megs, such that Nathan really had no idea how it would all come together. Pretty much the only thing he'd had a say in was the guest list. Everything else, even down to how he and the other soldiers were to dress in their military finery—complete with swords on hips— had been dictated by Evelyn.

As the assembled wedding party and guests were now positioned well out on the lawn, Nathan was having a difficult time imagining how Evelyn would make her grand entrance. Would she arrive in a carriage, or walk the long distance from the hotel across the lawn in her full wedding gown?

Even as he pondered this puzzle, the orchestra struck up a song he couldn't quite place, which seemed to be the signal for the ceremony to begin. The eight men of the honor guard had lined up four to each side at the end of the aisle, and now drew their sabers and stood to attention with the blades held tightly in front of their chests.

Out across the lawn, Nathan saw the foyer doors to the hotel flung wide, and two figures stepped out onto the patio, striding toward the lawn. One was a gentleman dressed in a black suit of the finest cut, and on his arm was the figure of a woman, but she was covered from the top of her head to past her feet by a cape of dark red velvet, whose hood disguised her features. The cape was held in front by a clasp of gold, and it was trimmed in what looked like white fur. As she stepped, and the breeze moved the fabric, Nathan could just catch a glimpse of the brightest white fabric underneath the cape, but he could not make out her face nor any details of her dress.

He could feel his heart beating faster, and he could not suppress a smile at the anticipation of seeing *her* for the first time this day. It took only a minute or so for the couple to reach the end of the aisle, but to Nathan it seemed like hours. As they came closer, the mystery of why Jonathan Hughes had not been in his seat was resolved, for it was he who was escorting Evelyn. In that moment, Nathan remembered Gareth Hughes saying that his father considered Evelyn to be, "the daughter he never had," and then it made perfect sense. Over the past few years, Jonathan Hughes had come to fill the role of the father she had lost years before.

Evelyn and Jonathan stopped just as they reached the end of the row of sword-bearing soldiers, and he moved behind her. She unclasped the cape, shrugged it off her shoulders, and he caught it neatly, laying it carefully folded over his arm.

And then Nathan saw her in all her finery: *Evelyn*—dazzling in her white gown, sparkling in the sunlight. To Nathan, her beauty outshone the sun. She caught his eye from across the gathering, and she smiled. He felt that his heart would burst.

The orchestra immediately began the now familiar bridal chorus from Wagner's opera *Lohengrin*, commonly known as "Here Comes the Bride," and the bride and her escort began their slow, stately procession toward the front of the congregation, as all the guests stood.

As she moved closer, he took in the details of her gown for the first time. From a distance, he'd thought the dress was purely white, but now he saw that it was not so: its intricate pattern of white lace was accented with brightly colored flowers that appeared real at first, but as she drew nearer, he could see had been meticulously embroidered. Her golden hair was neatly pinned up, with a long, lacey veil streaming down her back, tied on with a fancifully knotted silk ribbon of white. Her slender neck was accentuated by a gold necklace with a large emerald in front, and her otherwise bare arms were covered past the elbow by delicate white silk gloves. He thought the overall effect was stunning—queenly, even, as an image from out of the old tales.

And though he'd fully expected her to turn and meet eyes with everyone she knew as she moved up the aisle, to his great pleasure, she never took her eyes from his, the entire walk.

When Evelyn and Johathan reached the front, they stood before Reverend Holing as he addressed the crowd saying, "Dearly beloved, please be seated."

Then he turned, looked at Jonathan, and asked, "Who shall give this woman to be married to this man?"

"I will, on behalf of, and with greatest respect for, her beloved late father, Elias Hanson," Jonathan answered, then setting Evelyn's white-gloved hand in Nathan's with a bow and a warm smile, he stepped back, then turned and went to sit next to Angeline in the front row.

And as Nathan gazed at Evelyn's face, he took in all the magnificence of it, as if seeing it for the first time, though it was also the most familiar image in the world to him. Every curve, every line, the slight blush of her cheeks, the pink of her lips, the sparkling blue of her eyes, were as perfection to him. As she continued to gaze up at him, smiling brightly, he was almost surprised that there were no tears, not even of joy; only bright happiness and love.

And as the pastor began the ceremony, Nathan found he could not take his eyes from her, not even to acknowledge the minister's questions, nor when saying his vows. She did likewise, never averting her gaze from his. He felt as if he was sinking into her, such that the pastor's words for a time became a blur, until he suddenly came to himself, recognizing a Bible verse the preacher had just referenced.

Reverend Holing had said, "I shall now read from the Holy Bible, the first book of Corinthians, chapter thirteen."

> *Love is patient and kind; love does not envy or boast; it is not arrogant or rude. It does not insist on its own way; it is not irritable or resentful; it does not rejoice at wrongdoing but rejoices with the truth. Love bears all things, believes all things, hopes all things, endures all things.*
>
> *Love never ends.*
>
> *So now faith, hope, and love abide, these three ... but the greatest of these ... is love.*

And then, the ceremony was suddenly over, and Nathan and Evelyn shared their first kiss as husband and wife to the cheers and applause of the congregation.

As they turned to make their exit, Evelyn now paused to acknowledge and share a quick word of thanks with everyone they passed, and Nathan did likewise, such that their departure took nearly a quarter of an hour. Harry the Dog followed behind them, patiently enduring the friendly pats and greetings of the guests who were brave enough to come near him.

When they finally reached the back of the aisle, Jim Wiggins called out a command, and the soldiers raised their swords high overhead, forming the traditional army "arch of sabers" for the couple to pass under. The last two honor guards were the largest, Stan and Big George. These two giant men lowered their swords as the bridal couple approached, forcing them to stop, which, of course, they had expected—it being part of the long-standing military tradition.

"There is price to be paid for passage," Stan said with a huge grin. "Husband must first kiss bride."

Nathan returned Stan's grin. "Now *that* is a price I will happily pay, my good fellow," he answered, and proceeded to do so, which made the big man laugh with delight.

The reception was also held outdoors, but this time on a more level area of lawn on the uphill side of the hotel. And though Nathan and Evelyn greeted their guests who were queued up in a long reception line, they had already visited with most of them as they had arrived in the days leading up to the event, so the line moved fairly quickly.

In keeping with military wedding etiquette, the guests were greeted as they'd been seated at the wedding, in order of their "rank" or perceived importance. So the two governors were first—they arrived side by side so that neither could be perceived as "outranking" the other—followed by the two generals, and so on.

Francis Pierpont congratulated Nathan with great affection and enthusiasm, a reflection of their long friendship and working comradery, and likewise showed warm regards toward Evelyn.

Arthur Boreman, for his part, was more cordial, as he and Nathan hadn't worked together for as long. Nathan was effusive in his praise for all Boreman had done for the new state, and in his appreciation for Boreman's attendance at the reception and the honor that represented. Nathan's warmth seemed to touch the West Virginia governor, who acted more relaxed and genial thereafter.

Once the governors had departed and the two generals stepped up, Nathan shook hands vigorously with each in turn. Of all the generals in the conflict, these two had been the ones closest to him well before his own commission, and both had done him great favors at one time or another throughout the long ordeal.

Having exchanged the appropriate pleasantries, and even as Nathan assumed they were preparing to step aside to allow the next guests to come forward, General Rosecrans removed his cigar, then inexplicably looked over at General Saxton and said, "Damn it, Rufus. *Tell him* ... before I up and burst!"

Saxton laughed. "All right ... all right, William. Keep your britches on, for God's sake. I was working up to it ..."

"Working up to what? Tell me *what?*" Nathan asked, looking from one to the other in puzzlement. He shared a look with Evelyn, but she shrugged.

Rather than answer, Saxton reached into this jacket pocket and retrieved an envelope, handing it across to Nathan.

"What's this?" Nathan asked, unsealing the envelope, and extracting the half sheet of paper contained within. He noticed immediately that it was a bank check, though this was no ordinary check and had not been issued by any ordinary bank. This check was from the United States Treasury, made out to Brigadier General Nathaniel Chambers, in the staggering sum of $1,033,500.00.

Nathan turned to gaze at Saxton open-mouthed. "What is this, Rufus?"

"It's a check, of course," he answered with a grin.

"Well, yes, I can see that. But why? What for?"

Saxton chuckled. "After our side retook this area, we discovered that your property contained a ready supply of saltpeter in several caves near the surface, which the Confederates had started working. The demand for gunpowder being what it was, we naturally took over the operation that the enemy had started, improving the road and expanding the works. Fortunately, the officer in charge kept meticulous records, which I received in regular reports—three hundred forty-four and a half tons were extracted, all told. The officer reported that the neighbors told him the place belonged to an officer who'd been away fighting in the war. Naturally, I had assumed he was a *Confederate* officer, since the place was entirely abandoned. But when I discovered *your* name attached to the property, I submitted an expense voucher to the treasury on your behalf for the full amount: 344.5 tons, times 2,000 pounds per ton, times $1.50 per pound—the going price of saltpeter—which comes to exactly $1,033,500.00, the amount you see on that check."

Nathan just gazed at Saxton, entirely speechless.

Rosecrans reached out and slapped Nathan on the back, "Congratulations, Nathan. I reckon that makes you just about the richest Goddamned gentleman in West Virginia!" He beamed.

Saxton laughed, "I have to say, it's the best wedding gift I've ever had the pleasure of giving, though clearly, I can't claim all the credit, since I didn't actually have to pay out the money."

"Regardless … I don't know what to say, Rufus. I can't thank you enough for this," Nathan said, and then shook hands with Saxton, followed by Rosecrans, before looking over at Evelyn, and handing her the check.

She gazed at it in amazement. "I don't think I've ever seen such a large number written down before," she said, slowly shaking her head.

Then Nathan caught her eye and said, "Guess this means you may have that ball room added onto the house that you've been wanting."

She smiled and continued to shake her head in wonder. "Yes … but more importantly, you can complete all your plans for the farm, including giving all the freemen their own plots, and all the equipment they'll need to work them."

"True, true. What a blessing from God," he answered.

❧❧❧❧❧❧❧❧❧

After several pleasurable hours conversing and enjoying refreshments out on the lawn, the party had moved indoors to the massive ballroom of the hotel. As Nathan expected, Evelyn had taken advantage of Angeline's willing largesse to fill the room with flowers, ribbons, and many other colorful decorations, such that the place fairly glowed with elegance.

And once the musicians were in position, the dancing began, starting with the bridal couple dancing alone, surrounded by an audience of their "dearly beloved" guests. It was a waltz, of course, and Nathan met eyes with Evelyn and chuckled a quiet laugh when he recognized it as the same Chopin tune that had started the now famous "Big Wedding" at Mountain Meadows, now seemingly ages ago.

She returned his laugh with a smile. "Do you like it, darling?" she asked.

"Very much … the more so for its … *familiarity*," he answered. "*Grande Valse Brillante*—the 'Great, Sparkling Waltz,' I believe you named it."

"You remember," she answered.

"I remember everything that has had *you* in it," he replied.

She frowned, and said, "Oh, *God forbid!* Some memories of me are certainly *not* worth remembering. And further, I beg of you to *forgive*, and then to *forget* them!"

He chuckled and said, "I can never forget a single moment I've spent with you, Evelyn, even if I tried. But there has never been anything to *forgive*."

She smiled and patted him on the arm as they spun, then answered, "Well, thank you for saying so."

Hours later, after dancing with nearly everyone in attendance until their feet were sore, they found themselves once more dancing together as the evening wore into night. As the present waltz was coming to its close, Evelyn leaned in and whispered in Nathan's ear, "I find I'm feeling a little … wearied, my darling. And I also notice that no one is paying any mind to us at the moment. Would you … be so kind as to escort me to my bed, sir?"

He looked into her sparkling eyes and smiled, "I can think of nothing I'd rather do, my dear."

She laughed, then took his arm, and they slipped through the back door of the ballroom into a night shining with stars. They strolled along the walkway, through the moonlit gardens to the front door of the hotel. There, they re-entered the building and made their way to their room, to spend the night together for the first time as husband and wife.

☷☷☷

Wednesday, October 25, 1865 – Greenbrier County, West Virginia:

"What is it you wish to show me?" Nathan asked, as Evelyn led him by the hand across the driveway toward the farm's various outbuildings. Nathan's constant, huge, four-legged companion plodded along behind them, as usual. Although it was fall, the day had dawned bright and clear, and the warmth of the sun's rays warming their backs belied the lateness of the season.

"Well, it's not a roll in the hay, if that's what you're thinking," she answered teasingly, flashing him a playful smile.

He laughed and returned her smile. "Well, a fellow can hope, can't he?"

She returned his laugh easily, but continued to lead him past the horse stables and the hog sheds, finally stopping in front of a small tool shed.

"What's this?" he asked, gazing at the small, nondescript shed.

"It's a tool shed, I believe," she answered.

He rolled his eyes, "Yes … that I can see. But why are we here, pray?"

She smiled. "Because I have a gift for you that I've kept out here. It was the only place I could think to hide it where you'd not discover it."

"Oh. Well … what's the occasion? Have I forgotten some important event that we're celebrating?"

She laughed, "You'll see … Wait here a moment," she said. She pulled open the door, which creaked on its hinges as she ducked inside.

Hmm … ought to oil that, he thought, as he heard her moving around inside. Harry seemed entirely disinterested, sitting down heavily beside Nathan, his prodigious tongue hanging out to the side in his usual comical manner. Though he still followed his master everywhere he went on the farm, Nathan noticed the old boy seemed to be slowing down a bit. *Well, after all, he has spent the last four years fighting a war*, he decided. *That's enough to tire anyone, and he's not as young as he once was.*

Evelyn came out after only a moment holding a crude, clay flowerpot extended in her hands. Growing in the pot was a robust-looking plant about two feet tall with broad green oval-shaped leaves with a slightly waxy surface.

Nathan looked up at her quizzically, but she just smiled in return. So he took the pot from her hands and gazed at the plant, trying to decide what its significance might be. He didn't recognize what it was at first, though it seemed to him there was something familiar about the look of its leaves. And then it hit him, "Why, it's a magnolia! Like the great one that we lost."

"Not just *like* the great one, it is the very child of that same tree. I found a seed pod from the felled tree, and have planted it and nurtured it ever since. Waiting for the right moment to gift it to you."

He smiled brightly as he gazed at the healthy seedling. "This is … most thoughtful of you, my dear, knowing how sad I was over losing the original."

"I knew you'd appreciate it," she beamed.

"It's … like a new, fresh beginning," he said. "I shall plant it next to where the old one stood, and we can watch it grow taller and stronger year by year."

She nodded her agreement, but continued to gaze at him with an odd, unknowable look that made him think he was missing something—something important. But he couldn't quite fathom what it was, so finally he shrugged and asked, "You've hinted at a special occasion … that you've been waiting for the right moment to give this to me …?"

She grinned, "Yes. But … can't you *guess*, darling?"

He gazed at her odd, happy expression, but could think of nothing, so again he just shrugged.

She laughed, a joyful, happy smile lighting her features. She reached down, gently patted her stomach, then looked him in the eye and said, "The tree's seed was not the only one that has been planted."

"*Oh, my God, Evelyn!*" his beaming smile now matched hers, and he embraced her, then kissed her with great enthusiasm.

Then he held her at arm's length and gazed at her stomach. She laughed. "Nothing to see yet. But very soon, now, we will start doing as you say: watching a young thing grow taller and stronger every year. An onery boy—tall, strong, and handsome like his father."

"Ha! I have always pictured a girl, as mischievous, beautiful, and full of life as her mother."

"Well, whichever it is, he … or she … will surely have a wonderful life," she answered.

"Amen to that, my love. Amen to that."

If you enjoyed *Resolve*,
please post a review.

If you enjoyed the ***Road to the Breaking Series***
please post a review
and enjoy the first volume of the **new series by Chris Bennett**:

THE ROAD TO REVOLUTION SERIES:

"One of the greatest adventure stories in American history ..."

Ethan Chambers' life is suddenly changed forever when his father suffers a horrific accident, only escaping death by the timely intervention of legendary frontiersman, Daniel Morgan. But the calamity has left Ethan's father permanently disabled and unable to work, forcing the teenager to take his place as the family breadwinner, a role for which he feels entirely unprepared.

And then, even as Ethan struggles to find work, leaders of the American colonies come to blows with an ever more violent and imperious British monarchy, at Lexington, Concord, and Bunker Hill. Ethan and his new hero Daniel Morgan find themselves swept up in an irresistible tide of conflict as the defiant American colonies ignite a full-scale war against the mightiest nation on earth.

Despite his doubts and fears, Ethan joins Morgan's Virginia Riflemen in the fight for freedom. But as the company embarks on a treacherous expedition through the Canadian wilderness, battling both nature and the powerful British army, Ethan begins to question if he is truly capable of living up to Morgan's expectations.

As the stakes grow higher and winter approaches, Ethan, Daniel Morgan, and a ragtag band of determined patriots must defy the odds and fight for their country on the perilous *Road to Revolution*.

Get started today on book one of the series:
THE ROAD TO REVOLUTION

Resolve – Facts vs. Fiction

I get asked all the time whether this or that person or event in one of my books was factual, or invented for dramatic effect. This volume, like the others in the series, contains a good number of interesting historical facts and circumstances that may, at first, seem made up. I thought you might enjoy the following enumeration and explanation of these details. – *Chris Bennett*

Petersburg Siege – contrary to what the popular name for the engagement implies, this was not a typical siege, where a city or fortress is encircled and entirely cutoff from re-supply while being constantly bombarded. Instead, the Union's campaign against Petersburg consisted of nine months of separate battles, eventually devolving into trench warfare that presaged the stalemate fifty years later on the western front in World War I. The Union's attempts to break through at Petersburg to gain access to the Confederate capital at Richmond eventually succeeded, forcing Robert E. Lee to withdraw his troops to the west, where he surrendered a week later.

Brigadier General Joshua Chamberlain – one of the most notable and heroic figures of the Civil War, Chamberlain was a college professor in Maine when the conflict broke out, eventually working his way up to the rank of Brigadier General, after General Grant believed he was bestowing the honor posthumously when Chamberlain was "mortally wounded" in battle. But Chamberlain recovered from his wounds and returned to the field in time for Lee's surrender at Appomattox, which he had the honor of overseeing. He is best known for his heroic action at Gettysburg, leading a desperate Union bayonet charge that prevented the Confederates from turning the Union lines, and for which he received the Congressional Medal of Honor. After the war, he was elected governor of Maine by the largest landslide in state history at the time.

Battle of Fort Gregg – as described in this book, approximately three hundred rebels held the small, mud- and log-walled fort for several hours against a Union onslaught estimated at fifteen regiments in all. And it was in fact the Twelfth West Virginia regiment that helped to finally break the stalemate and overrun the fort, including breaking in the back sally port door. For their actions that day, several members of the regiment received the Congressional Medal of Honor. The only *fiction* is Nathan Chambers and his men's involvement. Otherwise, the events described herein are factual.

Burning of Richmond – Confederates under the command of Lieutenant General Richard Ewell did in fact set the town ablaze before retreating westward with Robert E. Lee's army. The arriving Union army, ironically mostly black freemen, subsequently extinguished the fires, saving much of the city from what is now considered needless destruction instigated by its own supposed defenders.

Appomattox Court House Surrender – the fiction here is that the surrender did *not* actually take place in the court house, as the name implies. In those days towns that hosted a court house were very proud of that fact, and would sometimes change their name to reflect their new status—thus the town of Clover Hill was renamed Appomattox Court House when the Appomattox county seat was moved to the town. The surrender signing actually took place at a private residence within the town, owned by Wilmer McLean. Ironically, McLean had also owned a house at the place where the first major battle of the war took place, Manassas Junction (or Bull Run), and had moved to Appomattox in an attempt to avoid further involvement in the conflict. Guess that didn't work out too well for him.

Battle of Mountain Meadows – fictional, of course, but clearly one of the most important culminating events of the series. The factual part is that the Thirty-Sixth Virginia Cavalry Battalion— depicted in the book as being led by Elijah Walters—did in fact break out of the Union encirclement at Appomattox and fled into the west before disbanding.

Tragic Consequences of Lincoln's Death – the succession to the presidency of Andrew Johnson and his subsequent conflict with radical Republicans triggered the divisive period of American history called Reconstruction, which saw decades of ongoing conflicts between various factions in the North and South, conflicts that continue to have repercussions to this day, especially concerning race relations. Historians generally agree that had Lincoln remained in control of the nation for the rest of his second term or even longer, many of these problems might have been avoided by his thoughtful, firm hand on the rudder of the ship of state, especially where it concerned the transition of former slaves into productive and prosperous members of a free society.

Buffalo Soldiers – the *fact* is that the so-called Buffalo Soldiers, composed of black soldiers, were initially formed at Fort Leavenworth Kansas in September, 1866, and served with distinction during the Indian Wars that followed. The *fictional* part is the source of the name "Buffalo Soldiers," as related in this book, coming about during a conversation between Ned Turner and Lieutenant Auggie Gordon. In fact, no one knows exactly how the name came about, though several theories have been floated. One is that the Indians named them this, due to their curly, kinky hair, like a bison's mane; another is that they were called that due to the coats made of bison pelts that they wore in cold weather.

Union Army Ranks – If you're not a military buff, there can be plenty of confusion about the different ranks, their hierarchical order, and their insignia. Confederate ranks were similar, but their insignia were mostly different. Leaving off specialized ranks, such as surgeons, quartermasters, etc., below is the general list on the Union side.

Also, if two soldiers have the same rank, then seniority (that is, the date of enlistment or commission) would generally serve as the tiebreaker, unless explicit orders from a superior overruled that (for example, General Grant could place Major General Jones in charge of a division, even though Major General Smith, his subordinate, has seniority.) You may have also noticed that an officer's commission might be backdated to give him seniority over other officers of the same rank. This would be done to reflect things like battle experience, superior performance or capability, etc. In the series, Nathan Chambers, when he is finally commissioned, has his commission backdated to the beginning of the war in recognition of his previous service and combat experience in Mexico and Texas. This allows him to take command in a situation where there are no generals available, as he would typically have seniority over any other colonel in the field.

Note also that when addressing these men, the secondary part of the rank was typically omitted, that is, both a first or second lieutenant would be addressed as simply "Lieutenant Smith," a lieutenant colonel would be addressed as "Colonel Smith," a brigadier general as "General Smith," and so on, which can also be a source of some confusion when reading. However, when introducing *themselves*, officers were obligated to include their sub-rank, for example, "Hello, I'm Lieutenant Colonel Smith. Pleased to meet you."

- **Enlisted Men** (corporals and sergeants are also referred to as **Non-Commissioned Officers** or NCOs):
  - **Private** – no insignia, or single V-shaped stripe
  - **Corporal** – double V-shaped stripe
  - **Sergeant** – triple V-shaped stripe
  - **First Sergeant** – triple V-shaped stripe with flat stripes across the top
  - **Sergeant Major** – triple V-shaped stripe with rounded stripes on top (a.k.a. a "chevron")

- **Commissioned Officers**
  - o **Second Lieutenant** – shoulder patch with no additional insignia within
  - o **First Lieutenant** – shoulder patch with two single bars within
  - o **Captain** – shoulder patch with two double bars within. **Interesting aside:** A *naval* captain is a higher rank than an *army* captain. A captain in the navy is the military equivalent of a colonel in the army (see below).
  - o **Major** – shoulder patch with two *gold* oak leaves within
  - o **Lieutenant Colonel** – shoulder patch with two *silver* oak leaves within (yes, this does seem backwards, since the gold oak leaves indicate a lower rank than the silver oak leaves)
  - o **Colonel** – shoulder patch with a single silver eagle within (which is why a "full" colonel, vs. a lieutenant colonel, is often referred to as a **"bird colonel"**)
- **General Officers**
  - o **Brigadier General** – one star
  - o **Major General** – two stars
  - o **Lieutenant General** – three stars (only Ulysess Grant held this rank during the Civil War on the Union side, while the Confederates used this ranking more freely, though often temporarily, as in during the course of a specific campaign)
  - o **General** – four stars (this rank was not used by the Union during the Civil War, but Robert E. Lee effectively held this rank in the Confederate Army)
  - o **General of the Army** – five stars (this rank was not used during the Civil War)

Union Infantry Formations – the nomenclature and hierarchy of military formations (regiments, divisions, corps, etc.) can also be baffling. The following list (from smallest to largest formation) represents the *typical* numbers of soldiers, the rank of officers in command, and standard nomenclature at each level for the *infantry*. These lists are different for artillery and cavalry, and all varied slightly on the Confederate side. Note that the numbers of men could vary greatly and were never consistent, so the numbers I'm listing are to give you a general idea of the sizes, and to make the math work in a logical fashion, which it almost never did in the real world.

It is important to note that the one formation that was static for a given soldier in the Civil War (except for higher ranking officers, who might be moved from unit to unit as needed) was the **regiment**. Once a soldier was assigned to a regiment, he would stay there, and would identify himself, if asked, by that regimental number. For the Union Army during the Civil War, there were three types of infantry regiments: regular army, volunteers, and colored troops. Both the regular army and the colored troops were identified as "United States" regiments, while the volunteer regiments were designated by their state. So if you asked a soldier who he was, he might say, "Private Smith, Twelfth West Virginia," by which he meant the unit officially designated "Twelfth West Virginia Volunteer Infantry Regiment." He would never say, "Private Smith, Army of the Potomac," or "Private Smith, Third Brigade," for example, because his regiment might be moved around to different army formations as circumstances warranted, but it would always remain a cohesive unit.

- **Squad** – 10 men, sergeant, uses commander's name ("Sergeant Smith's Squad")
- **Platoon** – 50 men (5 squads), lieutenant, uses commander's name ("Lieutenant Smith's Platoon")
- **Company** – 100 men (2 platoons), captain, uses single letter ("G Company")
- **Regiment** – 1,000 men (10 companies), colonel, uses region designator and assigned number ("United

States 3rd Infantry," "12th West Virginia Infantry," "United States 23rd Colored Infantry"

- **Brigade** – 3,000 men (3 regiments), colonel or brigadier general, uses a number within the division ("3rd Brigade.") Occasionally a brigade would acquire a nickname based on their performance in a battle, such as the "Stonewall Brigade," or the "Iron Brigade," but these were unofficial names only.
- **Division** – 9,000 men (3 brigades), brigadier general or major general, uses a number within the corps ("2nd Division")
- **Corps** – 18,000 men (2 divisions), major general, uses roman numerals within the national army ("XXIV Corps")
- **Field Army** – 54,000 (3 corps), major general, uses the name of a region, typically a major river valley, in which the army typically operated ("Army of the Potomac," "Army of the Shenandoah," "Army of the James," "Army of West Virginia")
- **National Army** – all field armies, General-in-Chief of the Armies (Lieutenant General Ulysess Grant), Secretary of War (Edwin Stanton), President of the United States (Abraham Lincoln), ("United States Army")

Author's Note

To the avid reader Owen Garthe: my wish for you is that this special note inspires you to keep reading, and in a few years when you are old enough (and your parents say it's okay), I hope that you will read, enjoy, and absorb the entire Road to the Breaking series. I pray that you will take away from it some useful lessons not just about American history, but especially about the courage and resolve of ordinary people to do extraordinary things for the benefit of their friends, family, country, and fellow man.

Best wishes,

Chris.

Acknowledgments

Special thanks as always to my editor, Ericka McIntyre, who keeps me honest and on track, and my proofreader and fellow Tolkien fanatic Travis Tynan, who makes sure everything is done correctly!

And, as always, I can't thank her enough for all she does for the Road to the Breaking team—our "head coach" and my most excellent partner in crime, Keri-Rae Barnum. *You are the best!*

Recommended Reading

For excellent non-fiction accounts of the events in this book, please see:

- *A Southern Woman's Story*, by Phoebe Yates Pember

- *Appomattox: The Surrender of the Army of Northern Virginia*, by Joshua L. Chamberlain, Major-General, US Army

- *The Last Citadel: Petersburg, June 1864 – April 1865*, by Noah Andre Trudeau

GET EXCLUSIVE FREE CONTENT

The most enjoyable part of writing books is talking about them with readers like you. In my case that means all things related to *Road to the Breaking*—the story and characters, themes, and concepts. And of course, Civil War history in general, and West Virginia history in particular.

If you sign up for my mailing list, you'll receive some free bonus material I think you'll enjoy:

- A fully illustrated *Road to the Breaking* **Fact vs. Fiction Quiz.** Test your knowledge of history with this short quiz on the people, places, and things in the book (did they really exist in 1860, or are they purely fictional?)

- **Cut scenes from *Road to the Breaking*.** One of the hazards of writing a novel is word and page count. At some point you realize you need to trim it back to give the reader a faster-paced, more engaging experience. However, now you've finished reading the book, wouldn't you like to know a little more detail about some of your favorite characters? Here's your chance to take a peek behind the curtain!

- I'll occasionally put out a **newsletter with information about the Road to the Breaking Series**—new book releases, news and information about the author, etc. I promise not to inundate you with spam (it's one of my personal pet peeves, so why would I propagate it?)

To sign up, visit my website:
http://www.ChrisABennett.com

ROAD TO THE BREAKING SERIES:

Road to the Breaking (Book 1)
Enigma (Road to the Breaking Book 2)
Sedition (Road to the Breaking Book 3)
Breakout (Road to the Breaking Book 4)
Insurrection (Road to the Breaking Book 5)
Invasion (Road to the Breaking Book 6)
Emancipation (Road to the Breaking Book 7)
War (Road to the Breaking Book 8)
Inferno (Road to the Breaking Book 9)
Resolve (Road to the Breaking Book 10)

ROAD TO REVOLUTION SERIES:

The Road to Revolution (Book 1)
The Crossing (Road to Revolution Book 2) – Coming in 2025